TATTOO
GIRL

www.stmartins.com

Book design by Michelle McMillian

Library of Congress Cataloging-in-Publication Data

Stevens, Brooke.
    Tattoo girl / Brooke Stevens.—1st ed.
      p. cm.
    ISBN 0-312-26910-2
     1. Foundlings—Fiction. 2. Mute persons—Fiction. 3. Circus performers—Fiction. 4. Tattooing—Fiction. 5. Clergy—Fiction. 6. Girls—Fiction. 7. Ohio—Fiction. I. Title.

PS3569.T447 T37 2001
813'.54—dc21   00-045865

First Edition: March 2001

10 9 8 7 6 5 4 3 2 1

TATTOO GIRL

GIRL

BROOKE STEVENS

ST. MARTIN'S GRIFFIN
NEW YORK

To my loving wife, Karen, and our son, Fenner,
And to my mother and father

ACKNOWLEDGMENTS

The following people will know the special reasons for which I am indebted to them for helping to bring this book to life: Madison Smartt Bell, Ron Bernstein, Francesca Lia Block, Phil Borack, Paul Carrol, John and Andrea DePreter, Stephen Dixon, Deborah Garwood, Judy Katz, Mary LaChapelle, Eduardo Lago, Craig and Lu Marcus, Sophie Muller, Bonnie and Courtney Nussum, Nelly Riefler, Lucy Rosenthal, Oren Rudavsky, David Schifren, Lyde Sizer, and Celia Wren.

Special thanks to Gideon Weil and Kim Witherspoon for helping to shape this novel from its earliest drafts.

And to Jonah Winter for his encouragement in all stages of the writing of this book and the last.

And finally to the support and the invaluable insight of my editor, Bryan Cholfin.

And lest I should be exalted above measure through the abundance of the revelations, there was given to me a thorn in the flesh, the messenger of Satan to buffet me, lest I should be exalted above measure.

For this thing I besought the Lord thrice, that it might depart from me.

And He said unto me, My grace is sufficient for thee: for My strength is made perfect in weakness.

—SECOND CORINTHIANS, CHAPTER 12,
KING JAMES VERSION

Say, you're in the country; in some high land of lakes, take almost any path you please, and ten to one it carries you down in a dale, and leaves you there by a pool in the stream. There is magic in it. Let the most absent-minded of men be plunged in his deepest reveries—stand that man on his legs, set his feet a-going, and he will infallibly lead you to water, if water there be in all that region. Should you ever be athirst in the great American desert, try this experiment, if your caravan happen to be supplied with a metaphysical professor. Yes, as every one knows, meditation and water are wedded forever.

—HERMAN MELVILLE, *MOBY-DICK*

TATTOO GIRL

1

At 2:01 A.M. Harold Parks, the security guard of the Blue Night
Mall, a tall, soft-spoken black man in his midfifties, left his office
with his checkpoint keys in hand and walked past the gated windows of the sporting goods store, the blue jean shop, and the closed
metal curtains of the hamburger and hotdog stands. The mall was
empty and quiet enough to hear a pin drop. It had been that way
at this time of night for the last twelve years of Harold's shift. That
may have been why the sight of somebody's head from behind, a
person seated on the wooden bench behind the fountain under the
atrium in the center of the mall, struck Harold as peculiar. Even
from his vantage point through the wide-leafed, tropical plants,
Harold could sense the tranquillity of this person. As he rounded
the octagonally shaped fountain, he saw a teenage girl, fifteen or so
years old. Twigs, bits of leaves and dust were woven into her matted
black hair; her face was pocked with dirt worn deeply into the skin.

Harold stared at her. He'd never seen another person in the mall
at this time. It suddenly occurred to him that she might have been
separated from her friends or parents, though the mall had been
closed for over two hours. He smiled and walked toward the bath-

rooms. He'd already checked them once that night, but it was always possible that he had missed somebody in a stall. He swung open the door to the men's room and walked along the urinals. "Anyone here?" He pushed open all the stall doors and then turned around.

Down the corridor he could see the placid girl sitting on the bench near the fountain, her hands on the wood beside her. Harold knocked on the women's room door. "Hello? Anyone here? I'm coming in. Security guard, got to make my check." After a brief silence he strolled through the lightly colored room that was always far neater than the men's room. He would never have walked through this room if it had not been on his list of duties.

Back in the corridor Harold squatted in front of the girl. "Hello," he said. She turned to him and he thought her pupils dilated. "Are you okay?"

She stared without saying a word.

"Your friends, where are they? Out in the parking lot? Did they leave you here?"

His own question gave him an idea. Maybe they had been locked out and were outside trying to get in.

"Do you want to come with me or stay here?"

She didn't answer.

He got his keys out and made his way to the alarm box near the front entrance.

A yellow moon had risen over the lake at the edge of the mall parking lot since his shift had begun. The light mingled on the water with the faint lights of the far shore. A wind caressed his cheeks. He left the front door open and followed the sidewalk to get a look around the back.

The brake lights of a pickup truck parked near the guardrail at the far corner of the lot kept blinking on and off. The truck was too far away to see inside but as Harold approached he made out two figures inside kissing passionately, teenagers. The boy in the driver's seat must have had his foot on the brake pedal without realizing it.

Harold turned and headed back to the towering flat-roofed, windowless building with the neon lit sign, THE BLUE NIGHT MALL, crackling against the sky of stars and stratus of thin white clouds. The pickup truck peeled out, the rear tires smoking and shot through the wide empty lot toward the exit.

At the fountain the girl was in the same position, arms to her sides, staring down the corridor. He put his hand down for her and she reached up and took it. "Come on," he said and led her along the slick tiles, past all the closed stores to his office where his dinner lay wrapped in tinfoil getting cold. He always ate it right after his final check while listening to the news on the radio.

"Hungry?" he asked. He peeled the top of a banana. The girl took it from him, holding it in her hand without eating it. "Go on, I'm going to make a telephone call and we'll find your friends or parents, whoever you came with, sure as the sky is blue. Okay?"

As long as he'd been working at the mall, Harold had never once needed to call the police. A female dispatcher came on.

"This is Harold Parks, security guard at the Blue Night Mall. I just found a young girl in here. She doesn't talk, she seems lost or something. I don't know how in the world she could have gotten in here."

The dispatcher asked that he describe her.

"She's fifteen or sixteen years old, a white girl. Her hair's all matted and dirty, her shoes covered with mud. Seems her shirt's got some stains on it or something, something's dried on it. What's on your shirt?" he said. The girl held the banana without eating it. She seemed to understand what he was saying. "I don't know what her name is."

After Harold hung up the telephone, he knelt next to the girl. Now he noticed the crusty stains were all over the back of her shirt and pants. "Somebody spill their dinner on you?" he asked.

Something dark caught his eye through a small tear in the fabric. He got up and bolted the door, despite the fact that the mall was empty. Then he came back to the girl, knelt down behind her and carefully lifted her shirt. She stood there without moving.

He had thought there would be another shirt under this one. But there was only skin. Surely it was skin for it was alive and moving as she was breathing. A pattern, a fine mesh of tiny overlapping *U*'s making her look almost as dark as Harold. Scales, fish or snake scales, drawn evenly across her smooth white flesh, obviously by a person adept at the art. The scales went up as far as Harold dared lift her shirt. Turning her around, he saw they were on her stomach, too. He reached for the cuffs of her pants. The tattooed scales extended all the way to her ankles. "Mercy," he whispered. "Look what somebody did to you. You poor baby." He lifted her shirtsleeve. The pattern came down her arm all the way to her wrist.

Ten minutes later he was standing next to the girl at the mall's glass doors as a police cruiser parked next to the sidewalk. Perhaps the officer was having a bad night, or perhaps he wasn't sympathetic to what he saw: a black man holding the hand of a young white girl alone in this wide-open country. He kept his narrow eyes low as he silently stepped out of the cruiser. Sneering, he lifted the girl onto the seat.

Harold leaned down to the open window. "Excuse me, officer, but do you think it'd be possible if somebody down at the station could give me a ring and let me know why this poor girl's out here? I'll worry all night." He knew he was going to worry longer than that. Despite her silence, he already felt a connection to this girl, something he couldn't put his finger on.

"Sure," the officer said. He turned away as if he'd said too much already and put his car in gear.

An hour later, Harold called the station.

"What do you want to know about her?" the dispatcher said.

"Just if you found her parents. I'm about worrying myself to death here."

"Nothing yet."

"Oh," Harold waited, hoping she'd say something more. The dispatcher was quiet. "What a shame, somebody leaving a young girl like that all alone."

"A lot of creeps out there," the woman said.

"Sure," Harold said. "Sure is."

The dispatcher hung up and Harold carefully put the receiver on its cradle. The image of the beautiful young girl was still in his head. The three times he had to walk by the fountain, he thought he could feel her presence again. Her soul's innocent, he thought, but somebody put something around it, some darkness.

On his way back home to his small apartment that morning he bought a newspaper. Far more tired than usual, he crawled into bed and fell asleep. At one-thirty in the afternoon when he went to the kitchen for breakfast, he opened up the paper and searched through the articles as if the story could possibly have written itself while he'd been sleeping. He thought better of calling the police, and then his telephone rang.

"Mr. Parks?"

"Speaking."

"I'm a reporter at the *Morton Chronicle*, name's Tom Grant, maybe you've seen my name."

"I don't know the reporters there."

"We were wondering if you might want to answer a few questions concerning the girl who turned up in the mall last night for an article."

"I can't tell you much more beyond the fact that she was sitting by the fountain around two A.M.," Harold said.

"But you were the one who found her, is that correct?"

"Yes, I did. Is she okay? I'm—"

"You're what?"

"Worrying about her."

"Did you notice anything unusual about her? Did she seem shook up?"

"Maybe."

"Anything else?"

"She didn't say a word the whole time we waited for the police car."

"Well, she's evidently in shock. Once they took her clothes off she livened up a little, I'll say. There were stains on them, Mr. Parks, blood stains—not her blood, either."

The sadness that had settled on Harold's shoulders the night before grew heavier. He could feel it in his stomach.

"Human blood. All over her," the reporter paused.

"No," Harold said and put his hand against his stomach and kept it there.

"They don't know whose, but it seems from more than one source."

"Lord have mercy, what happened?"

"That's just what the homicide squad is looking into . . ."

"That doesn't make any sense."

"More sense than the other thing they found out about her. Did you notice anything on her skin when you found her, Mr. Parks?"

"She was all dressed up with a sweater around her neck."

"So, you didn't notice anything on her?"

"Nothing."

"Scales tattooed all over her. Yes, indeed," the reporter said. "The needle of the perpetrators of this crime against her spared nothing except her hands and feet right up to her neck. Nothing, no part of her body whatsoever, Mr. Parks. It's no wonder she can't talk. They blamed it on a cult, but there aren't any around here. Somebody thought she must be from a circus, but none have passed close by in quite a while."

"Who in the world—"

"A sicko, she's just a little kid."

"Just a *little* kid," Harold said.

On his way back to work that afternoon he bought a copy of the *Morton Chronicle*. For the first time in his life he saw his name in print.

CIRCUS GIRL FOUND IN MALL

Morton, Ohio. An apparently speechless young girl in blood-splattered clothing was found in a state of shock at around 2 A.M. inside the Blue Night Mall by the night watchman, Harold Parks. Though the girl was said to be otherwise unharmed, police said that tattoos were discovered covering over 90 percent of her skin . . .

2

The Good Friends Adoption Agency, a small, white, cement building stood in a fallow pasture of clover on a deserted country road. The building was windowless with only a single door and a set of cement steps leading down to a broken tar lot. Parked in this lot over shaggy tufts of grass were two rusted cars. A third vehicle, a fifties Buick, painted bright green with fins and round taillights, was just cooling down, ticking with heat, steam rising from its grille. In the rearview mirror, Lucy, a woman in her late-thirties, sweet and kind, God-loving and lonely, attempted to fix her curly yellowish hair that fell to her shoulders. She kept poking her fingers into it, drawing it down, and then bending her head back to get a better look at the shape in the narrow glass. Her face was pinkish and wide, her eyes small and sunk into her head. She was a little overweight; even small tasks such as getting out of her car and straightening her faded flowery skirt started her breathing harder than normal. Unaccustomed to high heels, she crossed the rough lot to the cement steps, careful not to turn an ankle on a stone.

Across a long narrow lobby of linoleum and potted plants, she saw a reception desk where a young secretary was busily tapping on a computer keyboard.

"Mornin'," Lucy said. Lila Peterson, a woman in her late twenties with a long neck and blond curls cut close to her smallish head, looked from her screen to Lucy and smiled. Despite being a dozen or so years older than this woman, Lucy suddenly found herself more nervous than she'd been in a long time.

"I've come to inquire about the girl," Lucy's nerves made her stutter slightly.

"The girl?" Lila said.

"Yes . . . in the papers."

Lila nodded her head. "Yes?"

"I've come to ask about adopting her."

Lila shook her head. "She's only been under our care for a few weeks. She's not up for adoption. No, at this point we're waiting for the parents—"

"Does she have parents?"

"We don't know. She doesn't talk, as you must have heard."

Lucy held her pocketbook against her stomach and looked down at Lila. "If she did have parents, you wouldn't want to put her back with them," Lucy said. "Whoever did that to her—"

"Well, we'll see," Lila said. "First they've got to be located."

"Yes," Lucy said. "I understand."

Lila went back to typing on the computer. "Can I help you with anything else?"

"I was just wondering if I could fill out the forms now, maybe."

Lila opened a drawer, pulled out a packet and handed it to Lucy. "Bring these in when you and your husband fill them out. It's a long process, you know, but you've got to start by filling these out."

Lucy held the packet against her chest. "That's somethin' I wanted to talk to you about," she said, gently. "You see, I'm not married just yet. But I have every intention of getting married some day, yes I do."

Lila looked Lucy up and down. "No, Mr. Lark never makes exceptions."

"Oh." Lucy's thumb caressed the envelope she held. "I came all the way up here from Millville."

"Millville?"

"It's over an hour's drive south of here."

"You should have called us before driving all that distance. You'll find that's the policy most everywhere you go. You've got to have a husband and you both have to come."

"I understand." Lucy hesitated, thinking of something more to say, but then she turned around and walked sadly toward the door. A rectangle of harsh sunlight from the open door fell across the linoleum of the windowless lobby. She began feeling dizzy. Everything in her line of sight became distorted as if she was looking down a watery tunnel, a kaleidoscope of sorts, parts of it growing bigger and smaller as she moved her head.

She stopped herself, took a deep breath and turned around to Lila at the desk. "Miss? You might hear stuff like this all the time. But—" She mustered the courage to speak, to tell her what was really on her mind. "I . . . I think I'd be just right for the girl . . ." She took a deep breath, closed her eyes and tried to emphasize the truth behind her words. "I know I would, more than right." Lila stopped typing again and watched Lucy. "I don't think it's just speculation, it's more than that. You see, I got a feeling about it when I read the newspapers, a special feeling in here." She touched her heart. "I don't know what it was about the story, the black lines on her body maybe or just that she doesn't talk, there's something about her. She's already like kin to me. I feel it so deep right here." She touched her heart again. "That's truth talking to me. You see, I live alone. I've been counting on—I've had my heart set on taking care of her. I mean, if I could just say hello to her, she might take to me, and then if she's up for adoption and all. I've got such a nice little home in the country and it would be hers, too, for the rest of her life. . . ."

"Right now the address where she's at is confidential, very confidential," Lila said. "She's attracted quite the interest, but we've got a very strict rule about that in a case like this where you never know who or why people want to see her."

"Lila," a voice called from another room. "Did you finish the memo? That was that pain in the neck from the *Register Herald* again."

A thin, middle-aged man in a too-small blue sports jacket stood in a doorway across the lobby.

"Mr. Lark?" Lucy said.

Mr. Lark raised his eyebrows. He had a long sensitive face and bags under his down turned eyes. Lucy walked toward him.

"I'm . . . Lucy Thurman."

"I don't recognize the name," Mr. Lark said.

"I live in Millville . . . You see, I haven't ever tried to adopt somebody before now . . . but . . ."

Mr. Lark glanced at Lila for assistance.

"She's by herself, no husband." Lila shook her head. "I told her that the girl is not even—"

"But . . . this is a special case," Lucy said. She had never before been so bold. "Because of the tattoos on her . . . it's a special . . ."

"What's special?"

"I told her she's not up for adoption," Lila said.

"Please, Mr. Lark, could I talk to you for a moment, please?"

Lucy moved toward Mr. Lark. He turned and stepped into his office and behind his desk, drawing a chair under him. "I'm very busy," he said, straightening papers. Lucy wiped the back of her hand across her wet forehead. "Go ahead, take a seat."

"I prefer to . . ." Lucy remained standing. "This is a special case, Mr. Lark. I know what Lila said, but that girl can't ever go back to where she came from and I know wherever she goes she's going to have a hard time staying away from where she came from—it's so difficult moving forward in life after something like this happens, believe me. The tattoos. Kids in school will make fun of her and she's always going to be *marked*. I know, I know what it's like . . ." Lucy spoke so emphatically that she suddenly found herself tongue-tied, unable to think of anything else to say.

Mr. Lark tapped a new yellow pencil against his lips. "Exactly how would you help her? She's severely traumatized."

"By bringing a special understanding to her. I've got a special understanding, I do. I think I know the kind of stuff that she's been through."

"You've never even met the girl, what do you mean?" Mr. Lark said.

"Well, she's going to be looked at as a . . . *freak*." Just as she said this, Lucy noticed that Mr. Lark was missing his two smallest fingers from the hand holding the pencil.

Cringing at the word, Mr. Lark dropped the pencil and closed his hand. "She's *not* that, Ms. Thurman," he snapped.

"I didn't mean it to sound like that. Being a freak isn't a bad thing. No, it's not a bad thing at all. But she's still going to be looked at that way and if she doesn't have somebody who . . ." Lucy suddenly felt sweat running under her arms. This meant so much to her that she was terrified of saying the wrong thing. Droplets gathered on her chin. ". . . who knows."

"Knows what, Ms. Thurman?" Mr. Lark jerked his head back, annoyed.

"Well, Mr. Lark," Lucy looked down as if in shame. "*I'm* a freak myself." She looked at her hands holding her knees. "I was in a circus for many years . . ."

There was a long silence. When Lucy heard Mr. Lark's voice, she detected a softer, gentler tone. "You look like a perfectly ordinary woman, Ms. Thurman."

"I was in the circus . . . and I was a big . . . I was a fat lady." Aware that she had gotten his full attention, she sat down and looked at the floor, afraid of raising her eyes. "I used to be much heavier than you see me now. I had my own tent . . . And I know, that young girl, she's going to have a hard time like I did. I can help her, even though I'm not married."

"We've never made an exception," Mr. Lark said, but again Lucy could detect a further softening of his voice, as if she'd found a crack that she could get through.

"But you've got to," Lucy said passionately, her eyes growing wide. "You've got to make an exception for her sake . . . and for *mine*."

Now she looked up at him. Seeing that his expression had changed, she felt that there was a chance she could talk him into this, if only he could see what was in her heart. "I knew a boy just like her . . ." She stuttered, unsure of where to go with this. "The thing that I'm talking about started with him when he was very young and he used to live in foster homes, but he didn't feel much at home with anyone and so he'd run away from each place one after the next. And it got so that every time he ran away, he'd get a tattoo." An awkward silence came down between them.

"So what?" Lark said.

"So, so those things were the only thing that stayed the same in his life, those tattoos were. He told me once that they were like his parents almost . . . Problem was, he ran away in the first place because he didn't feel close to anybody, but every time he got a new tattoo, it made things worse and put him even farther away from the other kids and he felt even less at home and so he kept on running. By the time he was sixteen, pretty much of his whole body was covered and there wasn't any place in the whole world for him to go but a mud show. That's how it happens, you see. That's how he joined the Crown Circus. That isn't any place to grow up in, I know, Mr. Lark, believe me, I know."

There was another silence. Lucy stared down at the floor hoping that he might be open to what she asked for.

"Well," Mr. Lark said. "The problem at the moment is we still have to wait. She doesn't talk, as you must know, and at night . . .

she's trying to hurt herself." Lucy shook her head. This did not surprise her. "The first night she was found lying in a bathtub trying to keep herself underwater. Believe it or not she was sleepwalking, trying to kill herself in her sleep. It's a rare phenomenon, but it's very real and very dangerous. The nurses couldn't even wake her up . . . well," Mr. Lark said. "Nobody knows what she's thinking or what happened to her and that's part of the problem. But something terrible happened to her. Something awful."

Lucy swallowed and looked away. She had known this all along but it was still difficult to hear. "I'd sleep next to her," she said. "I'd wake right up if she moved a muscle. A girl like that needs a body next to her, a soul who cares."

"I appreciate your concern, Ms. Thurman. Why don't you fill out those forms and let me review your answers and then we'll wait and see. I don't know exactly what to do. I'll be honest with you, I'm in a quandary about this one."

Lucy stood up, holding her pocketbook against her stomach.

"If it's ever possible, Mr. Lark," she said. "I can assure you of one thing, you would not, you would definitely not be making a mistake."

Soon after Lucy was gone, Carl Lark got out of his chair and asked Lila for the forms she'd filled out and brought them into his office and read them over carefully. Her handwriting was messy; many of the words were misspelled or crossed out. He read, *Lucy Thurman, 12 Scoville Road, Millville, Ohio.* In the space on the back, entitled "Reasons for Adoption," he read, *I got something to give to this young girl, it's something that I learned after all those years of being a freak in the circus.*

3

Something that I learned after all those years of being a freak in the circus. Carl lay in the dark next to his pregnant wife, Corva. Their child was due in less than a week. Carl could smell the flowers that he had placed in a vase next to their bed that evening. He'd remained awake for some time now; the last two nights had been among the worst of his life.

Years ago, when Carl was a teacher in a Cleveland ghetto high school, his work so consumed his life that Corva insisted that he get a more manageable job. The Good Friends Agency fit the bill. Placing a child, particularly one who had been through numerous homes, in a nurturing home was satisfying, and Carl gained far more control of his life than when he was looking after too many teenagers in the overcrowded school. Since then Carl had rarely brought his troubles home with him, but the young tattooed girl, whom Carl had named Emma, changed all that.

Emma's exact age was difficult to determine. One moment she looked like a young, melancholy adult full of sad memories; the next, she was fifteen years old at best, a sophomore in high school, someone who might have been playing soccer or field hockey after school, laughing with her friends about boys. Her face was beautiful and her dark curly hair shone richly once it was washed. There was a strange kind of depth to her innocence as if an encroaching cloud of darkness had seasoned her viewpoint but left her integrity untouched.

Every night after work, Carl drove to the Children's Hospital to bring Emma presents. It gave him pleasure to be near her, to hold her hand and talk to her. She listened attentively, but didn't even nod to questions, as if that might lay her heart open to people. There was an aura around her—she filled the hospital with a certain light—and everyone who came in contact with her seemed to regard her as if she were a precious secret. No matter how hard Carl tried, whenever he walked into the room, he couldn't take his eyes off her. He felt sure that he knew her or had seen her before. She reminded him of the subject in an old Italian or French painting or a sculpture that had come alive.

Corva sensed his preoccupation with her. She did not like the fact that he often came home later or that he called the hospital two or three times an evening to see how she was doing. Besides the tension with his wife, Carl began having violent nightmares that involved men searching for the girl. A number of things may have triggered these dreams. When she was first put under the auspices of his agency, she was kept in the nearby girls' home that the agency usually used. But after a day, the police department, fearing that she might be taken again by whomever had tattooed her, requested that Carl sequester her elsewhere. Soon afterward, reporters learned that Carl's agency had her in its care—that in itself had been kept confidential—and they called repeatedly requesting Emma's location. Carl fielded a few of these himself, Lila the rest. Once he heard her speaking quite sharply to somebody: "I said, we don't give that information out. Call the police department if you want to—"

It took a lot to rile Lila up. "Who was that?" Carl called to her.

"These guys. I think they're the same ones. They're trying to find out where she's been sequestered. I don't believe that they're reporters."

That night, the night after Lucy Thurman had filled out her application, as Carl drove toward the Children's Hospital to visit Emma, he noticed a van following him. He turned his car around, headed back home and gave Corva the flowers intended for Emma.

Late into the night, Carl woke up and stared at the ceiling in the dark. Corva had been breathing deeply but was now quiet.

"Awake, darling?" she said. "You're fidgeting, you know."

"I thought I was perfectly still."

"No, you were fidgeting—your toes."

"Toes don't fidget. They do something else."

Silence.

"Emma again?"

"Yeah."

"You *don't* know what happened to her, darling. Save your worrying until you know."

Corva was quiet, and soon he could hear her breathing deeply again. He took note of his toes. *They're quiet*, he thought.

"Your dreams, are you worried about them?" she said.

"I don't feel like having another one if that's what you mean."

"I figured it out today. You're worried about the baby, *our baby*. It's the last week—those classes—they scare the hell out of everyone else who takes them, too."

Finally, Carl fell asleep and as he did he had a tacit understanding that this dream was going to be worse than all the others. He was trying to smuggle Emma across an unmarked border somewhere in the midst of an African desert. The task should have been easy; there were no fences, just a lot of sand and a house that Carl realized, as he got nearer, he could easily have avoided. Three men stood behind the windows staring down at Emma.

"What are you looking at?" Carl called. A man pointed and Carl turned. He saw that the young girl's shirt had split wide open, exposing her stomach and the tattoos. It was a terrible sight to see; the shredded shirt barely hid her chest. *What an idiot I am for bringing her here.* He slammed his palm against his forehead, then realized his hand was bleeding. Suddenly, the men came out of the house and began approaching across the sand. *Oh my God, Emma.* He tried to pull Emma's shirt together, but pieces of fabric came off in his hands, then her pants split at the seams, exposing her thigh and rump covered with black scales. The men stopped in the sand. Then one of the men drew back his arm and threw a knife that shot past Carl and stuck deep in Emma's back, and then another struck Carl in the heart.

He woke up clutching his chest and thought for sure he'd been screaming out loud, but Corva slept soundly next to him. The dark feelings of the dream seemed like a sign that Emma was in danger of being discovered. He did not know why; it was a premonition that told him that he should act immediately. *I need to hide her right away.* He dressed quickly and quietly without waking Corva up, then stepped into the hall and wrote her a note on an envelope.

> *Darling, Gone to office. Couldn't sleep. I'll call you very first thing in the morning.*
>
> Love you as always, C.

Downstairs he opened the door to his station wagon and quietly pushed the car through the garage door to where he could start it without waking Corva.

He didn't drive into the lot of the hospital but instead parked on another street and cut through a dew-covered playing field. The security guard with gray bristly hair got up and unlocked the glass doors in the front. "Carl?"

"Is she still here? The young girl?"

"What? Of course."

"Are you sure?" He ran down the hall, opened the door to her room and flicked on the lights.

Emma sat up, rubbing her eyes.

"Hey, sweet girl," he said, kneeling in front of her. "I know where your home is. Sometimes things just come to you—intuitively—and you know a match is there waiting for you. Come on." Emma's large eyes glared at him. She wore a turtleneck shirt—she had refused to wear anything else, even to bed. "We're going to take a drive, maybe an hour. When it's light out, you'll be at the most wonderful house in the world, okay?"

And only I'll know where you are, not even Lila will know. He led her out of her room, down the hall.

"You're taking her now?" the guard said.

"I've found a place for her. Best to get a kid in the right home as soon as possible."

Even on the highway Carl still feared the possibility of being followed. On a flat stretch he pressed the accelerator so hard to the floor that the old station wagon rattled and smoked.

Checking the rearview mirror, he saw nothing but darkness, not a single headlight.

An hour later he was following a narrow country road through cornfields. The rising sun shone against shadowy telephone poles, long grass, and barbed-wire fences. He could smell manure and freshly turned soil. Cows with swollen udders stood on the cement ramp outside a barn waiting to be milked. Flocks of starlings and highflying crows appeared against the white sky.

Lucy's two-story yellow house was small but with spacious fields around a raked lawn. A birdbath with two plaster bluebirds, one bathing, the other drinking, stood in the front yard. Colorful flower boxes decorated the windowsills. He parked behind the old green car with its fins and circular taillights. Then he got out of his own car, shut his door, and waited. He could see three quarters of a mile across the dewy fields in both directions. All was silent except for a farmer calling his cows far away. There were no cars around. He was relieved that nobody had followed him; nobody knew he was here.

Holding Emma's hand, he brought her to the welcome mat on the rectangular stone step in front of Lucy's door and knocked. No light came on in the dark house. He knocked again, still holding the girl's tender hand.

On the back lawn, he stood looking up at the drawn shades of a second floor window. "Ms. Thurman," he called. "Hello!" Finally a yellow light came on and the shade moved to the side. An eye peeked out. "It's Mr. Lark of Good Friends. Look what I have for you." He raised Emma's hand and smiled. The eye stared out from behind the shade for a long time.

Lucy opened the front door, half asleep. She was dressed in a purple terrycloth bathrobe and black slippers that had fallen down at the heels and her hair was loosely bobby-pinned on her head. After staring at Emma for a moment, she put her hand out for her and led her and Carl into the house to a couch where a present wrapped in blue tissue paper lay.

Emma tore off the paper and lifted from the cotton a silver necklace with small wire circus performers hanging from it. She put it on over her black turtleneck. Carl was amazed. Had the necklace been meant for somebody else or did Lucy somehow know that he was coming? He smiled. He could tell just by the way Lucy was looking at the young girl that he had made the right decision, however impulsive. "Could we talk in private for a moment?" he asked.

Lucy and he stepped into the kitchen. Carl explained what had transpired that had led him to bring Emma here. "It may all be in my head, but you were certainly right about one thing—whoever had her before shouldn't ever go near her again." He noticed that Lucy's small eyes had become wet with tears. "Now, I also want you to know, I may have to come get her again sometime. If that happens, well . . . Do you understand that?"

Lucy stood watching Carl for the longest time, tears running down her face. In the living room, Emma was looking at the silver wire figures of performers on the necklace. Carl kissed her on both cheeks and then went to the door. "Don't hesitate to call me at home," he said to Lucy who was now holding Emma's hand. "Don't call the agency. I may check back here in the next few weeks, but only if I feel it's safe."

At seven A.M., when he arrived at the office, the sun had already dried the dew on the fields. He unlocked the doors and went to Lila's desk to complete his task of making it impossible for somebody other than himself to trace Emma's whereabouts. He had to get rid of anything Lila might have written down about Lucy. He checked her message pad, then dumped out her wastebasket, searching for scraps of paper with addresses or telephone numbers on them. Finally, he carried the basket to the incinerator in the back field, dumped in the papers and lit them on fire. Flames and ash rose up and he poked them with a stick. He felt relieved; such precautions may have all been unnecessary, but now he felt free of responsibility.

He turned to the beeping sound of a van backing around the side of the building. Two young men hopped out and strode up the path in the long grass toward Carl. *There they are, there are the people I've been running from.* For a moment he felt relieved to see the embodiment of his fears, as if they were proof that he was not crazy. Then he felt deeply frightened.

But he remembered that Lila had mentioned something about workers coming to clean out the septic system in the morning and his feelings shifted again. He smiled. "Good morning."

"Mornin'," the first man said. He put down a small tank that looked like the kind used by exterminators.

"You want to know where the pipes are?"

The man's young face was glistening in the early morning light. His nose, his cheeks, and his chin seemed incredibly smooth, much closer to a woman's than a man's. He wore a plain wool knit cap rolled up around the edges.

"What'd you do with her?" he said in a deep, commanding voice. Carl stared at his lips.

"With who?" Carl said.

"With the girl."

"The girl?"

"Yeah, we've been to the hospital, she's gone from there. Somebody took her."

"You're looking for her?"

The man nodded.

"Well, you're out of luck."

"Are we?" the first man said.

"Oh yes," Carl said and he felt the convictions that had guided his life come over him. He was somebody who had dedicated his life to helping children in trouble. "Not only that, if you had anything to do with what was done to that poor child, you're in a lot of trouble, right now."

"We asked you a question."

Carl caught his breath. He was sure now that his own righteousness could overpower these men, whoever they were. They were both in their twenties, not that much older than the high school students he had taught. He regained full confidence. "I think we should go talk to the police." Turning his eyes to the ground, he began walking around the men toward the building. A fist dug deep into his stomach. He buckled over, fell to his knees holding his shirt, gasping.

Then he felt something cold against his nose and realized it was a pistol barrel. "I asked you a question."

Carl couldn't seem to catch his breath to tell him. "No—" The man turned Carl's face with the gun. "No." Carl shook his head. "You can't—"

The second man lifted Carl to his feet and threw him in a head-lock. "Now we're going to ask you again." Carl couldn't move his arms or head. The man set the tank down in front of him, lifted something to Carl's face—a rubber gas mask—and clamped it over his nose and mouth. Holding it there, he said, "Now, you want to talk to us or to the water?" Carl tried to shake his head in the mask. The second man released a switch on the tank. The mask filled with water. Carl struggled, but the headlock was too tight. Water blasted into his nostrils and rushed down into his lungs.

"Let him go!" the one man said. They pulled the mask from his face. Carl fell to his knees, half conscious, almost choking, and then vomiting streams of water all over the grass. "Now who do you want to talk to, us or the water?" Through the water that blurred his vision, Carl saw the men, two brackish figures moving back and forth in front of him.

4

An hour later when Lila turned off her Chevy in the Good Friends parking lot, the engine did not quit right away; it turned over, coughed, then ran for a second longer and finally died altogether. A mechanic once told her to press her foot all the way down on the gas when that happened and flood the engine to a stop, but she never had the nerve to try that, sure that the car would then take off on its own. Instead, she just sat there, her foot on the brake as the car bucked and coughed to a stop.

It surprised her that Carl's station wagon was in the lot already. He always stayed later than she did, but he never arrived earlier. She grabbed her pocketbook and a bag of rubber bands she'd finally remembered to buy the night before and got out of the car. She could hear the robins and redwing blackbirds in the fields and smell the dew on the grass. At the front door she turned the knob without taking out her key. The door was always open when Carl was there, but now it was locked. She put her face to the small glass window in the door and saw that all the lights were out. Maybe there was work to be done out back. There were things Carl didn't tell her, plenty of things. She walked around the building.

A white van was backed up near the rear door, nobody in it. The septic system service had called to say they would come a day later.

But maybe they've come early anyway. All she could see were black birds rising and landing in the grass of the field. Besides a distant farm she could see the new yellow timber of a house under construction a quarter of a mile away.

She returned to the front door, put the key in, and entered the lobby, the fluorescent lights flickering on. Working with a man as kind as Carl made up for this depressing windowless office that had once been a machine shop. Her wastepaper basket was gone. Then she noticed somebody had moved her Rolodex to the other side of her desk.

Carl's door was closed, but she could see underneath it the lights were out. "Carl?" she called. She knocked on the door, waited, then turned the knob and opened the door. The office had been turned upside down. The file cabinets were open, papers scattered all over his desk. She stepped in a little farther. A hand grabbed her wrist and flung her into the arms of a man who clamped his hand over her mouth.

"Recognize my voice?" a man held a gun in her face. Lila's eyes were almost popping out of her head. "Do you realize you got a stupid boss?" Lila sucked air in through her nostrils. "Stubborn, yes indeed, and stupid. He wouldn't tell us where that little girl was, but you're not going to follow him down that path, right?" Lila kept staring, she tried to nod her head. The second man spread his fingers so that she could talk.

"Children's Hospital," Lila said.

"No. He picked her up from there last night."

"That's where she is," Lila cried.

"Now where did he bring her?"

"What? Where?"

"He brought her somewhere last night."

"I don't know," she said, tears streaming down her face.

The man pushed the gun against her cheek. "You really don't know, huh?" The gun barrel pressed harder into her cheek.

"He didn't tell me anything. He took her?" she said in hysterics. "He brought her home."

"You're a little liar—"

"There was a woman," she said, "a woman who came in here yesterday."

"Yeah?" the man said.

"Maybe he took her there. He said he liked her, he told me he liked her," she was still weeping.

"Okay, that's a start. Where's the woman's house?"

"Well, it's written down—there are forms on the desk . . . She filled out a form."

"Find it for us."

The man let Lila look for it. She pulled Carl's desk apart, drawer by drawer, went through his files. "Her name was Lucy—I don't know her last name."

"Find it."

"I'm trying!" she screamed. She was on her knees, going through the scraps of paper from one of his desk drawers. "He must have taken it with him."

The man with the gun picked up the telephone, dialed a number, and told the operator it was a collect call. He told the person that they'd had an accident with Carl, he'd been stubborn and wouldn't talk. Then he told the man that they had Lila. "I don't think she's lying. She don't seem to know." The man listened then handed the receiver to Lila.

Lila heard a smooth voice on the other side. "Hello there, young lady. You think Mr. Lark took my young girl to some woman named Lucy? What's her last name?"

"I never heard it."

"You're sure? Where's she from?" The voice spoke slowly and carefully.

"I don't know, she never said, just that she drove a long way."

"You think he brought her there?"

"That's the only person."

There was a long pause, the man was thinking, she could hear him breathing. "Now listen, Lila, you're going to type a little letter, just like you were my secretary. Is that clear?" Lila stared at the baggy pant legs of the man who stood in front of her. "You got a boyfriend, Lila?"

"No," Lila said, crying.

"Okay," he said. "What's Carl's wife's name?"

"Corva."

"Now, listen to me carefully, Lila, you set down in front of your typewriter just like you're taking dictation, hear me? Just like you'd do for Carl. Go on, get up and move to the typewriter." Lila got up and moved to the typewriter in Lark's office. The man with the gun followed her. "You got yourself a piece of paper in there?"

"Yes."

"I want you to type this note for me," the man said. " 'Dear Folks . . .' You got that, Lila?"

"Yes," Lila said, typing.

" 'Carl and I love you all.' " The man hesitated, thinking and waiting for her to stop typing. " 'We love our families.' " Another pause during which she typed. " 'But now we also love each other . . . We pray to the Lord Almighty that some day you'll forgive us both.' You got that down, Lila?"

"Yes."

"Now sign it 'Love, Carl and Lila . . .' Do it in pen, you hear me?" he said, and the other man took the phone and spoke to him and then hung up.

"Come on," the man holding Lila said, walking toward the back door, carrying the tank.

"Where?" The other man pushed her toward the back door. Outside she could see the van, one door open. "I'm not getting in there!" she yelled.

The man behind her pushed her down the steps. As soon as she tried to run, he grabbed the back of her shirt, then threw a headlock around her neck. The other man lifted the tank and mask out of the back of the van, approached her with the rubber mask and then jammed it on her face. She held her breath to avoid taking in whatever was inside. Water gushed in, filled the air space above her nose, above her eyes and she continued to hold her breath. The second man slapped her on the back. She coughed her air up, blew bubbles in the mask.

She had to breathe in. In came water, filling her lungs to the very brink then her throat exploded. She coughed, sucking in another lungful of water. She pushed these lungfuls out harder and then harder. If she could only expel all the water from her chest, it would be all right or at least better, but then it came time to suck in and she sucked in more water deeper into her lungs. *If only she could suck it in deeper, so deep that* . . . She tried to expel this lungful but it didn't seem to want to go and so she sucked in again. Not much came in and then she thought it would be okay everything would be okay *if only she could suck in more of it, more water and then she'd have enough* . . .

5

From that morning on, the morning Mr. Lark dropped off Emma, a deeper happiness than ever before drifted down into Lucy's life. Her prayers for a daughter, a companion, somebody she could love and nurture had been answered. Shopping, cleaning the house, going back and forth to work were entirely different experiences than when she had been living alone. The great emptiness that had plagued her since leaving the circus six years earlier vanished; now her life had a purpose that brought joy into every aspect of daily living. While driving or hanging the wash or cooking or shopping, she'd hum or whistle a tune, not knowing where it had come from. She never sighed as she had been in the habit of doing before. In the past she had woken up frequently during the night, afraid of the emptiness of her life, unable to make sense of her isolation, her shyness around most people. But now she slept peacefully and at daybreak she opened her eyes with a smile on her face.

Her coworkers at the nursing home, the Eagle Rest Home, told her that they could sense a change for the better had come over her. Because she was afraid of losing Emma, Lucy didn't bring her to work and mentioned her to but two friends. She was afraid that if people started asking about her, they might realize that Lucy's adoption of her wasn't necessarily legal. Maybe somebody would report her to the police.

Lucy's only other worries centered on doing the right thing for Emma. As a caregiver at the rest home, she was adept at working with the elderly, changing linens, bedpans, bringing them their trays of food, feeding them by hand if need be, helping them to their bathrooms. It had taken her a number of years to build her confidence in this simple job, but her supervisor had given her such consistently high marks in her reviews that she eventually began to trust herself. But taking care of Emma was entirely different. Whereas the old people talked to Lucy endlessly about their problems, Emma was always silent and entirely independent if Lucy let her be. Because it was nearly impossible to tell what the girl wanted, Lucy always worried whether or not she was doing the right thing for her. She took her on frequent short trips to shop or sightsee. Although the Blue Night Mall was the closest large mall, Lucy would drive in the opposite direction to shop. She brought Emma into music shops, clothing shops, boutiques, places that she thought Emma might be interested. One day she drove all the way to Cincinnati and they went to an art museum and then a zoo together. Another day they visited a wax museum, another time they took a tour of a cave. Emma was attentive to her surroundings, but it was hard to tell what she really liked or didn't like. Even when they stopped at a restaurant it was difficult for Lucy to tell what she wanted. Emma would hold a menu in her hands and stare at it, but eventually Lucy was the one who ordered.

Lucy left her alone during the days she worked. When she came home, she'd usually find her outside on the back in one of the lawn chairs, looking across the great fields toward the farmhouse, a placid, if distant, look on her face. "Did you have a good day?" Lucy would say. Rising to her feet, Emma would stare at her and then follow her into the house. She moved from one room in the house to the next without leaving a trace. Sometimes Lucy would find her staring out a window.

Once a week on the way home from work, Lucy stopped off at a thrift store and bought Emma clothes that had been donated that week. She'd hold them up for her then set them down on her bed. Sometimes the following morning Emma would come out of her bedroom wearing one of the items. She only liked outfits that adequately covered her skin such as turtlenecks, blue jeans, and long socks. Never once did she put on a skirt or a short-sleeve blouse. Once when Emma was taking a bath, Lucy tried to slip a towel through the door and saw that a chair had been wedged against the inside knob.

Lucy was a woman of many small rituals that helped her get through life outside of the circus. These rituals didn't change with the arrival of Emma. If the weather was fine in the evening after dinner, they would sit out on the lawn under the tree and watch the light fade and the stars come out. A herd of black and white cows were always visible, moving from one field to the next; sometimes they were in so close against the fence that Lucy and Emma could hear them chewing and their tails whipping flies from their backsides. As the evening shadows grew long, Lucy found herself telling Emma stories about her life.

She never had any desire to tell anyone the stories about her life. She had few friends, mostly from work at the Eagle Rest Home, and these friends considered her a quiet, introverted person. Even her closest friend, Margie, did not know that she had been Mrs. Big in the circus. Lucy had grown up in this very house before running away to the circus at the age of fourteen, but upon her return not a single person from town seemed to recognize or remember her. Though she made a point to stay to herself and do most of her small shopping in a neighboring town, occasionally she would step into the Millville supermarket and pass a face in the aisle or behind a counter that she remembered from grade school or junior high.

Now with Emma by her side, Lucy opened up and found her voice and discovered things that had happened to her that she had buried deep inside of her. There was a good reason for telling Emma her stories. Things had happened in Lucy's life before the circus that had led her to join it, and other things happened during the circus that she had somehow or another learned to survive. In her heart, she knew that something terrible had been done to Emma; in many ways she was a young girl without hope, a young girl whose memories would plague her forever, a fragile girl who would be lucky to survive her adolescence. Lucy was trying to pass on what she had learned to Emma.

Lucy was in her late thirties, but the wrinkles around her eyes made her seem much older. She knew her face, scarred with sadness and worry, would never be attractive to a man. She had been on a long journey that had started early in her life.

After a month together, Lucy saw that Emma had begun to pick up books around the house and read them. This seemed a good sign that a change was taking place in her. Soon she was picking up every paperback and *Reader's Digest* book in the house, even old copies of magazines that Lucy herself had never opened. She became absorbed in her reading, not looking up for hours, her eyes moving quickly across the pages. Often she pressed her palms against her temples and Lucy thought that perhaps she had a headache and offered her aspirin, which Emma took.

One Saturday Lucy drove her to the library and climbed the steps with her, holding her hand. There were other children in the library. Emma stood at the threshold of the big wooden door for a moment, nervous, looking back and forth. "Come in, darling," Lucy said. "It's just a library." Emma turned down an aisle and began scanning the books. Lucy followed. "Take anything you want," she said.

Emma came back with half a dozen novels.

"You're going to read all this, darling?" Lucy said, stepping outside with her pile of books.

It was the young girl's smile that Lucy watched for so carefully and there were certain mannerisms, ways Emma had of turning her head that indicated to her that she was happy.

One day they drove to a farm that leased horses for children and Lucy put down money for an old retired mare named Audrey McBride. Of all the activities they had done so far, this seemed the most successful. Emma's spirits rose whenever they drove into the yard of the ranch. They would chase Audrey McBride with grain in their hands until she got tired of her game, slowed down, and let them slip the bridle around her neck. Emma would ride while Lucy led the horse through the fields.

On the drive back home, Lucy encouraged Emma to squeeze up next to her and take the car wheel. Lucy called the old car Elvis. Master Howard, the ringmaster of the Crown Circus, had given it to her on her last day with the show. It had been painted with red and white polka dots at the time, but shortly after arriving home, seeing the attention that the car attracted, Lucy had it painted bright green, a color that was unfortunately almost as conspicuous as the polka dots.

Emma put her foot against the gas and brake and Lucy helped her with the wheel. She apparently liked to drive as much as she liked to ride horses. In the fields on the grassy roads in the back of the horse farm, Lucy sat in the seat next to Emma and gave her full control of the old vehicle. At first she started and stopped and chugged and wove back and forth in the tractor tracks, but after she got the hang of it Lucy even let her drive all the way home on the back roads, passing cars going the other way and stopping and going at intersections.

After work one day Lucy brought home a sketchpad and some colored pencils, unpacking it all before Emma on the living room floor. It seemed a good idea to encourage Emma to at least hold a pencil in hand in case she ever wanted to communicate. Crossing her legs on the rug, Lucy began drawing stick-figure people, cows with sticks for legs and ears, holding them up and showing them to Emma. A few days later after Lucy came home from work she found five pages in one of the sketchbooks filled with colorful squiggles, nothing that she could identify, just lively little marks on the page.

"Emma, these are gorgeous!" Lucy said, ecstatically. "I'll hang these on the refrigerator."

A proud smile came over Emma's face as she saw Lucy's enthusiasm. She then filled up every page with lines of all different colors. Lucy pulled some out of the pad and put them up over Emma's bed. "Beautiful," she kept saying.

As Emma filled more sketchbooks, her drawings became more skilled; at last Lucy could see what she was depicting. "What's this?" Lucy said, holding a drawing up.

Emma stared silently at Lucy.

"These are fish," Lucy said. "Beautiful fish." Lucy wrote *Fish* at the bottom of one of them, hoping that Emma would write something also.

Emma kept getting better at drawing; the fish had scales and gills and fins that were fairly well defined on the page. Though she continued to read, not once did she write a single word. "Words are something else altogether, aren't they?" Lucy said. "Maybe you're just not ready for them."

6

One day Lucy climbed through the hatch door into her attic and brought down a wooden box full of memorabilia from the circus. She had not opened this box since her arrival home. At times she wondered why she had not thrown the contents away. Now she knelt next to Emma on the rug and opened it. Within this box was another small wooden box, and in this were photographs that she had collected over the years. She laid a curled black and white photo on the floor in front of Emma: a dwarf, standing on the hood of a car. The dwarf wore a gray suit and had a very sad expression on his face; it seemed he did not like standing on this car, that he was there only for the photographer. "This is the man I loved. His name is Pidge," Lucy said quietly and sighed. She had wanted to keep the sadness that now crept into her voice away from Emma, but such a feat was nearly impossible. She had not laid eyes on Pidge for years and now the picture evoked all the feelings, the tenderness, the love for him, the dreams that she had created in her mind of being with him. So too did it evoke the disappointment, the morning of reckoning, the sharp pain that had sliced into her like lightning splitting open and blackening the trunk of a tree. Emma took the picture in her fingers and brought it close to her eyes. "He was a clown, but he hated doing that more than anything in the world.

I don't blame him; if you're born like he was, a dwarf, well, you don't need to make fun of yourself—the world will do it for you. You see this man here?" Lucy showed her a picture of a ringmaster in a tall black hat. The man had a long horselike face; his skin was brown and his eyes dark. He wore a double-breasted tuxedo buttoned tightly over his rotund chest and his tall black boots shown in the sunshine and he held a black whip in his hand. "Master Howard. He used to call himself the master of the universe, but in truth he was just a ringmaster of a tattered old run-down circus. He had me fooled for a long time. I thought he knew everything about everyone in the world—me included. Some stuff I still don't understand how he knew, but mostly it was just guesswork. He was real good at that."

Emma held the photograph up to her eyes and Lucy could see her pupils scanning the scene, the whitish tent in the background, the rear end of an elephant, the decorated trailer to one side.

"Pidge and I, well, we were married," Lucy said to Emma whose wide eyes turned to her. "Well, not really. Not in real life, in circus life. You see," she said. And then she handed over a picture of a huge woman in a great big flowered dress. She had a cane in her hand to balance herself. "Do you know who that crazy lady is?" Lucy said, quietly. "Me." She could hardly bear to look at the picture, let alone to admit to Emma that this was who she had been. She never thought it possible that she would share this picture with anyone in her life, but now she felt it important; it would help Emma somehow, though she had no idea how that might come about.

Emma examined it carefully and gently and Lucy could see her taking in tiny breaths of air and she thought she saw her face soften with compassion. It was hard to tell what she was thinking, but Lucy felt that she was understanding her. "I know, I can hardly believe that was me. I don't know what I was thinking in those days. I guess I felt pretty bad about just about everything, but that's all over with," Lucy tried to change her tone of voice. "I hope, anyway. I'll tell you something, I sure feel different since you got here . . ." She touched Emma's shoulder, then her own heart. "You pretty much changed my life." She tried to smile, there was so much pain in these pictures, and she didn't want to bring Emma down into it. "You see that guy?" she pointed at the picture of Master Howard. "He didn't help my problems much." Lucy tried to take the picture of herself back, but Emma moved her hand away. "Here, you can give it back to me." Emma pressed it against her chest. "Hey, now," Lucy said and finally Emma gave it back to her. "I don't want you to remember me like that." Emma reached into the wooden box, and Lucy's heart jumped as if she had just been set upon by a stranger, but she did not stop her as she lifted another picture, this one showed her in a white wedding gown when she was still very heavy, holding the hand of Pidge who was now in a tuxedo. "That's what I mean about married. There used to be a wedding at the end of every show. It was a big attraction that year. That was my husband—or everybody was made to think so. I don't know what he thought about me, but I fell so awfully in love with him. So darn in love with him, Emma, I didn't know what to do that year, what with the wedding going on every show." Lucy's eyes moistened. "You know how it is when things don't work out the way you want them."

Lucy closed her eyes—she could not go on. She had done such a fine job of blocking this out of her mind, and yet here it was again . . . that feeling of helplessness. Then she felt something against her cheeks. Emma was wiping them with her palm.

"Hey, there," Lucy said. "I meant to tell you the fun stories about my life. I don't want to get you all worried, too, you've got enough you're dealing with right now."

Emma shook her head. It was one of the first direct signs of communication that she had made to her. "Hey, you can hear me all right, can't you?"

Emma nodded her head ever so slightly.

Lucy smiled. "You're getting better . . . it's like that, that . . ." Lucy looked around the room, but she couldn't find an example to express her feelings. Emma again indicated that Lucy should talk. "What do you want me to say?" Lucy said.

Emma picked up the picture of Pidge and her and Lucy smiled or tried to; it wasn't easy remembering those days.

"That was me, Mrs. Big." She sighed. "And that was old Pidge, Mr. Little." She took a deep breath and tried to think of where to go with this story; there were so many sides to it that she hardly knew where to start. She smiled. "I think he took to me at one point. He must have. Maybe something turned him off to me. I don't know. Maybe it was all in my head to begin with." Again she laughed. "But I . . . I think for sure . . . no, maybe . . . I don't know what he really felt because he was like you—he wasn't much of a talker." Lucy paused. She herself had never been much of a talker, not until she had to fill up these silent moments with Emma. "He was the best mechanic the circus ever saw—oh yeah. That's what he lived for. We had a lot of beat-up old trucks and generators, but we were never in a bind. If one of them broke down, he'd be under the hood and have it up and running in five minutes flat. He came into the circus to do that, fix things, but Master Howard made him do the clowning during the show. God, how Master Howard kept control over things like he did, I'll never understand. Sometimes I wonder if I'd have—he said to me once, 'I made you who you are, made you from the ground up,' and I wonder if he didn't mean that he made me into the fat woman. Well, that was because of a lot of things, Emma, things that happened right here back at home in this town, bad things. But look at me now. I don't look like that lady in the picture anymore, do I?" She smiled and thought she saw Emma smile, then Emma's eyes met hers and moved quickly back and forth in the most expressive way, as if she were letting the world in or as if she were searching her memory for a word. Lucy could feel something opening up in the child, a tiny sprout of green in the hard-packed earth, something was pushing up into the light. Then, too, Lucy knew that this was the first time that she herself had ever declared that she was no longer the fat woman, even to herself. "Whenever you're wondering about something, Emma, you should just come right out and ask it . . . You see, I'm a living example of how come it's important to ask a question when you're curious. I should have just asked Pidge what he was thinking . . . but I was just too scared to, of rejection, do you know what I mean? We were just kind of thrown into this marriage thing; it wasn't his choice or mine. But there I was spending most of my energy hoping what was just a show would become real." She took out another picture; this was of a banner hanging in front of the Crown Circus midway. It said, COME TO THE WEDDING OF MRS. BIG AND MR. LITTLE. THE MOST UNUSUAL COUPLE OF ALL TIME. "Pidge was such a quiet fellow, he didn't have any more friends than me, but I'll tell you something, he had a kind heart. That's the most important thing, is kindness. Reverend Williams told me that that's more important than believing in God or in money, or anything in the world. Kindness is the crown jewel of humanity. It's as far up as man can go. And he had a kind heart . . . He just didn't know how to express it, being that he was too shy." Lucy tried to laugh at herself. "Now that's where I get into the problems, it really is, Emma. Pidge did something terrible to me—at least I think he did, but I don't know. Maybe Master Howard put him up to it. You should forgive people—if you can, that's what I think. But I don't know about that, I mean about Pidge. I don't know if I could ever forgive him. Ever. It don't matter. I don't reckon I'll ever see him again."

After Lucy put the pictures back in the box, she realized that Emma was still holding the one of herself when she was heavy. Lucy pointed at herself.

"You want that?"

She nodded.

"You won't show it to anybody, right?"

Emma shook her head and then looked back at the picture.

"Well," Lucy said. "Maybe that'll be a lesson to you. Whatever's happened to you don't mean a thing. You can always change, fight back, don't listen to what they tell you about yourself, only listen to this." She touched her heart. "This is your best friend, your very best friend. You can always get better." She smiled again. "I'm better. I don't have to be what people want me to be, I can be exactly who I am."

Lucy knew that Emma would have to fight what somebody had tried to make her. Yes, somebody had tried to change Emma, to mold her, paint her, change her mind into something that she wasn't. Lucy had no idea what sort of person was capable of this, but at times she could feel the presence of this man when she was with Emma.

The next morning things took a sudden turn for the worse. Emma woke with a wild, unhappy look on her face; her eyes were all puffed up as if she were reliving something in her dreams and all that next day she seemed as worn out as the old people Lucy cared for at the home. Lucy wondered if her stories hadn't triggered something. She wondered if she was doing something wrong with Emma. All day at the home, Lucy prayed to herself that Emma would learn to speak. After dinner, she asked Emma questions. "Are you okay? Did something happen?" But she got little response. Before bedtime, Lucy hugged Emma, but Emma merely stayed still between her arms.

"You've got to talk what's on your mind, darling. Otherwise everything that happened to you is going to sit inside you and fester and rot. You've got to speak what's on your mind. You can talk to me. Nothing you say will ever shock me."

7

Lucy was woken by a loud strangling, gurgling noise coming from another room. She jumped out of bed in her nightgown, wondering what on earth the noise could be. Then she decided that somebody else was in the house. *Somebody's trying to kill her!* She rushed into Emma's room only to find the bed empty. The sounds were coming from a room farther down the hall. Lucy rushed into this room. It was pitch-dark, the noise got louder, the intruder was in here. Lucy screamed and frantically fumbled for the light switch. "Get away from her! Get away, get away from my daughter!"

Finally she found the switch and turned on the light. On the floor between the bed and the window Emma lay, a lamp cord wrapped tightly around her neck. There was nobody in here but the girl herself who was holding both ends of the cords. Lucy grabbed her arms and realized that she was still fast asleep. She pushed the girl's hands together to relax the pressure from the cord, then pulled it away from her neck and began to shake her. "Up, wake up, Emma, please!" Tears flooded Emma's eyes as they opened and Lucy got down on her knees and hugged her.

The rest of the evening, Lucy slept in Emma's room, a cot pushed up next to her bed. "Darling, I'm right here," Lucy reassured her anytime she heard her stirring.

Besides what Mr. Lark had told her, Lucy had never heard of people trying to kill themselves in their sleep. Surely they'd wake themselves up or at least pass out before actually damaging themselves. But then one night, Lucy woke to a slightly different sound, a gagging noise coming from downstairs. This time Lucy ran straight down to the kitchen and found Emma on her back with a black garbage bag pulled over her head. "Lord help us!" Lucy ripped the bag into pieces and then picked Emma up into her arms and hugged her tightly against her chest. "Oh, Emma, oh, little darling, why, why are you doing this to yourself?"

From this night on Lucy drew the cot up next to Emma's and tied a string between their wrists. Three nights over a period of a month the young girl got up in her sleep and pulled on the string and Lucy jumped up and shook her awake. Lucy thought she had things under control.

Early one morning Lucy's eyes opened to the rising sun coming through her curtains and the sounds of sparrows chirping. She turned to see the covers of Emma's bed pulled back, the string on Lucy's wrists dangling to the floor where it had been broken. She got up. *She's done it, this time she's done it!* She pulled on her bathrobe and walked to the stairs, listening intently. Except for the birds and a gentle breeze that blew the white curtains in the window over the stairs the house was quiet. One step at a time she went down, her hands gripping the railing, listening for any possible sounds. *Bad luck like this can't happen all to one little girl.*

She looked across the living room to the sofa and love seat and television with the coat hanger antenna. In the kitchen a chair was pushed against the counter, the cabinet where Lucy had hidden the garbage bags high up was open. The screen door to the backyard was unlatched.

She stepped out onto the back step and looked across the yard beyond the single tree. "Emma!" Lucy called and waited. She could see the neighbor's cows filing into the barn for milking. She crossed the yard carefully as if one wrong step could bring the world down on her head; her heart beat hard against her nightgown. Across the barbed-wire fence the pasture grass was long and dry and full of thistles and small flowers. Then she spotted a black plastic bag caught on the branches of a dead bush.

Lucy crawled through the fence, her hands and knees trembling, hardly breathing, getting up and stepping carefully as if Emma's life depended on her every move. She followed a path of pushed over grass. The silence she felt was bigger than the clearest Ohio sky.

In a little grassy gully she saw her daughter in her tights and long-sleeved turtleneck shirt lying facedown in the grass. Kneeling next to her, Lucy turned her over. The young girl had spit up what looked like pieces of grass. There was saliva mixed with dirt smeared across her face and hair. Lucy picked her up carefully in her arms and carried her to her car.

8

"You've got to hope that she starts to talk again," said the nurse on duty at the Eagle Rest Home. She was Lucy's friend, somebody she could trust. She examined Emma in the doctor's room. "What I know about cases like this—they're almost impossible to treat if the doctors don't know what happened. If you think she could talk at one time, then you'd better hope she gets talking soon. She's got a fragile sense of self. Don't you want to take her to the police or something?"

"No," Lucy said.

"Maybe they'd know what happened to her by now."

"I can't go see them." Lucy remembered what Carl Lark had said about that. She felt sure they would take her away.

"Well, I think you should take some time off. Don't you have vacation due you?"

Lucy had been saving up her vacation time since the beginning of the year. "Some," she said.

"Just stay close to her. Watch her. Maybe you'd better take her to a psychiatrist."

"What would somebody like that do?"

"Figure out what happened to her, I reckon."

"Yes," Lucy said.

"And help her face it."

That night in bed Lucy woke up next to Emma with the nurse's voice in her mind. *Help her face it.* Nobody had helped Lucy face things after she was fourteen years old, nobody, not a soul after Reverend Williams died when she was fourteen years old. That was one thing that Lucy felt was different about herself. Most people had at least an uncle, a brother or sister who understood them while they were growing up. But not a single member of Lucy's kin had been there for her in any way, especially her mother. Sometimes Lucy wondered if that was why she had nearly killed herself by eating herself to death.

She left Emma's side and went downstairs. In the dark living room she sat down in her sofa chair and said the name *Master Howard* aloud. This ringmaster of the Crown Circus had hurt her more than he had helped her. But if Lucy believed anything about him, it was that he knew more about human nature in his own crude way than any person she had ever met or read about. Over the years he told Lucy things about herself that she had never told to a soul; others in the circus claimed the same sort of experiences with him. There was a brilliance about him, though it often expressed itself in a certain cruelty and an ability to swindle. He was also well acquainted with the criminal world in most small towns in Ohio and Kentucky and even parts of northern West Virginia. Among his many conceits he sometimes called himself *the Creator* and once told Lucy that it was his goal to convince *his* performers that they had not been born but rather *he had invented them.*

Lucy kept tossing in her sleep, slumped over in the chair, half dreaming and half envisioning what it would be like if she were to return to this man whom she had told Emma about. Half awake, she could hear the sounds of the circus barker in the midway selling T-shirts, popcorn and hotdogs. She could hear the circus band that consisted of one musician with a drum machine and trumpet and sometimes a slightly out of tune violin.

At five in the morning she climbed the stairs and peeked in at Emma who lay on her back. Her eyes were large, like a doll's, her eyelashes seemed to rest on her cheeks. Maybe it was the way her eyes were closed, but it seemed like she was deep in a kind of peaceful rest, as if the spirits that had been haunting her, driving her to destroy herself, had finally taken a break from her. *I don't want to take you there, not yet.* Lucy took some clothes out of Emma's dresser, then went into her room, and packed them in a bag with her own clothes. Then she lay down on her bed and slept until nine. When she returned to Emma's room, she found the young girl standing at her bedroom window looking out toward the neighbor's farm. "What are you looking at, darling?" Emma did not turn around. Lucy crossed the room and took her small hand that was cool to the touch and led her down the stairs.

By noon Lucy was driving through Sayerville Township, some eighty miles north of Millville, looking for the show. She found it in a large field that had already been worn thin; empty popcorn boxes and cotton candy sticks were blown up against the wooden snow fence surrounding the grounds. The big top was fashioned from the same canvas as years ago. Patches had been sewn across it and painted over. It looked like the sail of a ship too long at sea. A brand-new flag dangled from the center pole. That was something that Master Howard kept fresh. It had on it what he claimed was his family insignia: two vicious snakes, coiled together in battle, both with their yellow fangs bared ready to strike the body of the other. To one side of the field, the horses, llamas, and goats were tethered to a single chain strung between iron stakes. Fresh hay had been dropped in front of them and they were leaning over eating. Inside a small tent close to the snow fence in front of Lucy's car were Master Howard's three Bengal tigers. A groom was washing down their cages with a powerful hose and using a squeegee to clean the bottoms. Trailers, campers, and Winnebagos were parked at intervals around the big top with a series of clotheslines draped with costumes and workers jumpsuits strung between them. All alone in a clear place between the trailers, Lucy saw the show's only elephant, Marcella, swaying back and forth, curling hay up to her trunk and Iggy the elephant boy near her, brushing down a white llama.

Lucy parked and sat still, holding the steering wheel, looking straight out over the hood. "Well," she said. "I swore I'd never be back. But here we are. Here we are, my child."

9

"Just give me a moment, darling," she said to Emma. "And I'm going to get out of old Elvis and march right down there with you and find out what I can do to help you out. This is where all those people I showed you in the pictures are. It's not going to be too easy seeing them again." Emma stared as wide-eyed as a deer toward the city of faded colors. "This is the place where I used to sit and let people look at me, where I forgot sometimes that I was a human being because other people didn't consider me so. I was just something sitting there, to be laughed at good and hard. Except for that doctor, Doctor Marshall, who helped me leave the circus when the time was right."

It was strange that Lucy had to come all the way out here, away from her house, to be visited by memories of things back where she had been living. These memories began around the time of her first year in high school, a regional high school in a different town than her elementary school. For years Lucy had been waiting to move on to this new school, believing that the mere change in locations would make things happen in her life. Her peers and teachers would treat her differently; she would be somebody—not necessarily popular—but certainly a part of something that other children her age were part of. But when high school did finally come, students continued to ignore her except on occasion when they poked fun at her. One day well into the school year, her math teacher forgot her name entirely and asked her if she had been in his class all year long and she had said yes and the other students had laughed heartily at this.

Lucy started thinking of herself as a ghost. Somewhere she read that ghosts cannot speak to people or to other ghosts. *Yes, that is what I am, a ghost.*

All would have been lost in those days had she not had one good friend, Reverend Williams. Afternoons after school she would go over to his house for tea and knock on his door and he'd smile down at her and then lead her inside to a checkerboard that was usually all set up. Every so often he would indeed show off and jump six or seven of her players, but he usually let her win, pointing out to her some of the moves she should make whenever she was stuck.

Later they would sit on his back porch. He smoked his pipe and worked on his sermons while she read books from his house. Sometimes he helped her with her homework and he always kept track of her grades and congratulated her whenever he read her report card. She loved every inch of his house. The antique rugs, the smell of candles, even the smell of mothballs in his closet. Everything seemed to reflect his own mild manners, his quiet, personal voice. Sometimes he reached out and stroked Lucy's hair and she would feel a tickling along her spine. She dreaded going back to her house where her mother and friends always shouted at each other, where all the fine things in life were overlooked. She never once heard this man use a profanity. Though she only knew him for a relatively short time, it seemed an eternity back then.

One afternoon Lucy confessed her feelings to him about thinking that she was a ghost. They were sitting on his porch. He put his paper down and stared straight at her, then drew his pipe from his mouth.

"Say that again," he said.

"I keep thinking . . . I keep thinking that I'm a . . . a ghost."

He put his pipe down. "How could you be a ghost?" He laughed gently. "No, you're hardly that." He watched her for a while. "Do you know what you really are?"

Lucy shook her head.

"You're the opposite of a ghost. Do you know what that is?"

Again she shook her head.

"A freak."

Lucy's heart sunk and she looked down; she'd been called that before in school, too.

"Don't be ashamed, that's what I am," Reverend Williams went on. "I'm a freak."

"What do you mean?" Lucy said.

"Well, I don't know what I mean." He thought about this for a while. "I know this is a little strange, but all of us are freaks, there are just some people who don't want to admit it."

"Why not?"

"They're afraid of it, afraid of showing their differences, do you know what I mean?"

"Maybe."

"Most people strive for perfection. They want to be the best salesman, minister, mother. They want to look perfect like everyone on TV or they want to be a star or they want to make a lot of money. There aren't many people who just accept who they are. And at school, the kids who poke fun at you? Well, kids used to make fun of me all the time."

"For what?"

"For my big nose, big lips, and big feet. I could never say anything back to anybody because I couldn't think of what to say. I felt terrible. I wanted to be perfect like everybody else."

Lucy thought about this. She knew that he looked unusual, but she never thought of him as ugly. "I never wanted to be perfect."

"I know," Reverend Williams said. "That's why I liked you right away. You have a special knack for being a freak."

Lucy's gaze rose to his and slowly she let herself look into his warm eyes. He winked at her and smiled and she, too, smiled. Later that same afternoon, he told her something that he made her swear to secrecy between them forever. "If you tell anybody this, Lucy, I'll lose my parish and have to move away. You promise you won't tell?"

Lucy had nodded her head.

"Well, I don't believe that Jesus Christ is any more God's real son than I am the Son of God or you are His daughter. You see, Christ was just a human, born into the world like you and me, and Mary was not a virgin as they say, she was just a mother. But Christ's message *was* one about God, though I'm not sure it came directly from Him or whether Christ was just a very spiritual person who understood things on his own. His message said don't believe in God or even in religion per se, believe in humans, in humanity. Only we humans can save each other. To be saved is to realize you are human, which is to accept that you're a freak." Over the years Lucy had kept this a solemn secret.

She heard the news that Reverend Williams's heart had failed one Sunday afternoon after his sermon. She said nothing to her mother about it; she even went to the reverend's house after school on Monday morning as if he would be there. When her mother came home from work that evening and asked her where she'd been that afternoon, Lucy realized that she had lost her ability to speak. For the next three days she could not answer to her mother, her teachers, or her classmates. Her mother thought she was doing this on purpose to attract attention and spanked her hard. But much later, perhaps understanding that something serious was going on inside of Lucy, she stopped bothering her and went off with one of her men for a few days.

The morning of the funeral, Lucy dressed up in her Sunday

clothes that she bought herself from a thriftshop with money the reverend had given her, and she walked to the church alone and sat to one side in a pew. After the hearse left the church for the cemetery almost three miles away, Lucy, realizing that she did not have a ride and might miss the burial, ran across the fields and arrived at the grave just after the casket had been lowered and the few people who had attended were dispersing. She stood near the picket fence of the cemetery and watched the backhoe drag the pile of dirt into the hole. She kept thinking about what he'd said about Jesus Christ not being God's son, but carrying a message from God and she wondered what had become of Reverend Williams in the afterlife.

The simple white church where Reverend Williams had preached closed for services and notices for an estate sale were posted. Lucy went to the sale and there saw many of the belongings that she had turned over in her hands for so many years and cherished as she had cherished the company of the reverend, while people passed down a line, picking and choosing what to take home.

Because her pockets were empty, Lucy stole something for the first time in her life: the checker set that they had played on and an aromatic tin of tobacco. She hid them in a box outside across the fields until she was sure that nobody would come looking for them.

Soon a big yellow moving van appeared in front of the reverend's house and a large family moved in. Lucy watched the children running in and out of the house; she knew that they did not know what that house meant to her, that the house had been her little paradise, her refuge from the battering she was taking both at home and at school. Meanwhile Reverend Williams's little white church remained closed, the black shutters drawn over the stained-glass windows, and a damp paper sign on the door curling around the tacks that held it said CLOSED UNTIL FURTHER NOTICE.

It was one of the worst periods of Lucy's life. She spent every afternoon alone, walking through the fallow pastures, circling Reverend Williams's house and wondering where he had gone to.

Then Lucy saw a colorful tent set up in the field near the closed church. It reminded her of the tents the firemen used when they had their country fair in Millville, only this one had a sign on the great big white trailer parked in front that said PASTOR JOE'S BIBLE REVIVAL and it gave the times for the sermons.

That first Sunday, Lucy joined with many of the townspeople who crowded into the tent for want of a minister in their church. Pastor Joe had a big smile with even teeth. A generator ran the tinny microphone and the lights and the tent flapped in the gentle breeze and Lucy could smell the cows of a neighboring farm as the man gave his sermon.

This charismatic man had control of his audience like a concert pianist his piano. He knew exactly what people wanted to hear, how to allay their deepest fears and promise them what they hoped for. At times he paced the aisles, dragging the cord of his microphone, proclaiming his outrage and indignation at Satan's encroachment upon the territory of God and the angels. But then he would purposely turn his stern message to something humorous and to Lucy's great surprise the entire congregation, riveted to their chairs, would burst out into laughter and guffaws. Soon many more people were visiting his tent than had ever visited Reverend Williams's small church even on Christmas Eve. Everyone in town and even the children in school were murmuring the name Pastor Joe. They showered his collection basket with large and small bills.

One afternoon after school Lucy was walking along the long empty roads next to the pastures past the dormant church when she saw Pastor Joe sitting on the steps of his white trailer. He had strung a clothesline between his trailer and the tent, and his socks and black pants and shirts were drying in the balmy breeze. He himself wore blue jeans, cowboy boots, a baseball hat, and a turtleneck shirt. He waved to her and she waved back and continued on before realizing that he was waving her over to him. She crossed the field that was matted from where the cars parked on Sunday.

"You're the little girl who always sits in back," he said, smiling. He had been clipping his fingernails, the shards lay in the grass at his feet. "I don't see you with your ma or pa. Do you come listen to me alone?"

Lucy nodded her head.

"Where are they? Where are your folks?"

Lucy shrugged her shoulders.

"Do you have a ma and pa?"

"My ma doesn't like to go to church. I don't know if she's ever been."

"But you do." Looking her up and down, he seemed fascinated by this fact. "Isn't that something. What brings *you* to Pastor Joe's tent?"

Lucy shook her head.

"Does the body of Christ draw you in naturally?"

Lucy nodded her head slowly, though she wasn't quite sure exactly what he meant by this question.

"Your ma doesn't believe in Christ?"

"I don't know," Lucy said.

"Well, I guess you know better than your ma, then. That's okay, God works in funny ways sometimes. Sometimes he gives the daughter the knowledge and not the mother, or the son and not the father." He chuckled. "But then Satan has a strange way of choosing his disciples, too. You got to be on the lookout for that, Satan will send you up something that you think is one thing, then turns out to be another. Like *you*. I got to be careful with you, don't I?"

Lucy shook her head.

"Heck, you look like one of God's children, as innocent as a lamb, you are, but how do I really know? You might have come right to me from the hands of Satan." He smiled and then laughed a little. "Who sent you?"

"Nobody."

"Well, I'm sure you're one of God's, I pretty much can sense it. You've got a good heart, don't you?"

Lucy nodded her head, then took a deep breath. She didn't feel comfortable talking to this man who was far more animated than Reverend Williams.

"Come on now, pull up a seat. There's something special about you. I don't know what it is, but I do believe there is something real special about you. You're a brave one, you are."

Later he said, "You don't have many friends in school, do you?" Lucy shook her head.

"How come? How come the other kids stay away from you?" Again she shook her head.

"Well, maybe they can sense something *in* you." He didn't explain what he meant by this. Lucy became even more uncomfortable; she was not sure he was talking about a good thing.

"Well, well, I didn't have a friend in the town where I lived. Not a single friend." He held up his finger. "Not one." He smiled. "But look at me, I'm happy now. I'm doing what I was destined to do all along. Are you going to come visit me tomorrow?" he said when Lucy was leaving. She did not know what to say.

The next afternoon she saw him again and he called her over and asked her if she would help paint the side of his trailer. Then she had a paintbrush in hand and was standing along side of him as he reddened the letters: PASTOR JOE'S BIBLE REVIVAL.

The days passed and she got to know him. He talked about his plight growing up. "I might have been the loneliest boy who the Good Lord ever decided to invent. That's quite possible." They took short trips to the store together, fixed things around his tent and trailer. He never invited her inside his trailer. If he needed something from inside, he always told her to wait, then he'd slip in and out without letting her see inside.

Lucy began to care for him and trust him. The emptiness that she felt from Reverend Williams's death disappeared. She knew Pastor Joe had emotional problems. He had a fierce sense of humor, which he used to charm people, but also a wicked temper that flared at moments entirely disconnected from the rest of the world and from Lucy. At times she heard him talking to himself and this, too, was startlingly disconnected to the present, unlike the way her mother talked to herself, which always had to do with immediate things, something that she had forgotten or a lack of money or a man that she had been dating. Pastor Joe's talking to himself had a more philosophical bent to it. It was more like a conversation than a reaction to something specific.

Some afternoons Lucy would ride around the countryside with Pastor Joe in his truck, visiting farmers, walking down the main street of neighboring towns, Pastor Joe using his disarming sense of humor to make people laugh and to talk to them, then handing them a flyer and shaking their hands.

"Come on by the tent," he'd say. "We have an awful fun time, don't we, Lucy?"

One day while it was raining she stopped by his trailer and knocked. He came to the door and stared out at her. She was soaking wet and cold. She could see him hesitate before standing back and saying. "Well, you come on in here. You just don't touch anything, you hear?"

The interior of the trailer had piqued her curiosity long ago. But what she saw once inside more than equaled her high expectations. Wild objects covered every inch of wall, floor, and shelf space. They looked like they had been thrown in here chaotically. But then she realized that everything had been neatly arranged; the room had a kind of beauty and style.

Much of the furniture had been customized with a paintbrush; two wooden chairs were meticulously decorated with tiny seahorses amidst underwater grasses. On a painted table a tropical fish tank was bubbling quietly. Lucy approached the tank and put her fingers on the glass and he asked her not to touch. Inside the tank, baby flounder and rays skittered along the colored stones of the bottom. An eel poked its head out of a wrecked ship. Out of the corner of her eyes, Lucy saw two stuffed bright green parrots perched on painted branches mounted on the wall, their heads cocked toward her. On a table next to the couch, a stuffed black mink with tiny black marblelike eyes was poised with one raised paw. A stuffed red squirrel was climbing a vertical log, turning its head around as if frozen in time. The faded skin of a rattlesnake was curled around the base of an oriental lamp on the shade of which was a hand-painted figure of Christ on the cross.

Pastor Joe's clothes hung neatly from a rack. They, too, seemed part of the décor. Among his ministry clothes were costumelike outfits, a cowboy shirt and pants complete with a white hat, snake-skin boots with spurs. A white tuxedo with long tails.

Set against the wall among the many collectibles, Lucy noticed a series of framed pictures of circus freaks taken with a cheap Polaroid camera with a flash. Lucy's eye fell on a man standing against a brick wall, smoking a cigar. His body looked like it was put on backward—his legs and feet were pointed backward while the rest of his body faced the camera. In a small box was a woman, her body curled inside the tight wooden walls like the folded wings of a bat. In another photo Lucy saw two people with tiny heads, their sex unclear, then a woman without legs or arms set upon a pedestal like the bust of a statue. She had a cigarette in a long holder between her lips.

"Aberrations," Pastor Joe said. Lucy turned from the photograph to Pastor Joe. She wasn't sure what the word meant. "God's sense of humor. He likes a laugh like the rest of us, don't you think?"

Lucy shook her head. "No," she said.

"Sure, He's got to have a sense of humor."

"I don't think He would laugh if they weren't happy." Lucy was thinking of what Reverend Williams would say.

"That's not true. He would laugh his head off."

"No he wouldn't."

"If he makes them like that he does," Pastor Joe said.

Lucy shook her head and Pastor Joe watched her. "How come you're defending them ugly people."

"I don't think they're ugly. Why do you have their pictures here?"

"To make me smile."

"I don't think it's funny," Lucy said. "No, not at all."

"My, my, aren't you—" He tilted his head like a dog trying to understand his master. "Have you ever known a freak?"

She hesitated and then nodded her head. "I like them."

This took Pastor Joe by surprise. He stared at her, mesmerized and then mumbled, "Well, well." She sensed a sadness in his voice, a kind of resignation.

That rainy afternoon, Pastor Joe gave her a ride home and introduced himself to Lucy's mother. "You've got yourself a mighty fine daughter," he said, taking off his hat.

"You think so?" her mother said. "I guess you're trained to see light where everyone else sees nothing but darkness."

"I don't see darkness in her," he said to her. "I sure don't see any darkness in her, no, ma'am."

"You would if you had to live with her."

"I don't believe it's there," he said, politely.

"Ha," her mother said. "I've heard that one before." He sat down and her mother made him an iced tea, then invited him to dinner. That evening Lucy's two uncles came over to join them; one was drunk and rowdy as always. After Lucy was sent to bed, Pastor Joe stayed at the table and Lucy hid at the top of the stairs where she could hear the pastor telling stories; they were stories about circuses.

He had never before mentioned to her that he knew circus people, but in front of these adults his memory came alive with yarns about them.

"Circus folks are the hardest folk in the world to convert. I don't know if I've ever met a single soul in a show who gave a second thought to what Jesus did for mankind. People do not join a circus as you might think. They're cast into circuses by God. Personally, I hate them. I'll certainly never go near one again, if only because of the darn freaks," he said with disgust.

"Freaks?" somebody said.

"God's dirtiest souls. God didn't grant them a half body for nothin'. If you got to know a few of them, you'd understand." Then he told a joke, something about elephants and midgets and everyone laughed, everyone except Lucy. It made her sad to think that this was the way he really felt.

One day in his truck he said to Lucy, "Does your ma bring a lot of fellows home?"

Lucy started to shake her head. "Those were my uncles."

"I know, but I heard rumor that she likes her men. Meets them in bars."

It was true what he was saying; Lucy said nothing.

"It's a shame, you know. I didn't want to talk to you about it, but I thought I'd better say something." He shifted the gears of his truck and drove around a wagon full of hay bales. "It's a shame when a mother does something like that around her daughter. It's one of the few things I find most difficult to forgive in a person." Then he paused. "Could I ask you something?"

Lucy said nothing, she was afraid of this attention.

"What makes you so different from them?"

Lucy looked down at her bare knees.

"Don't be ashamed. I can see you *are* different, you're like nobody I've ever met before, you've got the goodness in your heart, plenty of it, too. Where did you get it from?"

"I'm not good," Lucy said.

"How do you mean?"

"I've been real bad at times."

"Who says? Your mother? How would she know? She just takes it out on you, that's all; I could tell from her tone of voice. She just doesn't see you for who you are."

"Who am I?" Lucy said quietly.

"I don't know," he said almost to himself.

That sunny afternoon Pastor Joe drove down a narrow road that ended at a corroded asphalt boat launch to a lake. A farm was on the far side of this oval-shaped lake; there were cattails and long grass and a few cows standing in the water. The farm itself sat on the horizon like a little dollhouse in the distance. He parked the truck and they got out and sat on a low cement barrier that had been knocked askew a long time ago. "It wasn't just the folks in my town that were so messed up. It was my folks, my ma and pa, too," he said.

She stared at him across the cement barrier on which they rested. He looked at her, then back at the boat launch.

"Sure, more messed up than your ma, way more messed up. People who don't have no regard for human life. People who wouldn't give Jesus Christ the time of day if He asked for it. People who never understood what it meant when God sent his Son down to die for their sins. People who would never have bothered with such a concept, not if it hit them in the face."

How many times had Lucy heard his sermons: Jesus died for your sins on the cross, but all the suffering, all that He was put up to do had been for naught since mankind refused to learn even the basics of His lesson.

Pastor Joe threw a rock in the water and said, "Sometimes I like to judge sin this way. I think of all the water in the world, all the oceans and rivers and ponds, and then I think of all the sin in the world, then I try to figure out which is more, the water *or* the sin."

Lucy didn't like it when he got on the subject of sin. His voice changed, he became serious and often on edge, ready to snap at her or at somebody else.

"Indeed." He stood up and paced in his cowboy boots and blue jeans with the cuffs rolled up and put his hands in his pockets. "Did you ever wonder where I get my power?" He squatted down in front of her, picked up a small stone and dropped it on the pavement at her feet, then picked up another and dropped it and it bounced under his legs.

"Right there," he pointed behind him. She looked out at the water. "You see that?"

Lucy said nothing.

"Nothing but water, right? Sure, nothing but blue water, cows drinking from it, fish swimming in it. Sometimes it falls from the heavens and moistens the dry grass. Other times it's sucked up in the air and turns to clouds that drift dreamily across the sun and the stars. Sometimes it flows down a beautiful river, over stones and under fallen logs, carrying leaves, a home to brook trout. Sometimes it turns into a wave and breaks on a shore of white sand and clay cliffs. We wash our feet and hands in it, shower in it, drink it. Dust to dust. Dust is death and water is . . . perfection," he said and got up and tossed a smooth stone through the surface of blue. "God's perfection. Now, where do you think I get my power?"

Lucy said nothing.

"Perfection," he said. Then he laughed at himself. "I know it sounds funny, but I made a pact with God long ago. Never to be like the people who brought me up. My ma was more of a bitch than—" Lucy cringed at the word "bitch." Pastor Joe noticed and didn't finish the sentence. "My pa, he was a cruel man without remorse. It took me years to understand that God had banished him from the ranks of normal society, banished him to the underworld even while living on earth.

"During my upbringing I was beset with temptation, over and

over. At age twelve and a half I was stripped naked and thrown in bed with a naked lady. I know this is tough to hear, Lucy, but I was put through the trials of Job, just about. And I've stayed clean, like you and other children. I'm like Christ that way, like water." He threw another stone into the blue lake water. "Ever think of what it would be like if Christ had children? If Christ had a daughter or son?"

Lucy shook her head.

"I wonder if He felt left out, regretted it, you know. Strange thought, isn't it? Well, I'm the same way." Lucy could feel his sadness. "You don't want to be my daughter, do you?" he said suddenly.

Lucy looked right at him, then turned away. He was blushing; she sensed that it had been difficult for him to ask this.

"Do you know what virginity is?" he asked, taking a deep breath. Two dragonflies came buzzing by, pausing near Pastor Joe then darting down to a thicket of reeds near shore. "It's the key to Christ. It's perfection, the only true way to serve Christ. I don't want to be boastful, but people should be so lucky as to get me as their preacher. Everything comes from my pact with God. You think I'm too cocky, don't you? Well, I'm sorry, sometimes I do get awfully heady." Then he became softer, his voice sweeter. "We make a good pair, the two of us, even if we aren't really father and daughter, just pretending that way. But if I were your father, I'd be a good one to you, I would. I'd do just the opposite of mine. That's how I learned my lessons from him, yes indeed," he said.

Lucy closed her eyes.

"You just need to trust me," he said. "You're a good girl, you don't even know who your real father is, do you?"

Nobody had ever asked this question directly to her. She felt a sadness in the back of her throat. Again she closed her eyes.

"Well," he said, "you just consider it a done deal. You're my daughter, I'm your dad."

After that afternoon he never mentioned the term father or daughter to her, though she felt that he was thinking about it often. He instead frequently said "the two of us." Nobody but Reverend Williams had ever used this expression with her, no adult, and she could not help but lean on him and accept his offer of friendship. It was a different kind of closeness than what she felt with Williams, but it was a closeness nevertheless that helped her accept his many odd qualities, his talking to himself, his ranting about God and Satan, even his talking about being a virgin. "You've heard of the Virgin Mary, now you've heard of the Virgin Joe," he said once and laughed.

Sometimes she understood that if she had a normal friend, she would never have befriended Pastor Joe; she recognized her own desperation, but she was unable to do anything about it.

But then one week, around the time another minister was suppose to move into the town church, Pastor Joe seemed to change. All along he had expressed jealousy of ordained ministers. Most ministries looked down on people like himself who worked out of tents. He had plenty of followers, but the establishment had never legitimized him.

Somehow or another as he sat outside his trailer with Lucy, he got onto the subject of Reverend Williams. He wanted to know everything about the man, what he had thought, how he had lived. The more Lucy told him the more jealous he became of him and their relationship.

"Sounds like you liked him better than me," he said.

"It was different."

"Sounds like you liked his civilized ways. You must miss him."

"I do."

"How come?"

"Because he was a freak."

"What? What was wrong with him?"

"Nothing."

"How do you know he was a freak then?"

"I don't know, because I loved him. He told me things, he told me a secret."

"What kind of a secret?"

"I can't say."

He stared at her and then he got up and asked her inside his trailer. She had only been in it a few times since he'd first shown it to her.

"How about a Coke?" he said.

She accepted and he made them glasses of Coke. "You can tell me your secret now," he said, handing her a glass.

"No, I can't," Lucy said.

"But you must, you and I are such good friends and I'm a minister, too, and Reverend Williams meant for you to keep it a secret only from other people who are not ministers. You can tell me."

"No," Lucy said.

"You know, some people consider their pastor the person closest to God in their life. Did you know that?"

"Yes."

"Am I that to you?"

". . . Yes," Lucy said, thinking this was true, at least at the time.

"You know, I'm not even going to be around much longer," he said. "It's very important for you to tell me the secret the reverend told you not to tell before I leave."

"No," Lucy said.

He thought about this a moment. Then he said something very quietly to her. "I'll show you a secret." His quiet voice masked his rage at her stubbornness. "Come here."

Even now as she sat in her car outside the circus holding the hand of Emma, she could not remember what that secret had been. Whatever it was it had terrified her so deeply that she had lost its memory.

"Now, what's your secret?" he turned to her and pressed the question again.

She shook her head.

"Did the reverend ever do something to you?" he asked.

"Checkers, we played checkers," Lucy said.

"I know, you've told me you played that stupid game."

For a second Lucy thought he somehow knew of the checkerboard she had stolen from the estate sale. Then she remembered him grabbing at her pants. He exploded with rage.

And pain shot up between her legs, an excruciating pain that went to the core of who she was.

After he made her put her clothes back on, he paced back and forth; sweat was pouring down the side of his face and neck. He turned to her, pointed at her, his face red with rage. "That's why you were hanging out in the back of my tent, huh? Is that why?"

She shook her head, crying. He lifted his hand to swat her across the face, then lowered it.

"You came into my world to bring me down, didn't you? Somebody sent you, didn't they? You . . . you freak lover!"

She kept shaking her head.

"Yes, yes of course, you were sent to me. You didn't come here with that little innocent face all on your own. No way, no way! Why?! Why?! Please tell me, please!"

He got down on his knees and put his hands together in prayer. "God, I have failed you. God, I should have known who sent this little girl. I should have known she came up from the depths. Why couldn't I see it? Why was I so blind?"

He went back and forth between hysterical tears and a murderous rage.

"You're not one of God's children. I can see it now, I should have seen it before, it's so obvious now." He was staring at her as if seeing her for the first time. Lucy was shaking. "Yes, we must atone for what we've done." Then he paced back and forth, tearing at his hair, biting his hand, slamming his fist into his leg. "We've got to do something. Yes, we've got to, I don't know what it is." He fell to his knees, closed his eyes to pray, and then bounced back to his feet again. "I know what it is," he said. "We've got to die for this, oh yes, there's no question about it, we've got to. It would be Christ's will, it's what Christ would have done!"

"No!" Lucy screamed. "No!"

Twice he grabbed her around the neck, cut her air off, and she blacked out only to wake up covered with his tears as he was kissing her, begging her forgiveness as well as that of God's.

Finally Lucy found a moment while he was praying to slip out of the trailer and run through a nearby stand of trees to a pile of old dry hay in a barn near her own house where she tried to wipe the blood from between her legs. She hid in the barn and cried until the sun went down and she couldn't cry anymore, then she headed home. It was dark, the crickets already sounding, the full red moon bathed in the sad mist of the sky.

"Where've you been, little girl? Your supper's in the compost heap, I told you to get on home here." She could still hear her mother's words years later.

There were tears in her eyes. "I'm sorry, Momma," Lucy had said.

"Pastor Joe stopped by, he told me where you was at."

Lucy froze for a moment, as if it were possible that he had told her mother what he had done. "What did he say?" she said.

"Said you was hanging out with some bad boys." Lucy stared at her mother, her eyes puffed up. "Told me he'd told you to get home for supper, that he could tell you were up to no good. He'd been waiting for you all afternoon, he said."

She shook her head then turned and went upstairs to her room.

She had slept about an hour before waking up and then she began trying to figure out whether or not to tell her mother about what had really happened. That was the loneliest night she had ever experienced.

The next day when she got up she saw her neck and face were black and blue where he had hit her. She waited for the school bus, then got on it and sat in the back. The bus route ran by Pastor Joe's lot. She closed her eyes as they were passing, but somebody tapped her on the shoulder and pointed and she looked.

The tent and trailer and flatbed truck were gone, not a sign left, just a yellowish circle where the grass had faded without the sun.

What had happened to her had already begun to seem unreal, but now it was even further away: all the apparatus that had made up this man's show had vanished.

She hid her wounds from her mother. For several months she went back and forth about whether to tell her what had really happened. She instinctively knew that her entire relationship to the woman who had given birth to her rested on how she would react to being told the truth that her daughter had been raped and nearly killed. Somehow she understood that if her mother didn't come down on her side, she would have to leave home. Leaving behind the few things that she really did love would be a kind of suicide, but staying around would be another kind, a more sure form.

All that time and Lucy wasn't even thinking that she would have to tell her mother anyway, that what he had done to her was to put something inside her that was growing. "What's the matter with you, crying every morning?" her mother said a few months later.

"I'm not crying," Lucy said and fell silent.

"Well, you're getting fatter than you are, sitting around eating. You should be getting some exercise. Your tummy isn't getting any smaller, neither."

That was the first time she'd been aware of it. She stood in the mirror in the bathroom and saw the bulge and knew that there was something funny about it, just as there had been something funny about throwing up in the morning. She thought that was all just part of the crying, which was all related to the darkness of that afternoon with Pastor Joe.

"I saw you with those bad boys and I told you countless times, you can't be flirting with snakes and not expect to get bit."

"But—it wasn't any boy . . . he was lying."

"Who was lying?"

". . . Pastor Joe . . ."

Her mother lifted her hand to slap her, then lowered it. "You're on your way to hell like that."

By the time she was showing it was too late to even get an abortion. Her mother took her out of school and brought her to a doctor who directed them to a clinic clear across the state that dealt with adoption agencies. Two days before the baby was due, her mother brought Lucy to a cheap motel near the clinic and waited for her to go into labor, the television blaring and empty boxes of take-out food collecting on the tables around the room.

Lucy never did see the child, her mother forbade it, said it would make the separation even messier. Lucy cried all the way back home and did not get out of bed for nearly two days until her mother took her to school herself and said, "You get back into things and you don't tell anybody where you've been. I hear about that and you're in even deeper trouble."

One rainy afternoon soon afterward, on her way back from school, Lucy froze in her tracks on the shoulder of the road near her house. Parked in the driveway was the flatbed truck that Pastor Joe used to carry his chairs and tent, covered with droplets of rain.

She remained frozen, staring at the truck as if in a bad dream. Then she sneaked around the back of the house to where she could hear Pastor Joe's voice. Her mother was laughing heartily and it was evident that he was charming her.

"I did what I could with her," Pastor Joe said. "But there's an old saying, Jesus can't save everyone. He's got His hands full with all those niggers singing hymns, you know."

Lucy's life would have gone down an entirely different road had she overheard her mother giving him hell. But among the raucous laughter of her mother, she heard some broken dialogue that Lucy knew was about herself. "Don't worry about her. That lazy kid does as much fibbing as she does pigging out on the cookies lying around here. You should see what I found in her room laying up under her bed. Only the Good Lord knows how I ended up rearing a kid like that. Sometimes I have a mind to take her over to the farm and drop her off in one of the pig stalls. But I'll tell you something, Pastor Joe, I sure appreciated you lettin' me know about her evil ways last year, turned out you was right on the money, she gave birth to a little girl last week . . . She keeps calling that hospital, too—and she'll pay that long distance bill, I'll tell you. She's a stubborn one, she wanted to keep that child born of her sin."

Every time Lucy considered turning back for home, even on that first rainy night while hitchhiking near the tollbooth three miles from her home, she would replay in her mind these words spoken by her mother. She headed across the state for the hospital where she'd given birth and had heard the cries of her baby. After rides from truckers and drunks, she came at last to the hospital, and mounted the steps and walked down the hall to the nursing station in the hospital wing where she'd already been. Luckily, the nurse who had held her hand during labor was behind the desk.

She looked up, amazed at the sight of Lucy.

"I'm here to get my girl back," Lucy said.

The woman shook her head. "No . . . That's impossible."

"Where is she?"

"She's in good hands, but you can't contact her."

"Who has her?"

The woman was silent, at a loss as to what to say.

"I need her back," Lucy said. "I got to have her back."

The nurse came around the side of the station, put her arm around Lucy and said, "Come now, how did you get here?"

Lucy struggled to lie; she wanted to say that her mother brought her, but she could not seem to muster even this simple prevarication; she instead remained silent.

"Well, whoever brought you must know, you can't reverse it when you give your baby up for adoption. Some day the child may find you."

"No," Lucy said. "I can't wait that long. She's all I got right now. I got to have her back."

She began crying and the big nurse pulled her against her bosom. "I know how you feel, I know."

"I came here to get her. I did. I came here to get my baby."

At last Lucy left the nurse and went outside and began walking down the road away from the hospital, wondering what to do, when a great big red truck pulled right up along the curb and a man rolled down his window.

"Where you headed?" he said. His sleeves were rolled up over his bulging forearms and he spoke as softly as his rough voice would allow.

"Nowhere," she said.

"Then you belong back there."

"Why?"

"Well, look on back there, would you?"

She looked and saw the words THE CROWN CIRCUS on the side. The idling truck followed along side of her and she began to remember what Pastor Joe had said, that a circus was one place he would never go.

"Go on," a woman reached over the man and stuck her head out of the window. "He's right. Get on in back."

Then Lucy was among bundles of canvas similar in smell and color to Pastor Joe's tent. She could smell animals and hay and see garish little signs among the rattling equipment. It was only after the wind of the moving truck whipped her hair that Lucy realized that other trucks were following now in a convoy. The truck right behind her was carrying an elephant whose trunk kept reaching out for the leaves of low-hanging branches that the convoy passed under.

Late that night the truck turned into a bumpy field off a country road and stopped. The man called to her, but Lucy had grown more frightened of this ride. She hopped down and ran across the road to the dilapidated stables of an abandoned race track with long grass growing along its oval course; there she lay down to hide.

He called her again and for a moment she thought she heard him say her name, though she definitely hadn't told it to him.

Later she heard pigeons cooing, then mice, hundreds of them, scurrying up and down a beam just over her head. *Busy tending to their babies*, she thought and her eyes became wet before falling asleep.

The next morning as soon as the sunlight slanted through the slats of the dilapidated barn, Lucy climbed up to one of the open doors of the stables. Across the street the circus had already set up its spacious tent, now covered with a glistening coat of dew and surrounded by a wooden snow fence. To one side of this barrier, she could see the elephant that had been grabbing leaves, swaying gently, a German shepherd asleep in the hay at her feet. Lucy crossed the road and stood near her; the elephant watched her through one gray sagging eye.

"Well, I got to thinking things over last night," Lucy whispered. "Maybe I don't have anything to lose, maybe I'm going to come join you, maybe this is where I really belong. I hope you don't mind." The sound of her own voice made her very scared because she had never really wanted to join a circus.

The elephant stopped swaying for a moment, her eye squinted as if to say okay. Then the shepherd woke up and started to bark wildly.

Lucy stepped behind a trailer where she saw a girl with a very long neck washing the aluminum siding.

"Pardon," Lucy said. "Could I help you?"

The girl stopped scrubbing and looked at her.

"I could do that," Lucy said.

"Are you the girl they picked up near the hospital yesterday?"

Lucy nodded. She had not been that close to the hospital when they stopped.

"There was talk of you. Master Howard said you'd run away from him last night, but he said it didn't matter none, you'd be back. He's always right, that *wicked* man," she said almost adoringly. The long-necked girl began laughing and Lucy moved forward and took the sponge from her. "Well, I guess you're working for him now," the girl laughed again and Lucy began to clean off the side of the trailer.

"Hey, fat girl, what's up?" she heard much later once the metal was shining in the sun.

"I'm working for Master Howard," she said, recognizing him from the truck.

"You're working for Master Howard, are you?"

"Please, you don't have to pay me nothing," Lucy said. "I heard you were a nice man."

Master Howard roared laughter at the words "nice man." "Liar!" he said and dropped a pair of boots in front of her and a tin of shoe polish. "Have you ever heard of a spit shine?"

"No," Lucy said.

"Well, you don't use spit, just slap some water on them before they're all shined up, then buff 'em good 'till you can see the pimples on that face of yours. If you're workin' for Master Howard, the shoes is how it starts, hear me? You'll get along okay."

For years in the circus, Lucy would wake up in the middle of the night crying into her pillow as silently as possible. She told nobody of the chain of events that had led her here to the show. It was partly shame and partly that she could find no apt words even in her thoughts to describe what had happened in that trailer that day with Pastor Joe. There was only a kind of stuttering that would eventually lead to a silence deeper than the deepest ocean. Each time she went through this period of silence, she became ever more wary of trying to speak about it again.

But what was on her mind most often was the baby she'd lost; she'd overheard her mother tell Pastor Joe that it was a girl. At times Lucy wondered if she herself had made this up, whether her mother had said anything about the child to Pastor Joe. But then she remembered the child crying and she was sure that these were the cries of a baby girl. For several weeks the milk from her breasts stained her shirt and she kept changing her blouses, afraid that somebody would notice. But each time she saw these stains the feeling of missing the child grew stronger.

She had never experienced anything as powerful as the deep and sad longing for this child. It was as if the entire world rose up around her to create this feeling of missing something that was more important than she herself was—as if her fears of her new life in the circus came to be represented by this one feeling of longing for the baby that had come out of her womb never to be heard from again. If she let herself dwell on it, she'd suddenly realize that her arms were cradling the air. At times especially when she first joined the circus she could hear a sharp scream in the distance coming from behind the tents or even from the sky; it was the baby that she had secretly named Lily, calling for her mother.

Every year that passed while she was in the circus, Lucy wrote her a birthday card and kept it in her trunk. At times Lucy found herself speaking aloud to the child when she was alone. At night she dreamed about the child in her arms, about mothering her, fixing the blankets around her face. At one year and three months, she imagined that Lily was speaking already. She seemed to know this in her dreams. Lily had a bright red, healthy face, and she smiled all the time and showed her incoming teeth.

Lucy began looking for Lily among the children who visited the show, maybe the parents who adopted her might bring her along. But how would she know whether the baby was really hers? It was all speculation, just the same she would check every baby's face with the mother's to see if there was a match. If they did not look alike, even if the child's hair color was different than the mother's, then this would set Lucy to wondering. She would watch the mother and child, follow them for as long as she could, even out to the parking lot where they got in their car.

"There's something about you," Master Howard said to Lucy after she was in the circus for less than a year. "You're a black sheep among black sheep. That's not to say folks around here don't like you; they like you plenty, but they like to make fun of you . . . It's something about that look on your face, like the Lord—if there is such a thing as a Lord—didn't quite finish you when He fashioned you from the dust."

Lucy spent hours looking at her face in the mirror, trying to determine what it was that attracted the scorn of so many even in the circus, even in a place where everybody could be in some way considered a freak.

During the shows, she worked with Mrs. Cookie, selling cotton candy, snow cones, and fried dough. The overweight Mrs. Cookie talked to herself all the time; occasionally she scolded Lucy, but most of the time she said nothing to her. At night after a show, Lucy always walked by Marcella the elephant and stood near her and spoke to her as she had that first night. She said, "How're you doing tonight? I'm not doing so good myself. I want to get on home. I don't like this life, no, I don't care for this way of life, I was never meant to be in a circus. I bet you feel the same way, don't you? I bet you just want to be with the other elephants in Africa or something, some place you call home."

Marcella would sway back and forth; her eye would kind of squint as elephants' eyes do, and sometimes she made a certain snort that Lucy was sure was to let her know that she understood.

"Well, maybe you're used to it, old girl, I don't think I'll ever get used to this life myself."

As much as she wanted to be in one place, she knew she could never go home to Millville, not as long as her mother was there.

"I know you ain't happy in this miserable outfit," Master Howard said, "but you're alive, aren't you? That's something after what you've been through." He would invite her to sit in his trailer while he drank or played poker or solitaire, then he would talk to her. "I don't know what it is about you. You just bring out the mean old clown in most everybody. I can't stand to see you without doing something to you."

Lucy was just sixteen years old at the time. It was easy to make her cry.

"Heck, cut that out now, what's wrong with you. I'm just trying to tell you the truth about yourself."

She couldn't stop her eating. If she skipped a meal, she would eat three times as much the next meal, if she refrained from eating the cookies Master Howard gave her, she would devour an entire bag an hour later. Eventually she started spending the night in Master Howard's trailer. She did not think that the things he was making her do to him at night had anything to do with sex, she just woke up one day and realized that she had been sleeping next to him.

10

Now Lucy got out of Elvis with Emma, put her arm around her and started walking with her toward the show, Emma staring wide-eyed at the faded canvas. Passing inside the gates, Lucy heard somebody call to her from under one of the trailers. "Well, look who's come back to the show," Shorty said in his gentle nasal voice. His short, blond jaggedly cut hair was often stained with oil and grease, and he had a long face, the face of someone much bigger and perhaps older than he actually was. He was not a midget, but he was not of normal height either. "I'll be damned if you're not half of what you was before." Shorty's broken nose laid flat against his face so that his nostrils flared out. He was lying on the ground under one of the trucks, parts strewn around the grass amidst blotches of spilled oil. "Is that your kid?"

"Yeah, she's mine, her name's Emma," Lucy said and she introduced Shorty to Emma.

"She's a beautiful little kid."

"That she is, Shorty. Where's Master Howard?" Lucy had often thought of what it would be like to return. She was afraid to linger, as if the old quicksand that had kept her before could take her back.

"You come to see the old man?"

"Is he in his trailer?"

"Go on over and try. He's going to think you're bringing him a little circus girl."

"She's not that," Lucy said.

She crossed to the fanciest trailer of the show, adorned by a mural of Siamese twins locked together at the hips in a bloody fight with each other, one with an axe raised in one hand, the other a hammer. Performers and circus workers stood around them, gaping at the sight. Every year Master Howard had a painter touch up the mural to keep it fresh She knocked on the door.

"Yeah?"

"Lucy."

There was silence, rustling around inside, then the door opened. Master Howard liked to dress the part of ringmaster because he claimed it was good for business. He wore tall black boots, a vest with gold buttons and a mustache that he waxed and curled at the ends meticulously despite the filth around him. His fingers were crowded with rings. He started to smile. Lucy squeezed Emma's hand. "Looks like somebody threw you in a washing machine and shrunk you." It was the same cutting voice. "I told you, girl, how many times do I have to tell you, you can't get away from this place. I knew you wouldn't gain no traction. It's all silliness otherwise." Lucy turned away from the tall man of black and red clothes, black hair, and black eyes. "What happened to you? What happened to that beautiful body of yours, huh? I can't hire you like you are, you'd better get back to your old ways with food if you're—"

"Shut up," Lucy said under her breath. She had thought she had toughened herself to his cruel comments, but they were still cutting below the surface.

Master Howard laughed. "Shit," he said. "I knew you'd be back. I haven't been livin' in this mud hole for forty-two years for nothing."

"I'm not back."

"Shoot." Master Howard came out and walked to the rear of the trailer.

"What're you standin' there for?" he said when he returned, holding a saddle against his hip. "You want to work? You know I'm going to hire you. Now clean out the cotton candy machine. Hey, who you got with you?" he said suddenly as if noticing Emma holding her hand for the first time.

Lucy shook her head. "My daughter here—"

He looked Emma up and down. "What's that?"

"Somebody's messed her up. I need to know what happened. She doesn't talk because of what they did to her."

"Well, what do you expect from me?"

"She's been marked. She's got tattoos all over her body."

"So?" Master Howard spoke loudly. "There are tattooed girls all over the damn country, you know."

Master Howard was heading inside of his trailer.

"No, not like her," Lucy said. "Somebody's put scales over every inch of her skin, like a fish." Master Howard stopped with one foot in his trailer. "Her skin is dark with them," Lucy repeated.

He held his eyes on her for a moment, just long enough to let Lucy know that she had jogged his memory, then he continued into his trailer silently, leaving the door open. Lucy turned to Emma and told her to wait outside, then she stepped up into the smell of saddle leather and cigars and dirty socks and flat beer at the bottom of open cans. In the shadowy darkness, she saw the foldup table and the same unmade bed that she had slept in and the dark green blanket. Bridles and saddles hanging from hooks on the wall. He started unbuttoning his shirt to his undershirt. Lucy backed toward the door, shaking her head.

"No," she said. "I'm asking you for help."

His fingers stopped. "Then you better do what I say."

"Do you know something about my girl? Do you know what

was done to her? I don't need to know who did it, just what they did. She can't tell me herself."

"Maybe I do, maybe I don't." He started unfastening another button.

Lucy kept backing toward the door. "Tell me what you know. My daughter . . ." She stared at him. "Do you understand what I'm saying? This is worse than what you put me through."

"What I put you through?"

"It's much worse."

He stood there, his dark green eyes resting on hers, the painted harnesses and bridles hanging from the wall behind him. Lucy wondered if he had any idea how destructive the trick he had played on her years ago had been, she wondered if he even thought about her.

Then he reached for his belt buckle.

"No," Lucy said.

"Well, get out of here now. Go on home."

"Tell me what you know about this girl. Please—"

Master Howard went about his business in the trailer. It was obvious that he wasn't going to budge from his demands, but just the same the thought of lying in bed with him again was more than she could possibly bear.

"What do you think's going to happen to her?"

"Something in her's going to kill her if I don't help her get at it. She's got to get talking about it. I could get a doctor to treat her if we knew what happened to her?"

"And you think if you find out what somebody done to her, that's really going to help her."

"Maybe."

"That's stupid."

"Maybe it is," Lucy said.

Master Howard nodded and smiled, then again reached for his belt buckle.

"No," Lucy said. She could tell she was about to cry.

"Well, get outta here now. Go on home."

Lucy stepped back into the sunshine. The blond-haired elephant boy, Iggy, was washing down Marcella, spraying the hose on her back and hindquarters while rubbing down her gray skin with a long-handled brush. Marcella swayed back and forth, squinting her eyes as if she were smiling. Lucy brought Emma forward, holding her hand, and Marcella put her trunk out to Emma's hand, sniffed up her arm to her neck.

"Do you remember me, old girl? I still wish I could take you home, let you roam around the fields behind my house."

Marcella snorted and her eye squinted softly and Lucy rubbed the underside of her trunk below her mouth.

"Hey, get away from there," Iggy said. He had been twelve years old the last she'd seen him and now he had tufts of blond hair on his Adam's apple and under his chin.

"Iggy," she said. The blond-haired boy, nearly an albino, came over, water running from the hose into the hay, and he stared at her. "I knew you when you were no bigger than my girl here. You stole Camel John's false teeth. He would have killed you if I hadn't saved you."

"Where you been, lady?" Iggy said. "You just up and left the show, don't write, don't visit or nothin'."

"Let my girl sit up there, would you?" Lucy pointed at Marcella.

"Master Howard 'bout shit if he sees that," Iggy said, then he picked Emma up and commanded Marcella to kneel.

"Looks like a little princess," Iggy said when Emma was high up on the elephant's neck. Emma didn't smile, but Lucy thought she looked happy. "You take care of her. I've got to go talk to Master Howard."

"I'm no babysitter, ya know."

Lucy turned and looked back at Master Howard's open trailer door. She thought of how the mention of the scales had stopped him in his tracks. And yet the mere thought of letting his dirty fingers touch her own skin . . . She returned to Master Howard's trailer door and knocked. He stared at her through the cracked open door.

"You git in here and take care of me first. Do I have to say it again?" She stepped up and into the shadowy yellow light of his trailer and he unbuttoned his shirt, opened his pants and let them fall. "Shit, I bet you have plenty of loose skin on you, sure." He pulled her over to the cot, unfastened her slacks, and put his hand inside around her behind. "Where you been?" His fingers pressed into her flesh like the claws of a hungry animal. She kept her eyes shut tight and did her best not to cry.

After Master Howard was finished, a change came over him and he started kissing her and telling her that he loved her, then he put his head back, his arms around her and fell sound asleep. There was nothing innocent about him, even when he slept. Constricting her throat to try to choke down her cries, Lucy waited, the smell of semen creeping up from where he'd gotten it on her belly. She kept her mind fixed on a memory she had of Emma sitting on top of Audrey McBride, smiling. It was the first time she had ever seen her smile, the first break in those dark clouds.

Outside the trailer she could hear Uncle Pat playing the harmonica. It was Uncle Pat all right. He never learned how to play well, he'd just sit on a hay bale blowing and sucking on the instrument with a certain rhythm and Lucy remembered this rhythm well.

She rubbed Master Howard's chest to wake him up. "Well?"

"You wanted it, too, didn't you?"

She lied, nodding her forehead against his chest.

"What's the matter with you?"

"My daughter . . ."

"Maybe I don't know nothin' after all."

"You know something. I saw it in your eyes." She had never before been this firm with him.

Master Howard's small green eyes looked straight up at the dented aluminum ceiling of the trailer. Lucy could clearly see that he was contemplating saying something. "After you left the show years ago," he spoke slowly. "I didn't think much about it. Not until a few months later, then I got to feeling something, I started kind of missing having you around—can you believe it, me missing somebody? Whatever happened to my Lucy? I started wondering. Why did she up and leave me like that?"

"You know damn well why I left. You know what you did to me."

"I know," he said. "But you two were the best darn thing this show ever had going for it, then he left, too."

"Pidge left?" Lucy said.

"Sure," he said. "He quit circuses altogether. Renounced them like somebody in one of them hokey AA groups."

Lucy caught her breath and studied the face of Master Howard to see if he was telling the truth. It was impossible that Pidge wasn't with a circus of some kind somewhere. Somehow she felt intuitively that Pidge was at an even bigger loss as to how to live his life than she had been, perhaps that was what attracted her to him to begin with. He had gone along with the trick that Master Howard had played on her and yet there was something just as vulnerable about him as there had been about her. She had rarely seen him so much as talk to his fellow workers and she had felt his loneliness as palpably as a woolen sweater. How could he have sworn off circuses?

"After you left the show, he came down with a fever . . . Sure he did, girl." Lucy knew he was telling the truth by the way his forehead came down over his eyes. "That fever stayed steady at about 105, put him right on the brink of the abyss . . . Doctors were pulling their hair out to figure it out . . . They had him under ice packs, looked like a little Eskimo."

He tried to look at Lucy in that cunning way whenever he was telling her a lie. But somehow she knew he was still telling her the truth.

"If you ask me it was psychosomatic, you see."

"What?"

"In his head . . . didn't feel right about what he'd done."

"He didn't plan to hurt me; you did. I figured that out later."

"I think he must of had feelings for you after all. But I'm no head doctor, you know me, just a second-rate impresario in a run-down, two-bit, mud show with enough debt to—"

"You want to mess with me until I just lay myself down in my own grave, don't you?"

"You were already laying in your grave when I rescued you," Master Howard said. "Think of it. You were getting fatter every day, you'd be dead by now if I hadn't done something to jar you out of your trance with food. I wouldn't have done it if I didn't think it would cure you."

"Cure me?" Lucy said. "You tried to kill me."

"Think whatever you want. You told me once that life was all about the angle that you looked at things. You're the one who claimed that."

"Tell me what I come here for," Lucy said mustering as much authority as she could.

He sighed deeply, stared up at the curved ceiling; she could see his black widow's peak.

"About the time I started thinking about you I had a dream with you in it," he began slowly. "It woke me up—so strong I thought it had really happened. That preacher whose name you used to say in your sleep? Well, he was in my dream and he was baptizing you in a river. Only thing, he stuck your head down underwater and kept you there, kept you there on purpose and I could tell it was for good. You struggled like hell to come up, but he kept you down there until your eyes began to pop open and your tongue came out all white and finally you stopped struggling." Lucy did not necessarily believe that this was a real dream since he lied about everything. "Then I saw your body floating downstream. You were drifting along, dead as a shoe. Every new angle, your body changed to a different color, getting brighter each time and then smaller. Finally I decided I'd go out there, swim out there and fetch you and give you a proper burial. But by the time I got there, you'd gone under and there was just a black barrel with a yellow rope tied around it, and I dove down, fifteen feet, at least, and followed the line beneath it and there I saw a coin attached to the end of it, resting on the river bottom, about the size of a quarter. I swum back up and put it in my pocket and then suddenly I realized that that little piece of change was the key to everything, the token to the next world and it was going to free me forever from this miserable poverty that I've been living in all my life."

"What's that have to do with my daughter, Emma?" Lucy was becoming impatient.

"I didn't say it had anything to do with her. I thought I should tell you something, and I did."

"What else? Go on."

"Okay," he said. "I will say this. A long time ago before you joined the show some fellow brought a girl by. He said he'd found her walking down the side of the road. She was dirty and frightened and lost. Her skin was just about covered with tattoos, some pictures on her, some words written across her stomach, all messed up and crazy. The fellow who brought her by figured she must have come from the circus. She didn't talk, didn't say a word. I saw her for about five minutes, then I had to go off to town and so I left her with Pidge." He smiled and examined her as he had done when he first mentioned Pidge's name. Lucy could hardly contain the many feelings that the mention of his name brought up; they were still there whether she liked it or not.

"What happened to her?"

"Some young men showed up when I was gone to town to say the girl belonged to them. Pidge tried to stop them because he saw that she didn't want to go. They threatened him pretty bad."

"How old was she?"

"I don't know. She was young."

"Did she ever say where she was from?"

"The fellow picked her up in Gainston, in West Virginia, up in the hills."

"Who were the people who came for her?"

"One of them had a white van. That girl's skin was as pale as that light bulb right there. You could practically see through her. And her eyes were about that big around." Master Howard made a circle with his finger and thumb. "And yet if you looked under her shirt, you could see her skin was scribbled all over, pictures on it, like somebody had been practicing his art on her."

"Where did they take her?" Lucy said. Her heart was beating hard. If Master Howard told her this, she would at least have a place to start from.

"How should I know? I wasn't even there when they come to get her. I figure they took her back to Gainston."

Lucy was quiet, staring at his face. He was looking up at the ceiling.

"I'll tell you something. That girl brought a world of bad luck down on us. From then on it was a month of hell. A lot of bad things happened and I figured it was because of her."

"Where's Pidge at?" Lucy asked.

"I don't know."

"Are you sure?"

"I told you I don't know. Now you get on."

Lucy was silent, and so was Master Howard, lying on his back, smelling of sweat and semen and the nasty French cigars that he smoked. "Go on now," he said.

. . .

"Hey, Momma, did you make him happy?" Iggy was brushing down a white llama, collecting the hair in his hand that came from the brush. Emma was standing in the sun near him. "She's my princess," he said.

"She's mine, too." Lucy took Emma's hand. "You take care now, Iggy."

"I hope you made him happy," Iggy laughed to himself and continued brushing the llama.

On her way out she passed by a trailer and she could see Shorty's legs sticking out from under it as he was turning a bolt over his head. "Shorty?" she called.

He swung around and looked up at her. Master Howard had told her that Shorty's father had broken his nose when he was six years old. *That boy had to crawl to the damn show to join it*, he'd said. *You at least walked your fat ass here.* "Are you headin' out of here already?" Shorty said.

"Where's Pidge at?" A sudden feeling that Pidge must be dead shot through her unexpectedly. Somehow, deep in her heart, she felt that Pidge could not survive without the circus; he would dry up and die.

"I haven't seen him."

She almost considered leaving it at that. "Are you sure?"

"Can Opener seen him working in a junkyard, Dom's I think it's called, up Tarville way."

"A junkyard, huh, in Tarville?"

"That's what Can Opener told me."

"How long ago was that?"

"Oh, about three years ago." Shorty thought for a moment. "You best get yourself a map."

Lucy got into Elvis with Emma and drove to a gas station outside of town, filled up and took a free map, and asked a grease-covered teenager if he'd ever heard of Tarville.

"Nope."

She found Tarville on the map and saw that it was only an hour's drive away and happened to be on the route to Gainston, which was two or three hours into the hills of West Virginia. As Lucy started her drive she remembered Pidge. How was it possible, how could he of all people have survived without the circus?

11

Pidge had been a part-time clown in the Crown Circus, not a very good one and only one because of his dwarfism. It was evident to Lucy and to everyone else who saw him perform that he got far more pleasure from working as a mechanic on the broken-down cars, trucks and trailers, covered as he often was from head to toe with a thick black coating of grease. Lucy had not known him well until Master Howard came up with his plan for the promotion of that season's show. That year he had posters printed up headlined: COME SEE THE MOST CURIOUS MARRIAGE IN ALL THE LAND: THE WEDDING OF MR. LITTLE AND MRS. BIG! POSSIBLY THE MOST UNLIKELY SPOUSES IN THE MIDWEST!

At the end of every show, Master Howard would summon the entire circus in full regalia, and, acting as Justice of the Peace himself, would marry Pidge and Lucy in the ring.

"Do you take this woman as your lawfully married wife?"

Pidge would put the wedding ring on Lucy's finger and say into the microphone, "I do."

Master Howard's plan to increase the show's revenues worked unexpectedly well. The money from the highest ticket receipts ever went into fresh paint on all the trailers, two new trucks, and a chimpanzee named Kiki. COME SEE MRS. BIG JOIN HANDS IN

HOLY MATRIMONY WITH MR. LITTLE. Pidge dressed up in a small black tuxedo and Lucy wore a long white wedding gown, the children in the show carrying the hem.

As the weeks and months fell away, what had begun as a mere performance sank deep into Lucy's heart. She found herself looking forward to the end of each show; at night she'd have dreams of the ceremony and look to the ceiling of the tent and realize it was the dome of a church and see in the place of Master Howard a priest in flowing white robes. With each show she found it more difficult to restrain her increasingly fertile imagination. Once a tear slipped from her eye as Pidge placed the ring on her finger and she had to wipe it away with the back of her hand. At times she wondered almost aloud whether Pidge was feeling some of the same hope and elation as she was.

Then one day midseason, she found a bouquet of flowers, a wedding bouquet, on the doorstep of her trailer and looked for a card but found none. Suspecting Master Howard of a trick—perhaps he had detected her feelings for Pidge and was jealous—she tried not to raise her hopes about it. Then she began finding cards slipped under her door with a heart drawn on them. Was Pidge carried away by this wedding, too? During the show he seemed to play the part with greater conviction. Had it been his secret wish to get married also and was he now courting her in reality?

Her hopes grew higher at every new present she found, though she continued to try to hold them down. She looked more and more carefully at Pidge to try to tell if he was concealing his love for her. After the show was over and Pidge was dressed in his mechanic's jumpsuit, she'd watch him crawling under the motors of the cars and trucks, wrenches in his hand, grease spotting his face. Was he thinking about her as she was about him?

Then she got a card that said, *Your most secret admirer in the world would like to meet you for a walk next to the lake tomorrow morning. You see, I've let you inside. It's been real hard because you know how shy I am. Please don't let me down. I'll meet you on the town beach at 5 A.M.—Your Most Secret Admirer in the World.*

There was no stopping her hope now that he had written this. At five in the morning she got up from her trailer and followed the path at the edge of the field that led to the lake. Pidge, she saw, was sitting on a log by the shore, his back to her and his porkpie hat on his head. As she looked at him from behind, she could feel something raining down from the heavens. It was not merely moon and starlight, but something crystalline, like the tiny flurries of snow shed in the far North.

"Pidge," she said behind him.

He didn't move. She thought he must be afraid, as shy as she was inside. But when she walked to the side of him and looked down, she saw the face of a newly acquired chimpanzee. At that moment she heard rustling in the bushes and then the thundering laughter of Master Howard and the roar of at least ten other men, all of whom had risen from their cover to watch Lucy's rude discovery.

Lucy knew who had masterminded this trick, but it didn't matter; Pidge was among the men watching. In the very least, he had loaned him his hat and clothes.

She fell to her knees on the beach of that lake, then onto her stomach, pounding the cruel earth and weeping. After the men had finished their laughter, a change came over them and they tried to get her to snap out of it. But she would not and she lay there in the sand until they were gone and the sun rose.

Pidge did not go and remained standing near her, shuffling in the sand, making a clucking noise with his tongue. The clucking was a nervous tick he had whenever he wanted to speak but couldn't. Lucy could hear him clucking, trying to speak all morning. He had something to tell her, she knew, something important. But she kept staring straight up at the sky, birds flying high against the white clouds, doing everything in her power to make him vanish from her reality, to make him go away forever.

Without ever saying what he had stayed to say, Pidge backed away and Lucy got up and went to her trailer. Master Howard opened her door and stood looking at her as she lay on her bed. "It's time to get dressed," he said. Lucy looked away and Master Howard did not so much as try to coax her back into the show. Perhaps he, too, had been touched by something for he even gave her the car that would take her back home to Millville. Later she heard him announce to the crowd at the beginning of the performances that the wedding had been cancelled. "These two odd ones are not exempt from the wily and whimsical rules of love that we who call ourselves normal are subject to. A disagreement over the business of sleeping arrangements has led to a termination of their engagement. Anyone wishing for their money back before the show begins can line up in front of our ticket booth. Our sincerest regrets."

Two days later a lawyer contacted Lucy to tell her that her mother had died and left her the house in Millville. A few days after that, a doctor by the name of Paul Marshall visited her tent to examine her and then told her that her health was in grave danger if she didn't lose some weight.

12

"A fellow named Pidge work here?" Lucy asked at the office of the Tarville Vehicle Recycling Center. "He's about this tall," she put her hand a yard above the oil-blackened earth. She could have said dwarf, but she remembered the look on Pidge's face whenever he had heard that word. She had never said it then and would never say it now.

"We got a guy named Tommy like that," the stout man with horn-rimmed glasses said. "Never heard of no—what'd you call him?"

"He work in a circus once?"

"Never mentioned where he used to work," the man said.

Lucy took Emma's hand and started walking up the steep, oil-drenched, muddy road between crunched and rust-bitten cars stacked four and five high. At the top of the hill she could see the vast layout of the junkyard: at least half a square mile of cars. In several places yellow front-end loaders dragged upside down vehicles through black mud, piling vans on top of vans on top of trucks, blue diesel exhaust billowing into the air.

Lucy kept going down hill into the jungle of cars, passageways of wrecked metal where she could only see the sky. A crane was lifting and dropping engines into a pile where another man in a blue jumpsuit was checking over each one.

Lucy waved to the driver of the loader and he stopped and let his machine idle.

"Where's Tommy at?"

"Clear the other side, over by the station wagons." Taking Emma by the hand, Lucy continued through the maze of passageways to another open lot.

Pidge was driving one of the front-end loaders, a flattened hand-rolled cigarette stuck to his lower lip, a German shepherd next to him on the seat, proudly watching his little master manipulate the hydraulics. The machine's pedals were rigged with wooden blocks so that Pidge could reach them. It was obvious how skilled he was, zipping back and forth, tipping and balancing cars like the loader was an extension of his own body.

She watched him, his narrow shoulders, his muscular greasy biceps popping out of his sleeveless T-shirt. Every time he shifted he slid forward on the seat. He saw her and she waved. He didn't recognize her and wave back. She approached him with Emma, and called, "Pidge," when he backed up near her. Right away he shut off the tractor, squinted his eyes. "Do you know who you're looking at?" Lucy asked.

He watched her, then barely nodded his head, the flat yellow cigarette bobbing up and down.

"You're not too easy to find all the way out here," she tried to smile. He rested a hand on the dirty coat of his shepherd. "Shorty told me you were working out here. Thought I'd stop by. I've been to the show, they said you'd quit. I got to thinking about that, you know," Lucy said. "Got to wondering."

Just standing here looking up at Pidge as he stared down, Lucy could feel how lonely he was. "Come on down, meet my daughter, Emma," Lucy said, trying to sound cheery. She held up Emma's hand.

Pidge climbed down the tractor tread and wiped his hands on a dirty rag, his dog jumped down behind him.

Emma and Pidge looked into each other's eyes.

"She don't talk," Lucy said. "But she'll understand every word you tell her." Pidge looked at Lucy with such intensity that she thought he, too, might have lost his power of speech. "I guess you didn't expect to see me today, huh?" Pidge pulled a silver lighter from his back pocket and lit what was left of his messy cigarette. The big flame flashed across the deep wrinkles in his face. "You don't look much different than when I saw you last."

Pidge spit out a shred of tobacco, then exhaled a long plume of smoke. A voice over a loudspeaker echoed across the acres of cars, asking the operators to keep their eyes out for a Ford Fairlane '63 engine. "She yours?" he asked finally. He turned away to wait for an answer.

"I adopted her." Pidge took another drag of smoke and looked off at a tower of rusted station wagons next to a pile of rubber tires. It seemed like he was trying to come up with something to say. "How come you left the show, Pidge?"

Pidge grimaced, looking down at his small laced-up work boots and the rolled-up cuff of his jeans. "I figured I'd get out of the circus business."

"And you like being out here in Tarville?"

Pidge sighed. "It's not the brightest way to spend a lifetime."

"Well," Lucy said. "I think we can put everything that happened back in that show behind us. What's done is done."

Lucy could hear a dog barking on the other side of the junkyard, and then a man operating a front-end loader came sloshing through the black mud between the stacked cars, an engine dangling from a chain on the end of the bucket. After the loader passed them by, Lucy said, "I came up here to tell you something, Pidge."

Pidge stared at her and for a second Lucy didn't really know why she'd come here. But then a thought rushed into her head—as for she and Pidge, they'd gone through something together, a marriage and a divorce. And while Lucy had found a way to recover or almost recover, Pidge had not even known how deep his feelings had become. She knew this by the mere fact that he was out here alone in this junkyard trying his hardest to survive, she knew it by the look on his face.

She could see him swallow hard, then he took off his work gloves; black grease had seeped deep into his pores. "Don't beat yourself up for what happened."

As he looked away his lips moved and Lucy thought she heard him thank her, but she couldn't tell for sure. Then there was more silence; his German shepherd was sitting by his side, his tongue out.

"I was awfully mad at you," Lucy said, "but feeling that way really didn't do me any good, either." Then she took a deep breath and tried to move on. She let go of Emma's hand and stepped closer to Pidge. "I went up to visit Master Howard. Emma here, you see, somebody did something terrible to her. I'm trying to find out what it was, trying to find out why. Somebody tattooed her from head to foot. Master Howard said there was a girl who joined the show who somebody had messed with, drawn all over with words and pictures. A girl."

Pidge nodded his head.

"Well, I was wondering if you knew anything about those folks who came for her. You see, it's not much but it's about all I have to go by right now."

It took Pidge a long time to understand what Lucy was asking, then he said, "Don't go messing with the folk who came to take that girl away."

"Who are they?"

"You know how it is, you come across all kinds of down-and-out folks in a mud show, sure, but these were a bunch that—well, Master Howard, soon as he saw them, he was scared of them. Don't go looking for them."

"Did the girl ever say where she had come from?"

"I don't know anything about those people. Master Howard didn't tell you anything?"

"Nothing much," Lucy said.

"Well, I think he knows more about them than he's letting on. You just leave them be."

Lucy nodded her head. "Yeah, I'll try to," she said. "Only they haven't left my daughter alone, not yet. What they did to her is still haunting her. But thank you anyway."

Pidge nodded his head. Lucy was about to turn around and leave, when she said, "If you ever need a place to stay, my place is over in Millville, four hours north. Scoville Road, the yellow house with the pink birdbath. You're welcome there anytime." She could tell he wanted to say something but couldn't. She went on. "I might just head back there tonight, but even if I'm not there right away, you'll find a key under a brick near the back door. Go on in there and make yourself at home. I know Emma would appreciate getting to know you. Won't you, darling?" she said to Emma. Emma stared straight at Pidge, her eyes as wide as a deer's.

13

"Emma, I'm going to leave you for a few days with Dr. Marshall," Lucy said as they were driving away. Lucy had already told Emma about this doctor, describing how generous and caring he had been to her, having taken an interest in her in the circus. "You'll feel comfortable with him; he may be able to help you, too."

Emma seemed to nod when Lucy said this, then Lucy reached across the seat and held her hand. "Don't worry, I'll be back before you can say jack rabbit, besides, it wouldn't hurt to have a good doctor like him keep an eye on you." Dr. Marshall had told Lucy that he would be of service to her anytime she wanted to call on him, but she had not taken him up on his offer. Every Christmas she had dropped him a card saying that she was doing well.

Fifty miles south of Tarville, Lucy turned off the highway for a town called Persia and stopped in a general store to ask directions. "Most likely you'll find him in his clinic."

The clinic was in a brick building with ivy climbing the crumbling walls, a Laundromat and a hairdresser shared the ground floor with the Paul and Frances Marshall Health Clinic. Lucy and Emma stepped into the waiting room and Lucy asked the nurse if she could talk to Dr. Marshall.

"Do you have an appointment?"

"No," Lucy said. "Dr. Marshall told me—"

"You need to make an appointment. You can see how busy he is." It was true that the waiting room was crammed full of children and adults, obviously poor, crying, and coughing and waiting patiently for his assistance.

"Yes," Lucy said. "I'm um . . . would you tell him that Lucy Thurman is here?"

"Are you a personal friend?"

"No," Lucy said. "But he most likely will remember me."

"You need an appointment . . . Is this your girl?" she said pointing to Lucy.

"Yes . . . But right now, it's very important just to speak to him. He told me to come here whenever . . . He told me to come see him." As the woman left her little office, Lucy called, "Would you tell him I'm from the circus . . ." Then quietly, "Tell him it's the fat lady."

The confused woman stared at Lucy, then at Emma, then disappeared into the back. A moment later a tall red-haired man with a long pale face and yellowish glasses came to the door, his eyes darting around the room. Without ever looking directly at either of them, he waved them both into an examination room in the back. "My, my," he sighed with relief. "This is something, this is really something." He looked to the side of her, behind her, to the wall, his small eyes darting back and forth without ever resting on Lucy. "You must have worked hard. How did you do it? My, my," he said again proudly and then he pointed at Emma. "And who is this? Who is this darling little gem? Is this somebody dear to you?"

"Yes, that's my daughter. She *is* my daughter, yes indeed." Lucy could feel her chest rising proudly.

"What a beauty, what an extraordinary face. Have I seen you before?" he said to Emma. Emma watched him. "You remind me of somebody," he smiled brightly. "Maybe in a movie or a book— you're a princess, aren't you, the daughter of some great king?"

"She doesn't talk," Lucy said. "Could I have a word with you?"

After admiring the young girl for the longest time, Dr. Marshall stepped into another room with Lucy while Emma waited outside. "I know you're busy," Lucy said. "There have been many times I wanted to call you. I know the number of people you're treating . . . But this is very important."

Dr. Marshall sat back against the metal table and crossed his arms and now he stared at Lucy, as if he finally trusted her enough to do this. Lucy explained all that led up to her visit, from the loneliness of living alone in her home in Millville after the circus, to the adoption, to Emma's worsening condition. "Can you help her?" she said. "I'm going to try to find out what happened to her. I don't want to take her with me. It might be dangerous."

"You mean, you want me to take her home? To my house?" he said. He was shocked by this request.

"Well, you see, it would be safer that way. I think, I'm not sure, but you see—she was found in the Blue Night Mall this spring. She doesn't talk, but she will soon—I can feel it, I feel the words coming out of her."

"Is she deaf?"

"Oh no, no, that's not it. Something was done to her. Nobody knows what it is and I don't think she even knows. You see, she's tried to harm herself in her sleep."

"In her sleep?" Dr. Marshall was alarmed.

"Three times she tried to kill herself and she almost succeeded. You must keep a close eye on her, let her sleep in the room with you and your wife. I have to look into things and I'm afraid to take her with me. It will help her in the end, even if I find out nothing. I must do it for her."

"Well—" The more Dr. Marshall thought about it, the harder he shook his head. But Lucy begged him to do her this favor.

"You helped me, Dr. Marshall, you helped get me out of the

circus. I have a regular job now; my life is so much better. Now I need to help this girl. It will be a few days."

A woman walked into the room with a stethoscope around her neck and Dr. Marshall introduced her to Lucy as his wife, Frances. Kneeling down, she took Emma's hand, and Lucy could see that Emma was at ease with her right away. When her husband told her Lucy's request, Frances said to Emma with a smile, "Well, well, we do need an assistant after all. What can you do? Are you good with children? I'll bet you're good with children." She took Emma's hand and brought her into the other room.

Dr. Marshall asked Lucy questions about Emma's health and all that she knew about her psychological history. "I need to give her a sedative at night to assure she doesn't do anything rash."

"You do what's right for her. If I could have your number I'll call tomorrow night. Either way I'll be back in two or three days," Lucy said. Dr. Marshall gave her a card with both his clinic and home number on it.

Lucy found Emma kneeling among children in a room full of colorful plastic toys. Emma stood up and Lucy hugged and kissed her for a long time. "I'll be back soon and we'll fix everything together, you and me. I'll try to call you soon."

After Lucy was gone, Paul's wife, Frances, a pediatrician herself, took the young girl back to their house early. Later when Paul arrived home, Frances and Emma had already prepared dinner and they seemed to be getting along very well. Paul was sorry that he had given Lucy such a hard time for asking him this relatively minor favor. Frances and he always enjoyed company and this quiet young girl seemed especially precious.

14

It was late afternoon by the time Lucy got to the weather-beaten sign just off the road next to a farmer's barbed-wire fence that said WELCOME TO GAINSTON. The road passed into a gorgelike valley where a shallow, fast-flowing river ran. The deeper into the valley Lucy drove, the more run-down the houses became with FOR SALE signs planted in the midst of every shabby lawn. The trees and fields got darker from the shadows of the mountains. She could feel something inside her, some sort of weight. She wasn't sure what it was, but she slowed down and drove with caution. Yes indeed, something about this township felt familiar to her, or was it simply the name Gainston? The name rang a faint bell from a long time ago. Then she noticed a sensation within her body, a heavy weight at her center similar to the way she'd felt inside the circus before she'd dieted, a time when she came to believe that every place she visited would be her last on earth. Still following the river, the road climbed a hill, then leveled out where it hit the main street, the center of the town or what was once the center. Lucy stopped the car and got out, convinced she had motion sickness. In an alleyway gnats circled a Dumpster filled with rocks and cement. The shops were boarded up with plywood, signs spray-painted on them said OUT OF BUSINESS, JESUS LOVES YOU.

Lucy saw the sign THE GAINSTON GUN SHOP above broken store windows. Shattered glass and trash littered the sidewalk. On the corner of the first street was a small, long-abandoned grocery store, the door open, the shelves inside empty.

The limbs of trees covered the sidewalks in front of the houses where the strip of stores ended. Furious grass and weeds choked the lawns. It felt like something had swept through the entire town and everyone had fled in fear. She got back into her car, then stopped again just outside of the center where she saw a dilapidated motel, the doors open, the windows broken. On its side in the grass was a large metal brown bear in blue pants, holding a coffee cup in one paw. The other paw had fallen into the deep grass. There were fresh truck tracks in the field near it. It looked like somebody was dismantling it and moving it away piece by piece. An old sign on the roof of the motel said THE SLEEPY BEAR MOTEL LODGE.

Lucy drove back through the town and up the side of the mountain behind it. On a hillside a man wearing a ragged straw hat, an undershirt on his back, worked in a vegetable garden next to his house. Lucy stopped her car and got out and crossed the yard to him. He worked on his knees, gloves on his hands. "Hello," Lucy called so as not to scare him.

The man looked up from his plants.

"I'm not familiar with the town of Gainston. What happened to the folks down there?"

The man stood up from his task, took off his gloves, and set them on top of a cedar post. Lucy could see vines with ripe tomatoes, heads of lettuce and broccoli. "Have you got five, six thousand dollars? You could buy yourself a good-sized house and ten acres for that. You drive on up Hemmels Way, you'll know as soon as you get to the end of it."

"What's there?"

"Go on up, you'll see."

Following the contours of the river, the well-traveled dirt road of Hemmels Way climbed into the shadows of a deep ravine. No houses on either side, just thick dark trees and a rushing river, NO TRESPASSING signs posted every twenty feet on posts and tree trunks. She stopped in a dirt parking lot where a chain-link fence had been erected. Near the fence was a kind of cement platform with a pipe railing. A couple was standing at the railing taking pictures of a wide concrete dam, at least one hundred feet high and several hundred feet wide. The man and the woman passed Lucy as she made her way to get a better view of the dam. The water rushing underneath it was loud and Lucy could feel a fine mist on her face. Looking over the vast expanse of concrete, she saw large words inscribed across it in Roman lettering. *I will destroy man whom I've created from the face of the earth; both man, and beast, and the creeping thing, and the fowls of the air; for it repenteth me that I have made them.* Then below it was a separate sentence: *Herein Lies the Body of Jesus Christ, Our Lord.* Then another line read: *Iesous CHristos THeou HUioS* and below that *ICHTHUS.*

Then Lucy noticed buried into the concrete at the base of the dam were seven large metal gates that looked as if they could be opened at a moment's notice.

Lucy headed back through town to the highway to an exit where she'd seen a sign for a motel that advertised a price of eleven dollars a night. The neon sign buzzed and snapped on the roof of the motel as she got out of her car and walked across the broken tar to the front door. The pale trim of the screen door was marked with fingerprints. Lucy could hear a television, children yelling in another room and she could smell something fatty cooking. She pressed the doorbell that had a bare wire attached to it. A young boy peeked around the corner. "Ma! Somebody's at the door. *Ma!*" Lucy heard cursing, and then a woman in a yellow shirt came around the corner, wiping her hands on the front of her dirty slacks.

"Have you got a room?" Lucy asked.

"That sign out there? That's all wrong. It's twelve dollars and fifty cents a night, that doesn't include the tax either, you know," the woman said.

Lucy went into the bathroom of the small dirty room she rented and cleaned out the tub with a washcloth, lifting a clump of hair from the drain. As she lay back in the tub, she kept the water running and scrubbed her body, closing her eyes. "I promised you I'd never do that again," she said to God, whom she sometimes still mixed up with the image of Reverend Williams. Time hadn't dulled the nasty bite of Master Howard's words; she could still feel them as she lay in the cool tub. "It's different, what I did this afternoon was different," she reassured herself.

Lying in the tub, washing under her arms and legs, Lucy recalled seeing the newspaper articles in the *Morton Chronicle* about Emma. *Those black lines over her body, that's what I got over me*, she had said to herself then. And now she began to see the abandoned town below the dam in her mind.

15

Before bed Paul gave Emma a mild sedative as he had promised, then he lay in bed himself next to Frances, thinking about Lucy. He had seen many patients over the years, but Lucy was one whom he had often wondered about. Something about her suffering, perhaps her lonely singularity in the world, had touched him.

Paul had a rare illness that had been difficult to diagnose because the symptoms of this disease were false symptoms—they were psychosomatically "borrowed" from the diseases of other people. Paul first began noticing this phenomena during the opening days of his practice while preparing to draw blood from a young boy covered with hives; hives had sprouted on the back of Paul's own hands, too. Another day during a house call to the ramshackle hut of an old woman crippled by arthritis, Paul's own joints stiffened. He couldn't move his neck and when he tried to give the woman a shot of cortisone, he could hardly move his fingers.

Little by little over the years Paul had built up a resistance to contracting the symptoms of his patients' diseases, rarely making eye contact with the sick, cutting them off if he found himself getting swept up into their problems and trying to look at people, old and young, as objects rather than sentient beings.

One weekend six years back, the mother of one of his patients delivered tickets to Paul for the circus. Paul had read enough about circuses, particularly small, impoverished ones to know that he should keep away. But one thing led to another that evening and he decided to go to the show.

Once the performances were under way, just as Paul had imagined, he became deeply depressed by the whole affair. At times he broke into a sweat, other times he had trouble swallowing. But for some reason on the way out of the show he dropped twenty-five cents into the hat at the door of the freak tent. At the sight of Lucy in her special chair, her huge arms spread out, wearing a tank top, her head sunken into the rolls of skin around her neck, Paul let down his guard and stared into her eyes. Right away his heart beat unevenly and the longer he looked at her the worse it got. The crowd, surrounding and staring down at Lucy, was silent.

Then the father of a small family burst out laughing and, turning to leave, muttered under his breath loud enough for everyone including Lucy to hear, "She must eat like a hog. Looks like one, too."

The cruelty of this comment snapped Paul into action and he followed this man across the grass toward the parking lot, his heart beating with an even more irregular rhythm. "That was a person in there, a human being," he said, catching up to the man.

The man turned around and faced Paul and Paul practically ran right into him. "Are you trying to make some kind of point, mister?" the man snapped.

"Do you think she's immune from words like that? She's got a disease, that's what she has."

He pushed Paul with both hands and Paul fell back against a bale of hay, losing his glasses. "Why don't you go back to that big old mamma and kiss her big fat butt." The man left Paul feeling in the hay for his glasses.

Paul walked quickly over to his car, popped the trunk and took out his leather medicine bag. At the door to the tent he dropped another quarter into the hat and walked right up to Lucy and told her that he was a doctor and that he wanted to test her blood pressure.

Lucy shook her head.

"Now wait a minute," Paul was all worked up. "Do you want to die this way? A blood pressure test is one of the most effective means of determining somebody's health."

Again Lucy shook her head and mumbled something under her breath. "Master Howard wouldn't—"

"It's not a matter of who would or wouldn't, this is a matter of life and death."

He wrapped the inflatable bandage around her wrist and pumped it up, taking her pulse and watching the gauge as he counted.

Never before had he witnessed anything like the figure he rapidly calculated in his head, even on somebody who was overdosing on drugs. He found her pulse again, pumped up the bandage and counted. It was real; it was what was happening inside of her at that moment. "Have you been this heavy your entire life?"

Lucy shook her head.

"Something happened to you, didn't it?" He didn't look at her as he continued checking her over with his stethoscope. "What happened? Somebody did something to you, something you can't talk about? Sometimes the armor you develop to protect yourself gets so cumbersome that it's the very thing that kills you. Now, cough, here."

Lucy coughed.

"Cough again."

Again she coughed. He took a small light from his medical bag and began probing her ear. "I'm going to ask you again. Did something happen to you back then when you started putting the weight on?" Lucy was silent as Paul prepared her arm with alcohol to draw a blood sample. "You've got to tell someone your story," Paul said.

"You don't tell somebody your story then this happens to you. That's why you're like this."

Paul heard a noise in the other bedroom of his house. At first he thought it was some kind of animal caught in a trap. He jumped up, throwing his bathrobe on and went into Emma's room, turning on the light. Emma writhed on the bed, her eyes closed, covered with sweat, moaning as if she was in great pain. Paul grabbed her arms and started shaking her awake. The moaning went on for quite some time before he could rouse her from sleep.

Then he looked into her eyes. Already Paul felt something, a knot in his throat, some sort of tightness preventing him from swallowing. He touched his Adam's apple, then Emma's throat which also seemed tight and swollen. "My God," he said to himself quietly. Laying her back in bed he turned out the light, then went downstairs to his medicine cabinet and unlocked it. He took out an even stronger sedative, filled a glass of water and brought it up the stairs. "I don't want you going anywhere in your sleep, Emma, this will knock you out for the night at least. Tomorrow you'll help Frances at the clinic. We'll all get to know each other."

16

That evening in his trailer Pidge had lost his appetite for the beans and franks he'd heated up on the skillet for dinner. Not a minute had gone by since Lucy's visit that he had not been thinking about her. He put his full plate on the floor for King, then got into his pickup truck and drove to the Wagon Wheel and climbed onto his favorite stool and gazed down the long dark bar at the television.

I will go where I've never been before and keep going where I've never been before and end up where I've never been before. Pidge had come up with this motto twenty-two years ago in a drunken stupor; the motto had become his guide, his moral plan, his new father. It led him from the house where he grew up to a bar twelve miles away where he practically lived for the entire eighteenth year of his life. Then into the back of a police car, then a jail cell, and finally into detox where one sunny afternoon Master Howard spotted him from one of the circus trucks, sitting in the sun on the back steps. He gathered everything he owned into a paper shopping bag with a broken handle.

Soon he found himself deep in the belly of the circus, a great leviathan that had swallowed him like a modern-day Jonah. Pidge began to believe that it would vomit him up somewhere on dry land after forty days.

Forty days and I'm outta here. Pidge worked and traveled with the show and waited, counting off every hour before he would be delivered from the show, not knowing which town they'd be in nor even which state at the end of that period. For thirty-nine of those days he worked without a break, fixing trucks and trailers and generators during the morning and walking around the ring in a clown costume in the afternoon and evening. On the fortieth day he rested and sat on a hay bale next to the tethered camels and llamas, watching the rest of the show work, waiting secretly for somebody to arrive and pull him out of it, take him to jail or deliver him back home. As he sat on that bale listening to Marcella snort and rustle the dry grass into her pink mouth, he thought of going to the police department and confessing to crimes that he hadn't committed.

Fourteen years later at the age of thirty-three the thought of leaving the circus was long gone, replaced by the idea of getting married, of being swallowed up by and of being born of a woman who would deliver him from his ultimate estrangement from humankind.

A deep, cruel irony lay beneath Master Howard's promotional wedding plan. Every spectator in Ohio, Kentucky, Tennessee, and Arkansas would believe that Pidge's wife was the fat woman.

After Pidge flat-out refused to do it, Master Howard said he'd guarantee him a *real* wife within four years if he changed his mind. Pidge turned him down again. And so Master Howard told him that if he didn't do it he'd guarantee that he wouldn't work in another circus ever again. Since Pidge had never come close to meeting another woman who wanted him, he agreed to participate in a ceremony that mocked what had become for him his only life ambition.

The first few weeks of the staged wedding were easily the worst in his life. He despised himself for smiling as Master Howard had ordered him to do, despised himself for performing this sacred ritual in front of all of the people who came to the show as well as all the circus people. Inside he had secretly come to hate Lucy.

The only way he got through the ceremony was to imagine different ways that his so-called wife might die before him. When he saw her eating in the dining tent, squashed between tables, he hoped almost out loud that all the food she took in would clog up her intestines and veins and kill her.

And Master Howard, what was he doing to her in his trailer in the middle of the night? What could this master of the universe be doing with the so-called fattest woman in the Midwest at one o'clock in the morning? One evening Pidge crawled under the trailer and put his ear to the underside and heard Master Howard grunting. Though Pidge knew he could only be having sex with her, he imagined that Master Howard was really inflicting pain on her. He waited, crouched underneath the trailer, his head cocked to the side so that he could listen. When it finally stopped he heard cursing and then the sound of Lucy crying and whimpering weakly, fraily like a small animal with a leg caught in a trap. And that sound of her in pain had given Pidge pleasure, he'd laughed to himself, clicked his fingers together, skipped as he made his way back to his bunk. "Master Howard's going to kill her," he said out loud quietly. "For being fat and ugly, yes, that's what she gets for ruining my life."

Lucy's misfortunes became a staple in his emotional diet. For some reason he couldn't make up the stories of her misfortunes himself, he had to find them, overhear them, discover them in other people's mouths, nuggets of gold that he'd pocket for the afternoon.

Lucy's falling in love with him, acid in an already painful wound, churned out strange nightmares whereby he was drawn deeper into a relationship with her, resigned like somebody acknowledging a terminal illness that this was it, this was the woman he'd been looking for, the one his unfortunate destiny had delivered to him.

The possibility of relief came soon after he'd first heard about Master Howard's plan.

"I want you to play along," Master Howard had said.

"I ain't lookin' at her," Pidge said.

"I haven't had a good laugh going on a couple of years now and this affords me the opportunity of a good one."

Despite all of the dastardly misfortunes that Pidge had hoped and prayed would befall Lucy, he suddenly realized that he himself was totally incapable of bringing any of these things down on her himself. He could hope but he could not do.

"I want you to write on this 'your secret admirer.'"

Pidge took up the pen, and fixed his hand to make the first letter Y.

"Well, go on, now."

"I won't mess up your plan, but I can't write that myself," Pidge said. "You do what you want. I won't get in yer way. I ain't gonna look at her, and I ain't gonna write nothin' for you."

"You ain't got no fun in you, little man," Master Howard had said. "I didn't think you were that far gone."

For several weeks Pidge tried not to pay attention to what was happening; he saw some of the things that Master Howard had left for her, the flowers on her doorstep, the little present wrapped in pink paper with the card on it.

Maybe this'll fix things, it'll do somethin', I don't know what the hell it is, he said to himself, *but surely somethin' will change.*

Then Master Howard asked Pidge for some clothes.

"We're dressin' up Kiki to look like you."

Pidge just walked away.

"Well, little man, you gonna give us some of yer clothes?"

"You want 'em, you get 'em yerself. I don't lock 'em up, you know that."

"You're right there. Nobody's gonna steal 'em."

That night a knock came at Pidge's door and Pidge got up and saw Master Howard, three other men standing next to him, and Kiki on his shoulder dressed in Pidge's clothes, which fit uncannily well. He'd put Pidge's hat on her, his scarf and his little patched blue jeans. Earlier that night Pidge had made up his mind that this trick would exorcise Lucy once and for all from his wounded psyche. Her spirit would crumble, all of her idiotic love for him would disappear in a tornado of surprise, maybe it would kill her.

As Pidge followed Master Howard down the trail to the lake shore where Lucy had been instructed to come for the moonlight rendezvous, he could see Kiki had turned her head clear around. Her innocent eyes seemed to say, *You too?* No animal, no human being except a man, not a woman, could think of such a trick with so many levels of evil.

They came to the beach where a smoldering mist rose from the wide dark lake. Pidge waited with the men as Master Howard carefully placed Kiki on a log and commanded her to stay. Kiki leaned against the log and looked out toward the water. She was an old and wise chimpanzee; she'd stay until he told her to move. Master Howard retreated, waving the men to a wall of brush. Pidge squatted with the rest of the men.

"Maybe she'll marry Kiki, Pidge, and not even realize it ain't you. She's smitten enough."

The faint dawn blossomed above the horizon, thin, beautiful vapors rose from the placid water of the dark lake. They listened carefully for footsteps.

A rustling of leaves turned out to be a yearling that stood proudly at the trailhead looking down at the chimpanzee dressed in a man's clothes. She sniffed the air, then snorted violently and took off back up the trail. Another time a raccoon crunched twigs and branches as it waddled down the beach to the water to wash its paws; without noticing Kiki it turned around and headed back into the bushes.

Then Pidge saw Lucy's figure in the darkness moving more quietly than any of the animals. It was eerie, her silhouette against the bushes, as if she'd found a way to lighten her step, as if she'd been thinking if she took a wrong step the love that the world was offering her would vanish forever.

She was dressed up in an outfit Pidge had never seen and he wondered where she'd gotten it. It looked like she'd made it herself, something between a circus costume and the vestments of a priest. It was ridiculous, more so than all of her other outfits, and yet he could not help but to admire some absurd beauty that it radiated.

Her whole body appeared to be trembling more delicately than the deer that had paused behind Kiki.

Pidge's body convulsed. He would jump up and tell her what they were doing. But Master Howard laid his powerful hands on Pidge's shoulders and he watched her cry out, then fall in anguish into the sand and heard the roar of laughter that rose up around him. Pidge did not laugh; he felt something inside himself crumbling.

A few months after Lucy had left the circus, Pidge became so physically tired that he went to his bunk before finishing the show. Soon Shorty and Tommy Henry carried him to a hospital where a number of doctors attempted to diagnose his mysterious illness. In his heart Pidge knew what had been eating away at him. He desperately wanted Lucy to forgive him, and yet he felt that the only way it would count would be if she did so without being asked to. Even though she was long gone from the show, he tried to send her mental SOS messages that he was in far more trouble than he'd ever been in his life.

His sickness brought a fever of 105 degrees and summoned almost everyone in the circus but Lucy to his bedside; a doctor had told Master Howard that Pidge would die. Pidge knew that his high fever was the only way he could plead for Lucy's forgiveness, if only she would show up by his bed, if only somebody would go and get her and she would see what he was doing to himself for what he'd done to her. And yet, he was ashamed of himself for even hoping that she would do this.

Days later as his fever was mysteriously letting up, the circus faraway in another state, Pidge kept thinking of the time his father had dumped him over the side of a rowboat while they were fishing, fished him out, and then laughed at him as he rowed them in. On the way home that evening, in the neighboring town of Tarville his father drew his arm across Pidge's eyes in order to point at something outside the window. It seemed apt that his father would point at something and blind Pidge with the arm that was pointing. When the father finally lowered his arm, Pidge saw a rusted metal sign set atop a fence of corrugated metal and barbed wire that said VEHICLE RECYCLING CENTER. "Why the fuck don't they call it what it is—a goddamn junkyard," he had steamed. "If you're working in a junkyard you might's well admit it. If you clean out shithouses for a living, you're not a sanitation engineer are ya? It don't make you a sanitation engineer, does it? You're just a shithouse janitor's all."

"A junkyard," Pidge said to himself when he finally walked out of the hospital doors. "I reckon."

"You had one too many, fellow. What's with you?" the bartender said to Pidge that night. "I've never seen you looking so down."

"I just got to thinkin'," Pidge said. "That's all."

17

First thing in the morning Lucy drove back to the highway and got off at the exit that said Gainston. She drove around the village and up into the mountains. Late in the morning, on a rise well above the flood plain, Lucy passed a sign tacked to a tree that said SHEAR ELEGANCE HAIRCUTTING SALON. The sign was in the front yard of a ramshackle farmhouse with a rusting blue Buick parked in the muddy driveway. Lucy backed up parallel with the house where a light shone in the bay window facing the road. Then she parked and climbed up on the porch and pushed the doorbell and heard a woman's voice inviting her to come in. The hairdresser, Sally, a woman with curly hair the color of yellowed newspapers, was sweeping up a customer's gray locks in the makeshift parlor. A hair dryer was leaning over a ratty sofa chair. "How much is a haircut, just a trim?" Lucy said. She sat down as Sally spread a plastic apron over her lap and tied it behind her neck. "Half an inch off, everywhere you see. Keep it the same shape," Lucy said.

Sally sprayed water on Lucy's curly hair, then combed it out, looking at her through the mirror. She started to clip, the hairs falling onto the apron. "Just passing through?" she asked.

Lucy's eyes met with hers in the mirror. "I don't know," Lucy said. "I may be staying in the area for a day or two."

Holding a shock of Lucy's hair between her fingers, Sally paused. "Oh yeah?"

Lucy nodded ever so slightly. Sally went on clipping. "What happened to everyone here? Looks like there was a plague or something," Lucy said.

"Might as well have been one, people act like it's the same damn thing. What brings you around these parts?"

"I'm just looking around. Curious, you know. I take drives, see the countryside, things like that," Lucy said. "I thought Gainston was a regular town. I guess I thought wrong."

"It used to be, sure. It used to be a happy little place; business was good. I wouldn't call it booming, but people did make a living here and there. Look there," she pointed to a color postcard of the town with cars parked on main street and an American flag on the green. "That was a decade ago."

Lucy nodded. "Things have changed, having to do with that dam up there?"

"How'd you know?"

"I was up there yesterday."

"Yeah, well, the dam's got a lot to do with it. In fact it's got everything to do with it. You didn't see what's behind that concrete wall, did you? Three quarters of a mile of water back there and it isn't at all shallow judging from the depth of the valley that it filled. Thing lets go, I guess everybody who sold out of here will be glad they did."

Lucy moved her head away from Sally's scissors and turned around to look her in the face. "Whose idea was it to build something like that above a town? I'd think it would be against the law."

"Hey, wouldn't you think?" Sally said as she went back to clipping hair. "I don't believe anybody in this town knows the real story behind it except Johnny Ranch. He owns the property where the dam was built, used to set his trapping lines along the Pemagawaset River, used to lease his land out to a fishing club every spring and summer. That was about his only income. But here he comes five or six years ago, king of construction."

"Did anybody ask him where he got his money from?"

Sally laughed, "Sure, people asked him. He claims he didn't build it, he's just the leaseholder on it. He says he didn't have any money and never did, and if you look at the wreck he drives around town or the shack in which he lives you might tend to believe him."

"Then what's his explanation?"

"It's simple. The Son of God built it. He himself had nothing to do with it."

"What?"

"That's what he says, says that with a kind of smirk on his face, a devilish little smirk, I'll add. Jesus Christ put up the money, hired the workers, laid out the plans. Ranch just watched it happen, he says."

"How about the workers who built the dam, where did their paycheck come from?"

"They keep mum, too. I guess nobody likes to bite the hand that feeds them, but it helps that none of them are from around here. Did you see the gates built into it?" Sally walked over to the counter and sat down. She hadn't finished Lucy's hair, but she was getting worked up as she told the story. "Those gates were built for one and only one purpose: to lift up all at once and let the entire lake come down the valley in one big old wave of water. In Gainston, a bunch of folk got together to sue nasty old Johnny, said he was threatening their property values, let alone lives. But old Johnny turned out to have himself the services of a law firm outside the state, not a cheap one, no way. They produced a little piece of paper they got from the mayor of this town years ago. I guess Ranch thinks we're suppose to believe Jesus is footing the bill for that, too.

But all that don't matter no more. Four years ago people panicked and sold out and somebody came in and snatched up most of the property for a song." Sally went back to cutting Lucy's hair.

"I saw some people taking pictures up there."

"Yes indeed," Sally said. "That dam attracts a Jesus freak or two. Don't help my business any; they come traipsing up here from all corners of the state to take a look. Preachers like to visit Gainston, too, setting up their speakers and microphones on what's left of the town green. 'Man's used up his quotient of sin,' they cry. 'God has manifested Himself up on the hill and the river will soon rise and flood the entire earth.' " Sally was cutting the hair over Lucy's forehead. "I'll tell you something else, one morning about five years ago, folks came out on their doorsteps to a note that said: 'God repenteth that He created ye, when this river floods so shall the entire earth!' that sort of thing. Then one morning everybody woke up to the sound of water running, their outdoor faucets had been turned on. Now, I didn't listen to a word of it back then, but I've watched my business dwindle and my friends leave town in droves. Occasionally I see Johnny Ranch swinging through town in his beat-up old pickup truck with that crazed look in his eye. I wouldn't mind spittin' in it, but it wouldn't do any good."

Through the window behind Sally, Lucy could see a fence and fields, willow trees that must have been growing near the riverbed. The sun was out and white clouds were drifting over the deep green mountains. "So, who's really behind the dam?"

"Don't know."

"You really don't, no idea?"

"None. Just whoever it is has got money and likes the commotion around this thing, likes to uproot people."

"Have the newspapers—?"

"Well, yeah, sure. But it's pretty much a dead story, pretty much accepted. Now I'd bet there'd be a commotion from all those Jesus freaks if anybody did try to tear that dam down."

Sally was putting the finishing touches on Lucy's hair. Finally she said, "A couple a years ago, there were some fellows who wanted to put a bullet between Ranch's eyes. I talked them out of it. It isn't Johnny behind that dam, no way. He's just been put up to it, I remember him from high school." Sally picked up a mirror and showed Lucy the back of her head with it. "How's that?"

Lucy hardly looked at it. "Fine," she said. "I've never heard a story like this before."

Lucy got up from the seat and Sally stepped over to the cash register and rang her up. Lucy handed her the money, then a sizable tip.

"Hell, are you hungry? I made a pot of soup that'll go bad if nobody helps me eat it."

After fixing bowls of chicken soup, Sally and Lucy sat down at the blue-and-white checked table and began to eat. "I came here nineteen years ago. This house was nearly fallen to the ground . . . ran away from home when I was twelve," Sally said.

Lucy sipped her soup and watched for an explanation. "You, too?" Lucy said.

"Sure? Why not?" It seemed like it hadn't registered with Sally that Lucy had run away, too. "Of everything I ever did, and I've done quite a lot, that's the one thing I did right. I left, didn't look back once, not once."

There was silence, a fly buzzed in through the open window and landed on the tablecloth. "Somebody hurt you, didn't they?" Lucy said.

"No," Sally looked down at her half empty bowl of soup. "But nobody did anything for me, either."

"Then I know why you ran away," Lucy said.

Sally's round face went from outgoing and talkative, to withdrawn, wrinkled, and tired. Her eyes seemed deeper and smaller. "You know, huh?" she said. She moved her spoon in the broth.

"I was in a circus, most of my life," Lucy said. "I ran away and joined one, isn't that corny?" Lucy had rarely if ever told anyone this story and now she was embarrassed. "I had to do it. I couldn't stay in the town I grew up in. I was nothing back then, not to anybody, even my ma, then somebody did something to me and I became even less than that, that's how I ended up in the circus. Besides, I was running from somebody and I knew he hated circuses. Next thing I knew I was eating day and night. I didn't get much fatter than some people get in Ohio, I mean I've seen a whole lot of bigger people, but I at least had a title. The fat lady."

Sally looked Lucy up and down compassionately.

"Having a title didn't help any," Lucy said, looking down. "I nearly died."

Sally stared at her for a long time, nodding her head. Then Lucy went on to tell her the story of adopting Emma, how she had read about her in the paper and how she had known in her heart well before she'd even laid eyes on her that she would feel incredibly close to her if she adopted her.

". . . Right in the middle of the night, he brought her up to my door." Sally's eyes opened wide as Lucy told the story, as if it were a tale about great danger. If Emma hadn't been delivered to her, she would never have survived. "I've had her now for quite a while now. I'm not a superstitious person, you know. But all those secret feelings I had when I read about her in the paper? They turned out to be true. Just as true as that vase right there," she pointed at one of Sally's vases on the table. "She and I have gotten closer than any two people you can imagine. She gives to me, and I, I try my best to give to her. I'll admit it right here, right now. I need her very much. I try to love her the right way, the way that will help her, but I do lean on her."

"Where is she now?"

"Right here," Lucy said, and she pulled a small square picture of Emma out of her shirt pocket and laid it on the table. Sally picked up the picture and began to examine it.

"My word," she said.

"She's had some trouble at night." Lucy stammered. "The doctor I left her with is going to put her on medication, she's been sleep-walking. And I've come down here to see what I can find. Some-body told me there are some men up this way. I've come to talk to them. I've come to lay my eyes on them, to see what they're all about. I guess in some way I'm just trying to do for Emma what was never done for me. It may not sound like it makes sense, but it does to me. You see, I don't think there's anything more impor-tant in this world than knowing somebody tried to help you, even if they bungled it and all and made a big fool of themselves, so long as they tried." She tried to make light of this, though her whole being was behind these words. "And I, well, I'm inclined to bungle most things." The two women stared at each other and Lucy could feel that every word she had said had gone deep inside of Sally.

"Well, you got yourself a place to stay right here, understand? I've got all kinds of spare bedrooms." Lucy went outside to her car and brought her bag upstairs to the bedroom. Opening it up she saw Emma's clothes were still packed, she'd forgotten to leave her a change of clothes at the Marshalls'.

18

At around two o'clock in the afternoon Lucy drove out of the yard and back to the road that led up to Hemmels Way. She didn't know what she'd say to Ranch, but she thought she should lay eyes on him, assess him herself. His driveway, she had learned, began where the road ended and was well posted with NO TRESPASSING signs. She drove right by and up the steep hill. At the crest she could see a long field speckled with sheep that led to the dam's lake, so big and expansive that she paused to take it all in. The water was dark in some places, blue in others. On the far shore a thickly forested mountain rose with a fire tower on its summit; flocks of geese and pairs of ducks drifted under the mountain's reflection. Directly below Lucy where the road ended she saw a tall, narrow shack of warped plywood and tattered tarpaper, partially covered with stretched animal pelts.

The road was washed out in places, deep ruts that made Elvis rock and scrape bottom. Finally Lucy stopped the car, fearing that if she went any farther she wouldn't be able to back out. She got out to walk the rest of the way.

Suddenly a shotgun blast rang out over her head, the blast returning in triple echo from the lake; ducks and geese flapped their wings against the water as they took off. A man was walking up the hill from the crooked shack toward her, a shotgun dangling between his arms. He was a skinny, scarecrowlike fellow wearing a crazy patchwork hat of animal fur, some kind of bright but stained orange hunting vest, and baggy army fatigues.

"Can't you read?" he called. He was still far away.

Fear anchored Lucy to the earth, she couldn't move backward or forward. "I need to talk to you," she called back. Her voice echoed over the wide lake and returned faintly, like the voice of somebody who has just died.

"I *don't* need to talk to you," the man called back as he approached her.

She still could not move, thinking how reckless it was for her to just drive up here. "I came all the way down here from Ohio. I don't want anything from you, just to talk."

"Who the fuck are you?"

She could see the man's small eyes and his dirt-streaked face. "Just a woman."

"What the fuck's a *woman* doing up here?" The man stopped; his forehead wrinkled as if the word woman confounded him.

Lucy was silent, trying to center herself, to arrest her fear so as not to show it. "I need help, I'm asking you for help, that's all."

"I don't need none of your lady bullshit, none at all. I've had enough of that in my life time from *bitches* like you."

Again Lucy was silent. A cow started mooing in the field near her. She could hear the flapping of crows that the shot had flushed.

"Get on back into your vehicle," the man waved the barrel of his shotgun. Lucy didn't move; she didn't even turn away from him. She felt she was in a kind of trance, caught between fear and courage.

"I need your help," she repeated. "I'm not here to ask you about the dam."

Now the gun was pointed directly at her. "Get on back into your old junker there, otherwise you'll be fillin' turkey buzzard guts for the next month or so and I'll have to smell you. I can smell you bad enough from here."

Holding her breath, she watched the twin barrels of the gun. Then words came out of her mouth automatically. "They wouldn't touch me." She surprised herself as much as him.

The man was silent, trying to figure out what she'd meant by that. "They wouldn't, huh?"

"Nope."

"Why not?"

"Because I'm a *freak*." Again she surprised herself and she saw that Johnny was taken aback, lowering the gun and raising his chin a little.

"Oh, you're a *freak*, huh?" he said.

"That's what I am," she said. "That's why I'm here." Then she said quietly, "*Here on this earth.*"

"And what's that have to do with coming up here and getting your head shot clean off. Blasted away like a crow on a post."

"It may not have anything at all to do with it. I was the fat lady in a circus."

"No shit," Ranch said. "You ain't big enough." He used his shotgun as a pointer, up and down her body.

"I'm staying with a lady down in the valley who cuts hair. She said you're the only one left in these parts; maybe you would know about some other kind of freaks—" She stopped short as something caught her eye on the lake behind him: two black barrels with bright yellow rope wrapped around them exactly like the ones Master Howard had described in his dream. *He was lying when he said he dreamed them. He's been here himself. He's seen these things.* They bobbed far out in the water. Sleek black ducks floated near one of them. It occurred to Lucy that she shouldn't let Ranch know that she was staring at them and yet she could barely pull her eyes away.

The moment she did she realized that Ranch had raised his shotgun again and was aiming it right at her face. "Listen, ugly, I'll give you ten seconds before I Swiss Cheese your face, okay?"

Lucy quickly turned and walked up the rutted dirt road to her car. She didn't turn around until she reached the car and got into the driver's seat. Ranch had followed her up and stood twenty yards away from her, aiming the gun at her through the windshield.

19

Lucy spent the rest of the afternoon driving around the area. She found but few occupied houses, all of which were outside of town safely above the flood line. A few of the people she talked to seemed to believe or at least half believe some of the myths surrounding the dam. One woman said, "Well, you never know, they don't have any other explanation for it. I've known the Ranches all my life. The father never had a dime; the mother, well, thank God, she never had a dime. She was in jail most of his growing up for killing his younger brother with a paring knife. And yet the whole thing is deeded to Johnny. Now you explain it." Lucy showed people pictures of Emma, but nobody had ever seen her before, nor did they know of anybody even associated with this pretty young girl.

Off a mountain road Lucy stopped into a bar called the Watering Hole. Five or six pickup trucks, dented, rusted cars, and a farmer's tractor with a manure spreader attached were parked among the potholes of the lot. The building looked like a shed with big brown linoleum shingles, some of which had fallen off, and a red neon Rheingold sign in the window. Inside she was told by the barmaid, a red-faced woman with a fly swatter in her hand, that Johnny Ranch came in every night around eleven for three shots of whiskey and two beers. "Soon as I get off, he come in."

"Every night?" Lucy said.

"Frank'll tell you about him. Johnny leaves him the exact same tip, too. Zip," the barmaid smiled.

That night Lucy and Sally had dinner together. Afterward, Lucy took the Marshalls' card out of her wallet and called them to see how Emma was doing. Frances answered and said, "She's wondering about you."

"She is?"

"Yes, she's been staring out at the road from the living room. She's waiting for you, every car door that closes, she gets up and looks. I'll put her on."

Lucy could hear the phone changing hands. "Emma?" she said. She thought she could hear Emma breathing through the line. "I miss you. I'm going to be back soon." Lucy waited, trying to think of what to say. "You see, I'm looking into some things—for me and for you. I'm trying to figure some things out for both of us." Lucy again told her how much she missed her and loved her, then said goodnight.

For safekeeping Lucy put the Marshalls' card in Emma's pants pocket in her suitcase.

Just as Sally was about to go upstairs to bed Lucy said, "I think I'll stop up to that bar, the Watering Hole."

"At this time? You'll get yourself in trouble. That isn't any place for decent folks."

"I've been in plenty of those kinds of bars. Don't you worry, I'll take care of myself."

It was a twenty-minute drive across the river to the bar. Lucy parked near a wooden rail fence, turned her lights off, and went to the door. She opened it and looked for Johnny among the half-dozen men drinking and smoking and the barmaid who was just turning her shift over to the bartender, and then she went back to Elvis and waited. There were at least a dozen cars, mostly old wrecks, parked in front. The barmaid came out and got in her car.

Soon a pickup truck swung quickly into the parking lot and pulled up to the front door. Ranch jumped out, a red bandanna tied around his head, a ponytail reached halfway down his back. He slammed his truck door twice to get it shut then took three big steps and pushed through the door of the bar. Lucy started up Elvis and drove quickly back down the road to Hemmels Way.

Before the crest of the hill where Ranch's property began, Lucy backed down a small logging road she had noted earlier until Elvis was well out of sight of the main dirt road. She got out and started on foot toward the top of the hill. Then she stopped. She did not want to carry identification on her and so she went back to the car and hid her wallet and the car's registration behind a log. Then she continued on over the hill to where the fields began. Looking at her watch she saw it was 11:38. By midnight at the very latest she'd be back in her car and driving back down the dirt road.

It was dark and quiet except for the high-pitched yaps of foxes across the mountain. The reflection of the half moon glittered near the center of the lake. Sheep lying down in a corner of the field looked like gray rocks arching out of the earth. Lucy cut through the field, moving as quickly as possible toward Ranch's shack next to the lake.

She could see the animal skins splayed across the sides, and near the foundation were metal barrels, a rusted truck without tires on cinder blocks, a clothesline, some farm equipment, and an out-house. Ducks quacked loudly on the other side of the lake, then flew close to the water, their wings beating against its surface, then they landed again with a splash.

The grass had been worn away from the borders of the shack by Ranch's feet. A string and a nail secured the door that faced away from the road toward the lake. She took the string off the nail and stepped inside. The shack smelled of stale beer, cigarettes, dirty socks and the faint trace of urine. A worn couch covered with news-papers, boxer shorts, beneath it a deerhide rug and a pair of army boots. On the walls were the upper halves of beaver skulls with their two teeth bared, several sets of antlers. Rows of empty beer bottles stood on a shelf next to a basinlike sink. There was no bed down here, but a ladder leading up to a sleeping loft.

On a desk spotted with melted candle wax, Lucy saw notebooks with scribbled pen marks and on the floor next to them an empty cardboard box inside of which were two plastic bags and a handwritten note that said:

Come with me and be fishers of men.

There was oil or Vaseline coating the inside of the two plastic bags and a faint trace of blood. Lucy tried to understand what this meant and what had been in the bag.

She looked at her watch: 11:47.

She stepped out of the shack, closed the door, placing the string over the nail, then she headed up the road. She stopped; again she looked at her watch, then back to a sagging dock where an aluminum rowboat was tied. *What's under those barrels?* She wondered why Master Howard had described these barrels in such detail. She remembered him saying, "And I dove down, fifteen feet, at least, and followed the line beneath it and there I saw a coin . . ." Why had he told her this? She'd have to move fast if she were to have a look.

She tested each dock plank carefully, and then climbed down into the rocky boat, stepping on a pile of steel-jawed traps and their chains. Lucy quickly put the oars in the locks and started to row away from Johnny's shack. She carefully watched the top of the hill where the road passed out of sight, meanwhile glancing over her shoulder to guide herself toward the nearest barrel at the lake's center.

She came up alongside of it, the bow echoing as it touched. Bending over she pulled the yellow nylon cord up from underneath the barrel. There was something heavy attached to it; the wet rope dripped over her knees and shoes as she drew it in, hand over hand.

Perhaps there was just an anchor on the end of the line; she didn't know.

Finally, she brought something to the surface; a rock that was much heavier coming over the gunwale than it had been in the water. *A rock.* She almost laughed to herself nervously. *Another trick Master Howard another trick and if Ranch comes back*—but there was more rope attached to the rock and she began to pull that in; something was floating right near the boat. She pulled it up into the moonlight.

A hook big enough to catch a large shark. Skewered on it was what looked to be a chunk of bacon fat, bait of some kind. She was about to drop it back when she realized what it was—a bloated human foot cut cleanly off at the ankle, skewered through the arch by the barb, tiny toes curled downward. The skin had not wrinkled because it had been treated with something that repelled water, Vaseline or motor oil. It was as white as a squid and now under the moonlight it glistened.

She turned her eyes away, gagging, trying to keep from throwing up, putting her mouth against her shoulder. After a few minutes she scanned the hill past the sheep to the road. *He'll be back soon.* She threw the rock and the rope and then the foot spun out of the bow throwing a spray of water around it.

She began rowing back. Ripples around the barrel dissipated. Mist rose from the mountainside, clouding some of the stars. She could almost hear Master Howard's horrible laugh again. The foxes' high-pitched yapping started up.

Then it occurred to her that if she had the foot she could go to the police, evidence of crime, a murder. She turned toward the second barrel and grabbed the yellow rope from underneath and began to pull it in.

Look, he's your suspect, she'd say to the police. *Anybody capable of doing this is capable of marking up a little girl.* She came to the anchor rock then kept pulling. Another hook, only this one had something much smaller beneath the barb. She thought it was the head of some rodent, white and viscous, but then she could make out a thumb wrapped across fingers, a hand. She dropped the line and nearly cried out in disgust. Then she reached down, closed her eyes and started to pull it from the hook. Its fingers slipped through her own hand and she saw that there were fingers missing, two fingers missing, healed before the hand was cut off. *I've seen this hand before* . . . She immediately thought of Carl Lark holding the yellow pencil in his office, the same two fingers were missing.

Again she could feel her throat closing as she gagged. She closed her eyes, dropped the hand and stepped on it and began to twist the hook out of it. But the barb held stubbornly. Leaning back she pulled with all her might.

The hand ripped free and she fell backward against the gunwale, nearly tipping over. Steadying the boat at last, she threw the bare hook and rock over the side and grasped the oars and began to row quickly. A humming noise in the faint distance, a persistent humming like a pain from a sore tooth worked its way to her ear. She didn't know how far away the vehicle was. She headed toward the dock, rowing quickly—she would tie the boat up. *If he sees the boat isn't tied—*

She was twenty feet from shore when headlights flashed across the sky as the truck crested the hill. Reaching the dock, she dropped the oars. The headlights were coming down the dirt road on the other side of the house. *Find the rope and tie the boat up.*

She couldn't find it. Instead she grabbed the slippery hand. The truck stopped on the other side of the shack, the truck door slammed. She ran toward the side of the house and squatted down next to some barrels and a pile of rotten lumber and chunks of firewood. She could hear Ranch slam his truck door again and then his footsteps as he walked around to the side of the house that faced the lake. The boat was floating freely from the dock. *But he won't know I'm here, the loose boat doesn't mean somebody's here, it could have happened on its own.* Lucy was just around the corner at the other end of the shack, in the shadows, right up against the warped plywood and torn tarpaper that made up the wall. She felt around for a rock or anything that she might throw at him if he found her, but she kept coming up only with dirt.

"You great big old stinking bitch, you!" he shouted so loud that for an instant she thought he stood right above her. Echoes came back from across the lake and she realized he must be facing away from her, toward the water. She squatted down harder between the barrels, one of which had the bitter and pungent stink of human dung. It was dark where she squatted, but not dark enough for cover if he did happen to walk down to this side of the building.

She heard his footsteps and realized that he was only feet away from her. She pulled herself into a tighter ball. He came closer and he stopped. She could feel his presence, was he looking at her? She remained still, afraid to move a muscle.

Suddenly she felt something on the back of her neck like somebody had laid a hot water bottle down on the nape. The sensation was a strange one. It was cold but, as it quickly spread, she began thinking that it was red hot like molten lava rising up the back of her head. Then it seemed much more like a color than heat, a purplish-red that ferociously engulfed the top of her skull.

20

When she opened her eyes, she was lying on her back in a barn with cathedral ceilings and wooden beams. She tried to move her hands but found them tightly strapped to a hard bed, like a doctor's examination bench. When she tried to move her legs, she found they too were securely strapped down. Her face was numb, her cheeks swollen. She now remembered Ranch beating her on the face. There was swelling around her nose that must have been broken. She could hardly see through her eyes. Her head felt like a sheet of ice with a hairline crack that widened slightly every time she moved. It occurred to her that her skull had been fractured and that the ice was an image of this break.

She called, "Help!" at the top of her lungs and the pain spread, the crack widened. Then she was quiet and tried to reassure herself that anyone who had gone through such effort to strap all of her limbs and torso to this bed must intend to return.

"Help!" After the pain she could hear nothing but the sound of sparrows chirping somewhere. Time went by, minutes, hours, afternoons—she didn't know how long or what time of day. Emma's eyes, she kept seeing them inside her head. Why were they so familiar? Why had they always been so familiar from the time Mr. Lark brought her to her house at dawn three months before?

One time during the middle of a performance one of Master Howard's tigers escaped and ran outside the tent to a tethered baby elephant and jumped on her back, and the mother, loosely chained by one leg, had rolled over both her baby and the tiger, scaring the tiger off.

The tiger leapt on a mare horse named Vera and began to eat the flesh on her back. From the door of her tent Lucy could clearly see the scene. The strangest thing she noted was that Vera didn't move while being mauled, but stood almost peacefully up to her hocks in hay staring out at the pastures. Perhaps she knew that it wasn't going to do any good, or perhaps it had all happened too fast; she stood perfectly still, drinking in the world with her beautiful clear eyes as the tiger tasted the dark sweetness of her blood.

Lucy could hear the squealing of the cage as Master Howard and his groom wheeled it up behind the tiger. Master Howard drew his whip down on the orange and black fur and a strip of blood appeared in it, then the tiger jumped from Vera's back into its cage where the groom dropped the bars and quickly wheeled the cage back up the hill to the tent.

Vera still did not totter, perhaps her legs were trembling but Lucy couldn't see them from where she stood on the hillside. Then Lucy observed that her belly had been ripped wide open by the tiger's claws and her intestines and stomach and other organs had spilled into the hay beneath her.

Lucy heard the bullhorn of Master Howard calling everyone into the ring, deflecting the panic that had ensued after the tiger had fled. But Lucy herself had not been able to move. Shorty raced past her, heading toward Vera. In his hand was a dark object. Not until he raised it to the side of Vera's beautiful head did Lucy realize that it was a gun in his hand. Then she heard a crack, and Vera's legs folded like a marionette whose strings had been cut.

Later the horse trainer, a blond woman with long false eyelashes and a tight costume that showed off her breasts, came down to the stables to see her lovely horse being drawn into the back of a pickup truck with a winch. The trainer said, "It's always the best ones, the most beautiful, the most innocent that fall victim to these accidents. I don't understand it, such a lovely creature."

Now as Lucy lay here strapped to the cot she realized that Emma's eyes were similar to the innocent eyes of the mare that had gazed out at the pastures with a tiger on her back.

Lucy heard a door open. She couldn't turn her head toward the person who walked into the room and around her as if he were observing her from different angles.

Lucy opened her mouth to talk, but for some reason she couldn't say a thing. It was like trying to run in a dream and not being able to. Then the person stepped around the back of her head and came up to her and looked down.

Lucy focused on the mask the person wore, blue and yellow with scales and a long snout. A rubber fish face. The man carried something in a pair of pliers. *Oh my Lord*, Lucy thought. It was a metal rod that had been heated so that it was red-hot.

In his other hand he held the small square picture of Emma that Lucy kept in her pocket.

"Where is she?" the man said.

Lucy shook her head.

He brought the red metal rod an inch from her neck and she could feel heat pulsing against her skin.

"Where's my girl?"

21

Two hours after Lucy had left her house that night and not returned, Sally telephoned the Watering Hole and spoke to the bartender who said he had not seen a stout, curly-haired woman all
night. *She must have gotten lost.* Sally waited in a chair next to the
telephone in the parlor. She had not known Lucy long but she
already trusted her to be a sane and considerate person, who would
call the minute she was able to. At around three A.M. a candle
she had lit went out on its own and she continued to sit there in
the dark.

Headlights cast windowpane shadows against her ceiling. She
got up to see a car pulling into the drive. In the light of the
dash she saw two men get out of the front seat and climb up on
her porch and knock. Sally stood behind the door. "Who is it?"
she said.

"Are you Sally Finch?"

"Who are you?"

The man threw his shoulder against the door and knocked it
open enough to put his foot in it. "We got a search warrant."

"A search warrant? For what?"

"Come on, lady, you know what."

"I don't know what you're talking about."

"You got a girl in here, don't you? We heard you got her."

"What?"

"Don't play dumb."

"I have no idea what—"

The men threw their weight against the door again and knocked Sally back.

"Oh, go ahead, search the place!" Sally said. "There isn't anybody here."

One man ran upstairs, flicking on light switches wherever he found them and the other went into the back of the house. They were looking under beds, in closets, under chairs, anywhere a person might hide, including the cabinet under the bathroom sink. "You're wasting your time," she said to the man. "Whoever sent you has got the wrong house."

One man came running down the stairs with a handful of Emma's clothes, two turtleneck shirts and two pairs of pants.

"Look at this!" he said to the other man. "Whose clothes are these? Huh? He said she likes her turtlenecks, yes he did!" He turned to Sally and grabbed her shirt and pulled her right up against him. "Listen, lady, do you believe in Christ?"

"Let go of me!" Sally screamed.

"I asked you a question," the man screamed into her ear.

"Yes."

"You tell us where she is for Him?!" the man said, yelling.

"I never saw the girl in my life."

"Where is she? She must have told you."

"She didn't say—"

The first man looked at the other as he held Sally by the shirt. "Get the tank," he said.

"Wait a minute," the second man said. "She might be—" He stepped up to Sally. "Where's the girl?" he yelled into her ear.

Tears burst out of Sally's eyes. Holding her by the blouse, the man began slapping her face with the back of his hand. "Where?"

Sally kept crying. The other man ran out the door and came back moments later. "Let me take her," he said. He held a mask with a hose attached to it. Sally screamed. "You want to talk to the water?"

Sally kept screaming and crying. "I don't know where she is."

The man with the mask started to wrestle Sally away from the first man. "Let me take her."

"Wait a minute," the first man said, then stared at Sally. "She must have told you."

"Maybe . . ." Sally said. "Maybe . . ."

"Let her talk," the first man said to the man with the mask.

With tears falling from her eyes, Sally said, "She left her down the road, down the road at a motel, Motel 6."

"Where?"

"The one, the one," Sally said, catching her breath, "on Route 202 going out of Blair."

"Are you sure of that?"

"She brought the kid down there," Sally said. "She didn't want to bring the kid into town."

The first man threw Sally on her back to the floor. "Are you lying?" he said, standing above Sally who lay against the wall under a window. A lamp had fallen over next to her and the hot bulb was against her ankle.

"No, she's there, call, go ahead call," Sally said.

"Shit," the man said and kicked her with his boot. "She ain't there, you'll have your dialogue with the water."

"Let's go," the other man said. They both turned and went to the door. One man had gathered the few belongings that Lucy had left in Sally's room.

22

Sally got up off the floor and staggered to the porch where she saw their taillights disappearing along the road. She stumbled down the steps to her car, determined to get away before they returned. Unsure of where to go, she got on the highway heading east, still in a daze and trembling from what had happened. She drove for an hour at which time dawn was breaking, then pulled into a rest area and fell asleep. Soon she was awake again and driving and a voice came into her head: *They came into to my house, inside my house. They tried to kill me inside my own house.* Sally had not told Lucy the whole story about running away. From when she was very young Sally kept moving from city to city and state to state for almost seven years. The house she lived in now had belonged to her dead grandmother. Sally had ended up there just as she had reached the end of her rope. The place at the time had been abandoned, water pouring through the roof when it rained. Sally had moved in, camping in the kitchen, gradually bringing the rotting structure to life.

She could not help it; her outrage began to mount as she focused on her lovely house and what these men had done to her, of how they had violated her, violated the person that she had made herself. *They kicked me in the head in my own house; they nearly beat me to death in my own house. They had no right, no right to do that.* At the next exit she turned around and headed back. *Nobody has the right to do that to another, nobody!*

She parked in her yard. Her door was open; a window next to it was broken. The men must have returned. She went up to the attic and removed a shotgun from a trunk that had belonged to her grandfather.

Sheets of plywood had been sitting between the barn rafters for years. She brought them one at a time over to the house. Using a Skil saw to cut them, Sally boarded up all twelve windows on the bottom floor and sealed the back door. In the front door she cut a hole in the plywood just big enough for the barrel of a gun. She finished just before evening. She did not bother cleaning the place up. Instead she pulled a chair to the boarded up door and waited. At times she nearly forgot what she was waiting for, she just sat there quietly, listening to the birds and insects and a few cars.

As dark was falling, she heard a car pull up into the yard and she peeked out through the hole she had cut in the door and saw the two men get out at once and climb up toward the porch. They were in their mid- to late twenties. They had a certain arrogance about them like they knew something that only men were allowed to know. Before they got up to the porch, Sally slipped a board over the hole and sat there against the door, listening to them talking to each other, no more than two or three feet from her.

"If you aren't looking for trouble you come on outta there; a couple damn boards aren't going to stop us from coming on in." They knew she was behind the door.

"I don't know if I agree with you about that," Sally said.

"You open up now."

Sally carefully moved the strip of wood from across the hole, squatted down and looked through it. She was staring right at the leather belt of one of the men. She moved the strip of board back and stood up straight, the shotgun in her hand.

"Come on out of there, lady, otherwise we're going to get rough with you. We just want our kid back, that's all."

"I told you I don't have your kid."

"Come on, lady."

"You're trespassing, that's what you're doing. You can't walk in and do that to somebody. No way."

"You're holding our property."

"That girl isn't anybody's property, she sure isn't yours. One thing I know, it's not right what you did to her and you've lost the right to her, whoever you are."

"Now that isn't for you to judge, lady," the man said, arrogantly.

"It isn't for me to judge that you cover a child's body with tattoos?"

"If you get any nastier on us, maybe we'll draw some lines on your body, too." He snickered.

"Yeah, well, I've had plenty of lines drawn on my body already, deep lines, lines that I'll never forget," Sally said. "If anybody ever tries that again, I warn them."

"Well, if you don't want that to happen, then you come out of there right now."

Sally slid the board down again, put her eye to the hole and again saw the man's belt, then she raised the gun barrel and pointed it at the hole. "No, I don't want that to happen," Sally said.

One man laughed. "Don't get too cocky in there, little lady."

"Come on out or we'll paint you up good."

Sally pulled the trigger; the gun kicked back against her arm, practically knocking her over, but she caught her balance and kicked the door open all the way, surprised to see the man she'd hit had been knocked clear across the porch. The other man dashed down the steps and raced across the yard. Sally lifted the gun again and pulled the trigger. She caught the second man in the back of the leg. He went down on one knee, flipped forward, then got up, dragging his torn leg toward the car. Sally tried to break the gun to get the other cartridges in, but the man pulled out of the yard, tires kicking gravel, then smoking on the pavement.

She finished loading and walked over to the man she had caught in the stomach. He was holding his wound, grunting, his eyelids fluttering and the whites of his eyes showing. She stood over him, aiming at his chest. "You happen to know where that woman is, the one whose kid you're after?" The man looked up at her and nodded. "Are you going to tell me or what?"

He stared at her, drooling, his mouth was now crooked. He started to say something about Christ but then, almost by accident, she pulled the trigger and the gun went off.

He broke the spokes of the porch railing behind him and fell back into the grass, upside down, his legs over his head like a child trying to stand on his head.

She walked down the porch steps, looked at the side of his stomach to see if he'd stopped breathing and then headed back to the barn and started up her car and backed it around to where he lay. She tied a rope from her bumper to one of his legs, got in the car and dragged him behind the barn into the field. She got out and slid to one side the circular cement cover top to a well that was plenty deep and no longer of use to her. She had some trouble getting the man to fit down the stone well because she hadn't taken the cover completely off, fearing she'd never get it on again.

Back at her house, she packed a few of her bags, brought them out to her car, turned and looked at the house where she'd lived for almost nineteen years and took off.

23

That evening the Marshalls had to return to their clinic on an emergency call, leaving Emma sitting at the wooden desk in front of her bedroom window that faced the dark backyard. She was alone. A pencil was in her hand above a piece of notebook paper that she'd found in the desk drawer. Before her, through the window, she could see the rear of the neighbor's house, the wooden fence that ran between the two yards, and beyond the fence, a tied-up dog had been barking at nothing in particular, but was now quiet. She looked down at her hand holding the pencil, slowly touching the lead to the paper, then lifting it up again. Then she closed her eyes and touched the paper again; this time she made a letter, the letter *D*, then she slowly carved out the letter *E*, then an *A*.

After a moment she looked down at what she'd written, *Dear Lucy* and covered it up immediately with her hand and took a deep breath; she had pushed past something inside of her, something that was important to get beyond. And nothing bad had happened to her for it. She lifted her hand and looked at it again. Then she started making more letters and words, slowly at first, then faster:

Come back home. Please come back . . .

She paused to take in what she had just done. It was important, an important step. She put the pencil to the paper again. Suddenly she felt as if somebody was watching her. She turned her head. There in the doorway she saw a man in a dark suit and minister's collar. She got up and backed around her desk. He was familiar, but more than just his features; she recalled a feeling that she was shrinking, rapidly becoming smaller, tiny, while his body grew in stature. Already Emma's legs trembled so hard that she was unsure she could even run. "It is you, it is you, but I must see for myself, I must see for myself. Lift up your sleeve," he said. "Do as I say!" He approached her slowly, having shut the door behind him, his arms out to keep her from running away. "Lift it up, I said!"

Emma backed into the corner of her room into a bookcase; her fist gripped her wooden pencil over her head like a dagger. "What's gotten into you?" he yelled. If ever she needed to speak it was now, but the silence that she had lived in for so many years continued to envelop her. He came toward her; she stabbed at him with her pencil, but he grabbed her wrist and twisted it, then slid his hand up it so that he could see the black scales on her arm. Then his hand locked so tightly around her wrist that he might have broken it if he snapped it hard enough. She sucked air in through her nostrils.

He quickly wrapped a piece of clothesline cord around her wrists and pulled her out of her bedroom to the top of the stairs. Without realizing what she was doing, she bit the back of his hand and he threw her down in front of him and kicked at her like she was a stray animal. Then he yanked her to her feet again and shook her so hard that her head snapped back, nearly blacking her out. "What've they been doing to you? Tell me!"

He dragged her to the top of the landing. She didn't resist, her legs folded under her and he dragged her down the steps, her heels clapping against each one until she reached the bottom. He tried to make her stand up, but she had no use of her legs.

She remembered the smell of this man, his voice, even the way he breathed. He dragged her through the kitchen to a door into the garage and shoved her into the leather seat of a black car and slammed shut the door. She remembered this car door—he'd removed the handles and lock from this side. He jumped in next to her and backed out of the garage. "Don't you move, don't you do anything rash," he yelled so fiercely that she stared straight down under the dash and held still, she was trembling from head to foot. He flipped on a radio, full of static and broken voices, a police scanner.

Slowly she raised her head and looked out the window at the highway grass, the wide fields where small herds of deer grazed in the dark. Despite the darkness she hoped to see somebody on the side of the road, a woman, catch her eye, let her know just with her expression that she was in trouble, to get the police. "What did you do? Did you tell her about me? I told you never to bring anybody into our business," he said. She looked at him, vaguely aware of who he meant by *her*. He smiled. The word *Lucy* came into Emma's mind; the man was looking at her. "Now Audrey's making a mess of that old meat locker. All because of you. Audrey McBride."

The familiarity of this name confused Emma for a moment until she realized it was the name of their horse. She felt relieved, maybe the man didn't have Lucy, maybe he was talking about somebody else, but then the reality of the situation came to her. He must have somehow gotten Lucy. Lucy had lied to him, told him her name was Audrey McBride.

Emma's body convulsed, she lunged at the man to scratch his face, but he drew his arm down to push her off and she fell onto his lap and slipped in front of his knees beneath the steering wheel. She was trying to bite his leg; she sunk her teeth in below his knee; he kicked wildly at her face and she fell further, now to his feet and now against the pedals. He jammed his shoe into her chest.

With the pressure of his foot against her chest, her back pressed against the gas pedal, the car blasted forward, careening wildly down the road and he cried out for help at the top of his lungs, reaching down and firmly grabbing her hair. She turned and got hold of his forearm with her mouth, she clamped down and bit clear through it and he screamed. But it was too late, the car must have been clear off the road; it smashed into things, tipped down gullies, and cracked through something wooden; the man's foot pushed harder, clamping Emma down onto the gas pedal.

The car slammed into something solid, then lifted clear into the air and for a moment became weightless, then came down with such a furious explosion that the man was thrown out of his seat and Emma slammed up against the steering column.

Then again there was silence, weightlessness, and again a crash, this time turning the car upside down, knocking the wind so thoroughly out of Emma that there was a long moment of deadness in her fragile chest.

Finally the car came to a stop, rocking back and forth upside down. Emma's head was spinning, her breathing had resumed. She could hear the man's groan. It sounded like he had been thrown into the back seat of the car.

Despite the pounding in her joints, Emma focused on getting out of the wreckage. The door was wide open; there was grass before her. She dug her hands, bound at the wrists, into the earth and pulled her legs out from under the dash. She dragged herself over metal parts and into the field where the car rocked back and forth like an upside down turtle.

"Hey," she heard.

She staggered to her feet, fell down to her knees, then staggered again. "Where are you going?"

There came a moment of silence, then the sound of a truck on the road that was at least a hundred yards away.

"Don't go anywhere. I got to talk to you."

Then inside her head, Emma could hear Lucy's voice, *Run, run!*

She staggered forward. Her neck felt like it had been blasted with minute pieces of broken glass.

She was unsure where to go—toward the road, or the other way, across the field to a stand of trees. She could see lights on the other side of the trees.

She heard the wrenching sound of a car door pushing open and more groans from the man. She leaned forward, pain lurched behind her eyes with each step, ran up the back of her neck and dizzily through her skull; she could feel it in her shoulders, her chest, even the front of her neck, her Adam's apple. But she continued to thrust herself forward.

The man yelled to her across the field. She stepped into the deep darkness of this stand of trees, branches snapping into her face. She held her bound hands before her to avoid crashing into a trunk. Then her legs sloshed through marshy water and sank deeper, each step clear up to her knees.

Behind her she heard the man crashing through the brush, then the sound of him hitting the marsh, water sloshing. She crossed this shallow swamp, heading toward lights that she could see beyond the trees. All at once she came up against a chain-link fence and got to her knees, scooting down a tunnel-like space in the brambles that ran at its base. There was a hole in the fence, she slipped through this and came to the parking lot of some kind of industrial park.

A sign of life—a large white truck, the lights on, idling, nobody near it, the back door ajar and big red letters IMPERIAL CARPET OF BROOKLYN, NY painted on the side with a street address underneath. She climbed up and inside and crossed thick rolls of plastic-covered rugs stacked halfway to the ceiling. Soaking wet, covered head to foot with mud, she squeezed between the end of the stack of rugs and the back wall of the truck.

Her body ached; she waited patiently, listening carefully to the silence around her, holding her breath to hear more clearly, then releasing her air carefully.

Finally she heard somebody climb into the idling truck cab and close the door. The engine rewed and the truck backed up. But it stopped again and now the back door opened all the way and bright light shone near where Emma hid. "Get up, now . . . Ease it up, yeah . . ." They were dragging something heavy into the truck, another rug, then dropping it onto the stack.

She thought of standing up and showing herself to the men, but then instinct told her to keep still, to wait until she was far away from her pursuer since he would surely drag her away from the truck drivers. Then the door was closed and she heard the latch turn. The truck started to move.

It stopped abruptly and Emma heard the voice of the man, the familiar voice. "I saw her tracks up to where you were parked," he was yelling to the driver. "I think you got my girl in the back."

"What?"

"My girl, she ran away. She's in the back of your truck."

"Nobody's in the back there," the driver said. Emma could tell from the truck driver's tone of voice that he was full of defiance; this was a gift to her, she was lucky, this defiance might be the very thing that would save her. "We just threw a carpet in. Nobody's in back."

"She tracked mud up there. She's in there."

"What are you talking about? There's nobody in there." This defiant attitude was her friend.

But then the back door to the truck opened and Emma squeezed herself deeper into the space behind the rugs and she could hear somebody climb up onto the metal floor of the truck bed and begin to look around.

"I need a flashlight," the man said.

"Nobody's in there. Come on, let's go," the driver yelled. Emma closed her eyes; she tried in her mind to focus on the driver's short temper, let it rise, don't give in, release it at him, she thought. "I'm on a schedule here. I got to be at the warehouse in Brooklyn in the morning or lose my job."

"Wait a minute—"

"I don't have a *fucking* flashlight, *bonehead*, and I'm *fucking* late, real late. What the *fuck* kind of costume are you wearing, anyway?"

The man walked back and forth inside the truck ten feet from Emma holding her breath. "I'm telling you, let's go! Get out of my truck, *son of a bitch*!" the driver said.

Soon the door slammed shut. "I know she's back there. She's a mute and I saw her tracks!" the man yelled from outside the truck. The truck lurched forward again. *How lucky, how strangely lucky;* she did not think this in words, but she felt it inside her battered body. Soon they were on a highway, driving quickly, the roar filling Emma's ears.

24

She went back and forth between waking and dreaming without realizing it for many hours, each time thirstier. She could drink a cold gallon jug of water without pause if it were offered to her. The truck turned off the highway and now it kept stopping, starting. A siren passed by, other trucks, car horns. Emma tried to move her head; every bone in her body ached from the accident. Somehow or another the brutal reality of the crash gave her hope. She did not know how or why, perhaps it had woken something in her up.

Then the truck stopped and the engine turned off. Emma climbed out of her hiding place and stood near the door and waited quietly. She heard voices outside the door and pressed herself against the truck wall. Then came the sound of somebody unlatching the back gate. She considered rushing back to her spot, but it was too late, the door started to open. She sprang at it with her bound hands up, knocking it open and leaping to the ground. She smashed her knees and hands against the pavement, then jumped up and ran. Sure enough a man was behind her. He grabbed her shirt, but she continued to bolt and she slipped through his grasp and dashed like a rabbit making short turns between cars in a parking lot. She could see an open gate in a chain-link fence. As she approached it, the man grabbed at her shirt around her neck. But he stumbled forward, nearly landing on top of her and this enabled her to slip through the gate and run down the block.

She turned into an alleyway, crossed into somebody's backyard, around a blue aboveground swimming pool, then over another fence and down somebody's driveway. She crossed another street and ran into the backyard behind a row house. This yard had a shed and behind the shed a barking dog lunged at her against his chain and she jumped up on a brick wall and ran along it, then down along a cement driveway.

A heavy woman whose shoes were collapsed on both sides was pulling a cart full of groceries up to the front door of an apartment building. Out of breath and covered with sweat, Emma dashed up to this woman and held her tied up hands to her as if to show her she needed help, but just then somebody came out of the glass doors and Emma slipped into the lobby and ran down a flight of stairs, through a boiler room, past washing machines, and finally into a room full of wooden crates and cardboard boxes. Behind one of the boxes she sat down.

She closed her eyes and waited, listening to every noise, her heart pounding. She could hear a washing machine and dryer going, otherwise the basement was silent. The cement floor was cool on her legs. She closed her eyes; sweat continued to pour from her face, down her sides and under her chest. It soaked her turtleneck, pooled in her belly button; her jeans clung like a washcloth to her legs. An elevator's cables clicked and knocked in a shaft nearby. She had no idea where she was, how far she was from the Marshalls, though she knew she had been traveling in the truck a good long time. She knew one thing; she would wait here for as many hours as possible; she would sit out the man who was looking for her, defeat him with her patience.

Then she noticed a pegboard of hanging tools above a workbench. She cautiously rose to her feet and reached up for a hacksaw and sat back down. Clasping the saw upside down between her knees, she cut at the rope holding her wrists. Finally her hands sprung free; it seemed a good sign, as if she herself would soon be free. Her skin had broken under the abrasive rope. Her neck was so sore she could barely move her head.

She stepped into the laundry room and found a sink. Turning on the water, she put her mouth against the faucet. She drank and could not stop herself. Then she lifted her head to breathe and drank some more.

She returned to her hiding place and waited until she could wait no longer. She would take her chances and go upstairs to the street. She got up, the sweat on her clothes had dried; her pants and shirt clung stiffly to her. She passed through the empty boiler room, then up the stairs to the lobby door. It was late afternoon; she could see a gray street, a few cars parked along it, a tall red apartment building with small windows similar to the one she was in. She stepped outside and walked quickly without looking around, then turned on the street that ran behind the building in which she had hid. Now she was in a neighborhood of smaller buildings built on a grade. There were some young people on stoops, an old man walked slowly with a plastic bag of groceries hanging from his fingers. A skateboarder came down the street, wiggling back and forth, and a group of young boys were playing catch with a football.

She could feel a nervous pain in her stomach. It hurt so much that Emma was tempted to fall down on the street and hold her hands against her ribs. But she knew she must keep moving farther away from this neighborhood, she knew the man and perhaps other men would be searching the neighborhood. She wanted to get away, to get as far away as possible.

After turning onto a new street every block, zigzagging her way through one neighborhood after the next, she came to a cemetery surrounded by a spiked iron fence. She walked along its border for a while. There was a slight grade and between the buildings she saw an astonishing view: a skyline of skyscrapers. These structures were far taller than she ever imagined buildings could be. As she stared at them against the gray sky, she realized where she must be: New York City.

She was wonderstruck, the painful knot of nerves in her stomach contracted. She squatted next to the cemetery fence, holding her ribs, still looking at this sight, trying to tear her eyes away. Layers of thin clouds, gray and yellowish like cigarette smoke hanging in still air, gathered behind the buildings. A truck came up the street, shifting gears. Without even realizing it, Emma bolted across to the opposite sidewalk and ran down a hill between row houses.

When she stopped she realized how truly tired she had become. From the knot in her stomach down through her legs, she could feel a kind of blankness and yet a creeping heaviness. She began thinking of what she should do. People were entering and leaving their homes, others getting into cars. Maybe she should try to find a woman who would help her; she needed help as soon as possible, somebody to hide her. She began walking, staring at people, wondering what they would say if she went up to them. Each time she approached a woman, Emma turned away, too afraid of what exactly the person would do if she presented herself. Despite the exhaustion she decided she needed to keep moving, tramping farther away from where she had escaped from the rug truck.

Finally, she came to a busy street with many markets and hundreds of busy shoppers milling along under a metal bridge of train tracks that followed the curving street. The crowd was thick, and almost everyone was busy picking out melons, peaches, strawberries, and string beans from the fruit and vegetable stands. She entered the various meat markets, where strings of sausage and roasted chickens glistened, and the clothing outlets with bins of socks and T-shirts on the sidewalk.

She realized that she was looking at all of the women and that even though she knew better she was secretly hoping with all her heart that Lucy would be among them. She passed black women in colorful clothes, children dashing through the crowd under people's arms, old Asian men with crooked legs, men in black coats with long curly sideburns and black hats. From under a cardboard box she pulled a squashed felt hat and shook it of dirt, put it on and pulled the floppy brim over her eyes. She was nearly numb with exhaustion and yet she knew she would not be able to rest for a long time. She must push on.

She heard a metallic squealing and screeching that shook the metal bridge above her head. Looking up she saw the underbelly of a train. It stopped on the tracks above her head and soon a crowd came down the steps and poured onto the street. Other people climbed these steps and Emma followed them up. At the top she saw people putting coins into the turnstiles and passing through to the platform to wait for the train. Emma looked behind her at the crowd coming up the steps, then she thought that if only she could get on this train, she could travel far away and then surely the man would never find her. She stood here a moment, watching people pass money through the slot of the glass booth, then walk over to the turnstile and go in.

Reaching into her pocket, she was surprised to feel two wrinkled dollar bills—the change left over from when she had gone shopping with Frances Marshall. At the time Emma was so anxious to return to the house in case Lucy were to come that she wondered if she had not been rude and yet Frances had been so kind to her. Frances's kindness had been a reflection on Lucy; Lucy knew how to find kind people. That had been only a day ago and yet now it seemed distant.

She passed the two dollars through the slot and received a token and some change. Then she joined the crowd on the cement platform.

Finally she heard the squealing of metal wheels against the track. Sure enough old red train cars came bumping and jerking to a stop and the doors opened and Emma followed the crowd inside.

Through the scratched train windows, she could see the skyline again. These buildings seemed like they were truly from another world, a world that was far away from where she was now. Despite their fearful look, she felt instinctively that she would find refuge among them from her pursuers, at least temporarily.

She sat down, watching out over the buildings. Emma had never seen such a strange shade of powdery red light as the sun went down behind the skyline. The train descended into a tunnel and there was darkness outside of the windows and an occasional soft yellow light passed by.

25

Emma finally got off the train at what seemed like the busiest stop, following the people to the turnstiles, then up steps to the street. A siren screamed and the powerful horn of a fire truck passed through lanes of traffic. Shouts and grunts—a basketball game behind a chain-link fence. So many people ambled along the sidewalk that once again the thought, the fantasy, that Lucy had to appear came to mind. There were not this many people in the world for Lucy *not* to be included among them. She wound her way up and down small streets, sometimes she would see somebody far away who could conceivably be her and she'd run to greet her only to feel disappointment sweep through her, dragging her down in a flood of sadness and fatigue.

She stayed wherever there were crowds of people and light. She was in shock; she did not know where to go; she only knew to keep moving. Then she saw a clock and realized how late it had gotten; Lucy would have been in bed long ago, asleep. Where was she going to spend the night? Where would she be able to sleep? She kept moving from street to street, crowd to crowd and finally the crowds began to diminish, the sidewalks became empty of all but a few pedestrians. Then she came to a park where a dozen or so men were sleeping on benches. Unable to keep her eyes open, Emma lay down on one of these benches and fell fast asleep.

"Do you need a place to stay?" Emma looked up and saw a policewoman swinging her billy club back and forth. She tried to get up to run but the woman grabbed her shirt and put her club in front of her. "Hold on there. We're not going to hurt you." Emma shook her head. "Who are you? What's your name?"

Emma merely stared at her. The woman leaned down to examine her.

"Come on, I'll take you to Park Side, it's a place for young girls."

Emma stood up, still shaking her head.

"Come, come," the policewoman took her by the arm. "Even men aren't safe out here."

She brought Emma to a cruiser where a policeman waited. "What are you doing out on the street?"

Emma got in back; she was so tired she could hardly hold her head up.

"Run away?"

Soon they parked in front of a building with glass doors. A man came to the door as the two officers escorted Emma inside. "Sleeping on a bench, she doesn't seem to talk," the female officer said to the man inside the lobby. His puffy sleep-filled eyes looked Emma up and down.

"Can you talk to us?" the man said as if talking to a young child.

Emma looked down.

"If we put her in the dorm, we'll wake the other girls. We'll give her a room for tonight."

The policewoman turned to Emma. "Don't go sleeping on park benches anymore. Plenty of places to stay if it comes down to that."

The man led Emma down the hall to an elevator and up. "You stay here tonight. The linen hasn't been changed, but that's okay.

You'll have to get up early for the meetings, then breakfast. Then you'll be in the dorm room with the other girls, okay?" The bed in the narrow room he opened was unmade. Emma climbed under the covers with her clothes on and fell asleep.

26

Lucy woke up in pitch darkness unaware of how long she had been sleeping, two days, three, maybe a week. She was vaguely aware of what happened before blacking out. There had been questions, a crescendo of questions about where Emma was, but Lucy had not responded, had never even entertained the notion that she might give him an answer or even a clue, had steeled herself and had even come to grips with the assumption that the man with the fish mask would surely kill her. It was fortunate that she had left her wallet and registration behind the log in the woods because the man had also wanted to know her name. She had lied to him and said, "Audrey McBride." This name, the name of Emma's horse, had come off her lips so easily and naturally, as if something inside of her had taken over.

Lucy found that she was no longer strapped down, she could move her hands. Eventually she sat up in the dark and reached above her head to see how high the space extended. She put her feet on the slick damp floor and managed to stand, her back shrieking out with pain. Her hand touched a slick, wet metal ceiling only a few feet above her head. She began to move slowly, shuffling against the cool metal floor that smelled faintly of the earth, of ferns and mud. Moving down the length of her cot, her hands out, her fingers met with more cold metal. She followed this wall to another wall.

She discovered that she was confined to a rectangular space fifteen or so feet long by about six feet wide, some kind of a locker maybe, probably once used for food. She could barely hear the sound of a blue jay outside the thick walls. Was it daylight outside?

Groping further, her fingers found a fine crack, a gap that she followed in the dark and determined was the only possible door. At the base to one side of this door she found a plastic jug half filled with liquid, she poured some out and smelled it. It was water. Next to it her fingers landed on a plastic bag filled full of something—scraps of meat and vegetables. She opened it; the rancid smell stung her nostrils. She wondered how long ago the man had left it here, how long she had been unconscious.

After finding her way back to her bed, she lay down and began to feel her body for its many wounds, the tender blisters from where he had seared her. The ones that had popped were open wounds, painful to touch. Above her head she noticed holes in the ceiling, tiny air holes that had been punched through the metal emitting specks of daylight. Later these specks darkened and she realized that night had fallen.

She began thinking about something that caused her great stress, that ate away at her very soul, her very own sense of hope. Would Johnny Ranch remember that she had mentioned where she was staying to him the first time she visited his property? And how many of the details had Lucy told Sally while she was staying with her? She had not told Sally Emma's exact whereabouts but she had pulled the card that she had taken from the Marshalls out of her pocket at one point and put it among Emma's clothes. Or had she? Was it in her wallet or had she left it in her room at Sally's? The thought of that business card's whereabouts continued to eat away at her.

She began reconsidering her entire venture and a feeling of guilt took over. Maybe she had gone through all this trouble for herself rather than for Emma. What if the men found Emma because of this? Lucy started crying. What a mistake she had made. She should have moved somewhere with Emma, she should have run away again.

27

Emma was awoken into confusion by a loud rap the next morning and there in the doorway stood a large woman in a flowered dress whom she mistook for Lucy. "Now you listen, you don't have anything to worry about, you go on down to the office and they'll help you fill out the forms and then they'll send you to prayer meeting. You can wash up right down the hall and I suggest you do that, darling, I don't know what you got yourself into."

Emma's body ached so intensely from the car crash that she could barely get up. Moving her head, she heard the bones in her neck crack, even the joints of her fingers ached. She opened the door and went into the bathroom. Two girls stood at the sink, one of them was applying makeup to her eyebrows. Emma went into a stall, she waited until she heard the others leave, then she came out and looked at herself in the mirror. Her face was filthy, her hair matted and tangled and her eyes were puffy like Lucy's eyes often were in the morning. She dashed water on her face and began to wash down. Inside her arm a streak of blood had dried and she wiped it off with a wet paper towel.

She went downstairs to the office and there a tall man with large bony hands and bony feet in flip-flops greeted her warmly. He was slightly unshaven; short gray beard hairs were sticking out of his pointy chin. "Sleeping in the park?" he shook his head. "Tch, tch, don't have to do that, you know. Now the desk clerk said you don't talk, is that right?"

Emma carefully nodded her head. She did not even realize that she was responding to this man.

"Do you write?"

She nodded again and the man pushed some forms and a pencil across the desk and Emma began to read it and then slowly to fill it out. She slid it back to him and he looked it over.

"You don't know any of these questions?" He looked at her perplexed and she shook her head slowly.

"I find that hard to believe."

He paused and continued to examine Emma, then looked back down at the application and made a notation in the margin.

He gave her a copy of the rules for boarders and began to read from it to her. "The Park Side Residence for Wayward Girls is not a permanent residence; girls are only allowed to stay here for a month before paying their way. The maximum stay here is two months. The Park Side management will assist you in getting a job and eventually moving into a roommate situation. Dinner is at seven-thirty. You *must* be inside our glass doors by nine o'clock and lights are out in the dorm rooms by ten. We cannot make exceptions to this. Do you understand that? Girls who arrive after the doors are closed will have to sleep in one of the city shelters."

The man positioned Emma before a camera and told her to smile, then flashed a picture of her, and soon he handed her a laminated identification card that said, *Emma Thurman, Park Side Home for Girls.*

Emma filed into a large room with hard wooden benches and long felt prayer pads on the floor. Three women sat behind a table at the front of the room. Other girls came in until the room was filled and everyone was quiet, then the middle woman stood up and began to lecture to the girls.

The woman spoke of God; she was obviously Christian. However, she seemed careful not to espouse any particular creed or sect and instead spoke in generalities about spiritual problems that teenaged girls might experience. At one point she told the girls that the Park Side asks only that the girls pray to their God whichever God that might be. "All religions are accepted here."

After a short break a second leader stood up and told of something that had happened to her, a strange coincidence and then a surprising act of generosity on the part of a stranger that reflected without a doubt the existence of a higher power. When Emma closed her eyes during the ten minutes of silence, she imagined Lucy's house along the long straight road with tall grass growing under the mailbox and saw the farmhouse across the fields and the black and white cows out to graze; she could hear and smell and feel everything as if she were in her bedroom, even the individual birds singing outside of the window. *That house is my birthplace*, she thought to herself.

Her memories extended no further back in time than the night she had been discovered in the Blue Night Mall. When she tried to think back further than that, she envisioned a long dark corridor, the sort of image one remembers the morning after a vague, disturbing dream. There were doors along this empty corridor and rooms off it, but she could not seem to recall exactly what was in them. Other than this image, there was merely a kind of disembodied blackness, the surface of which shimmered and moved like water in the wind. There were no people in her memories, not until she felt the hand of the black security guard who had never told her his name and then the first kind words of Carl Lark.

Suddenly she remembered the face of the man who had yanked her mercilessly from the Marshalls' bedroom. She opened her eyes to the silence of the room and looked around at all the girls in the pews, their heads bent praying, and the three women at the table, their hands clasped in front of them and their heads bowed. One of the women's lips was moving as she mumbled something to herself.

After breakfast Emma signed out and wandered around the square perimeter of Gramercy Park. The private park was surrounded by a wrought-iron fence and was accessible only to those who carried a key. Through the fence she could see fine gardens, a fountain, a gardener working on his knees, another was watering the flowers. The sidewalk around the park was made of gray flagstones, settled and tilted into the earth, shoots of grass growing between them. After circling the park, Emma returned to the girls' home like a child having to touch home base. Then she ventured farther, following Twentieth Street to Park Avenue where there were two lanes of thick traffic. Her bones and muscles ached from the car crash and her neck bones continued to crackle as she moved her head. She felt a kind of ache in her jaw, like a toothache that ran up to her ear. One of her ears, she had noted, was ringing. There were constant butterflies in her stomach and a lump in her throat. The vast, intricate machinery of the city squeaked and rattled and ground its gears and backfired around her. Smells, some strange, some familiar, swayed her moods to and fro like seaweed. Cars and buses coughed and choked and spit out their blue and black exhaust. Restaurants and bakeries exhaled their warm, vaporous oven smells that vaguely reminded her of Lucy's kitchen. Delicatessens reeked of cold cuts and stale coffee and cigarettes. Lucy and Emma used to stop at a 7-Eleven outside of Millville that smelled like this.

Emma had seen images of these crowded streets on television but had never experienced what it was like to feel diminished and lost by such a vast array of human souls. Towering buildings cast their terrible shadows over the yellow taxicabs and trucks and threatened to fall upon her when she looked up. She was astounded by everything, street corner people jamming brochures and advertising flyers into peoples' hands, beggars with their paper coffee cups slumped in doorways or the gathering of a crowd at a crossing while the orange DON'T WALK sign shone. She noticed the many different shoes that people wore, tennis sneakers, sandals, high heels, shiny black dress shoes, hiking boots, leather clogs, and bare feet, the backs of these feet pocked with dirt and the rags dripping down the legs of such a person.

She kept careful track of the street numbers and names as she slipped through the fracas, scanning the crowd, even feeling surprisingly safe for brief moments—it seemed unlikely the man would ever find her among such a great mass of people. Once she saw a minister coming her way and she darted along the sidewalk and up a side street, not looking back, hoping, like a child ducking under the covers, that if she didn't look back he would magically go away. She kept circling farther away from the girls' home, gathering her thoughts among the cement and granite and asphalt.

At six o'clock, she entered back in through the double glass doors of Park Side and showed her identification to the overweight guard, a black man whose thighs hung over both sides of his plastic chair. She was hungry, famished, dizzy with the need for food that the pains all over her body had nearly made her forget. She stood in line in the dining room with a tray and the food server seemed to notice something about her and gave her several extra spoonfuls of mashed potatoes and an extra helping of meat. Finding a seat alone among the long tables with benches was a trick. She did not want to be asked questions, though she already knew that if worse came to worse she would write her answers down on a piece of paper. Finally she found a lone spot next to the yellow wall, sat down and scooped the potatoes with her fork quickly into her mouth. Her stomach was tight, she waited for the food to settle and then ate more, finishing everything on her plate.

After busing her tray, she found herself wanting but one thing and that was to get to sleep. The bones in her feet and her shins hurt, she felt her mind becoming hazy with the need for rest. She passed a lounge where some of the girls were watching television and another lounge where girls held cigarettes in their fingers covered with nail polish and chattered back and forth, laughing. She did not want to see another person for the rest of the night. She climbed the stairs to the dorm room and slipped her sheets back, kicked off her shoes and pulled the covers up to her neck. Another girl reading a book, leaning against her bed, introduced herself to Emma, but Emma merely shook her head and waved her hands, then turned over and put her face into her pillow.

She fell asleep, only to be woken hours later when the rest of the girls readied themselves for bed at ten. They were talking and laughing and slipping into nightgowns and pajamas. After the lights finally went out, Emma put her hands behind her head and stared at the ceiling. Suddenly she had a kind of hallucination. Lucy was standing over her bed in the refracted light from the window, talking to her, telling her to sleep well. Emma could see Lucy's hands, the gray-silver ring on her finger, the wrinkles at the joints, the deep wrinkles around her wrists, the loose skin on her arms whenever she wore short sleeves, her smallish eyes, kind and warm and squinted like somebody crying and yet happy and filled with joy and life and compassion and the excitement of being together with her. She was saying something that she had said many times in the past. "You don't owe me anything because you've already helped me more than I've helped you," Lucy said. "It's our little secret." Even then Emma knew this was not true, could not possibly be true, that Lucy was merely telling her this to make her feel she had a purpose. "I'm serious, Emma. Now I'm happier than a cricket. All because of you. Thank you, little one, and sleep well." She could almost feel her tucking in the sheets.

Emma knew that she would not fall back to sleep. The city that she had walked through all day rumbled through her every bone. It was a huge, raucous, indifferent, endless, and vast machinelike creature that Lucy, despite her many stories of the many places she had been, had never once mentioned. As Emma stared up at the fan shapes of light from the street coming through the high windows against the ceiling, she was faced with what she knew to be reality: whoever had marked her body, whoever had tried to crush without mercy her soul, drown her in darkness, that person now had in their possession the person who had given her life: Lucy.

A memory of the meat locker began coming to Emma. The slender trunks of maple trees growing around it. Leading up to it was a kind of earthen road where the man had dragged this great big metal box through the woods with his tractor. He had dragged it out here to hold people. Girls like herself? Girls covered with scales? She had not been the only one; there was a girl he had told her about, a girl he practiced on, developed his art. The very thought of this girl made her ache with sadness. It was one of the last feelings that Emma had before the man erased her feelings with his ways. "The path of God," he called it.

Emma watched the light coming through the high window and realized her first memories before the time in the mall were returning. She closed her eyes tightly.

One girl was snoring, another girl kept rolling over and the springs of her cot squeaked. Emma could smell body odor, shampooed hair, the stale breaths of many sleepers. The reality of her situation was coming into clearer focus to her: she was alone and she had not the slightest idea what to do, let alone how to find Lucy.

A girl began to stir in her bunk, a girl having a nightmare. She was making short squeaks and her breathing quickened. Then Emma heard another girl get up and try to rouse her. "Come on, little sweet, wake up."

"Huh, what?"

The overwhelming feelings and thoughts and memories brought on by this new world finally tore her from her many waking fears and dropped her into sleep. When she woke up to the bell in the hallway, she was struck by the very starkness of her situation: *The man who had me, has Lucy.*

She sat through prayer, thinking more clearly than she had since she was at the Marshalls. She needed to remember exactly where she had been for all those years before the Blue Night Mall, for surely that was where Lucy was, and she needed to get there by bus or train or even by car. *I need money to do that. Money. How can I get money?*

28

Emma contemplated this question all morning after breakfast as she again continued her explorations on the streets around the girls' home. She considered begging, but this she felt was too visible. Everyone would be looking at her and the man who was surely frantically looking for her—she knew now that she was valuable to him, more valuable than anything on earth—would be drawn to such a spectacle. After lunch she spotted a HELP WANTED sign written in black Magic Marker on a piece of cardboard set in the window of a delicatessen. Inside, a middle-aged woman worked the cash register. Emma now had a pad of paper and a pen. Standing out on the street, she wrote, *I am looking for work.*

The thought of somebody, anybody, friend or stranger reading these simple words scared her, made her quake in her shoes. She walked down the street and back with the note, thinking of a strategy. She put her felt hat on and adjusted it over her eyes. She must look at the note as a *means* to something else more important so that the importance of the words themselves would be lessened.

At last she ventured into the narrow delicatessen and stood near a metal rack of cellophane-wrapped cookies and potato chips. A stack of *New York Post*s with a headline about a rapist escaped from prison rested on a short shelf beneath the front counter. The cashier in a stained white smock looked down at her, and Emma reached up and handed her the note.

The dark-haired woman put her glasses on. Her eyes behind the distorting lens moved back and forth. She looked down at Emma and her eyes looked big through the glasses. "What can you do?" she said.

Looking to the floor, Emma stepped backward and shook her head.

"Well, we only have cashier open, that means dealing with the public, many people—you look too young anyway, my dear."

Emma felt her lips move upward into what would be perceived by the woman as a smile when it was just a reflex that she had no control over. It was strange to feel her lips in this position. Blushing, she backed out of the store, staring down at the dirtied linoleum.

Suddenly she bumped smack into somebody coming in and her felt hat fell to the floor. A tall, awkward man reached quickly to pick it up and held it over her head and was about to replace it for her when he smiled and said, "Hey."

He was astonished at something, though Emma knew not what. She took back her hat and pulling it down over her eyes, went quickly out the door onto the street. "Young lady, now wait a minute, please," the man was saying. "Don't run away." She ran a little, but her knees became weak, and something slowed her down. "Are you looking for a job? Did I hear right?" the man caught up. "Well," he was catching his breath. He had a small hooked nose, a wide face, stringy blond hair, and a friendly, almost innocent expression on his long face like a child who has an important story to tell. "A counter person pays nothing . . . but it just so happens I'm looking for somebody for my class, a life drawing model. I'm a teacher at a very respectable institute called the Artists' School of New York. Have you heard of it?"

She merely looked down at the sidewalk, a gum wrapper pressed into the dirty, gray pavement.

"Could you take your hat off again?"

She looked up at the tall man's red cheeks. His skin was otherwise very white.

"Didn't mean to offend you. I'm always looking for models for my class, that's all. Have you ever modeled?"

Again she didn't move. Something inside of her was paralyzed, she wanted to run but couldn't.

"It pays well and it's easy. It pays three times what you'd get back in there," he said, pointing at the deli.

The man paced back and forth excitedly. There was something harmless about him. And then Emma realized that he looked just like Giant John from the Crown Circus. Lucy had showed her a photograph of this man with his huge feet and white socks and pants that came up to his shins. This man's pants were too short also and he too wore white socks.

"Come now, show me your face for just a minute." He moved his head back and forth happily. "Would you like a job? You'll get paid twice minimum wage. You'll be able to save a lot of money." She wondered if this was not one of the coincidences that Lucy had told her about. Here was a man who looked like Giant John, whom Lucy had said was a generous man, offering her work. "A lot more than at a place like that. I've got to see your face . . . If I can see your face I'll tell you if I can hire you."

If anything the man seemed clumsy, incapable of catching her if she were to run. Emma turned away and walked toward the wall of a vestibule. Here she took off her hat and allowed the man to see her face from the side. "Ah, I knew you had an unusual face. Actually I've never seen anything quite like it. Did anybody tell you how unusual you look? You're very beautiful. Do you see that building right there?" He pointed to a granite facade with stone steps that fanned out onto the walk. Students were sitting in the sun on some of these steps. "That's my school . . . If you show up tomorrow morning at five minutes to nine sharp and ask for Mr. Glover, you've got yourself a job. What's your name?"

Emma shook her head.

"Could you write it for me?"

Again she shook her head.

"Oh, *come on*. I saw the note you wrote in there, you can write your name for me. I'm Stan Glover. Now, please, go on."

Emma took out her pad and slowly wrote the letters of her name.

He held the piece of paper up in the light and looked at it. "Emma, that's a fine name." He put his hand out to shake; she turned away.

"Will you definitely come tomorrow, Emma? You've got to promise me, otherwise I'll have to call tonight for another model."

Emma nodded her head.

"Is there a place where I can reach you so I can double check with you?"

She shook her head.

"All right, I trust you. Now remember, Glover's the name, okay?"

Emma returned to Park Side for lunch and thought about what had just transpired. She did not want to stay in the city a day longer than she had to; she wanted to get going though she was not sure to where. Committing herself for even a day seemed somehow wrong. She also knew that money should not come that easily; it certainly hadn't for Lucy. But then she was heartened by the thought that she had given only her word to Glover; she could break it and never see him again.

29

Lucy woke up and lay in the same damp darkness that she'd gone to sleep in. She had lost track of time. For the past few days two different men had dropped off food and emptied out the sanitation pail. They said nothing to her. She hadn't gotten a look at their faces, but one of them she suspected to be Johnny Ranch. He came in the morning.

Then she began to remember something that had happened the night before. The first man had come into the meat locker, blindfolded her, and then brought her outside and up the hill. On the way up the hill, she had not been able to see anything but a crack of light under the blindfold. She heard chickens clucking, a cow lowing, and the many birds in the trees. Now and then the man pushed and guided her from behind and said nasty things to her under his breath. He dragged her inside a building and she could tell just by the feeling of the space inside that it was the same one she had awoken in after her capture, and she was again strapped to the doctor's examining bed.

"What is your name again?" She thought she recognized the voice as Pastor Joe's, but she wasn't sure. If it was him, she wondered if her face was so badly beaten that he didn't recognize her.

"McBride," Lucy repeated the name she had made up before.

"McBride, what kind of a name is that?" She was really not sure whether this was the voice of the man from whom she had run for so many years. She had been thinking about him a lot since she'd visited Master Howard. Maybe she was confusing things. She considered telling him who she was, but then that would lead him directly to her house.

"Irish."

"You're Catholic, aren't you? Now, let's go over this again. Why don't you have a residence, Audrey?"

"I live in hotels."

"Then what were you doing with my child?"

"Taking care of her, they gave her to me to take care of."

"In a hotel?" the man was getting angry.

"I didn't tell them I was homeless."

"How did you get a car if you were homeless?"

"I told you, it was stolen."

"You're lying to me, aren't you, Audrey? Who do you know in New York?"

"New York?" Under the blindfold her eyes were shut tightly. She could hear him preparing his instruments.

"New York City—who do you know?"

"Nobody."

"Let's say if the girl were in that vile place, where would she go?"

"I've never been there." Lucy was trying to understand how Emma had gotten to New York.

"Who do you know there?" he asked again.

"Nobody."

She felt something touch her skin near her belly, then explode with pain. The electric tattoo needle was heated. She screamed, then clenched her teeth tightly; her fists gripped themselves.

"Who would she contact?"

"Contact?"

Again the needle blistered into her skin and she screamed out in agony.

"I've never been there."

"Who are your friends—who has she met?"

"Nobody," Lucy said.

"That's a lie. You must have known some people in those hotels."

"We never saw anybody together. She only knows me."

This time the hot needle touched her skin near her neck. She shook her head but the pain wouldn't go away. She blacked out.

"Don't move!" he said when she woke up. He was tattooing something on her stomach. She burst into tears. "You're going to mess it up."

She kept crying, then he placed something over her mouth, a cloth of some kind. Again she thought of Pastor Joe—he'd held a cloth over her mouth in the trailer that day.

She passed out and didn't wake up again until she was back on her cot in the meat locker.

Now she put her hand on her stomach and felt the raised design. She could not tell what it was; there were many lines, some thicker, some thinner, curling and winding around her stomach.

She thought of Emma in New York City. How in the world had she gotten there? Had the Marshalls sent her there? Suddenly the thought of that big city comforted her. What better hiding place for her? It would be difficult, if not impossible for this man to find her there.

These thoughts relieved Lucy, gave meaning to what she had just been through. Emma was still free of him.

For some reason Pidge began coming to mind, she did not know why. As she lay in the pitch-dark she could not get the image of the little man in the midst of the wrecked cars out of her head.

30

Just over the border of West Virginia into Ohio, Pidge pressed the hydraulic lever of the front-end loader forward and eased a rusty, half-crushed Pontiac station wagon dangling by a chain onto the top of a stack of three crushed cars and then examined the pile for stability. Unhooking the bucket's chain, he backed away, turning his machine around, half expecting to see Lucy standing with the girl in the same black, oil-covered lot where she had appeared just a few days earlier. Since she had walked away from him back then he could not forgive himself for not saying something that he should have said years ago that morning when Lucy lay on the beach. But to say what exactly? There was no way he could put his feelings in words. In the very least, he thought, he should have admitted to her why he had really left the circus.

His throbbing hangover fogged his vision and his eyelids were half closed and sweat stung his eyes. A dirty ring had formed around the hot sun as if even that was stained with what he had done wrong. He climbed down from the machine. King jumped over him, almost knocking him down. "Hell," Pidge said to the dog.

He walked through the myriad passageways of oil-soaked earth that led between the piles of wrecks. His hips ached as always, his short legs were sore at the knees. He opened the door of the so-called "smoke house" where Harry Gates puffed on his dirty cigars. Pidge crossed the floor covered with spare parts with white tags. "Mr. Gates," Pidge said. The short, fat man sat at his desk under dirty window light, paying bills. He wore a tie to work and demanded that everyone call him "mister." It was one of the ironies of working here. "I've got to take the rest of the day off."

"Who says?" Gates said. A wet cigar rested between his yellow teeth. "You've got cars to move before you quit. If you don't finish, you might as well take the next ten years off." He turned and Pidge saw his little eyes and wide cheeks.

"I'm not in any condition to do that. I'm strung out, that's what I am."

"You've got the delirium tremens, buddy boy."

"I had a visit by a lady."

"You had that visit from the lady quite a few days ago. She doesn't have anything to do with what you're doing to yourself every night. You were fucking up before she got here and you're fucking up now. Do you get my drift?" Gates turned back to his desk, mumbling to himself as he shuffled the stained papers around.

Pidge got in his pickup truck with King sitting next to him and drove out of the yard.

His trailer was on a plot of land hidden from the rest of the park by a little knoll that had been hard-packed by the feet of playing children. The children sometimes threw rocks at his trailer until he came out and then they laughed at him and called him Mr. Munch. He opened the padlocked front door, propped open all the narrow windows, and lay on his bed and tried to close his eyes. Soon he was fast asleep and dreaming.

In his dream he was running up and down hills spread far apart. At last he had found a way to get rid of his miserable throbbing headaches; all he had to do was run from them. And now that he was doing that, not only did the pain diminish with every step, but his legs grew longer until his head was in the clouds. Had he paused, he would have realized that he didn't know how to operate these long legs. "They're doing fine on their own," he said as he ran over mountains, around cities, reaching high speeds while airplanes flew by level with his nose.

He came to a very high mountain out West somewhere. At the top of this rocky peak, which was just slightly higher than he was, he saw a circular red tent and recognized it as Lucy's. Reaching forward with his long hands he opened the tent flaps and looked inside. There he saw Lucy, fat again on her tiny stool, the rolls of flesh bunched up around her huge neck, only this time there was something different about her. He studied her, wondering what that was. Something was moving in the rolls of her pink flesh around her belly. Hidden in her fat were tiny, hairless pink kittens.

31

The next morning Emma climbed the granite steps to the art school. It was noisy with young people crowding the hallways, many were just a few years older than she. They filed in and out of classrooms, waited in line at one of the offices, yelled to each other, traveled in groups, laughing and talking excitedly. The smells in the school were of dried wood, paint, and turpentine.

Many of the classroom doors were open, but Mr. Glover's was closed. As she raised her fist to knock, the door opened and Glover stood back and waved her in. The class had already gathered, a dozen students sat in chairs and on stools with sketchpads on their knees; others stood behind easels. Mostly boys looked over at her and she quickly looked away. "I'm glad you made it."

Glover seemed even taller and more imposing now that he was inside a room of students not much older than Emma. He took her to the side and asked her if she had brought any ID. She shook her head. "Well, if anybody asks, you tell them you're eighteen, okay?" She continued to stare without moving her head. He tapped a paintbrush against a stool and said loudly, a little like an impresario introducing an act, "This is our new model, Emma." Emma felt the eyes of the students turn to her. Not expecting to be the object of attention, she looked to the floor at the myriad colors of spilled paint. "Did you bring a robe?" she heard Glover say. She saw him seated on his high stool, his pallet on his knees. "Well, for today you can use the one over there." He pointed with the end of a brush to a stained and torn robe draped over a chair. "You'll do six five-minute poses and then three twenty-minute poses, all with short breaks in between." He went back to scraping paint on his pallet. "Don't be discouraged at first. It's boring as all get out, but your mind will figure out little tricks to get you through. Are we ready?"

She nodded her head.

"Now, go ahead. You can get ready behind the screen. The first pose I want you to do will be a sitting pose, in that chair. Cross your legs and put your hands in your lap."

Emma picked up the robe and walked toward the screen. She stopped and turned back to him. He pushed his blond hair away from his eyes with one hand and worked his pallet colors with the little metal knife. At the screen she turned to him again and he glanced up this time and then back down, waving with the back of his hand for her to hurry up. She stood behind the screen for a moment, the robe in her hand.

"Come on," he said. "Time is of the essence."

She put the robe on over her clothes, then walked around the screen and up to the hard wooden chair on the platform. Crossing her legs and putting her hands across her lap, she looked up toward a skylight high in the studio. Through the skylight she could see the line of a skyscraper stretching toward the clouds. She heard Glover laugh. "You've got to take your clothes off," his tone of voice was different now, sardonic. "We're not painting you with your turtleneck on." She turned and looked at his impatient smile. "Come on, you're wasting precious time, precious time."

She looked down at the torn robe over her slacks and shook her head.

"What? You're not going to undress? Well then, you certainly can't work for us here. You'll have to leave," Glover pointed to the door. "We'll have to get somebody else right away. My word."

Emma stood up and took off the robe, draping it over the chair where she'd found it.

"You didn't know that models have to take off their clothes?"

She tried to stop them, but there were tears coming to Emma's eyes as she made for the door, the class murmuring to each other as she walked down the echoing wood floor to the exit leading out to Twenty-third Street. As she opened the door to the busy street, Glover called to her above the din of traffic. "Hold on a minute, young lady." The very directness of his approach toward her frightened Emma so much that she ran down the granite steps to the street. "Would you hold on here?" A loud truck was shifting gears as Glover caught up to her. "What did you think I was asking you to do yesterday? You have to work for your money, you know."

She wiped her tears away, wanting them to disappear so as not to let him know even what she was feeling.

"Hold on there, would you?" Glover offered up the cuff of his sleeve to dry her face. "What's this all about?" His voice was softer and kinder and he touched Emma's shoulder to turn her around to him. "You agree to be an artist's model, you must know that you have to take your clothes off. Where are you from?"

Emma stared at her feet without moving.

"What are you doing here? Are you in school? You're such a strange-looking creature; you don't even seem eighteen years old. You'll get used to taking your clothes off, you realize, there are many models of all ages and they all do it and have been doing it since the beginning of time, since the Greeks. Nothing wrong with it, it's perfectly respectable."

Emma continued to stare at him and he at her. He seemed fascinated with her face and so she looked down at the ground, at her feet and allowed him to examine her, listening to the horns and squeaking brakes of traffic and the footsteps of passersby. When she looked back at him, he was still staring at her, but now his expression had softened considerably and he said, "Well, why don't you come back with me to the class. I know what I'll tell them, I'll say that you're too young, that I made a mistake. I'm going to ask them if it's okay if you keep your clothes on—it's sort of a funny request, you know—but just for today, all right?"

She hesitated. The thought of heading back into the classroom where she would be the object of attention was nearly unbearable, but just as she was about to pull away, she thought of Lucy. Lucy had done something like this; Lucy had survived it. Then the image of Lucy in the meat locker came to her. Yes, she would go back to the classroom, of course she would.

She followed him back up the steps and down the echoing hall to the tall doors with the fogged glass. "You wait here," he said.

He stepped inside and she could see him through the frosted glass, holding something that looked like a paintbrush in hand, explaining the situation to the students. A moment later he stepped back out and asked her to come in and sit on a chair on top of a pedestal. She climbed up, all eyes were on her, and then she put her hands on her lap and took a deep breath.

"Would you pull your turtleneck down a little bit?" Glover called.

Emma shook her head ever so slightly.

"You can't even show us more of your neck?"

Emma closed her eyes. She thought for a moment that he suspected something, that he might be guessing that there was something wrong with her skin.

"All right, all right, forgive me for asking," he said, then mumbled, "Class, let's begin."

At the end of the day, Emma had sat for two different groups of students, a total of six hours. Glover took her into the office and spoke to the model coordinator, a friend of his, who helped Emma fill out a form and submit it to the bursar who paid her in cash. Though she hadn't calculated the hourly wage, she knew just by the feel of the money that it was more than she'd ever had in her hand at once. Glover walked her down the wooden hallway to the exit. "Have you got a deep pocket or two to put that money in? Somebody will snatch it otherwise," he said. "Don't pull it out on the street, okay?"

Emma pushed the money deep into the pocket of her jeans.

"Now listen," Glover said, quietly and personally. "Are you busy tomorrow? Quite frankly, I started a very intriguing sketch of you, a few of my students mentioned that they did, too, and, you see, you've got a very interesting face, young lady. I'd have to change the whole focus of these classes, but if you'd like to come back tomorrow—"

On the way back to the Park Side Emma stopped into a clothing shop filled with booming rock music and bought herself a new turtleneck and two bras and long slacks and underwear and socks. Once Lucy had told her that she'd kept a diary in the circus. The diary, she said, became her home away from home. Emma stopped into a stationary store and bought a pen and a notebook.

After dinner she hid the money she had earned in her new socks and placed them in her locker. On her bunk, hiding her notebook with her arm so that nobody could look over at it, she lay very still and tried to remember her past. The task was daunting but she knew it was the only way she was going to find Lucy. She tried to remember how she had gotten into the Blue Night Mall, where had she been that night, whose blood had been on her clothes?

The harder she tried the blanker her mind became.

"Lights out, girls," a woman called into the dorm room. And Emma turned the reading lamp off next to her cot.

As she lay in the dark, she thought she could hear circus music. Then she could see a man staring at her, amazed, as if she were a circus sideshow, but maybe she had assumed Lucy's memories for herself or maybe the modeling had triggered this.

The memory became more vivid and she knew it wasn't a dream

at all. She was sitting inside of a white van. The side door was open and a man was outside staring at her, gasping, guffawing just like she was a circus act. He was a spectator; he had paid to see her. Suddenly something was thrown over the spectator's mouth, a mask of some sort with a hose and two men wrestled him down to the ground, struggling on top of him, holding the mask over his face while his feet kicked the ground.

Then the man, the spectator, was silent, lying on his back, his eyes bulging out.

32

Tired from a nearly sleepless night, Emma arrived early at the school the next morning and opened a classroom door, thinking that it was Glover's. But it was a different classroom, already filled with different students. On the pedestal, similar to the one she had been on the day before, Emma saw the olive skin of a naked woman with long silky black hair, reclining back against her elbows, her slender legs before her and her breasts resting upward on her chest. She was looking at the ceiling, apparently enjoying the attention as students and a teacher drew her.

It occurred to Emma that this was what Glover really wanted her to do and so she closed the door and turned to go back out the entrance to the street.

But Glover was coming in. His blond hair had been brushed straight back. His cheeks were flushed and over his broad chest was a faded red T-shirt with the silhouette of a dog on it. "You're early." His face was smooth and kind and he was holding the door open with his foot. "Come on, I worked on the sketch of you last night. I turned it into a painting. All we need to do is see your face, so you don't even have to pose, just sit there. How easy can life be?"

He headed down the hallway into his classroom and Emma followed, feeling strangely at ease with this man, as if he were one

of Lucy's story characters come to life. She sat down on the pedestal
and crossed her legs and Glover announced to the class, "A number
of you have told me that this young girl's face inspires you. We're
going to keep her. Actually, she's too young to be a life model—
that's what I've determined, but she's a fantastic subject nonethe-
less. Hey, *I* wouldn't undress in front of you guys, either."

The students laughed.

"If you have problems with this, let me know. Now let's com-
mence."

Emma had plenty of time to think as the students around her
began sketching and painting. She remembered the van again—
perhaps if she had a pen and paper she could sketch it, make it
vivid, draw it out of her memory. It was white and shone so brightly
she could see herself against the side.

During a break later that morning, Glover asked Emma to meet
him for lunch at a restaurant called the Blue Mile. "I'll pay of course.
It'll be good for you. You'll get a little culture. You seem so out of
it." He told her the address and asked her to meet him there at
noon. "I'm doing some terrific paintings at my studio *of you*, my
dear, and I need to pick up some supplies." He left the classroom
early.

The Blue Mile was a formal restaurant with white tablecloths,
wine glasses on every table, and waiters in black vests pouring wine
for customers with one hand behind their backs. A waiter led her
through the dining room to a table near the window where Glover
looked up from a novel. "There you are." He called to the waiter
and ordered beverages for them. Then the waiter placed an open
menu on the table in front of Emma and began to set one down
for Glover but Glover waved it away. "She'll be ready in a minute."
Then he turned to Emma. "Order whatever you want."

She looked through the menu for something familiar among the
long descriptions of the dishes.

"Do you live with your parents?" Glover was looking at her and she suddenly became uncomfortable; he would surely ask her more questions. She shook her head.

"What's the hat over the eyes all about? It's a shame to hide that charming face of yours. Have you ever modeled before?"

She shook her head, glancing at Glover who seemed to take great pleasure in her company. He threw his elbows out and raised his glass of wine to his lips. "Would you take off your hat? It's not polite to wear that thing inside."

Everyone at the surrounding tables was busy talking; nobody was looking at her. She took it off.

"That's better. You're staying with friends?"

She shook her head.

"In a hotel?"

Again she shook her head.

"A dorm?"

She nodded her head ever so slightly. She did not want to give away her whereabouts and she was unsure how many dorms were in the city.

He thought about this a minute. "Sounds like you ran away from home."

She looked down silently.

"Well, well, that's okay. Your parents I'm sure are worried stiff, you should call them." He watched her and she continued to look down. "Well, there are two sides to every story." He seemed to reconsider. "Maybe this is just something you need to do. You don't seem like the type to get in trouble. I know, I'll look after you, okay?" he stated brightly.

The waiter stepped over to take their order and Emma pointed at what she wanted. Alone with her again, Glover said, "You know, as a painter, I've been on a kind of quest, I've been looking everywhere for a certain face, but I didn't know exactly what that face looked like or anything, I just knew that I'd recognize it when I came across it. I've got an exhibition coming up and I've been com-

pletely panicked trying to complete this cycle of paintings . . .
Maybe it's all a big dream, I don't know, but when I saw you, even
though I couldn't really see what you looked like under that visor,
I was sure that I was onto something. Then when you took off your
hat, presto, I knew without a doubt that you were the very person
I'd been seeking all along to complete my portrait series. Luck,
that's all."

The thought that he had been seeking her out brought up disturbing feelings. She wanted to run away; she kept glancing at the
other diners and decided that if he tried anything she could run to
them for assistance.

"Now here," he said. "Here's what's strange: you absolutely refused to disrobe. Do you see?" Emma kept her glance averted from
him. "You don't see what's strange about that?"

She did not move her head, but Glover seemed to take this for
an answer.

"Here I am looking for a portrait subject. I take you to my life
drawing class and you refuse to disrobe—as if you knew all along
that you were meant to be a portrait." He laughed. "It's only your
face that I needed and you seemed to know that in your own way
quite well," he said again. "And the other strange thing—only a
few students have left the class after I've completely changed its
orientation. Now tell me, please, just a little bit about yourself, I'm
really curious. Please write it down."

Emma looked around nervously. Glover pushed a pencil and a
piece of paper in front of her. "Go on," he said. "Write it down."

She picked up the pencil and held it over the pad. Then slowly
she wrote. *Soon, I go to Ohio.*

He read the note, then looked at her. "What part of Ohio are
you from? There's something about you that reminds me of my
home." He smiled. "You must think I'm a nut and I'm going to
admit to you right now, I am a bit of one. I'm so full of superstitions
I can hardly walk down the street. I'm always looking for signs

from the heavens to follow. You remind me of my childhood, I don't know why. Do me a favor, would you? Would you smile just a little bit for me? You haven't smiled since I've met you."

Emma merely looked down at the tablecloth.

"My, my, that's not much of a smile. But it will come, I'm sure, with time once you realize that I do really want to take care of you."

He went on eating his lunch. "I know what you need, you need a room of your own, don't you? A place to collect your thoughts—you're a dreamer like me, you must be." It was true that she needed a room of her own and so she found herself slowly nodding her head. "Have you ever thought about a hotel? It would probably cost you about seventy-five dollars a night, something like that." The more Emma thought about a private room, the better it sounded—maybe that would help her remember more so that she would know where to go to look for Lucy. "I'll tell you something else," Glover went on. "I've got plenty of space in my loft. You're welcome to stay with me, you'll have your own room or maybe you're uncomfortable with that, maybe you'd prefer to stay in my studio, I'll give you the key, it will be all your own for—I have to charge you something, don't I?" he looked around the room. "How does fifteen dollars a night sound?"

She looked down at her fingers holding the edge of the tablecloth. She did need a place where she could sit down at a desk alone with the door shut, in order to remember things.

"I'm making you uncomfortable, I can see. Later we'll check out the hotels."

That evening after classes Glover stood on the granite steps of the school with Emma and said, "Where do you want to go? Back to your dorm or to my studio? My studio will be very private. I can show it to you now if you want, it's just downtown a ways."

Emma could not decide what to do.

"Is it the fifteen dollars a night, is that the problem?"

She shook her head.

"How about ten?" he said, smiling. "I don't want to charge anything, but I can see you like to pay your own way."

She continued to stare at him without moving her head.

"Come on, we'll take a taxi over and you can decide for yourself," Glover said.

Glover flagged a cab and Emma got in the slippery back seat, staring out the window away from him. She was not sure she had made the right decision, but she had not been able to sleep much in the dorm room. The taxi took them to a loft building in lower Manhattan where they climbed steep wooden steps that smelled of dust and dried paint and echoed beneath their feet. Emma grabbed the railing, afraid of falling backward. He pointed to a door and said, "That's my apartment." Then he unlocked the door across the hall.

Spilled paint speckled and streaked the floor of his studio. A large cathedral-like skylight covered with pigeon droppings crowned the high ceilings. As Glover turned on lights, portraits of Emma appeared around the room, small, dark, mauve, suspended on easels, some half painted, others finished and framed. In them she was wearing different clothes and sitting in an unfamiliar room where a strange yellow light shone on her face.

She stood in front of one and stared for a long time.

"Do you like it?" Glover asked. She turned to him, then stepped back; he was standing too close to her.

She shook her head, though she was hardly aware of it.

"That's not very nice."

She moved to another portrait and stared at herself and a vague uneasiness, a floating feeling, familiar and yet disorienting began to creep out from it, a feeling from long ago.

She couldn't understand the origin of the sensation that she got from seeing the picture. It was coming from deep inside of her and making her more and more uncomfortable; now there was a hint of nausea mixed in with it.

"I should never ask people if they like portraits of themselves. Everyone is so vain. Come, I'll show you your room."

Emma kept staring at the picture. What did it remind her of? She turned and followed Glover into a small bedroom just off the big room of the studio. An Indian print, elephants in black ink on dark orange fabric hung on the wall behind a low bed.

"I'll give you the key, you can lock the door and have the place to yourself or you can hang out in my apartment and watch TV if you want. I won't bother you," he said. "Do you want it?"

Had Emma not been convinced of the need for privacy to look into her past she would never have said yes to him. There was also something kind about him, he was indeed like Giant John of the circus.

She nodded her head.

Glover accompanied her back to Park Side in a cab and waited outside for her while she gathered and packed her few possessions.

That night Emma locked and latched from inside the studio door when Glover was gone and crossed the big room without looking at the portraits of herself. On her bedroom door itself was a full-length mirror, she stared at her face in that—it had been some time before she had looked into her own dark eyes. She could not believe that she was so far from home, so far from anything that she knew.

33

Late that night Emma's eyes opened so wide that she knew that she wouldn't get back to sleep again. She turned on the light and lay back on her pillow. The thought was of Lucy again, in the meat locker. It was unbearable. Her vision of this metal box out in the woods had gotten clearer. It was resting in her mind's eye and now she was sure that Lucy was inside of it and she was suffering, suffering terribly.

How much money did she have? She got up and counted it. Nearly three hundred dollars. That would certainly get her out to the Midwest, but where out there? Where would she go? Should she go to the police? What would she tell them? She needed a plan, but really she needed to remember more, much more.

She got up and went to her desk and sat with her pen in hand hoping to recall places that she had been. Had she ever known the name of the town where she had stayed? Did she even know what state it was in?

Something occurred to her, her body; perhaps if she studied her body she would learn things.

She had been afraid of doing this in the past even in the safety of Lucy's home; but now she got up and stood before the mirror on the door and stared bravely into her eyes. What did she see in her own eyes? Looking at herself, she could feel the presence of the man. What had he done to her? She could hear the words *daughter* and *Christ*. She closed her eyes and thought about this. The mere recollection of these words caused a lump in her throat to form. She tried to collect herself, to calm down. She stepped away from the mirror and sat on the bed and breathed in and out carefully. Then she reached down and pulled up her shirtsleeve and stared at the scales on her wrist for the first time that she could remember. She yanked her sleeve back down and shut her eyes again, this time even tighter and felt the presence of the scales as if they were alive, a kind of living shadow that threatened to climb up her neck and suffocate her, drown her with darkness.

Finally, she reached down and took off her shirt and kept her gaze averted, staring straight ahead at the wall above her bed. She backed up toward the mirror and looked over her back at her reflection. As she took in the intricately drawn lines that circled her shoulder blades, she felt an almost palpable silence deep in her chest. She saw something before her eyes—a lake. At the edge of the lake she saw the reflection of a man and a girl, presumably the girl was herself. The two figures disappeared. Emma realized she had been holding her breath. She sat down and slapped her hands down on the bed as if to confirm her own presence.

As she tried to get up again, she felt something pulling her back down, the weight of darkness. She lifted herself against this powerful force until she was seated; her head began spinning, she was dizzy. Again she saw the reflection of the girl and the man; the two reflections started to walk along the edge of the lake. Then she saw others, a gathering of men, many of them in ministers' black suits, others with ruddy faces and in work pants and shirts. They were standing on a slab of cement with a view over a valley, a dam of some sort.

The image of these men on the dam, their figures against the sky, died away and after a while she turned out the light and lay back in bed. It was early morning now; there was light coming in her window from the sky. She closed her eyes to fall asleep. Another scene in the van came to her, a memory: a stranger, another spectator who had been lured out of a bar was looking at her, staring, gaping. Emma was tied to a chair bolted solidly to the floor of a van. The man had lifted her trouser leg and rolled up her sleeve.

"What'd you do to this poor girl!" the stranger said. "I'm not paying no five dollars to see some chick done up like this!" He was shocked and outraged and Emma could tell at the time that something bad was going to happen. "What kind of shit did you put on her skin?"

"You tell me," one of the other men said. The van was parked near a Dumpster. The open door in which Emma sat was facing a chain-link fence with a forest on the other side. Then another man who had been hiding somewhere near the van stepped up to the stranger and pointed a shotgun at his head.

"Hey? What? What's this?" the stranger said.

"You wanted to see some skin, didn't you? You told me in there. Well, here we are," the man had said. "Now tell me what you're thinking about it."

"Hey, you do what you want, this is a free country," the stranger had changed his tune.

"All I'm asking for is your thoughts about her," the man with the gun demanded. "Do you like her?"

"Yeah, sure."

"Do you want to *do it* with her? Huh?"

"What? Like I said—"

"Yes or no?"

The man began shaking his head, not knowing what to say. He'd been trapped by these men with the van, lured by the prospect of seeing a naked body but he had been unprepared to see Emma's scales.

A third man appeared with a hose and mask and slammed it

over the stranger's face and all the men who traveled with the van wrestled him to the ground. There was a long struggle as they held the mask against the stranger's face, but this particular stranger must have been ready for them.

"He's got a *damn* gun!" one of the men yelled.

And there was a gunshot, then another shot and something hit Emma in the face that must have been blood. Then the two men lunged at the stranger and began to wrestle him. Emma managed to wriggle out of her loosely tied binding. She bolted from the van to a hole in the chain-link fence and ran hard, deep into the woods, expecting to hear footsteps behind her. But in the end nobody was following her.

Then she saw the sign on the side of the flat-roofed building: THE BLUE NIGHT MALL.

34

That morning Emma got up, crossed through the studio and un-locked the front door quietly. "Sleep all right?" Glover was just coming out of his apartment. "I've got plenty of fruit here and coffee and I'm running out to get the paper." She stared at him, startled by his presence. "Hey, are you all right?" She continued to stare, then backed into the studio space and sat on the bed to get her bearings again. It was too early to see somebody, to have somebody talking to her.

A knock came on the studio door again and when she finally opened it just wide enough to look out, she saw that he was holding a bowl of peach slices and freshly washed strawberries. "For you," he said, graciously.

After eating the fruit, she brought the bowl across the hall to his apartment and they went down the stairs together to the street. Glover pointed at his car, a rusty, yellow Ford Duster with torn vinyl seats and a runaway crack across the windshield. Opening the dented door for her, he told her to get in. "Come on," he said. "I've got to get rid of this piece of junk otherwise I'm going to keep getting these." He pulled an orange ticket from under the wiper as he got in. After he found another parking space, he handed Emma a subway pass and they climbed down the stairs to the train.

At the arts school Emma followed Glover through the halls as he waved hello to friends and stopped to discuss plans with students. Soon she was sitting before the class to model on the low platform and she was thinking about the scene she had remembered the night before. She needed to remember places most of all. Once again the meat locker in the woods came to mind, but where were these woods located?

At noon she strolled up Fifth Avenue for her break, deep in thought, but alert for the man who had kidnapped her. Suddenly, out of the corner of her vision she saw something dart across the reflection of a glass shop window. A quick shadowy movement, then something else shot by in the reflection. She turned around to look for its source, thinking it must have been a bird, then turned again to the window and saw a third object shoot by, this time she was able to follow it with her eyes. It was the reflected image of a small yellow fish. Another came by, then another, all swimming across the imperfections in the glass, getting longer, then shorter, then fatter, then wider before disappearing into the sill.

She stopped and watched these strange images: the window was reflecting an entire school of fish. Where were they coming from? Were they being projected onto the glass from across the street? There was no flash of light from the other buildings. She turned again to the glass and watched a school of tiger-striped fish swim by. They were so real she felt that she could reach out and touch them. Then all at once she began feeling lightheaded, and then very dizzy and finally she was stooped over at the edge of a small park, her stomach heaving. She was barely able to keep from throwing up.

The dizziness continued. Was she having some sort of relapse or was there something in her revolting against last night's inves-

tigation into her past? She finally straightened up and headed back
to the art school.

The next morning as she and Glover walked toward the subway,
she saw the fish again, on smaller windows. This time she could
almost feel them swimming out of her thoughts. They were feelings
that had been pent up for too long and were now desperately cracking up her brain in order to get out. She was afraid to stare at any
one reflecting surface, afraid that the images would bring her entire
life to a stop. In the subway, Glover asked somebody to give their
seat to her. "Are you okay? You're pale," he said.

The class got out at lunchtime that day and Emma had the
afternoon off. She walked toward Seventh Avenue. Having decided
to avoid glass surfaces, she kept her eyes on people and on the
sidewalk, but all at once she heard a crash above the din of traffic
that sounded like a thousand cymbals. She turned and looked up
at a glass skyscraper. Hundreds of feet up she saw a great blue whale
leap from one side of the glass to the other and disappear, vanish
into the sky itself.

She gasped, then caught herself and knelt near a building wall
and waited for the dizzy sensation to pass. After gathering her
thoughts and walking on, an idea took hold of her. If she stared at
some real fish, maybe their images would trigger memories. It was
a crazy idea, but Glover had mentioned the aquarium and amuse-
ment park in Coney Island and had even suggested she go there
when she had some time off.

She took the F train to the end of the line and climbed down
the elevated platform and walked out toward the boardwalk. Hundreds of colored umbrellas spotted the sand leading down to the
water. She strolled along the sandy walkway; crowds gathered in
front of the booths and shops.

Admission to the Coney Island Aquarium: Adults $3.00. Standing
in front of the ticket booth outside the ramp that led down to the

aquarium, she noticed that her hands were shaking; she felt light-headed; her chest trembled. She laid the money in the smooth metal slot for the ticket-seller. "How many?" the seller asked. Emma grabbed the money back and stepped away. Going inside would surely open something up inside of her, point her in a direction, but she could not help feeling that there was something dangerous lurking behind the walls of glass. The mad bubbling water from the hundreds of tanks and the echoing voices of children sent her out on the boardwalk again where she leaned against the railing, looking toward the beach and water.

She could see crowds of bathers, mostly in groups or families, sitting in low chairs, lying on towels; she could smell the scent of suntan lotion.

Suddenly the world—the ocean, the beach, the jetty, the wooden walkway, the sounds of radios, the tinny speakers of the shops—began to spin around her. She held onto the dry splintery wood of the railing as if she'd just stepped inside a kaleidoscope. She held on tightly until the spinning stopped. She knew what it was that had caused this chaotic movement around her—the strange déjà vu quality of the aquarium.

How did I get here? She knew well all the little steps that had led her here but she still didn't understand why.

She glanced back at the light blue cement wall that ran around the aquarium. What was so dangerous about an aquarium? Could a fish smash through the glass and rip at her flesh before dying itself? She climbed down the wooden steps from the boardwalk to the sand and walked in her shoes, past the many people in swimming trunks and bikinis, people playing paddleball, listening to radios, eating fried chicken, smoking, talking, and laughing. She couldn't imagine how they sat in public in mere bathing suits allowing others to look at their skin. She was astonished, feeling that the world and the people in it were even more foreign, more different from her than she had even suspected. Were these the same people she saw on the weekdays walking down the street fully clothed?

None of them have tattoos.

This understanding hit her, a shattering realization. For a second she almost smiled. Like firecrackers going off inside her mind, she had another realization: *Nor have any of these people been tattooed. If they don't have tattoos, they haven't been tattooed.*

Such a simple thought led to so many others. *I'm physically different from them. By showing their skin, they're not exposing who they are at all, they're just showing how similar they are, whereas if I showed my skin, I'd reveal how different I am, who I really am. And that will always be a secret, always . . .*

Even with her clothes on she felt as if people could see through her to her body, her tattoos, as if people could see fish swimming in her mind. *There is no hiding anywhere that there are people.* She found a place in the white sand twenty feet from the nearest blanket and umbrella and sat down and let the sun fall on her cheeks while she closed her eyes. It was hopeless, finding Lucy would be impossible. *I am too far away from my own memories to remember where I've been.*

She stepped through the turnstile into the first room and walked up to the glowing yellow light of a small tank set into the wall. She saw a tank of seaweed, which at first she thought was otherwise empty. Slowly an eel began to rise out of the grasses, tiny bubbles rising from its sharp little teeth, its jaw open just a little.

A strange sensation took her over as she became mesmerized by the underwater creature. It seemed to look at her, then turn away, its rolling body gently propelling it to the back of the tank. A voice inside her head shouted. *You're an eel!* A loudspeaker set up between her ears.

She answered the voice in her mind. *I'm a person, not an eel!*

She began to walk around the curved corridor, glancing into the tanks while the voice in her head spouted the names of the fish at her and she responded to the voice. *I am not a yellow fish, I am not a sea turtle, I am not a striped bass or a sunfish or a sea robin.*

I am Emma.

I am Lucy's friend.

I am me.

She walked through a curved corridor with tanks set into the wall. Through the room with the killer whales, the room with the sharks, the room with stingrays, the men-of-war, the sea urchins, the starfish. *I'm not a starfish, either, I'm a person.*

She could see a girl whose body was tattooed with scales like her own floating inside a tank of water. The girl was dead, the water was pinkish . . .

She ran through the exhibits, and out the exit and onto the boardwalk.

She grabbed the railing again, held on to it until she'd gotten hold of herself, then ran farther away from the building. Later she tried to relax, to calm herself down and write down in her notebook exactly what the voice was telling her, where it was coming from.

Why does he want me to return to the water?

To heal the two.

What is the two?

She remembered every word that Lucy said to her. "If I ever see the person who put those tattoos on you, darling, he'll never be the same after I get through with him. I'll stand there as a *witness*. I won't have to do anything else. But that will do him right."

35

After sitting on the beach for a while, she climbed up on the board-walk and strolled among the hundreds of people, many girls and boys her age who seemed without a care in the world. Suddenly she heard a circus tune coming from tinny speakers over a sign that said CONEY ISLAND FREAK SHOW & MUSEUM. In the lobby of the museum, a man with cropped blond hair and wearing a V-neck sailor shirt stood behind a glass counter of memorabilia. Tat-toos, most of women, were displayed on his hairy forearms. "Show's only a buck," he said to all those standing in the lobby. "Museum's a quarter."

Emma looked through the glass at a pack of playing cards of freaks and an *Encyclopedia of Freaks.*

Being a freak helped me understand what we humans were put on earth to do, Lucy had once said to her. *In some ways it was a divine privilege that gave me a special perspective.*

Emma pointed and the man reached inside the glass and laid the heavy book on the counter. She looked at the pictures on the front, and then read the back. *Monumental cataloguing of every hu-man physical anomaly since the Egyptians.* Emma opened it to the *T*'s and looked for Thurman. It went from Michael Teller to "Pis-tol" Thomas. She looked up "fat ladies" and began reading about the lives of the various fat women who had worked in circuses throughout the country. Then she came across a paragraph that said, *Lady Redman—Circus Fat Lady for the Crown Circus. Died of heart failure. A train car carried her back to her home in Winston, Ohio for burial. She had to be lowered into her grave with a crane. At one time she weighed 628 pounds. Her successor, Lucy Thurman, was unremarkable in size, hardly a true circus fat lady.* Something about this struck Emma as sad. A tear slipped out of her eye and down her cheek onto the open page.

"Hey, there," the sailor said. "You want to pay for that thing?" He pulled the book away from her. "What's with you?" She stepped outside and wiped her eyes. Then she came back in and paid her admission to the freak museum.

She stepped through the two black curtains, her eyes adjusting from the bright sunlight outside. There was a recording of a primitive drum coming from a speaker and under it she saw a photograph of *The Two-Headed African*, a tribal black man with two heads and two necks with white bone necklaces.

A photograph of the tallest man in the world. A pair of worn leather shoes in the case that were almost as long as Emma's arm. A hat the size of a laundry bag next to it. The man had a long face and long teeth and he looked a little dumbfounded, as if he'd just discovered his awkward body. Then she saw the worn shoes and gloves belonging to the smallest man in the world. Then the girdle of the biggest woman in the world. The enormous girdle was dirty and torn. Above it were pictures of this woman sitting next to three dwarves and a normal-sized man.

Then Emma looked over photographs of tattooed men and women. The men stood shirtless, one man's shaved head was completely covered with designs. A woman's breasts were covered with tattoos of vicious snakes with blood dripping from fangs. Nobody had fish scales over any part of their body. Hearing voices, Emma turned to see a beautiful young couple approaching arm in arm.

Feeling exposed somehow, Emma stepped down the wall to a long photograph of the so-called largest gathering of dwarves in the history of man.

"God," the boy said to the girl. "Aren't they the sexiest damn things in the world?"

The girl laughed. "What are?"

"The snakes on that lady's tits."

"What?"

"Don't they make you want to fuck?"

Emma turned. The boy was looking at her, smiling, as if he'd said it just to see her reaction. She turned and ran quickly out the exit and onto the boardwalk.

In the subway car bound for New York, she felt more lost than ever. At Borough Hall she got off and walked in the direction of the East River. Soon she came across two dark red-brick factory buildings with broken windows and an alleyway leading to a litter-strewn parking lot that ended at the river's edge. It was late in the day now, the sun was settling down behind the buildings of Manhattan. She walked out into the open air of the parking lot and put her foot on the splintery timber that kept cars from driving over the edge.

The East River's current was visible, small eddies and whirlpools shimmered in the late afternoon light. Emma realized that she was covered with sweat as she stared at the smelly water. Again the feeling of vertigo came over her, the feeling of being inside a kaleidoscope. She pressed her foot against the timber to steady herself and kept staring at the brown wood until the motion stopped.

Then she heard a voice: *Go on, jump* in the same timbre of the one she'd heard in the aquarium.

I'm going to stay here, on land. My feet on the pavement.

Before you do something else wrong, jump.

I've got to find Lucy . . .

You don't understand . . . what comes up from the sea must—

She turned to the sound of footsteps and saw a woman cutting across the dirty pavement toward her, a streetwalker in spiked heels, a skirt that barely covered her bottom and a white half shirt—her belly button showed.

Emma turned and walked along the wooden barrier next to the river's edge.

"Hey, you," the woman called, swinging her pocketbook. "Got a smoke?"

Emma ran to the alleyway and back to the street that paralleled the water, then turned again between two shorefront buildings for another empty parking lot that bordered the water. In this lot she saw a Jeep with smoked glass windows parked toward the river, the throbbing, rumbling beat of a stereo coming from it. She would have to get close to the water to hear the voice that had been talking to her. She saw plastic bottles in the water, cigarette butts, a Kellogg's cereal box. Celery sticks inside a plastic bag bobbed in the brown liquid.

You'll feel a hell of a lot better soon as you're home.

You're not my home!

You can't survive out there, little fish.

Shut up.

She stood listening to the voice and the pounding of the Jeep's bass. Suddenly another car pulled into the parking lot. "Hey, baby." Three young men were hanging out of the window. "Look at that," the driver was hanging half out of the window with his tongue out. Emma dashed up the alley to the street and made her way toward the subway. *Something horrible has been done to me, something so horrible that there may be no words for it*, she thought as she got back into a subway car. *Somebody tried to cheat me out of my life.*

36

For the next few days, Emma saved nearly every penny that was given to her, and tried to make vivid whatever memories came to mind. She now had enough cash to leave, but she was still without a destination. Then one night at Glover's, while sitting on her bed in her room, she heard a knock on the studio door. She went to the peephole and looked out into the hallway. Glover was holding something in his hand. "Am I disturbing you?" he called. She stared at him for a moment, then unlocked the door. In his hand were three black and white snapshots. He handed her one of the photographs.

It was a picture of a tattered billboard in a flat field with a mountain in the background. The billboard picture was of a little girl, eight or nine years old, one shoe on, the other off, standing in a pool of milk on the checked kitchen floor. She had lifted her shirt and stuck out her belly. WE'RE FRESH. ARE YOU? DRINK MILK! The girl was familiar; she looked exactly like Emma herself might have looked six or seven years ago.

"I took these on a road trip a few years back."

Glover gave her another photograph of another billboard in a field; this one was of the same girl reaching across a high table, tipping over a glass of milk. The milk had run down from the counter onto the floor where two kittens were lapping it up. A third was clinging to the back of the girl's pants, pulling them down just over the crack of her behind. THEY'RE LOVIN' IT. ARE YOU?

He handed her another picture. It was of the first billboard from a distance. From this angle Emma could see some sort of roadside restaurant or motel with a large metal bear standing on its hind legs, holding a cup of coffee. The bear stood taller than the actual billboard, at least two or three stories high. "I don't know why I kept the pictures, but look at the similarity," he said, holding one up to Emma's face. "You look just like her."

She took the clippings and backed into the studio. He stood watching her.

"Do you have a sister by any chance?" he said.

She looked up at him quickly, surprised by the word sister. She shook her head.

"Well, I guess these are why I thought I knew you when I asked you to model for me. You see, I'm not such a nut after all. You've got a soul mate out in the world somewhere. Do you want to keep them?"

He crossed the hall for his apartment and Emma locked the door again.

Her heart was beating quickly as she looked at the pictures. Though she wasn't sure how it was possible, she felt that this girl, whose face had been touched up a little, was herself. She did not remember the kittens or anything else about the pictures. She certainly didn't remember anyone displaying her image on a billboard. But then as she sat on her bed a memory mysteriously came to her of a man snapping pictures of her in a room under bright lights: hot flashes of white light, people fussing with her hair, dragging combs through it, spraying it. A makeup pencil against her eyelashes.

These faint memories became clearer. There were two other people in the room with her, her parents, her real parents. They were always watching over her, always asking her how she felt. They would hold her hand, show her to other people as if she were an exotic pet. Then she remembered a single-story house surrounded by a lawn in the suburbs.

She put her face in her hands.

She was nine, maybe ten years old when she had gone for a walk to a store six or seven blocks away. On her way back a van had pulled up near her and a man jumped out and yelled her name. "There you are!" She had stopped and looked at him, then he called her parents by their name and said, "Guess what? I'm coming for dinner. Your mom said to pick you up . . . Wait a minute, I forgot something." He held a small present wrapped in blue tissue paper. "I know it's kind of late . . . But I think you'll like it." He gave it to her. "Go on, open it," he said. She opened it quickly. Inside was a blue rubber fish that had been cut three times behind the neck. The moment it was in her hands he was behind her, lifting her up and pushing her toward the open van door, which he slammed closed as soon as she was inside. There were no handles inside; the walls were lined with Styrofoam insulation. Only a small caged window faced the cab. She kicked the door of the van, kicked its sides, and cried for help. Within minutes they were on the highway, the sound of the tires reverberating in the van.

A day later when he finally opened the door of the van, Emma's hands and feet were swollen from where she'd kicked and banged; half of her body was black and blue. She tumbled out onto a white crushed stone driveway near the front door of a large house. He carried her into the house and then into a special room, a room built into the corner of the living room.

And gradually she had forgotten every memory that had made up who she was, her self. He had accomplished what he must have set out to do. He eradicated every aspect of her humanity.

Emma placed the photographs on her bed. The floor beneath her began to shift and it seemed for the first time in as long as she could remember that she was beginning to understand something: *Do you know the sort of thoughts you've been inspiring? Satan's tool! Huh?* She could practically hear this man's voice.

She wrote a note to Glover that read, *Where did you take these?* and brought it across the hall to him. He was working on a small painting of her face in his dining room, a spotlight facing the easel. He put his brush down and wiped his hands on his smock and read the note.

"West Virginia. I was on a road trip years ago, at least six or seven years back. Is she your cousin?" he said, smiling.

Emma shook her head.

"Can I tell you something for sure?" he added. "You could have a career in modeling if you wanted it, just like that kid."

Emma meanwhile had put her pad down and was writing another note: *Which town?*

Glover climbed up on his stool and read it. "I couldn't tell you the town. I wasn't traveling on the main roads, just looking around for things that caught my eye. I think it was in Derrick County, something like that."

On a shelf in the main room of the loft, Glover found a road atlas and brought it to his kitchen table and opened it to West Virginia and pointed out Derrick County. By the look of the roads it was sparsely populated.

Emma continued to examine the three photographs, more sure than ever that the girl was herself. Then she studied the big bear holding the cup of coffee. Had she seen this bear before? She was sure she had. It had a peculiar smile and wore a straw hat with holes in it. She had definitely seen this bear before.

She sat down at Glover's dining room table and wrote him another note, gave it to him, and waited for an answer.

"You want to buy my car?" he said. "No, dear. I couldn't sell that thing in good conscience to anyone. But you're welcome to borrow it. I trust you're a good driver, aren't you?"

She was amazed at how much confidence he seemed to have in her. She nodded her head.

"In fact if you really do plan on going somewhere in it then I *have* to loan it to you, that way you'll *have* to bring it back and I'll see you again." He thought of this as he spoke to her. "When do you need it?"

She thought a moment, then wrote, *Saturday.*

"You'll be back to work by Monday, I trust?" he said, calmly, continuing with his work. He glanced at her and she nodded her head slowly, aware that she was lying. He went back to his painting. "Where do you plan on heading?"

She wrote, *To see the area around New York.*

"Oh, I don't think that piece of junk will make it too far." She continued watching him work. "Well, maybe it will serve your purposes."

37

Before daybreak Saturday morning, with car keys in hand, Emma
tiptoed out of the studio door and pulled it locked behind her. She
had left a note on her bed that said, *I may be back later than Monday.
Please forgive me. I will write you a letter and send you money for your
car. Thank you, Emma.* She descended the steep stairs to the door
leading outside and began to walk for his car. The streets of the
city were nearly empty of traffic. There were a few groups of people
walking home after a night out. She found the rust-eaten vehicle a
block away, unlocked it, and sat down in the seat that had been
patched with tape.

Taking a deep breath, she put the key in and turned it. The car
started right away, then popped and stalled. She started it again,
this time giving it gas as Lucy had taught her to do. The motor
rumbled underneath her seat. She began trembling, she pushed the
shift into drive and the car lurched forward into the car in front
and stalled again.

She quickly tried to start the engine again but it made no noise
at all, just a click. A young man walking a dog came over. He must
have seen her bump the car in front of her. He tapped on the closed
window and said through the glass, "Won't start?" She didn't look
at him. "You've got to put it in park," he called.

She had no idea what he was talking about. She turned the key again, but the car was still dead.

The young man tied his dog to a parking meter and came around to her side. He tapped on the window again and told her to roll it down. She rolled it down just a little ways. "Put the shift in park," he said. He had brown curly hair and a prominent nose and a long innocent face. "That's the gear shift," he said, pointing across her lap.

She nodded her head, remembering that Lucy had called it that.

"It's in drive. Cars won't start in drive," he said. She pushed it forward into park, then turned the key. The car began rumbling again. She touched the gas pedal and practiced revving it. The young man stepped back, watching her. "First put your foot on the brake," he said, "then put it in reverse." She did as he said, drawing the shift down. "Now let up on the brake very slowly." The car went backward, gently bumping the one behind her and then stalling. "Do you want me to get it out of there for you? You're in a tight space."

She shook her head and continued to start and stop and the young man began to instruct her on which way to turn the wheel. Eventually, the car made it out and lurched forward into the lanes. "Turn your lights on," the young man said. "They're the lever next to the steering wheel . . . Are you sure you know how to drive?"

She started and stalled, then started and stopped short at a red light. A taxi idled next to her and she could feel the driver's eyes on her. Then the light turned and traffic began passing her. She went through the intersection, trying to stay between the lanes, then stopped at the next light. She was out of breath. As soon as the light turned green she was off again, jerking forward, slowing down.

Finally she was driving through the streets of New York, headed toward the Lincoln Tunnel, which she had seen on the detailed map in Glover's loft. It was four in the morning; there wasn't much traffic and she had time to remember at least some of what Lucy had told her about driving. As she entered the tunnel, a car behind her got right on her tail and began honking and flashing its lights, then finally it sped around her. On the incline out of the tunnel she was assaulted by another tailgater, a truck who flashed and honked and Emma pushed her foot down harder on the gas. Ten miles outside of New York, she pulled off at an exit to rest. After another fifteen minutes on the highway, she rested a second time before going on. Before noon she pulled off at yet another rest area, parked before a stand of trees, locked her doors, and fell asleep.

38

"Quiet now," Pidge said. "And get in." His shepherd bounded from the dashboard onto the torn passenger seat of the rusty pickup truck. A blue vinyl tarp covered six cardboard boxes tied down in the truck's bed—all the belongings that Pidge now owned in the world. He drove past the landlord's trailer on the other side of the park and kept going. No sense in trying to get his security deposit back; he'd spent more than one drunken night slamming his fists against the flimsy trailer walls.

He had decided he was moving, but exactly where he was moving to he had not figured out, so long as it was away from here. Now was as good a time as ever to stop by Lucy's house.

On the highway Pidge's truck swayed back and forth, pulling this way and that against his bald tires. He kept thinking of Lucy—he had spent a great deal of time contemplating her after he quit the circus. It was true that he had been far from attracted to her, but then again no girl had ever been attracted to him, either. Nobody. Not even the shortest girl in his grammar school, a girl who was technically a midget, no taller than Pidge, would have anything to do with him. Lucy was the first one, the only one. But it had taken him a long while to even notice what she was feeling. He remembered her behavior change during the wedding—her taking more seriously all the details of the wedding. She would make herself immaculate for the ceremony, spend twenty minutes making up her face, she walked differently, cautiously. Her hand trembled when he placed the ring on her finger. Then he recalled the first tear he saw come from her eye. He couldn't figure out why she was crying, he wondered if she had gotten some bad news before the wedding. But then as the many weddings continued there were more tears. The last time he had wept, he was eight or nine years old. Slowly he began to understand that she was crying because of him, because she was feeling something for him, the ceremony had taken hold of her.

Even now as he drove down the highway, he was unsure what she could have seen in him—an alcoholic dwarf with a face and body that made children laugh regardless of a costume. There was nothing else unusual about him. He wasn't known as somebody with a sharp wit. He wasn't funny. His personality was not particularly sweet, in fact, he had a tendency to snap at people. *Irascible*, was how Master Howard had described him. But Lucy had seen through that or said she did anyway—more than once she had murmured things to him on stage that he couldn't get out of his mind.

She hadn't deserved what he had done to her, but over the years, no matter what he did to try to drown her out, he always came back to her eyes on him and the sound of her voice when she whispered things to him like, "Let me in, I can see who you really are," or "I believe in you." The way she said, "I do," had a certain conviction, a kind of tremulous quality that he could still hear.

What was it about her? Why had he spent so much time thinking about her? She had seen something inside him that he didn't even know had existed. She had pointed it out to him with just her gaze and after that he began to notice it in himself.

Now as he drove toward her house, he kept picturing himself ringing her bell and the look of astonishment on her face when she saw him. But he couldn't imagine what he would say. "You've got to have a first line," he said to his dog who sat upright next to him, staring straight ahead. "Then everything else will fall in place." *Sometimes people don't say what they mean. I don't know if you meant it when you asked me . . . for whatever it's worth—*

He kept rejecting these openers until he felt so frustrated that he got off the highway and pulled up to the offices of the Nice Motel. An Asian couple ran the motel. Pidge took a room, climbed into the large double bed and pulled the blankets up to his eyes.

Pidge's motel room door swung open without warning and the middle-aged woman from the front desk walked in, stopped short, and saw wet Kleenexes scattered on the rug. She bowed quickly and backed out of the door. Normally Pidge would have cussed at somebody for this mistake, but instead he pulled the covers over his eyes.

Later he heard a faint knocking sound and, assuming it was on a door down the hall, he ignored it. But the knock persisted and finally he opened it to see the proprietor holding a large bowl of noodle soup in his hands. "From my wife."

Pidge looked down at the steaming bowl with the porcelain spoon and chopsticks in it. "I didn't order anything," he said.

"It's because she walked into your room by mistake. She went into the wrong room." He smiled pleasantly. Pidge kept staring at the soup. "It's very good," the man said, and smiled again. "Come over to our house if you change your mind, visit our cats."

"Cats? I'm not a cat person."

"That's okay."

"Just 'cause she walked in on me? Nah," he said, shaking his head.

He closed the door and lay back on the bed. Within a minute his stomach was bubbling and gurgling so audibly that Pidge thought he could make out voices among the noises. *How did he know I was so damn hungry?* He got up and walked through the hallway to the parking lot and headed over to the house. He knocked and the man came to the door. "I guess I—" Pidge said.

The man called behind him in Chinese. There were cats everywhere, on every windowsill, on top of an antique chest, on top of a dresser, behind potted plants and porcelain sculptures and many were swirling around the floor. Pidge stepped into the room and they swirled around him, dragging their tails across his legs.

"I don't know, they seem to like you," the man said and his wife came in the room and they both watched him in the sea of cats and laughed. "Many people drop them off out there," the man said, pointing to the parking lot of the motel. "No home so they bring them here. They think we'll be nice to them because of the name of our motel." He smiled warmly.

A large orange cat passed between Pidge's legs and Pidge reached down and touched its back.

39

As usual that night the man swung the door open to Lucy's box, picked up the sanitation bucket, emptied it, and then dropped it back by the door with a plastic container of leftovers. He slammed the door shut. Lucy got up and felt her way over to the food. She always ate it as quickly as possible before it spoiled any more. As she felt for the container, she touched something else next to it, something metal, cylindrical—a flashlight. Her heart skipped a beat. She knew right away that the man had left it by mistake.

Somehow this little mistake seemed like it might lead to her escape. She didn't know how or why. She turned it on and shone the beam around the small metal room. She saw her damp brown army blankets, one of her shoes stuck in the corner, little beads of water hung from the low metal ceiling.

Disappointment sunk into her, deep into her. The flashlight did nothing but show her the impossibility of escape, something that she already knew after feeling every inch of the box in the dark with her fingers.

She sat down on her blankets and began shining the light on her feet; they were red and the skin was peeling off from the moisture. Her dark slacks were stained and torn. Then she lifted her sleeve and put the light on her arm. There were the scars from the hot rod all over her. The burn marks were healing over; some were full of fluid, bubbling up. Now that he had given up trying to get her to talk, he was probably keeping her in the hope that Emma would come looking for her.

Then she lifted her shirt and pointed the light at her stomach. A tattoo of Siamese twins locked together at the hips in a bloody fight with each other, one with an axe raised in one hand, the other a hammer. She gasped and turned out the light. She couldn't believe that she had been carrying this on her body without knowing it.

Suddenly the door kicked open and the man yelled to her to toss over the flashlight. She did as he said and he slammed the door and fastened the padlock.

All was silent again. She lay on her blankets in the pitch-dark, her mind spinning with what she had seen. It was a sketchy tattoo, but it was similar to the mural on Master Howard's trailer.

40

Pidge slowed down as he came up on the yellow house on Scoville Road with the pink birdbath in front. It was Lucy's house all right. There had been no others along this lonely stretch of farmland with a birdbath of any sort, let alone a blue one. The house was exactly as he pictured it, small and nearly square, yellow with blue trim, sitting along a lonely stretch of road among wide fields. The lawn had not been mowed and the driveway was empty. He hit the accelerator and drove right by to get a closer look. The windows and doors looked shut despite the hot day. He turned around in a field. There was something wrong with what he had seen of the house. *Was mail hanging out of her box?* He yelled at his dog to calm down, then drove back to the house. Sure enough he saw that her mailbox was so jammed full that a magazine and two curled letters had fallen into the weeds. Pidge turned onto the driveway, rolling over the long grass that grew through the gravel. His dog sprung over his legs as he opened the truck door. Pulling up his blue jeans, he walked through the long grass toward the closed front door. A lump had grown in his throat as he mounted her cement steps. He couldn't reach the high doorknocker so he used his knuckles to tap just once, not too hard and then he jammed his fingers into his pockets and turned to the yard to wait.

His heart beat quickly. What if she was here? He had no idea what he would say to her.

But nobody came.

Without even turning back to the door, he started down the grass for the truck. Lucy wasn't here, she was off somewhere: on vacation, or maybe she had moved. *I'm an idiot for waiting as long as I did to get here anyway, but that ain't news to me. I was born an idiot.*

"King, let's go!" he yelled from his truck. King was barking in the backyard. Pidge called him again and then got out and walked around the side of the house. The shepherd was jumping up against a tree after a squirrel. "Get over here, you jerk!" Pidge grabbed him by the collar and yanked him good and hard.

The windows back here were shut and so was the wooden door inside the screen door. Something about this did not seem right. He climbed up on the step and looked for the key under the brick that she had told him about.

The moment he opened the door he could smell something putrid and he knew that Lucy had not been back to the house since she had been to the junkyard. He opened the refrigerator door and realized that the refrigerator light was not on; it was warm inside. Milk had soured; vegetables on the shelves were rotting. He tried light switches and determined that the electricity was off in the house. He went through the front door to her mailbox and brought in all her letters and magazines. Some of them were two weeks old, among them was a final notice electric bill. Where was she? Something was definitely wrong.

He paced back and forth, trying to figure out what to do. Finally, he opened the windows and cleaned out the fridge. The thought crossed his mind that Lucy was in trouble, why else would she have left her place like this, food in the fridge, bills unpaid? He opened her front door and sat down on the step. As every car came along the road in front of the house, Pidge got up, expecting to see her.

That night he brought his portable radio in from his truck, put it on the floor near the couch, and lay down to fall asleep.

41

The heat was mounting on the fields and highway as Emma neared the West Virginia border and Derrick County. Her car windows were rolled down. Clouds on the horizon grew darker and other cars turned on their headlights. Emma drove into a downpour and had to pull over to find the switch for the windshield wipers. When she drove on, the car swayed back and forth on the wet road, passing trucks splashed water over her hood. The night before she had prepared a card that said, *I'm looking for a big bear. It is twenty feet tall. It is holding a cup in its hand and it wears a straw hat. Would you know where it is?* She also carried one of Glover's photographs.

She saw signs for Derrick County and got off on the first exit and went to a gas station. In the convenience store connected to the station, she gave the card to a young blond girl not much older than herself. "A big . . . bear?" The girl began smiling after she read the card and then she turned around and showed her a bear barrette in her blond hair.

After ringing up a teenager buying candy, the girl said, "If anyone knows where a big bear would be it would be Sherry's dad, he owns this place." Her hair was very blond and she wore rouge and a thick layer of powder and bright red lipstick. She pulled three packs of cigarettes out of the rack for a woman wearing bright orange curlers and rang them up. "Sherry's dad would know. But he'd have told me ... look," she said and pointed to a section on the shelf on which everything was in the shape of a bear, bear candy, a honey bear, a coffee mug shaped like a bear. "Come back when Sherry's dad is around. He'll be here later."

Emma nodded her head, tried to smile and then stepped out of the store. Just outside a young man with buzz cut and pale skin approached her and put his hand out for the card. Emma gave it to him and he read it. "So, that's what you were asking her. I know where one is, come on," he said and walked toward her car. A duffel bag was slung over his shoulder and a cardboard sign was under his arm.

Realizing that he was a hitchhiker and that he wanted a ride, she shook her head and got in the car without him. "All right, suit yourself," he said annoyed and turned around.

Later that day she was getting back on the highway at another town farther up the road when she saw a man with a cardboard sign that said ALABAMA; his thumb was up. As she passed she looked right into his eyes and realized he was the young man who claimed he knew about the bear. The sun was in his eyes. Without thinking she put her foot on the brake.

He ran down and got in her car. "Just get on the highway, heading south. I'll see it; you can see it from the highway. I saw it last year. Hell, it's down here somewhere."

The young man was already smoking when he said, "You don't mind if I smoke, do you?"

Emma said nothing.

"Are you from around here?"

Emma shook her head.

"You're from New York, aren't you? I saw the plates." She knew he was turned halfway around in his seat, staring at her, and that her nervousness would only make it easier for him to take advantage of her. She wasn't sure what he wanted, only that there was a crazy intensity about him and there would be no way to contradict him. She shrugged her shoulders.

The man stared at her, then burst out laughing. She could see his yellow teeth out of the corner of her eyes. "All you know is there's a bear where you're going, don't you know anything more than that?" He laughed again, not kindly, then said, "Somebody hit you on the head or something? You're downright peculiar, that's what you are. You don't have any idea where you're from except a big old metal bear holding a coffee cup?" He laughed to himself again, then reached for the radio. "Do you mind if I turn it on?"

She reached for his hand to push it away.

"Hey," he said, staring at her. "Have you got something against music? Boy, you've got shattered nerves, that's what you've got all right . . . Look at me, haven't got a dime, haven't got anything but a few cigarettes, and I'm just as happy as can be. Do you know why?" The young man filled the car with nervous energy. Emma began looking to pull off at the next exit if there was a gas station and try to get him out of the car. "I'm happy because Satan doesn't have his claws in me any more, that's why," the man went on. "These people driving around here?" He started pointing at others in their cars. "These people think they're free, but are you free if your master is Satan? Hell no!" he said and began coughing. "You aren't free. No, if that's who you're working for, you're a slave. Satan doesn't have anybody working for him but slaves." He started pointing at people passing them. "Slave . . . slave . . . slave . . . all a bunch of slaves," he said and laughed. "How about you, are you a slave?"

She kept her eyes on the road, and tried not to look afraid of him. He was staring right at her; she could see his gaze out of the corner of her eyes. "Whoa, aren't we the touchy type now," he said. "You're lost, a lost soul. Just as lost as they come." He put his cigarette out in the ashtray and lit up another. "What're they going to be putting a big old bear around here for if there aren't any . . .

Bears are a theme. They don't have that theme in West Virginia because bears are practically extinct. Horses and smelly old cows, that's all they got in this messed up state."

She put on her blinker for an exit. As she turned to get off, he reached over and grabbed the wheel. "You keep driving, you aren't dropping me off in this nasty old town. No way."

She slammed on the brakes; the car came skidding to a stop in the middle of the lane. A car behind her swerved just missing her. "Get driving, you'll get us killed!"

Another car swerved and honked. "Get driving, you damn Satan lover." He grabbed her around the neck, then reached over to yank her out of the seat. His fingers dug into her shirt and the shirt ripped right down the middle.

She heard him jump back against the door. There was silence, he seemed to take a deep breath, then he said, "Look at that! I knew it. Satan herself! Jesus, have mercy. Scales and all!" he yelled, then opened the door and jumped out with his bag.

She heard him screaming at her as she drove down the road. Her shirt had been ripped clean open.

42

Emma took a room in an inexpensive motel that night and ate dinner in a diner across the road. She was thinking about the billboard. In many ways she knew that finding it, if it still existed, would probably lead nowhere. Her only hope was that she'd recognize the land around the sign, perhaps it would trigger memories.

At the crack of dawn she checked out of her motel room and began driving on back roads. Derrick County was the smallest county in West Virginia but there were still hundreds of miles to cover. She began winding along a back road that passed through thick forests, then fields and farms, and then it passed through the midst of a swamp. Suddenly her car stalled and rolled to a stop. Though early in the day the heat was already rising from the dark water. Bullfrogs were croaking and a rasp of cicadas rose from the trees. She tried to start the engine, the motor turning over and over, before it occurred to her to look at the gas gauge. Sure enough the needle pointed to empty. How in the world had she let the tank drain? It frightened her and made her realize how deeply preoccupied she was becoming. There was nothing to do now but lock the car and walk for help.

By the time she came across the first house, the humid heat that seemed to rise in waves from the pavement had soaked her clothes and parched her throat. She climbed a knoll on which sat a small green ranch house. She heard a vacuum cleaner inside. She knocked on the screen door, the vacuum went off and a tall woman with gray curly hair opened the mesh. Emma handed her a note that read, *I ran out of gas.* After reading it the woman wiped her hands on the smock over her housedress and looked down at Emma as if to ponder why she couldn't speak, then she said, "Well, I don't have any gas for you, but I can call a tow truck. Would you like me to do that?" She disappeared in the house and came back with a tall glass of lemonade. "It won't be long. My, you seem awfully young, where are you headed?"

She handed Emma the lemonade and Emma pulled out the card she had prepared about the bear. The woman read it and shook her head. "What on earth for?" she asked.

Despite her desperate state, Emma had been extremely guarded about writing down exactly who she was looking for her. But now she sat on the step and wrote out a more detailed note. *I am looking for a woman, Lucy Thurman. Have you heard of her?*

The woman pondered the name for a long time and Emma wondered what she was thinking. "Always, always put plenty of gas in your car, dear," the woman said. Emma put the cold lemonade to her lips and drank.

Soon the tow truck pulled in the yard and the driver got out, a short man with bristly black and gray hair on the back of his thick neck. His hands were coated with grease. He opened the door of his truck for Emma and told her to get in.

"She doesn't speak," the woman said. The man swung around and stared at Emma and then back at the woman.

"Is that so?" he said.

"She'll write you a note."

"Do you know where her car is?"

The woman shrugged her shoulders. "Down the road a piece, I reckon," she said.

As the driver pulled out of the woman's driveway, he turned to Emma and Emma pointed.

"Do you know her?" he said to Emma.

Emma shook her head.

"Husband's black as the ace of spades." Emma stared at the man. "Sure," he said. "Don't believe me? We got a name for folks like that around here." He stared at Emma as if he was about to say it, then he shifted his truck and turned back to the road.

They found Glover's car and the man poured a canister of gas into it and Emma handed him the card on which she asked about the bear.

Now the man thought about this a minute, scratching his forehead. His fingers left a grease streak across it.

"Hell, you see those big fellows sometimes in front of places. But you never remember them or anything. Go ahead, start your car up and follow me. I might have an idea."

Emma took out a twenty-dollar bill and held it in front of her. "Hell, you don't owe me nothing," the man said. "Come on, just follow me."

She got in Glover's car and followed him down the long straight road past the swamp and turned up over a hill. On the other side he honked and put his greasy arm out his window and pointed and waved. She stopped her car in front of a long aluminum fence with a single strand of barbed wire running along the top and a great big sign on the roof of a house behind the fence that said SANTIE'S JUNK. A pickup truck was sitting in the yard.

43

"Come here," Mr. Santie said and handed her back the card. He was a big, potbellied man with a long pointed beard, red suspenders, and stains on his blue work shirt. He leaned back like a walrus and touched his beard, then turned and walked from the cash register to the back of the store. Emma stood by the door and watched him, unsure of whether to follow him. He turned and waved and she went along reluctantly through the tables piled high with junk—old vacuum cleaners, dusty fans, lamps, and musty rugs. He stopped at the back door that looked out into the yard and pointed.

Under a tall pine tree across yards of rusting lawnmowers, metal chairs and children's toys, Emma saw the bear she was looking for. It was certainly the right one; three stories high, holding a cup of coffee in one hand, though now it was missing the other arm. A rope around its belly secured it to the trunk of the tree and branches shaded the bear's head.

Emma approached it, walking around a refrigerator and stove. She stared up at its hat and pointed ears against the moving clouds of the sky, its big black eyes and long snout. He was not a particularly happy bear, in fact much of his brown paint had been scraped off and the metal beneath it was rusting. Emma had earlier started to doubt her mission, doubt even the possibility of finding this bear that Glover had taken a picture of years ago. But now a sense of optimism and hope came over her, making her hair rise on the back of her neck as if Lucy herself were standing before her.

Mr. Santie crossed the yard in front of her and picked up a rusted saw. "That the one you're looking for, little one?" he said, pointing with the saw. Lost in thought, Emma nodded her head. "I'm not going to sell him, I'm getting kind of attached to him. But you can name your price and I might change my mind."

Emma showed him the photograph that Glover had taken.

The man held the photograph. "Yeah, that's the one. And there's the Sleepy Bear Motor Lodge. Couple of months ago they asked me if I wanted to pay money for this old bear, but I wasn't going to pay nothing for him. I wanted him, but I held out. Then sure enough, they called me and said if I found a way to transport him he was all mine. Well, that was when the trouble started. That big old fellow cost me more to get here than he was worth."

Where did you find him? Emma wrote on a card. The man took it and read it carefully.

"He comes from Gainston, keep right on going up the road, little one. But you won't find nothing up there 'cept a bunch of empty houses."

44

The road to Gainston passed along a shallow, fast-flowing river and empty houses with weather-beaten FOR SALE signs stuck in ragged lawns. Refrigerators and torn La-Z-Boy chairs on porches, cars from another era rusting under the trees. In one muddy yard, Emma saw a great big sow rolling on its back, its small legs kicking the air. Nearby a donkey scratched its neck against a cedar fence post. Potholes shook the car, her tires bumped across the gravel of a washed-out section of road, then she crossed a steel bridge with low arches covered with flaking blue paint. At the far end of the bridge, she saw a faded sign that said, GAINSTON, POP. 201.

She slowed down near the sign. A feeling came over her, as if she had driven into a wave, the world was closing in on her, engulfing her; a weight that had been growing in her stomach grew heavier. Certain feelings that she had been living with for so long became more palpable. Suddenly she understood exactly where she was and what she had been doing all along—she was heading back into the silence, into the heart of what had already nearly destroyed her. She pulled off to the side to gather her thoughts. She could see the street rising up the hill to pass between two, three-story, red-brick buildings. That was the beginning of the main street. She did not recognize these exact buildings, but she knew where she was.

She was tempted to turn around, to drive back. But instead she remained frozen in place, staring at the short hill, the buildings rising against the clouds of the sky. She could make out a very green mountain behind the town. She was certain that if she proceeded on, someone—the man himself or the three or four who worked for him—could see her and snatch her from the car. She began to tremble, but then another feeling came over her, one of relief. She was back at last. It did not matter that she had run away from this place. Even when she was with Lucy she had been carrying this town around inside of her. Now at least she knew that.

She drove up the hill and cruised the main street—parking meters on either side, a brick bank with boarded-up doors, a five-and-dime store, a drugstore. Bushes overran park benches on either side of the street. Farther along, a yellow traffic light was blinking at an intersection. She stopped her car just after she passed this light.

She saw nobody, no people or cars. Two black crows sat on the curved metal overhanging bar of a streetlamp. She started driving again, cruising slowly, cautiously, observing the smashed buildings, the broken, weed-infested sidewalk, moving her wheel to avoid debris that lay strewn across the pavement. Slowly she began to recognize things: the split trunk of a fallen maple tree that had taken telephone wires down with it. A brown metal gate pushed flat onto its back in the yard of an empty Victorian house. Even the windows in the cupola were broken as if children had been playing a rock-throwing game. In front of a long low building with plywood across its windows, she saw a sign that had once said CLOSED FOR GOOD. But somebody had crossed out one of the O's so it read CLOSED FOR GOD.

She stopped her car again. A memory came to her. She had waited in the van while he crossed the street with a can of spray paint in hand and crossed out the O. When he returned, he sat quietly, staring at the new meaning he had given the words. He used to chew on a toothpick, moving it back and forth in his mouth.

He had almost always been quiet around her. In fact, he had been all but silent, choosing his words around her very carefully.

She took several deep breaths, gripped her steering wheel and went on.

Just outside of town, she saw a painted, wooden sign on the sagging roof of a brown building, the Sleepy Bear Motor Lodge. Behind it a billboard was set back in an adjacent field, its advertisement long ago faded off, its rusty metal, insectlike legs collapsing. As she stared at it against the mountain behind it, she vaguely remembered that her photograph had been on the billboard. Now another memory came to her. She had once stood in the motel parking lot while he pointed at her photo which had begun to yellow with age. It must have been years ago.

On the mountain face behind the motel, Emma spotted a strip of white cement, the dam. *He took me up there more than once . . . He liked to walk back and forth up there with me. He said that within the water lay the body of Christ.* She was terrified at the thought of him returning. She now felt as if she were completely surrounded by him; all this was him. Dark yellow sunrays broke through the high, gray clouds and fell against the black mountain.

Farther along, she came across a freshly painted sign that said BIBLE TOWN. This was new and she decided to check it out. A hand-painted arrow pointed down a road that led to a fenced-in construction site. Once she reached the chain-link fence, she saw a sign on a post that read:

COMING SOON: BIBLE CAMP CORRECTIONAL FACILITIES.

For those who have fallen from His grace, a chance to reconstruct their lives through hard work and the intensive study of the perfection of God as set against the imperfection of mankind.

These words triggered the memory of what the man had said to her. "They knew about me in this town. Every single person in this town knew about me. They knew about my father. They even knew what he planned to do with me. But would a single one of them throw me a line? Why not? Why would not a single one of them throw me a line? Now where do you see them? Where have they fled to? Where can they possibly hide? Where does God not reign? And the Lord prepared a great fish to swallow up Jonah!"

Behind the fencing, gravel roads snaked around piles of gray dirt; no other signs of life here. Suddenly Emma spotted a car parked inside the fence. It was quite far away and yet her eyes were drawn to it. Then she saw that it was Lucy's car. There was no mistaking the color and the shape of the tail. She had never seen another like it. It sat next to a pile of gray dirt, the window open and it seemed symbolic of something, though she didn't know of what. The car was alone, out of place. The sight of it struck Emma as fantastic, a stroke of luck that she had come across it. Steep rays of yellow sunlight broke free of the clouds and dappled a mound of dirt behind it.

Suddenly she saw a tall, gangly man coming down the hill on the gravel road through the piles of dirt. She couldn't see his face, but he strode quickly and seemed to be headed for Lucy's car. She backed her car up and drove away from the fence and then pulled into a driveway covered with overhanging evergreen branches. She waited, watching the road between the branches that lay against the windshield. A few moments later, Lucy's car went by and she caught sight of the man driving it. He wore an animal skin hat and he was smoking a cigarette. The car coughed and rumbled by. She was horrified and she froze, gripping the wheel. She wanted to follow the car, but she was incapable of moving. Moments later, she heard the car's rough, unmuffled motor and looked up the mountain to the dam and there it was making its way up the side of the mountain. It was far away, going in and out of the trees, getting smaller. Then it stopped near the dam. She could not see the car for a minute, then it continued on and she saw it again as it climbed over the shoulder of the hill right next to the white cement dam.

She drove out of the driveway and down several roads until she found one leading in the direction of the mountain. It was reckless following this man, but she also felt she had no other choice—she had already entered this strange wave of silence and there was no turning back. The road quickly turned to dirt and followed a gorge and then climbed the mountainside. Finally, she came to a parking lot at the foot of the dam. She could hear the water thundering as it rushed out of the base of the structure. Beyond the small lot was a locked gate with a KEEP OUT sign hanging from it. She stared at the gate, assuming the man must have gone through it with Lucy's car. She was unsure of what to do. She turned around and drove back down the side of the mountain and then turned onto a soft, muddy, logging road that disappeared into the trees. She parked the car, got out and made her way on foot parallel to the road and past the gate, slapping at mosquitoes, lifting branches, and crawling through the quiet cover of the hemlocks. The sound of crashing water below the dam became distant. At the top of a hill she crawled through thick, dead leaves to an old stone wall and looked down a sloping pasture past grazing sheep to the lake.

It was as if she were peering down at another country, a hidden world; this lake and field were enormous.

Near the shore she saw Lucy's car, tiny in the distance, parked in front of a tarpaper shack. A tall mountain rose behind the black water that was fed by the river on one side and ended at the squared-off shore of the dam on the other. In the water she could see buoys floating, barrels with yellow rope wrapped around them.

She sat down in the oak leaves and watched. She could feel the silence again, the silence that the man had imposed on her. It was as if the area up here was even more infected by it than in the valley. Now she remembered when the man had stopped speaking to her. It was a year or so after he had taken her from her parents. He stopped looking at her for a while, then he stopped speaking to her altogether and whenever she spoke he didn't answer her. Eventually, he must have punished her whenever she spoke. She did not remember the punishments, but she did remember understanding that her silence was necessary for her safety.

The sun went down behind the mountain and the reflection of the red sky shimmered on the lake and faded as shadows crept among the trees. She began to recall this lake more clearly . . . Before it was entirely filled with water, she stood next to the man on its shore throughout a summer and watched the level rise.

He had been satisfied by the rising of the water. *Some day you and I will descend into the heavens through this holy water for herein lies the body of Christ. You are important to Him and so shall I be.* Then he had taken her below the dam and showed her the gates; there were seven of them, brass-colored. Above them were metal cables. *As Christ receives us, these gates shall rise and so shall He flood the entire earth.*

Songbirds grew few in number until a single bird was calling high in the tree above Emma. It, too, stopped and soon a chorus of crickets chimed around her. Geese flew up from the lake's surface. A soft yellow light flickered on in the cabin window.

Emma did not know what to do. She could not seem to leave the sight of the shack with the dark silhouette of Lucy's car parked in front.

Suddenly a car door slammed shut and the headlights of Lucy's car hit the trees above her head as it climbed the rutted drive leading out of the area. The car passed near her and went down the hill and she heard the door slam again as the man passed through the gate. Then she could hear him driving down the mountain road, getting farther away. Except for the crickets, all was silent and now the shack itself was dark and she wondered if Lucy was inside.

45

Emma began walking and then running down the bumpy field to the dark little shack. The stars but not the moon were out and bright constellations shimmered on the lake. A night bird's call echoed against the far mountain. As she neared the small house she could see debris, rubber tires in the grass, a crumpled truck fender, an upside down wheel barrow without its wheel. On the far side, she came up to a screen door held fast by a loop of string and a nail. Standing very still and holding her breath, she listened for somebody inside. She wanted to speak, to call out for Lucy, to see if she was locked inside. She held her throat and concentrated on making a noise. Her throat constricted under her fingers, she pushed air, but nothing but a groan came out.

Unhooking the string, she stepped inside into darkness and stood quietly among the pungent smells of sweaty clothes, stale beer, pine pitch, and tarpaper. She spotted a candle and matches in the starlight from the window. Lighting the candle, she cupped the flame and walked across the room with it, the shadow of her fingers against the studs and plywood that made up the wall. Above her head a green sleeping bag hung over the edge of a sleeping loft. Emma held her breath to listen, perhaps Lucy was tied up somewhere in here. But she heard only the small lake waves against the shore. She looked down at the table covered with dirty paper plates, forms, a small chain. All of a sudden among the debris she saw a small snapshot of a face. It was at the edge of the desk; it was torn and wrinkled in places. The face was so familiar that the very sight of it stunned and disoriented her.

It was her own face, from two or three years back; her hair was cropped short. Candlelight flickered over it.

She knew she should stop staring at it but she could not help it; questions popped through her mind. The background included part of a black van and a mountainous vista that she did not recognize at all, nor did she have a recollection of having close-cropped hair. She could not see below the neckline and so she did not know if she had yet been tattooed. Her expression was almost smiling, an eerie smile that one could read as happy or melancholy or pensive or even afraid. She realized on some level as she was looking at the picture that she was actually looking through a window into a room inside of herself that she had not gone in for a long time. There were clouds in the blue sky over the mountains that she must have seen at one time. And the person standing behind the camera, she must have seen him, too. This room inside the snapshot would surely be connected to other rooms inside of herself, rooms and hallways and entire cities that she may have been to and then lost the memory of.

She began to put it in her pocket. *Drop the picture, put it down where you found it and go.* Again she seemed to freeze in place; there was no longer a reason for her to be looking up here. Then her eyes fell to a name on a flyer. *Pastor Grecco's Television Schedule, Channel 43*. The name Grecco rang a bell. *Was that his name?* She saw a list of programs and times beneath it. She backed to the door, replaced the extinguished candle and stepped out of the shack, hooking the string back on the door. Then she was running for the road that would lead her down to her parked car. She could hear the river rushing through the mountain gorge, the smell of pines rising in the mist; her nose was wet with the smell. The windows of the car were covered with white dew; she got in, turned on the wipers and drove away.

She drove back along the road near the river to a motel she had seen. It was no more than a strip of rooms and a house with flaking white paint. Emma rang the office bell. A woman came through her messy living room to answer it, scolding a boy who ran across the back of the room in just his underwear. From a dining table covered with plates of spaghetti, the woman picked up a form. "One night?"

The copied form she laid before Emma was fuzzy and almost illegible. Emma signed it and paid for the room. Outside, she walked on the crumbling sidewalk, passing several windows with drawn curtains. A television blared from behind one door and the smell of cooking hamburger leaked out of a cracked-open door.

She entered her bedroom, locked the door, and sat down to consider the photograph of herself. She did not remember the actual moment, but now she remembered that the man, Grecco, had taken her on a trip, a sightseeing trip and had photographed her repeatedly with a cheap, Polaroid camera. She had many miles of travelling behind her, highways, national landmarks, and now she could see a shimmering view of the ocean from some high cliff and then later a meal in a roadside restaurant. At the time the picture was taken, she had already lost her speech and now for some reason she was sure that some of her body had already been marked with the black scales. Yes, by the time the picture was snapped the wave of silence had already risen around her. *Perhaps he had yet to show me to his people.* Then a sudden frightening thought came into her head with great clarity. *He knows I'm coming back. He knows what she means to me and he knows I'll be back to try to get her.*

When she finally fell asleep—and it took her many hours to do this—she had a dream where she saw somebody slowly descending on their back from the sky. It was Lucy. She landed in water without so much as a splash. And then she was floating, her eyes closed, her arms out. She was dead and Emma knew that it had taken many weeks to kill her. The current of the river in which she lay spun her body at strange angles. The sun on Lucy's shoulder reflected sharply into Emma's eye and blinded her, and then she heard somebody laughing and saw a man on his knees looking straight up at the sky, his hands in prayer; he seemed like a holy man but instead of praying he was laughing. And she saw why the light from Lucy had blinded her: Lucy's body was covered with silver scales. Hers were not tattooed scales; they were real, silver fish scales and she was shedding them—some of them were floating around her like feathers of a bird that had been shot.

At five in the morning her eyes opened on their own. She'd been aware of voices through the wall, but now her room was silent. She took a deep breath and tried to recover from the dream she had just lived through. The conversation of a man and a woman broke out into an argument, then later turned to laughter. A handwritten note taped to the plastic wood top of the television said, *If the picture don't come on, bang the top.* She turned it on and the screen filled with static and then she hit it with her palm until the picture came clear. A preacher in a white robe with hair as white as snow was speaking. *"You've got your welfare mothers, single parent families, your homer-sexuals and your prostitutes and your . . ."* She flipped to Channel 43.

She saw a preacher walking back and forth in front of a choir. Then the camera moved close on his face.

Emma put her hand over her mouth. She fell to her knees. *It was him, the man!*

Then, almost instinctively, she swung around as if he was in the room behind her. She turned back to the screen.

There was no mistaking it, it was the man who had imprisoned her. He was short and wore a black ministerial suit. "The world is a frightening place, is it not?" The lilt of his voice was familiar. "You come into it through two parents: father and mother. That's about all you know, am I right?" He paused and walked quickly back and forth in front of a fireplace and mantle with a white cross resting on it. She knew his walk, his small white hands. "But every once in a while you get to thinking, where were you before your parents conceived of you, before that little seed and egg met up to kick things off?" He tightened his thin lips. "In the body of another? Out in space somewhere?" He sipped his water. "No, no, not through space, not through reincarnation, either. I'll tell you where you came from, yes I will." His voice rose. "You came here through a river, you were no more than that water when you arrived here. Nothing in this universe was you except the water of that strange and beautiful river. Let me tell you folks, that river is a miracle. The river of Jesus Christ, Our Lord. That river is not merely the taste of life; it is the very essence of life itself." The picture vanished and Emma banged the television again, then she hit it harder, then harder. Still no picture. Again she hit it. Somebody started knocking on her door.

"You woke us up in there!" a man's voice said.

She pressed herself against the wall.

"Are you listening?" The man started wrestling with her doorknob. "Who are you? Who do you think you are? You woke us up, now calm the *hell* down in there or we're going to get the manager and kick your ass out! God-damn it!" The man kicked her door and walked away.

Emma turned off the television and stood in the middle of the room. She felt like gravity had tripled and was pulling her down into the worn industrial carpeting.

46

Just after dawn Emma returned to her place behind the stone wall. Smoke rose from the stovepipe chimney of the shack and the smell of frying bacon drifted over the dew-covered pasture. What else could she do but to sit and watch and study the movements of this man? At one point he stepped outside to dump a pot of dirty water, then he dropped the pot and unzipped his fly to urinate in the grass. Emma turned her eyes away. When she looked back, she saw him cross his dock and step into his rowboat. He rowed out toward the middle of the lake toward one of the barrels. He stopped next to it, pulled up the rope from underneath and Emma saw him examining something at the end of it. Then he lowered it back in the water and picked up his oars again and began to row. There was a light mist on the still water, the oars echoed against the side of the boat, ripples fanned out behind him. He grew smaller and smaller until she could barely see him against the trees of the opposite shore. Then she noticed a clearing on the other side and something dark and angular, probably the roof of a house. She closed her eyes. She knew exactly where this was. This was where Grecco lived. She had known this all along, but she had not been able to bring herself to acknowledge it. That was the side of the lake where she had been kept.

She rose to her feet, dizzy from sitting for so long but determined to go to the house. Over there was the very heart of her problem, her sadness, her horror, her loneliness, and there she imagined Lucy to be. The irony did not elude her. The very person who had helped spring her from the hell inside of her was probably now inside the hell itself. She had the feeling that she herself was underwater, deeper underwater than she'd been so far. She crossed the top of the dam quickly, looking out over the town. Then she followed the grassy shore to the trees and began to traverse the underbrush and tributary streams, keeping the edge of the lake in view all along. She swatted bushes and branches out of the way. At one point she stomped through a marsh and her shoes and slacks became caked with black mud. Directly across the lake from the shack, she saw a barn in a meadow. Beyond the meadow of long grass and wild-flowers, she saw the side of a white Colonial-style house. It was his house, she did not need to contemplate it. She knew exactly where she was. Staying under the cover of trees, she climbed a rise behind the house, then lay on a rocky outcropping and peered down into the backyard of the compound. The house was two stories tall with black shutters. Between a second barn and the house, she saw a white van and a dark blue car with a crushed top that looked like it had been hit with a sledgehammer. She studied this car: a navy-blue American sedan with a square front and rear end.

Suddenly it dawned on her that this was Grecco's car, the one that had rolled off the side of the road. Emma's mind began to race as she looked at the crumpled metal. An even greater sense of fear came over her. She dug her fingers deep into the earth. As her eyes moved from the car to the house, she began to remember things clearly: a rubber tire on a rope that she herself had sat on hung from the high branch of an oak tree in the yard. She recalled this old tire; he had strung it up for her in a moment of good will. After it rained, the inside of the hollow tire would fill with water that splashed out when she swung it. A vegetable garden in the yard with many tall leaning stakes covered with vines was familiar. She had once stood by while Grecco had picked tomatoes from the vines and told her about the apple in the Garden of Eden. *The apple is the same as the word.*

The door of the house swung open and out walked the man from the shack, followed by another man, a short, middle-aged man wearing dark glasses, Grecco. She sunk down closer to the rocky viewpoint and held her breath. There was a rising sense of unreality to all of this. It was unbelievable that she had found him, unbelievable that she was back here. It was her will that had brought her here, but it was impossible not to believe that he had played a part in it. He had drawn her here. As she watched him walk with his companion, she wondered if he could not sense her very presence above him right now. Her throat was swollen and tight with fear. The fact that she was back in this hellish place was a fate that she could not deny, a fate stronger than she was.

The two men went into the barn and came out with a red gas can and a weed cutter and disappeared down the driveway behind the barn. She could hear the rising buzz of the weed cutter in the distance. She looked at the sky. White clouds in the otherwise sunny sky had gathered together and darkened, casting a grayish pall over the grounds.

47

Waiting for dark for what seemed like several days, not just one, Emma lay in brambles, staring down through the tangled branches at the house. The clouds continued to gather. Where exactly was the meat locker? Wasn't it below the pasture, below the house? Every so often her thoughts would start to spin and spiral almost out of control, the sense of unreality would take over, a feeling of helplessness, as if she would remain in this spot forever, unable to get her bearings enough to get to her feet. She would close her eyes and calm herself down, collect herself, use her head and focus on what she had come this long distance to do—to find Lucy. She suddenly had a kind of premonition: If she did find Lucy, Sue would cling to her like a helpless child. *I must simply take her hand and run with her, that's all.* She fought the feeling of inertia that fear kept bringing about.

Suddenly she saw the two men come up from their work cutting brush, put the tools away, and walk into the house. Moments later the man from the shack came out carrying what looked like a water jug and a plastic container, disappeared around the back of the house and returned, empty-handed. Could that possibly have been for Lucy? She was sure now that the locker was on the other side of the house, closest to the lake. The man said something through the screen door and then left in the direction of the path that had brought him up to the house.

Emma heard thunder in the far distance; rain was on its way. The sun set behind the hills and darkness rose up from the earth around her. In a way, she welcomed the idea of rain, the change would bring her down to earth. The rope of the swinging tire disappeared into the gloom; a light came on in the big house, the door into the barn became black with shadows, and finally she could not see the clouds of the sky nor even the rocks just yards in front of her. She continued to wait; more lights came on in the house, then a shade came down in one room. Grecco was settling in.

A light rain began to fall, wetting her face and soaking the ends of her hair so that it dripped down the back of her turtleneck shirt. It was indeed a relief, shocking her out of her crazy thoughts. She climbed to her feet and began to move. Once she began to move she felt all of one piece, she could do this, she could do what she had come to do and get away. She skirted the property, staying low behind brush and trees, getting wetter every time she touched a leaf. On the other side of the barn, she could make out a pasture, a vague outline of thistles and a barbed wire fence. Carefully, she followed the border of the pasture until she came to a gate directly on the other side at the bottom of the hill. At once she realized she was moving according to instinct, according to memories she was no longer in touch with. She was sure the meat locker was down here somewhere.

For several yards she followed a muddy path to a clearing with tree stumps and unruly brush. In the corner of this clearing, she saw something vaguely metallic, rectangular, and wet. She moved up against its metal side and touched it. At last she had found the thing the image of which had floated in her mind for so long. It was real and her fingers were against it.

She moved to one end of the meat locker, looking for the door. Grasping a leverlike handle, she pulled gently. It didn't move. She pulled harder. Again it didn't move. Too dark to see clearly, she felt around the lever until her fingers caressed a padlock. She yanked at the lock, but it was clasped shut. No doubt it was securing the door. Rain fell lightly on her face. She knocked as loud as she dared, but thunder prevented her from hearing any possible response.

She knocked again and waited. The sharp smell of urine caught her nostrils among smells of rain and earth. She knocked once more, then put her ear to the metal. She thought she heard a faint tapping.

She knocked back. More tapping came from inside. Rain fell harder between the high branches onto the flat roof of the metal box. With her ear to the metal, Emma thought she heard a voice inside, faint and frail.

The downpour soaked her hair so that water began to run down her forehead, into her eyes and over her chin. Her turtleneck and jeans clung tightly to her skin.

She found a fallen branch and lifted it to the door handle and tried to wedge it open, but the branch bent under pressure. Now she remembered a tool shop in the barn adjacent to the house. Maybe there was a hacksaw, something that could cut through the lock.

The rain sent a chill through her body as she climbed through the woods to the edge of the property closest to the barn. Lights were on in most of the windows of the big house and now an outdoor spotlight illuminated the sheets of slanting raindrops.

Entering the ground level of the barn she heard breathing that made her heart jump and she froze. She heard another breath and a snort: the cows had come in out of the rain and were lying in the hay. She could smell them in the dark and feel their body heat and hear them chewing their cuds. The thought of these placid creatures calmed her down—they were lying in the hay, chewing their cuds, breathing, swallowing, digesting.

She remembered now of once being afraid of these cows. Back

when she was living here it was one of those fears that had remained even though so much of her had become numb. She had stopped fearing Grecco, she had stopped fearing water and missing her parents, but she had become afraid of cows. She crossed around their warm bodies, leading with one foot. Faint light from the house came through the windows of the tool room, enough so that Emma could make out the door and the worktable. On the table, among screwdrivers and hammers, she spotted a thin strip of metal with tiny, sharp teeth. It was not merely luck that she had found this hacksaw blade, something inside of her, some long forgotten memory must have led here. Her fingers grasped it.

The rain outside lightened again and a gentle breeze sent a deep chill through her body as she made her way back to the clearing of stumps where the box rested. She put the blade to the padlock and drew it down. Afraid that the noise might carry as far as the house, she tried shorter strokes. She scraped her knuckles and the ends of her fingers as she worked. Her forearms stiffened with pain. Finally the handle broke off and fell into the dirt and Emma dropped the saw, swinging the door open.

A rush of warm air came from the dark box and with it the powerful odor of a human being in captivity. It was a different odor than that of the lion house or monkey house in a zoo, it had a different, a more terrible sadness about it. She stepped inside onto the slippery floor. "Oh," she heard in a frail voice. She moved toward the person, one step at a time, her hands out as if she were pushing through the sadness itself. "Oh." Emma got down on the metal floor on her knees. She felt a damp, almost wet blanket, then she put her hand out and felt a wrist and then a hand.

On her knees, Emma moved forward and grasped a thin body, a woman. She was different, thinner but she was Lucy, unmistakably Lucy. She pulled her tight against her chest and put her neck next to hers and began to hug her and squeeze her. She could feel the wetness of Lucy's body and the wetness from her eyes. Holding back her tears, Emma tried to lift Lucy, but Lucy was frail and thin and did not seem capable of standing up. Realizing the pain that Lucy was in, Emma suddenly fell down sobbing and pulled herself against her, kissing her neck and shoulders and finally burying her face under her chin and squeezing her thin, damp frame. She would never let go, never, never, never would anyone separate them, not again, not ever again, her face was buried against Lucy's matted hair under her neck.

And now she wanted to say something to her, to speak to her, to tell her what was in her heart, what had been in her heart for so long. She closed her eyes, she could feel the words rising up inside of her, they were coming up from the depth of her soul.

"Oh," Emma said. "Oh, Lucy."

48

Rain was beating hard on the locker roof. A gust of wind rose and slammed shut the door and the noise roused Emma from her embrace of Lucy. She scrambled to her feet and pushed on the door, but it wouldn't move. She threw her shoulder against it, but it still would not move. Panicking, she pushed as the floor kept slipping out from under her. Finally, she stood back and at that moment the door opened on its own, as if the wind had done it.

But there was a man behind it and from his squat, wide-shouldered silhouette against the trees, Emma could tell it was Grecco. He grabbed her by the collar and dragged her outside with such sweeping force that she could not fight back. Placing his wet hand snugly over her mouth, he shone a flashlight in her eyes and then continued dragging her up the trail toward the house. She tried to suck through her nostrils, but they were so clogged with rainwater that she choked. He handcuffed her to a gate near the barn and went back down the hill to take care of Lucy. Emma struggled against the handcuffs that held her fast to the gate.

"Help!" she yelled. It was as if somebody else was yelling, not herself. And yet it was *her* voice. She screamed out again for help, loudly and distinctly. The rain seemed to suck the sound away from her.

He came back, unfastened her, and dragged her toward the house. She fought against him, biting and kicking at him. He pulled her in through the front door of the house and then across a living room to a metal door that he kicked open with his foot and then he unfastened her handcuffs and tossed her down and slammed the door. With all her might, she threw herself against the metal door and then slammed her palms against it over and over.

49

The light went out overhead and the long narrow room was cast into pitch-dark, not the slightest crack of illumination showed. Emma backed away from the door, found the bed with her hands and sat down. She was trembling, she could not stop her trembling. At last she had found Lucy, had seen that she was still alive, had even held her in her arms and tasted and kissed her. Lucy's smell was still in her nostrils.

After settling down, her legs wrapped in a blanket and her hair drying crisply against her head, Emma touched her chest and throat and considered that her voice was back. For years there had been a kind of wall between herself and her body. Not that she didn't feel things; it was more like she didn't feel that her bodily sensations were hers or if they were hers they had to pass through a thick wall to get to her. They were muted and distant, and somehow always sad. Now she could feel her muscles aching; her throat burned from screaming; her hands were sore from pounding against the metal door. She had the distinct feeling that she had somehow descended into her body after being torn from it for years.

She heard Grecco walk away outside the room; she knew that he would try to bring the numbness back inside of her, disarm her and force the darkness and silence upon her again. To counter this, she got off her bed, paced back and forth, and spoke out loud as if to prove she was now stronger; she could speak, her body, her throat, her vocal cords were her own.

"Help us, somebody help us," she said quietly into the dark. It was strange hearing herself; her voice was higher pitched than it had been inside her head, reverberating against her chest, echoing against the walls of the room, and yet she was closer to it, more a part of it. "Somebody help us."

As if he had heard her, Grecco opened the door a crack, emitting only the dimmest light from outside and slipped in, closing it tight behind him. She crouched and pressed herself between the sink and the toilet in the corner. He stood still in the darkness near the door, breathing, shifting his weight. It was so quiet in the room that she thought she could hear him swallow. As she waited for his next move, she realized there would be no next move. He had done this before. Stood there in the dark. She waited as he too waited across the room from her. He did not speak; his breathing was nearly silent. Finally he opened the door and left, locking it—as always—three times behind him.

The light came on again and she saw something he had left behind. He must have moved silently from the door to the first table. On it was a clear plastic cup of liquid. She brought it to her nose and smelled it. It was only water. "You can't hurt me any-more," she said and poured it onto the rug.

Later he opened the door and stepped inside and Emma crouched under the sink, waiting, remembering this strange ritual, as if he was letting her absorb his mere presence and making her contem-plate his power over her. After he left and the lights came on, she discovered another cup of water on one of the tables. She remem-bered he had done this before and she knew what it was about. He was laying the groundwork for her to submit to his will entirely. *Not just my body but my thoughts.*

Once again he returned and again Emma scrambled for the back corner. Grecco now stood just inside the room, holding something in one hand, something steaming. Hiding most of his face were dark, wrap-around sunglasses. He stepped farther into the room and she could see he wore his black slacks, part of his ministerial suit. He set a steaming microwave dinner in its tray and a plastic spoon on the table nearest the door and backed out of the room.

Still in its plastic, the dinner was some sort of baked chicken, mashed potatoes and beans, and a Jell-O dessert. Emma was so hungry she couldn't wait for it to cool and lifted a forkful of potatoes to her mouth and burnt her tongue.

Suddenly she spit out what was in her mouth and backed away. *I won't eat unless I know that Lucy is eating, too.*

Gathering courage, she sat back against the wall of the bed, her hands across her shins and waited for him. The door opened and he walked over to the food and saw what she had spit out and turned his head and looked at her through the black glasses, pausing.

"Where is she?" Emma said. She could feel the sharp contractions in her chest and throat. Sweat beaded under Grecco's nose; he seemed as shocked as she was that she had spoken again.

"Are you feeding her?" Her voice felt closer to her now, a new-found tool, a weapon. She would use it to make him do things.

He did not move. He seemed stunned by the sound of her voice.

She grew braver. "I'm not touching anything until I know she's eating." She was defiant now, sure that her newborn strength would save her and Lucy somehow.

Grecco left the room, slamming the door behind him, then turning out the lights over her head.

Over the next few days Emma would not touch any of the sandwiches or bowls of cereal that he dropped off for her. Each time he returned to clear the uneaten food, he appeared more frustrated and angry and Emma became hopeful.

"I won't eat until I know she's okay," Emma stated, feeling the words rising from her chest and up her throat, feeling her own strength, despite her dizziness from the lack of food. He seemed to whither before her eyes and before her words; he seemed unprepared for her in this state.

"I can talk now, he can't do anything to me as long as I can talk," she said aloud to herself when she was alone.

He opened the door with a paper plate of scrambled eggs in his hand and set them down next to her on the bed and reached into his belt for a black handgun. He aimed it at her forehead and motioned for her to eat. She stared at the gun, surprised, slowly realizing its gravity.

She reached for the food, then she stopped herself; her confidence came back.

"No," she said. The strength was still in her chest. He came closer to her and brought the gun slowly up to her forehead. "No," she said again.

She heard a click as he lifted the hammer. Out of the corner of her eye, she could see his arm was trembling. She clasped her hands in front of her.

"You show me that my friend is all right. Otherwise I'm not eating," she said. "Get out of this room, right away." She got up from the bed and turned her back to him in the corner of the room, crossing her arms in front of her. "You can't make me eat! Now get out!"

He grabbed her from behind, one hand around her neck; the other brought scrambled eggs to her mouth and mashed them between her lips. She snapped at him with her teeth, gnashing the side of his hand, tearing into his flesh. He yelled, yanking his hand back, shaking it, and then running out of the room and slamming the door behind him.

After he was gone, she remembered something that she had known all along that must have given her confidence: shooting her would go against everything this man lived for. He lived to drown her. To drown her? she thought. To drown *with* her, to deliver her and thereby deliver himself. She began considering his logic. If he drowned with her, they would both be saved and she would be anointed the daughter of Christ, the granddaughter of God. Another memory came to her. *He's got to finish me first, for Christ won't accept me otherwise. I am his life's work.*

But there was something inside of Grecco, Emma knew, that had not really wanted to finish her. For months, maybe years, he had procrastinated, added new scales to her arms and ankles but left parts of her back and buttocks bare; he had purposely left her unfinished. *He must be afraid of it, too, afraid of his body in that great big wave of water he plans to release from the dam, afraid that it will not find its way to God, as he wants it to.* She began considering ways of talking him out of it.

After a day went by without a visit from Grecco, the door swung open and this time Emma saw the tall, lanky man from the shack, whose name she had remembered was Johnny Ranch, in his baggy jeans and an untucked camouflage shirt, his graying hair pulled back in a ponytail. "Get up, the boss has got something to show you," he said.

"Get out!" She knew right away that her words were not effective with this man.

"Shut up, *kid!*" He grabbed her by one arm, pulled her to her feet. She yanked away from him and he came at her again, locking his thumb and fingers around her wrist.

"Leave me alone!"

"Shut up, the boss's got something to show you."

He brought her to the threshold of the door and Emma screamed. It occurred to her that they had done something terrible to Lucy. Then she saw her across the room lying on the couch, a blanket covering her thin legs. Emma struggled, but Ranch's grip merely tightened. "Talk to her," Ranch said to Lucy.

"Emma, you eat. It's our only chance."

"Is he feeding you?"

"Yes he is. But he said he'd kill us both if you don't eat," Lucy said, her small eyes in her gaunt face; the bone of her nose showed. When she spoke, her lips only half covered her teeth.

"Enough chitchat, sinners," Ranch said. "Get the message, little one?" He dragged Emma back into her room. She screamed and kicked at him, but she was so lightheaded that she fell on her back as she tried.

After she was locked away inside, the door pushed open and Grecco set down several plastic glasses filled with different kinds of juices. As soon as he was gone, Emma started to drink them. Then she was eating again, regaining her strength.

50

To Emma this darkness that Grecco left her in for hours was as familiar as breathing. For weeks back when he had first kidnapped her, she would sit in it, listening only to the occasional shuffling of footsteps outside her door and the voices of the men that came from upstairs during their meetings. Grecco was a televangelist. Occasionally he still liked to work under a tent close to an audience. He once told Emma that working close to an audience generated ideas, kept him sharp, kept him in touch with his audience. Television was another thing altogether. It had opened up worlds to him. Sometimes after a show so much money poured in through the mail that for years he didn't know what to do with it. Then the Lord had told him what to do with it and he had built the dam and established an entirely different church than the one viewers saw on television. Among its members were a devoted group of young men. He treated them like his sons and they treated him like their father. Grecco had met these men at a Bible boot camp that he was connected to. They were repeat offenders, there was little they could do to stop themselves from committing their crimes, and Grecco had solved their problems for them by giving them a reason to go on doing what they liked to do. A dozen or so of these men came to him on certain week nights for their own private sermon. With these men he shared his true beliefs and Emma knew that she herself played an important part in them. *Water is the body of Christ*; she had overheard this many times. One time he had lined up his men at the edge of the dam and brought Emma out, a robe covering her skin. It was a cold, windy day and she had begun to shiver as Grecco stood with his men looking from the valley to the water behind him, his hand resting on her shoulder. He spoke the Greek words *Iesous Christos Theou Huios*, then said, "Jesus Christ, Son of God, Savior." He asked the men to gather around and then he lifted her sleeve a little. *So innocent as to be nearly one with the body of Christ.* Perhaps it was the closest he had come to showing his inner circle exactly what he was up to with her.

But then late in her captivity, near the time when she escaped, he began following yet another ritual. It seemed counter to the privacy by which he treated her. Perhaps it was merely another delay tactic. He would tie her to a seat facing his van door and drive with the man from the shack to "girl bars," usually far away. After parking in the rear of the bar, he would go inside sometimes for an hour and then come out with one of the customers, somebody he had met and lured out to see his own show in the van. After collecting five dollars from the customer, Grecco would open the van door to reveal her tied to the chair. Then he would step up and yank the robe from her shoulders, exposing her bare flesh, her tattooed scales.

"All I'm asking you for is your thoughts," he'd say. And once he heard this person's thoughts, the man from the shack would appear from behind the van with a tank and gas mask. *Cleaning up the filth*, he called it.

Now as she waited for Grecco's next move, Emma continued to speak out loud to herself frequently. Her voice was her newfound self. As long as she spoke to herself she could keep him out of her thoughts. *When Christ sees you, He shall anoint you and we shall be saved, we shall have eternal life.*

51

She heard the keys in the locks. She didn't know whether it was day or night. She counted the number of seconds it took him to open her door. Then the light came on and he slipped inside, holding a pair of handcuffs up. "No!" she said as he approached her. The windows were open in the living room and she could smell freshly cut grass outside. He came at her with the silver handcuffs. "No!" He slapped the cuffs on her quickly and just as quickly he pulled a bandanna across her mouth and gagged her. She bit at it and tried to kick at him, but he held her from behind firmly. Her words were muffled through the cloth.

He led her outside into the sun; there were but a few white clouds across the valley and she could see the parking lot of crushed white stone. To her right she saw the black rubber tire hanging from the rope over grass. A lawn mower was running somewhere on the property, getting quieter, then louder. They crossed the white parking lot to a mown trail and headed up the hill. Emma saw where they were headed, the windowless barn. She stopped. "No," she said through the gag, she sucked air in through her nostrils.

"Go on," he said, "And shut up." He pushed her on. She remembered this second barn, the barn on the hill, and she knew what it was for. He thrust her through the threshold of the door. It was cooler in here; there were high ceilings and she could smell the dried wood of the rafters and floor. Then, across the big room, Emma saw the high narrow bed with straps, the doctor's bed. Again he pushed her.

"No, no," her mouth was full of cloth.

"Quiet," he said. "Lie down. It's going to take two sessions anyway." He forced her to lie down on her back, then secured her wrists and ankles. These tight straps so restricted her movement that she suddenly panicked and began writhing on the cot, moving her belly up and down. Grecco waited, watching her. "Are you done?" He approached her and she moved crazily again and he waited. When Emma was exhausted, Grecco came up behind her and began combing her hair, carefully untangling it. She jerked her head forward and he yanked it back and continued drawing the comb through until the roots became sore. Then he wheeled a small table over next to her on which she saw the tattoo needle. The sight of this instrument did not inspire fear at first, just a heavy black sadness.

He grabbed her hand and pressed it to the hard mattress. Slowly he brought the needle down to the edge of the row of scales inside of her wrist. She jerked her hand back a little, but he held it firmly, pressing with his weight and waiting for her to stop moving. Then the needle came down again, right where the hand and the arm joined. Pain shot up her arm to her head; the familiar pain jolted her.

He was indeed filling in the few bare swatches of skin on her body, completing this project of scales. This unmarked skin was somehow the only connection that she had with the far past when her body had been clear. She began to cry like a child. Another memory of him taking her out on the dam came to her. It was around sunset, the shadow of the mountain lay over the lake and the water was calm. *After you and I are one with Christ, Johnny will open these gates and we shall travel in a great wave into the Kingdom of Heaven.*

"One more session," he said later, when he began loosening the straps.

52

At dawn the next day, Grecco dropped a bathing suit on Emma's bed and told her to put it on. Then he left her alone. Emma quickly changed into the suit, pulling her clothes on over it. She knew there would be no choice in the matter anyway. A moment later Grecco came in. "Good, good, you've got it on?" He was becoming more confident, even cocky around her and loose with his words considering he almost never spoke to her for years. She didn't like it. He walked up to her, holding the handcuffs and locked her wrists together, then brought her out the door and down the lawn below the pasture. In the woods she could see across the clearing of tree stumps to the metal box where he kept Lucy. The sun shone on the dew-covered box that sat to the side of the clearing, under the trees. Briar bushes grew against one wall. She heard a bird, a blue jay calling from a branch just above it. Grecco led Emma through a stand of pines down the final hill to the lake and dock.

On the wooden dock that flexed under their feet, Grecco unlocked her wrists and pointed for her to take off her clothes to her bathing suit. She stared at him and shook her head.

"No," she said. She felt he was getting the better of her, his techniques were wearing her down, the tattooing had taken a lot out of her. Now her own voice, her ability to talk, which she had counted on, was failing her. "No," she said hoarsely, mustering her strength.

He shook his head as he looked at her, perhaps realizing that she had become incrementally more resigned to her fate. He seemed to smile at her. "Do you want to swim with a gag on?" he said. "If you don't, strip to the suit."

She stripped to her bathing suit. He stood there looking her body up and down, admiring it, breathing hard as if to absorb the dark beauty. He fell into a trance and for an instant Emma thought she could do something to him, kick him below the belt, knock him off the dock. But suddenly he collected himself and pointed at the water. "Go on, get in."

It was almost as if some old memory of what she'd been trained to do took over. Emma walked to the end of the dock, slipped into the cool water and began wading out over the rocky bottom. Finally, she leaned forward and began to swim. She heard him behind her. He had gotten in the rowboat tied to the dock and now he followed her, rowing and watching her. She turned and saw his dark figure standing up, his legs against the gunwales, an oar in his hand, the boat gliding silently behind her. "Like a dream," he sighed. After a while she tired and treaded water, breathing heavily, then she tried to lie on her back to catch her breath.

"Return," he called, pointing toward shore. She was so tired she thought she might not make it. She turned around in the water and sidestroked with all the energy she had left.

Near shore he went ahead and waited on the bank, watching her barely make it in. She crawled up on the grassy bank and fell against the ground on her stomach. He stood above her, looking down.

53

Late that afternoon he brought her back up to the doctor's bed and began to work on the rest of her skin. She struggled at first, then stopped. The needle viciously pricked her ankle, piercing bone. He covered the top of her foot and around her toes, and then he came up to the back of her bare hand. The ink dove into her veins and crawled up her body like a dirty worm. He was meticulous, patient, standing back from his work frequently, sometimes sighting her from across the room, the pattern of the scales was crucial, crucial to Grecco's entry into heaven. "You must reflect the perfection of Christ Himself," he said to her.

Late in the afternoon, he took a break, leaning against a table, eating a cornbeef sandwich, mustard on his lips, watching her. She could hear him chewing, masticating, drinking and swallowing. A boorish confidence had come over him, as if the momentum that he needed to go through with his plan had gathered. He was more convinced than ever that the proper markings on her body had indeed been exercised and would somehow lead him into heaven. It was no coincidence that Jesus Christ had been depicted as a fish throughout the ages.

When Grecco finished his lunch, patting his mouth with the flat of a paper napkin, he returned to Emma, who stared straight at the ceiling. She was picturing Lucy inside the metal box at the edge of the woods. Grecco rolled up his sleeves carefully, wiped his hands a final time and picked up the tattoo needle. He bent over her neck and started against her windpipe, stopping whenever she swallowed. The pain lashed through her head. How far up her throat would he go? She wondered if he meant to tattoo her face or would he stop, would his mind tell him that he was through at last, he had at last satisfied his image of Christ's daughter.

Then Grecco's hand began shaking; sweat poured down from his forehead, ran around his eyes and down his nose, covered his lips and chin. A droplet fell against Emma's lips; she blew out so as not to swallow any of it. He stood back wiping his face off with a cloth, then approached her again. He was getting there at last; a few more lines under the chin and that would be it.

At last he came to that point and tossed down the tattoo needle onto the wooden barn floor and stepped away from her quickly. She heard the door open and slam closed behind him, then the sound of him crying, hard tears of sadness or joy, she could not tell. Maybe he was afraid.

The thought that he was afraid awakened her. Maybe he could be talked out of it; maybe she could still touch his heart somehow or somewhere and he would see the truth behind what he was doing. "There are no words to describe how much I love Lucy and she loves me. You cannot separate us, no God would forgive you for that."

The door opened and closed again and she could see him out of the corner of her eye, standing by the knob. He stood very erect, like a soldier ready to die for his country, a great boorish general. His shoulders were broad for such a short man and his arms were long. His cheekbones were wide and yet angular. He stepped forward, staring at her as if for the first time, examining her feet, her knees, her forearms, her belly, her breasts and underarms and biceps, and finally he brought his eyes up to her neck.

He shut them tightly and fell to his knees and began to pray. She could not hear individual words, just a murmur, an intensity of expression, as if it were perhaps necessary for him to convince himself of the truth behind his actions once again.

"You have the wrong girl," she said, quietly. He stopped his murmuring. He was listening to her. "It's not going to work, you're just going to kill yourself, you'll die for no reason at all. Heaven is not waiting for us. I'm just a girl."

He jumped to his feet. "What? What do you know?" he said. She hadn't expected him to snap back at her. "You don't know what you are, you've got no idea."

"I know what I am."

"What are you, then?"

"I'm a girl, a girl you found and marked, that's all and I have a mother and I love my mother."

"That's a lie, you came back to me, even."

"I came to get her back, my mother."

"Mother? Mother? You call that ridiculous—that—I wouldn't call that—she didn't give birth to you. *Your* mother, ha!"

"She *is* my mother."

"Oh, silly one. You don't know who your mother is. You are lost and a little afraid, that's understandable."

"I didn't come back for this," Emma said. "You're making a mistake."

"Oh, my word, listen to you now. *They've* indoctrinated you." He began pacing nervously. "Before their influence you understood your role. You understood the glory of Christ. He sacrificed Himself for you, didn't He? What an opportunity you've been offered."

"No," Emma said. "Nobody has indoctrinated me. You've got the wrong girl." She couldn't tell whether or not she was sowing seeds of doubt.

He kept pacing back and forth. Emma feared that perhaps she was making him even more confident by challenging his way.

"So you think I'm wrong. You think all this work has been just a waste of time?" He laughed a little. "Do you really think so? That's a heck of a way to die," he said, bringing his face close to hers. "I wouldn't want to be in *your* skin, thinking it was all a waste. There's nothing you can do about God's will anyway."

"Well," Emma said, feeling his deep sadism. "Are you so sure I'm perfect?"

It took him a while to stammer out the words, "I do, I think you're very perfect. Absolutely. You're as near perfection as anything has ever been on this planet. You don't agree?"

"I just wanted to make sure you think so. I seem to remember some slip-ups."

"Slip ups? What are you talking about, where?" he said, anxiously.

"When I was in New York," Emma said, "a painter did my portrait. He saw the scales. He did not think much of them."

"A painter saw your skin?" he said. "What painter?"

"A very famous one, known all over the world by everyone. I stayed with him. He was not impressed. If *he* wasn't, do you really think Christ will be? You told me He sees everything, He'll see the imperfections."

He seemed utterly taken by her words, then he laughed. "You're not going to fool me, no, no way. You are the finest, most perfect . . . you are indeed worthy to be anointed the Daughter of Christ. He knows that already."

She stared up at him, then said quietly and carefully, "As long as you're confident, as long as you're sure you have not made a mistake."

He rapidly unstrapped her from the cot, handcuffed her, and threw a bathrobe over her shoulders, then pointed her toward a door inside the barn. He pushed her through it and they went down wooden steps into the dark. He turned on the light.

The basement was full of collected objects, hundreds, perhaps thousands of them—stuffed bright green parrots with cocked heads perched on painted branches mounted on the wall. Driftwood with stuffed rattlesnakes wrapped around them. Cowboy hats, velvet tapestries of wild horses, old guns on the wall, a glass case of daggers. A couch covered with hand-painted fabric, trapeze artists, tigers, elephants, a ringmaster. A series of hand-painted chairs faced a podium that was also decorated. From the rafters hung fishing nets that held blue plastic fish. Sections of a large canvas tent were rolled up on one side of the room and on the floor was straw. Two aquariums in which small bright-colored fish darted were bubbling.

"Let me show you something," he said. "Some real mistakes." His lips tightened. He seemed a little nervous, unsure of what he was going to do. He walked over to one of six tables covered with a canvas tarp. He yanked it off. Before Emma could close her eyes she saw a long fish tank filled with a pinkish liquid. A naked girl floated inside. Emma closed her eyes, bowing her head.

"What's the matter? Can't you stand imperfection either?"

She swung around for the door but he stopped her short. She had seen what was in the tank. A fourteen-year-old girl covered with scales floated at the bottom of the pinkish liquid. Her long reddish hair was tangled around her neck and covered part of her face. Her eyes were open and her mouth slightly ajar like a fish.

She said nothing; she could feel her throat constricting as if her speech were descending into the silence inside of her. She braced herself, clenching her teeth. Her eyes were shut tight. He dragged her toward the other tables that were covered with canvas and began to yank the material off each one. After he was finished he shook her until she opened her eyes again, which she did for but a flash. She saw six tanks filled full of pink liquid. In each one a tattooed girl was suspended horizontally, her arms over her head, her legs straight and toes pointed. "This one didn't cut it, she moved around too much," he said. "Besides, she talked a lot. And this one, look at that cut. She broke a hole in the wall in her room and scraped herself trying to get out. A permanent scar for sure. What a waste! He would surely have loved her in Heaven. And this poor fool, I couldn't get food to stay down and she just kind of shriveled up. So you see how different you are?"

Emma was doing everything that she could to keep herself from slipping into darkness, slipping away forever. She kept her eyes steadfastly closed and bit down on her teeth.

He led her up the stairs, out of the barn, and down the hill to her room. Then he unfastened her handcuffs and closed the door. Then the lights went out.

54

That night after Grecco came and went in the dark, the lights came on and Emma saw that he had set down a most elaborate meal for her that included cheeses and fruits, a strip of steak, string beans, potatoes, and a bowl of ice cream for dessert. This was his exchange for her life—a meal. She dumped it onto the floor and jumped on it, squashing it into the rug. She heard a crack; her clear plastic cup of water had broken.

He came in an hour or so later, saw what she'd done with her food, then looked at her. "Well, well," he said. "Not very polite." He picked up some of it, went out, and turned out the lights.

She lost track of the hours. One moment she thought dawn had surely come and that Grecco was about to step inside with his handcuffs. The next moment she felt that no time at all had passed, that time was moving so slowly that not even an hour had passed.

She became more and more agitated. She found herself trembling with fright, her teeth chattering ever so closely together. She closed her eyes; nobody could help her now.

Toward what must have been dawn, she rolled from her cot onto the floor and began feeling around her bed on her hands and knees. She could feel scraps of food that he hadn't picked up, a string bean, a squashed slice of peach. Her fingers landed on just what she was looking for, a shard of plastic from the cup. She was thinking of what he had said in the barn basement about the one girl. *She broke a hole in the wall in her room and scraped herself trying to get out. A permanent scar for sure. What a waste!*

Sitting up on her bed in the dark, she brought the sharp end of the clear plastic against her forearm, pressed down, and dragged it across the skin.

She felt for wetness. She had merely scraped herself. She scraped herself again, this time pressing deeper. Again she had only raised the skin a little without drawing blood.

On the third try, she clenched her teeth, closed her eyes and gashed the plastic down her arm. Wetness of blood covered her forearm right away. She switched to the other arm and gashed it open, and then she took off her pants. She cut through both legs, her thighs, then she made an *X* over her belly. Blood dripped down over her underwear and legs and oozed between her toes. She kept gashing at parts of her body, even her neck, the part of her body that he seemed to admire the most. When she finally stopped, she realized her sheets were soaked with her blood.

Every part of her body was crying out in pain.

She went to her door and started knocking and then pounding; she kept pounding until the light came on above her and he opened the door. He stood there, his hair standing on end, obviously roused from a deep sleep. It took him a moment to see what had happened, to survey the inside of her room. "*What?!*" he screamed at the top of his lungs. "What?!" He spun around, holding his hair, pulling on it, slapping his forehead with his palm. "What have you done? What have you done, you little—you!" He slapped his leg and then the side of his head. Then he raised his hand again, as if to slap her. Realizing he would damage her even more, he slapped his own face. "You, you idiot! You shameful little—ingrate!"

He slammed the door and she heard him throwing things in the living room, overturning the couch and chairs, breaking lamps, win-

dows. After a while the sounds stopped and Emma, who was standing in bra and underwear, could see her body under the light that
he'd left burning. There were thick red marks over every inch of
her skin, some slashes that she didn't even remember making. Her
bleeding was slowing down, clotting. She put her clothes back on,
painfully and slowly; they were soaked with blood. Then she lay
back on the bed and closed her eyes.

The door kicked open. It was Grecco. "Do you see, do you see
what you've done to your *mother!*" he said, bitterly. He pointed
behind him across the room. There was Lucy slouched back in
Johnny Ranch's arms. Her eyes were closed, her chin resting on her
chest. Ranch turned her to the side so that Emma could see three
white strips on her neck, three large white puffy burn marks, blistered, red, white, and black. Emma lunged forward, but Grecco
threw her backward into the room. "You touch your skin again,
you so much as drag a fingernail down yourself, you'll be helping
me bury her—*you'll* dig the hole, not me, okay? Do you hear me?"
he said.

He swung the door closed with his foot. Emma fell forward onto
the door, banging on it, screaming and kicking and yelling so loud
that she began losing her voice.

"You let her go or I'll rip my own skin off," Emma screamed.
"I'll rip my entire skin off, you *fucking* animal! You *fucking* monster!"

55

In the sheer darkness of the meat locker, lying on the damp cot, Lucy opened her eyes and turned her head. The burns on her neck shouted at her, shot through from one side of her head to the other. She closed her eyes and tried to hold herself still, the pain throbbing like a poisonous pressing finger.

The memory of what had happened hours earlier came to her. Johnny Ranch had dragged her out of the meat locker. Outside, a man was seated on a tree stump; he was the man she had looked up and seen in the barn; he was wearing a blue rubber fish mask, the snout hanging down as he leaned over the blue flame of a hand-held propane torch and what looked like a fireplace poker. He rose to his feet, stepped over to her and seared her three times against her neck; some of her hair caught fire before she passed out.

Now in the meat locker she could still smell burnt hair and seared flesh. The attack was out of the blue. Had Emma somehow gotten away? Why this sudden attack? Her heels were raw from being dragged. Had he taken her somewhere after she had passed out?

Her life spun around her, spun around the pain she felt in the skin under her ear. She reached up and felt the three blisters and laid her hand back down on the cot. Where was this voice from the past coming from?

She was beginning to understand something. Her memory brought her back into Pastor Joe's trailer, the tight quarters that she had only just begun to trust back then. This was the afternoon that her life had changed forever, when she was thrust down into a hell that she had fought for years to get out of. "I'll show you *my* secret," he had said quietly after trying to get her to tell him the secret she said she had kept with Reverend Williams. "Come here." She had not remembered this moment until now.

He had sidled over on the couch next to her and pulled his turtleneck shirt down. And she had seen it. At first she didn't understand it. How could it be? It was made of flesh, living flesh, three pinkish flaps of skin on his neck. They appeared to be moving ever so slightly, pulsing, breathing. He turned his head and she saw three more colored slashlike scars on the other side. He had always worn his collar over them before. "Do you know what these are?" he said. His tone of voice was different; there was something childlike about it, sadistically childlike.

The fourteen-year-old Lucy shook her head.

"Take a wild guess," he'd said.

She shook her head again; this sight horrified her not so much because it was grotesque but because of what it represented.

"Oh, come on, what do they look like?"

Lucy had started crying back then. She felt the mere act of him showing these things to her was unleashing something inside him, something that she had known was there, that he had kept from her. Now this poisonous snake was out of its box, now she knew she would be bitten.

Even before he said it, she knew that somebody had humiliated this minister of God when he was little, not merely humiliated him, that was not a strong enough word; somebody had actually tried to take away his most basic sense of himself as a human.

"Gills," he said. Tears continued to fill Lucy's eyes. She knew there was no way out of this trailer and yet she knew that his telling her this story was not a good thing for her. "My word. I was known all over town for them when I grew up. I wasn't fully human—part of me was left in the womb. In a way, I wasn't fully born. And they convinced me that was true, everyone. Every kid, every man, woman, and child in the town I grew up in. My father decided to cash in on this. Can you imagine doing that to *your* son?"

Lucy shook her head.

"Can you imagine if your daddy did that to you?"

"I don't have one," she said, hoping the words would rescue her from this hell.

"Aren't you glad you don't?" For a moment he seemed to soften, but then he bore down on the point again and she saw that he was a different person. "Can you imagine your father selling you to some two-bit, second-rate circus? All for the price of a used car?"

He was silent; Lucy looked at him and saw that he was waiting for her to react.

"I spent plenty of time underwater amusing people. The rest of the time I was tied up in the back of a truck. I saw Satan for who he was, and Christ for who He was. I had a clear choice: obey Satan or obey Christ. I took up the latter. I ran away, ran fast and hard across this dirty land. Guess how old I was?"

Lucy shook her head. Pastor Joe was possessed.

"Go on, take a wild guess."

"Fourteen," Lucy said, crying.

"Oh, not close. I was an old man by then. I'd seen more sin at that age than most dirty old men who run in and out of bars see in a lifetime. I was seven. And I was a *freak*," he said, "Now what's yours?"

"I don't have one," Lucy said. Then suddenly she had an idea. "I'm a freak, too," she said.

"What?" he yelled, terrifying her even more.

"I . . . I am a freak."

"What do you mean? What part of you?"

"No part."

"Let me see—it's somewhere hidden, isn't it?"

"No."

"It must be. Where? Down there?" he pointed at her pants.

"No, not there." He moved toward her, grabbed her pants and yanked them off to examine her.

Lucy could still feel the explosion that had rocked her life forever back then, she could still feel his rage that was unleashed not only by what he did to her sexually, but by what he had shown her about his life. It all seemed to come out in that trailer, a black rage—in part because he discovered she wasn't a freak.

Now in the darkness, she touched her blisters. How could this be? How could she possibly have ended up back in his hands, this man who had sent her tumbling down this dark, unforgiving tunnel, who had shadowed her for all these years? Had the very image of a girl marked from head to foot with small black scales somehow evoked in her things that this man whom she'd known when she was fourteen years old had done to her?

The door to the meat locker opened a crack, light came in, and she saw Johnny Ranch's silhouette. He set a plastic jug of water down and picked up the empty one, then he dropped the usual bag of scraps.

For the following week Grecco looked over Emma's wounds after dropping off her meals. There were long scabs running up and down her limbs and belly. "Don't you pick those off now, otherwise, like I say, you'll be shoveling out the grave of that so-called *mother* of yours, you hear me?"

Her cuts were healing, the scabs crumbling off on their own and underneath she could see the black lines of the scales.

56

Pidge drove past the many trailers and trucks and the center ring tent with the flag on top, forked like a snake's tongue, flapping in the warm breeze. There were three white llamas and a camel facing the country road. On the far side of the grounds he could see Marcella's back swaying, hay around her front legs. For many years now Pidge was determined never to return to this show, never to cross its path, never to speak to even the people he had loved here. But the last ten days that he had spent in Lucy's house changed that.

Since arriving at her house, he had been waiting anxiously for her return more determined than ever to tell her something. He wasn't sure what it was but as the days went by the actual words seemed to matter less and less. He wanted to be there when she walked in the door and look at her and let her look at him. He thought perhaps that was all he needed to do before moving on. Exactly where he would go he had no idea. There were certainly plenty of other junkyards in the world, places to start over again.

But in many ways, by merely staying among her furniture and clothes and neat pictures on the walls, he was getting to know her. An embroidered picture of a flower box hanging above the couch said, *Welcome to All Who Enter This Domicile*. He noticed that she still had a predilection for elephants; there were some black and white photos on the walls of elephants on a grassy plain and a letter on the kitchen counter from the *Save the Elephants Foundation*. That made sense; she had loved Marcella and Marcella, everyone knew, was particularly fond of her. Being such an old and tame elephant Marcella was allowed to wander freely around the circus grounds between shows. She would graze and pick at things with her trunk and then somehow find herself pulling at the grass near Lucy's trailer.

As the nights passed inside Lucy's intimate house, Pidge worried about her safety in spite of himself. He was used to worrying about King but not about another person. He drove to the electric company to pay the balance of her bill in cash. Each morning from her mailbox, he collected her letters and magazines and arranged them by the date in which they came. A raspy-voiced man from the Eagle Rest Home called and asked when she would return to work and Pidge said that he didn't know. Then a woman in a pickup truck pulled into the yard and knocked on Lucy's door. Pidge opened it and the woman said she was Margie, Lucy's friend. She stepped inside and asked where Lucy had gone to but Pidge did not tell her what he had come to suspect.

After a while Pidge's curiosity got the better of him and he began to look through Lucy's papers. He found a wooden box under one of her beds and there he discovered photographs from the circus. He himself had kept but a single piece of memorabilia from the show when he had quit, just his blue jumpsuit with the name CROWN CIRCUS stitched on the back. He shuffled through the photos quickly. There were many of himself both as a clown and as a mechanic. He always seemed to be turning away from the camera and as in all pictures he'd ever seen of himself his face was washed out, featureless, blurry. He looked like a ghost. There were pictures of almost everyone else in the show, Shorty, Iggy, Mrs. Cookie, and some of Lucy herself in her various outfits. *She was big back then, my God, she was huge. No wonder I couldn't love her.*

That thought made him sad. Then he came across some of Master Howard standing outside his trailer. These snapshots shocked Pidge. He had hoped never to lay eyes on this man again, even in a photo, but now that he was looking at him, he couldn't turn away. Something about his eyes seemed to transcend time. It was as if he was in the room staring up at him. Pidge shuffled through them quickly and then put them back and closed the lid and shoved the box back under the bed.

On Lucy's dresser, Pidge opened a black, hardbound book. Inside he saw handwriting and dates and immediately knew that he had discovered her diary. The first word that caught his eye on the page that he had turned to was his own name. *I don't know if Pidge could have loved me as I was then.* He wanted to close the book right away and put it down, but now he could only continue to read on. *It is hard, if not impossible to know what his real feelings were, if he still thinks of me now. I wonder if he believed that I was a real freak. Maybe he just thought that I was a tub of lard as people used to call me. I was never able to show him how much we had in common—that I was a freak before I weighed a lot. Do not forget what Reverend Williams said.*

Nervous, breathing hard, Pidge brought the diary over to the bed and sat down. He believed that there were few meaner ways of invading somebody's privacy than flipping through her diary, but he was so fascinated, so curious as to her thoughts that he knew he would not close it until he had read every single page in it. The diary spanned many years. Sometimes she went six months without writing in it.

He read the first entry:

> Back in this house where I grew up. A terrible silence, a loneliness like a poisonous gas. I think I should go back, then I think of all that happened. I may be a freak, but I am not going to be a fat lady much longer.

I wonder who I am. I think back to the days when I thought I was a ghost, and Reverend Williams said that I was a freak and how hard to hear that was, but in the end it was such an important thing for me to learn. I miss him. He had a lot of wisdom.

The circus was the roar of life, I guess. Even if it treated me horribly, at least it was life.

Two years later:

I woke up thinking of the pastor this morning. All these years have gone by and here I am thinking of him once again. I could write him a letter. Why did you do that to me, was it worth it, was what you did to that little fourteen-year-old-girl worth it for that moment of pleasure?

I wonder where he is and if he is happy and if he knows how much sadness he left inside me. I wonder if he would care.

A month later:

Yesterday I promised myself I would not think about him or about Master Howard or about Pidge. I will think only of those I love. But that is a difficult task, because you cannot control your dreams, you cannot control what you see at night.

I had this dream last night that I was back inside the pastor's tent and there he was doing something up front near his altar. I couldn't really see what he was doing, but I couldn't leave his tent either and I couldn't hide. I just didn't want him to see me sitting there watching him. I wanted others to come inside. Then sure enough people did start coming in. People from the circus, filling the pastor's tent and I was feeling better the more that came in. But suddenly he began to preach about the evils of the circus people and I knew he was hurting me, that he knew I *was* there and that I would have to remain in his tent forever.

When I woke up, I suddenly had the urge to go find him, to tell him what he did to me, to let him know that this man who thought he was a man of God was somebody who—I cannot think of a word for him.

Three years later:

It is not good to live in the house where you grew up when something like this happens. But that doesn't mean that if I moved to another part of the state I'd still be able to leave him behind. You cannot leave something like that behind, you live with it all your life, you live with the man who did it to you. You must accept that, that is the trick, to accept everything that's inside you. I can't do that. Not after that.

I am back to thinking about my daughter. I have decided I will find Lily. I will look everywhere until I find her.

Six months later:

Yesterday I pledged to give up trying to contact Lily. The agencies that I've gone to have said that she may want to contact me sometime, but I will never ever be able to contact her myself. They say that I've given that right up. But I was fourteen years old at the time, I tell them. They say nothing to that, they look at me as if I'm crazy. No, I'm not crazy. I still love that little girl, love her with all my heart, think about her every day.

Dear Lily,

   Just so you know, I will always always be your mother,
though I never got to change a single diaper, though I never
once got to feel your lips on my breasts, though I never once got
to touch your beautiful skin and to comb your beautiful hair
and to smell your beautiful baby smell. I never got to bring you
to school for your first day, I never got to tell you how much I
love you and how much I miss you and I do miss you, I miss
you so. I just want you to know I've done everything in my
power to try to bring you back . . .

Your loving mother

Pidge remembered that there had been a rumor years ago that
Lucy did have a child, though she never mentioned it to anybody.
This memory brought to mind the peculiar circumstances by which
she had joined the circus. Pidge at the time had been with the circus
for four years. All the trucks and trailers of the show were headed
to a town in southern Ohio one afternoon when Master Howard
changed directions for no apparent reason. Two and a half hours
out of their way they came across a young girl walking down the
side of the road. Master Howard slowed down next to her and
began to talk to her, almost as if he knew her. Then she had climbed
into the back of the truck and the circus turned around and headed
back to their original destination.

A day later this young girl was part of the show. Pidge remembered thinking once he got a good look at her that something must have been done to her. There were circles under her
eyes. Then he remembered the rumors about her losing a child—
she stared at babies all the time and she could be heard talking
to the child as if she were in her arms. There must have been
something in her that needed to stay in the circus. So many
people in the circus had a reason to be there, but a reason was

hardly the word for it, so many people in the circus could not go anywhere else if they wanted to.

Pidge saw a line that said, *May have to go back to him.* To whom? he thought. Whom could she be going back to?

Pidge found newspaper articles from six months before the present date glued to the pages. They were about the tattooed girls found in the Blue Night Mall, her shirt covered with blood. There were six or seven short articles. Below the last one, Pidge saw Lucy's handwriting: *Why can't I stop thinking about her?*

A day later:

> Another dream about the tattooed girl. I have not even seen her and yet I feel like I know her. The papers say that she has been traumatized. I don't know what happened to her, but I do know what she will become if she doesn't find the right person. Tomorrow I will go to the authorities and tell them that I know how to take care of such a girl.

Two weeks later:

> I am happy. There is nothing else to say. All I'm worried about is being the best mother to Emma. I am doing everything I can, but I still worry.

Two days later:

> I started to feel myself become a freak again—in the way that Reverend Williams meant it, in the good way that I felt after I understood what he said. I am no longer a ghost. I think it is because of Emma. She too is a freak.

Two days later:

I'd rather die myself, than lose her.

Two months later:

All has gone to pot. She does not look well at all after so many months of getting better. I'm afraid that I'm failing her. Should I call Carl Lark and admit to him these problems?

I have been thinking about Pastor Joe again and what happened in the trailer. I have been thinking about the dreams I had before I met Emma. I wonder, if Emma could talk, what would she tell me? Why do I sometimes see Pastor Joe when I see Emma's unhappiness?

Pidge's finger rested on the name Pastor Joe. The name rang a faint bell. Master Howard had mentioned the name to him a long time ago. *I tell you, that son of a bitch makes more money in a night than this whole damn show makes in a week. I should have gone into preaching.* Then Pidge knew why Lucy must have gone to see Master Howard and he knew he, too, would have to return to this man he had been running from for years.

Now Pidge climbed out of his pickup truck with his shepherd and approached the grounds on foot, circling to the back of the tent and slipping his dog and then himself under the snow fence. Once inside the grounds, Pidge felt lightheaded, almost dizzy. He made his way to Marcella as King ran ahead.

Years before, Marcella and King had been close companions, King often running right next to her rear legs as she trotted around the ring. Whenever Pidge was away for a night, the shepherd slept in the hay near the elephant. Now Pidge could see her trunk sweeping gracefully over King's back, smelling him. Then as Pidge approached, she was reaching for him, brushing her trunk's leathery skin gently against his ear, pushing his hair up and smelling up and down his body from his work boots to his neck. It was not a lie about the memories of elephants. Pidge put his small arm around her trunk and patted the back of it.

"Pidge?" A soft voice came from behind him and he turned to see Elvin, dressed in his white tights, his tight blue shorts and elastic shirt that split to show his smooth, hairless chest. He had straight blond hair, fair skin, and a face that seemed perfect at first until you noticed his sharp nose ran crookedly down his face.

"Working for another show?"

"No," Pidge said. "I'm out of circuses right now."

"Well, it's good to see you, Pidge. You look as well as I've seen you."

Elvin was always so polite. Pidge recalled Master Howard announcing his act in his booming voice: "High in the hippodrome, the Crown Circus presents: a strange and beautiful man whose feet never touch the earth, who does not live here with other mortals, whose only interest in life is to perfect the flight of angels!"

Pidge could not take his eyes off the person who stood before him. He wanted to look away, but he was mesmerized like a dreamer. Pidge always remembered him standing tall on a tight wire or hanging upside down from his swing. "You're looking for Lucy, are you?"

Pidge kept his hand on Marcella's trunk and looked at him as if to say, *How did you know?*

"I saw her come up here. She looked totally different. The first thing that came across my mind when I saw her again was that she was looking for you. But she didn't want to see any of us, just Master Howard." Despite having come to see Master Howard, Pidge had hoped somebody else would have the answer to her whereabouts. "She was here about a half an hour, brought a girl with her, most beautiful creature you've ever seen . . . I was relieved she didn't stay around. I don't think the circus would be any good for such innocence." He shook his head. "And Lucy, too, she's a sensitive soul, you know." He smiled at Pidge in a strange way, as if to say that he too should be cautious during his visit.

Pidge crossed the grassy grounds that smelled of manure and canvas and headed for the trailer of Master Howard. The door was shut; Pidge knocked and there in the dark entrance, his dark eyes puffed up from deep sleep, stood the man who Pidge had sworn off for life. Pidge immediately felt this man's power over him.

"Pidgie." Master Howard raised his crooked smile as if he had just won a bet with the devil. "Back at last, are we? Back to see us, back to work."

"I'm not here for that," Pidge said.

"Well, there's a job opening. I just put word out that we're looking to sign up a dwarf clown."

"I've already got a job," Pidge stepped back, shuffling as if he were walking in place, the tips of his fingers stuck in his pockets. He was trying to hold his own.

Master Howard smiled and wet his lips with his tongue. "A job? Last I heard you were pushing wrecks around a nasty old junkyard in Tarville."

Pidge shook his head. "I quit that place a long time ago."

"Also heard that in your spare time you were still sucking down anything you could get your hands on, mouthwash included." The old feelings were coming back. Master Howard was judging him, making him feel a failure in every way. It was as much his tone of voice as anything else.

"I got another job since then, a much better one—pays pretty good, too," Pidge lied. He knew how transparent this was; his voice had changed, had weakened.

"Oh really?" Master Howard was smiling slyly. "How much a week?"

"A lot." It was too late to back out of this lie. "Sure . . . I'm fixing to buy a little place, too. A garage, my own garage. I've got a lot of customers lined up."

"Is your lady love in on this little scheme by chance?"

"Who?" Pidge said.

"You know who." And Pidge knew that Master Howard knew all along exactly why he was here. "Your lady love, your princess . . . your bride."

Pidge hunkered down. He could feel Master Howard's words pulling his legs out from under him.

"Where is she?" Pidge said firmly and clenched his fists.

"Boy, you're looking mighty fierce, all thirty-five inches of you. What's gotten into you?"

"What's gotten into me? A lot. I mean, a whole lot."

Master Howard laughed. "Well, go on, spit it out."

"First of all," Pidge stammered. "First of all, I'm not going to be pushed—and she's not—"

"She?"

"Lucy. She's different—me, too, and she needs help, my help, and I intend to give it to her."

"You?"

"Yes, me," Pidge practically shouted. "She came by to see you, where did you send her?"

"Well," Master Howard drew his Vaseline-coated hair up over the back of his head. "You're turning into a regular little hero, yes indeed."

"You didn't tell her where those folks who came after the tattooed girl harkened from, did you?"

"Oh jeez, you know me, Pidge. I wouldn't tell her nothing unless it was wrapped up in a cryptic code to flip her mind upside down."

"Did you tell her—what did you tell her?" Pidge said loudly.

"Not much, just a little bit about that tattooed girl who fancied you. And let's see, what else? I told her that you two, neither one of you can run away from me. Nope. Hell no, you'll always come back."

"I'm not back. Just tell me what you said to her."

"Nearly forgot to mention," Master Howard said. "I gave her some of this, I sure did." He pointed to his half-open fly. His smile rose even higher like a jack-o-lantern, showing three gold-capped teeth with stars in them. Pidge looked down at the ground. He knew the angle Master Howard was trying on him now and he was determined not to let it bother him.

"I asked you a question," Pidge said.

Leaning out of his trailer, Master Howard called to Iggy who was standing near a white llama on the other side of the grounds. "Hey, Iggy, you watched her girl while she was in here making me happy, didn't you?"

Plucking hair from his brush, Iggy smiled and then laughed in his lonely distant way and said, "Oh yeah, the girl, why, she set right up top of Marcella when Lucy was in there with you—making you happy!"

Pidge thought he had come prepared for the worst. He was ready to be laughed at by this man, to be teased about everything from his size to his drinking. But he had not expected his own jealous reaction to the thought that Lucy had gone to bed with him once again. True or not, blood rushed into Pidge's face and Master Howard could see him blushing.

"Hey, what's gotten into you? I thought you hated that bitch, *despised* her. She didn't lose her touch or anything." He made an obscene gesture with his tongue against the side of his cheek. Pidge turned and walked across the circus grounds to the gates. He could not bear it another minute. How could he now care about this thing that had gone on so often years before anyway? "Hey, come on back and put your jammies on, we do need us a clown, yes we do."

He walked behind the tent with King by his side, but he stopped before passing under the fence. He could smell the pleasant elephant smell of Marcella, the acrid scent of tiger urine and dried hay and horse and llama hair and weathered canvas and freshly washed costumes hung out to dry. There were so many feelings tied up with this place, the only place he had ever been where he felt people had known him. And yet it was here that he had allowed himself to be controlled by this cruel man, had lost nearly every bit of his own self-respect. Unable to go backward or forward, he found himself repeating his old high school motto: *Go where you've never been before and keep going where you've never been before.*

Shorty, covered head to foot with black grease, climbed out from under one of the circus trailers and came to the fence. "Hey, where are you going? Aren't you coming over here to talk to your old bud?" he said. He looked beaten by drink.

Pidge had never understood why Shorty had always looked up to him, but now he did; Shorty must have known all along that Pidge had the ability to stop drinking—he had virtually quit at Lucy's house—whereas Shorty himself could never muster that sort of strength. "What have you been up to?"

Pidge was almost speechless.

"You let the old man get to you?"

He took a deep breath.

"You're looking for Lucy, aren't you? She came by here asking about you."

"Was she really in his trailer?" Pidge said, pointing at Master Howard's trailer.

"I don't know about that. I know she was asking about you. That lady, she's got a big heart, you know. One of the biggest hearts I've ever seen. And she's got that ability to tell you things with just her eyes, you know."

"What was she doing back here?"

"She come up to find out about her girl. She also wanted to know how you were doing. I told her where you were. Her girl, well, she wasn't doing too good. Lucy was on a mission, I think, to help her out. I imagine she was the only one who could help her out. Anything she did in that trailer with him was for her girl's sake, let me tell you. I wouldn't hold it against her or nothing."

Pidge shook his head and looked away.

"I'm serious, bud, don't you worry about something like that."

"Did you ever hear of a guy named Pastor Joe?" Pidge said.

Shorty looked away, then down at the ground. "How come you're looking for him?" he asked.

"I think, I can't say for sure, but I think Lucy's in a whole lot of trouble because of him."

Shorty expelled a long breath.

"Who is he?" Pidge said.

"I've been thinkin' about Lucy, she was a good girl."

"Who is he?" Pidge said again.

"Well, he's a preacher, a televangelist, a mighty powerful one, a big one, I mean real big. Bucks land in his pockets like flies to shit, I tell you, only he goes by another name these days, it's Grecco."

Shorty looked toward Master Howard's trailer and then back to Pidge.

"Does Master Howard know him?" Pidge said.

"Knows him all right."

"How?"

"Well, he'd kill me and I ain't exaggerating, he'd kill me if he heard me tell you." Shorty looked over his shoulder to the trailer again. "But seeing what's going on . . . He grew up with Master Howard. He was a kind of boy slave to Master Howard's father. Then his father died and Master Howard had charge of him for a while."

"When did you learn this?"

"Heck, I've always known it." Shorty had been in the show ten years longer than Pidge. "But there came a time, and let me tell you, he made it clear that it was his secret."

"What do you mean a slave?"

"He was a kid born with gills, they didn't work or anything but he could move them up and down like a fish. He couldn't talk, but he made noises like a fish gasping out of water. Master Howard's father used to present him to a crowd by pulling a cloth off a glass tank. There inside the people would see a boy swimming around, apparently breathing underwater—he could move them three flaps of skin up and down pretty good. But it was set up so the boy would catch a breath from a hose just behind some fake plant. They kept the boy in irons the rest of the time. Then when the father died, Master Howard took him over."

Shorty's voice seemed to soften.

"Master Howard said it didn't affect him none when his father had him, but when he got control of him it was like a volcano of feelings come up inside him. Guilt or something that had been gatherin' inside him since he could remember. He is a human being that old Master Howard. He once told me it was the worst thing that ever happened to him, getting control of the boy. He didn't know what to do, but he tried to be nice to him. And then around that time, the boy started being able to talk for the first time and his first words scared Master Howard nearly to death. And he said things that Master Howard said were profound and had implications for him the rest of his life."

"Like what?"

"He said that his life underwater had given him a special perspective on life, a connection to God. Master Howard believed him. I don't know why, maybe it was just the way he said it to him because I don't think Master Howard ever did believe in God anyway. I never heard him mention no religion, did you?"

"No," Pidge said.

"Well, maybe he just felt sorry for him because he let him go and for a long time, he sent him money wherever he was and he even gave him a tent.

"One day right after Lucy joined he came over to me and said he'd cut my tongue off if I ever mentioned Pastor Joe to her."

Pidge stared at Master Howard's trailer and he recalled the peculiar circumstances of Lucy joining the show. "You suppose Pastor Joe told him about her?"

"How so?"

"I mean when the show went and picked her up."

"I never thought of that. Hey, where you going?"

Pidge started walking for the trailer. Somebody yelled his name out, but he did not turn to them, he just kept walking. Then he knocked on the door and Master Howard opened it and stood high above him in the doorframe.

"I came up here to ask you something and I want an answer," Pidge said. He was not really looking at him, just kind of blurring his vision and looking at his feet. He could feel his chest shaking a little. "I want to know where the guy who raped her when she was fourteen lives."

"What?" Master Howard was taken aback.

"You know damn well the guy I'm talking about."

Master Howard was speechless. He merely stared down at Pidge.

"Is that where you sent her?"

"Why would I do that?"

"That guy has a hold on you, that's why." Pidge drilled the words at him.

"Have you lost your little mind?"

"I don't think so. You might think so because you can't do what you did to me anymore and you can't do what you've done to Lucy all along."

"Do what?"

"You can't control us, you can't make us do what you want, you can't make us feel bad anymore. You can't do what"—and then something came to Pidge's mind—"the way that guy controlled you."

"Get out of here," Master Howard said. "Go on, play with yourself somewhere else." His tone had changed.

"When Lucy joined the show back then, she'd been raped and had been made to give away her baby," Pidge shouted. "And you knew that, even if she didn't tell you, you knew that. But you just wanted control over her. You pretended you had special powers, that you could see into people's souls. You lied to her and then you played on her weakness and you got her to pretty near eat herself to death, all so you could say you had made her into what she is."

"What are you talking about?"

"Everybody's ruled by somebody, and this guy is ruling over you, isn't he? He told you to pick her up off the side of the road."

"Who are you talking about?"

"Pastor Joe." He had not said his name because he was afraid of endangering Shorty, but the words came off his lips.

Master Howard stared at him with an intensity that confirmed to Pidge that he was right.

"Let me tell you something, you little shit, when I picked her up off the road, she was a dead person, as good as dead. It didn't matter what she did to herself, she was dead, that's all. What I did was save her, she'd have killed herself anyway."

"No," Pidge said. "You were afraid of some guy, afraid or something of some guy even crazier than you. That's why you sent her back to him. Because you knew he'd kill you if he found out that you knew where his tattooed girl was. So you sent her back there."

Master Howard had turned white and Pidge saw a knife in his hand. "It's time for you to get along now," he said.

"I'm not going anywhere. Not until you tell me where she is."

"I'll tell you where," Master Howard held the knife out, but Pidge didn't move. "She's dead. Do you hear me? Dead."

"Liar."

"You're wasting your time looking for her."

"No," Pidge said firmly but something in him had begun to believe that it was the truth.

"Now get on, go on."

"I'm not going anywhere."

"She's dead. She died a week ago. Pastor Joe killed her. He sent word to me that she's dead."

"You're lying." Pidge ran at him, despite the knife, and hit him in the leg with all his might with his fist. Master Howard jumped back and then lifted his foot and kicked Pidge to the ground.

"Go on, you heard it, little shit." Master Howard stepped up into his trailer and slammed the door.

Pidge lay on his stomach, his face in the grass. Somehow or another he believed him about Lucy; he knew he shouldn't but he couldn't help it. He began to weep.

Shorty tugged on Pidge's shirt and tried to turn him over. But Pidge held fast with his face pressed to the grass.

"Hey, you okay, bud?" Shorty said. "I don't think he really knows whether she's dead or not. If she did die, it would have affected him. But I haven't seen much of a change in him. I do happen to know the guy's address just outside of Gainston because Master Howard sent me up there one time to drop some things off for him."

Lucy heard footsteps outside of the meat locker. She wasn't sure exactly what time of day it was—afternoon or morning. She had heard birds singing earlier and she could see the spot of sunlight through the tiny hole in the roof.

Lucy had regained some of her strength shortly after Emma's arrival. Better food and more of it had been dropped off by Pastor Joe back then. But now it seemed to Lucy that he planned on starving her to death or maybe he was hoping she would contract gangrene. There had been no more water, no more food. The burns on the side of her neck had become raw; she did not touch them. Nor did she move her head; the pain was too much.

A person was pacing up and down outside of the box. Suddenly she heard something smash into the side of the meat locker, then another loud smash and another. Somebody was banging on the side of the box with a hammer.

"Are you happy? Are you happy in there, lady?" she heard the man yelling. "Are you happy with all you've done?" She put her hands over her ears as the banging continued.

57

Pidge stashed his truck on a dirt road near Grecco's driveway, tucked a flashlight in his pocket, and started picking his way through briars and around boulders through the forest to Grecco's estate. He had entrusted King with Shorty. At last through a stand of trees he could see to a stone wall with a crooked barbed-wire fence running along the top and a heavily grazed pasture leading into a shallow valley. It was early evening.

Approaching cautiously, he saw a ratty-looking horse and a long-haired donkey standing in the shade, their hind hooves lifted, tails swatting flies on their hindquarters. The setting sun lit up thistles and cast long shadows across the uneven grass. Far across the clearing, a white house with black shutters stood next to a red barn. His heart was pounding. He was struggling with what Master Howard had told him. The terrible feeling that she might be dead came in waves.

Under cover of the trees, he followed the jagged border of the farmland and got as close to the backyard as he could while still behind leaves. Sitting down, he tried to make himself comfortable for nightfall.

Evening was descending; the air became cooler and clouds that had earlier threatened rain went away. Stars appeared here and there in the dark blue above the trees. A car drove up the driveway, headlights flashing over the leaves, and stopped on the gravel lot. A door slammed and lights came on inside the house. A cow bellowed in the pasture.

After a long while, he saw the windows go black a few at a time, the ground floor and then the second floor, until only one light remained burning upstairs behind a shade. That too went out.

Carefully, Pidge approached the house, stepping up to the door and slipping his hand on the knob. He found it locked. He slipped around the perimeter, trying windows and another door. The only open entryway, he discovered, was a vent window leading into the basement.

Legs first, he slid through the narrow opening, the sill scraping his belly and ears as he turned his head to the side. He hung from just his fingers against the metal sill, his feet dangling over empty space. The metal cut deep into his fingers; he closed his eyes, held his breath, and finally let go.

He fell and then crashed into something wooden before falling the rest of the way to the basement floor, rolling onto his back. He lay stunned, wondering if he would be able to get up. Turning on his flashlight, he realized that he had landed on folding chairs stacked against the wall.

He heard footsteps just above his head and then a door handle jiggling. Shutting off the flashlight, he crawled into the space between the chairs and the wall as the door opened and the light came on, pouring through the chair legs onto the basement floor. As someone came down the steps, Pidge drew in his breath as deeply as he could. The man passed through the basement slowly, his feet crunching whatever dirt lay on the cement floor. Pidge lay as still as a rock. The man stood so still for such a long time that Pidge had to finally let out his breath.

But the man did not hear him and moved on, returning to the stairs, closing the door and flicking off the light behind him.

Pidge was not sure what part of the house the man was in now. He just knew that he would be alert and one more sound would bring him back down quickly. Pidge got up. He had brought a few index cards and a pen with him. In his truck, he had tried to compose the words he would say to Lucy if he did find her. Getting beyond those first words was crucial. On one of the index cards in his pocket, he wrote, *Dear Lucy, Sometimes over the course of a lifetime, a person can have some trouble with putting his thoughts into words, especially if his thoughts have been in his head for such a long time.*

Just above his head, he heard more footsteps—somebody was pacing back and forth in short bursts like a caged animal. He looked to the ceiling. The pacing went on, a quick back and forth sound. *Surely that's her.* He had no control over this thought. It came into his mind and he believed it wholeheartedly and now he waited impatiently, a sense of optimism rising in his chest. He tucked the card into his front pocket.

After the rest of the house was silent for a long while, Pidge got up and carefully climbed the stairs to the basement door and then turned the knob and pressed his shoulder against it. The door opened quietly and he stepped out into the living room and turned on his flashlight. It was an ordinary living room with couch and chairs and a television. But in the corner his beam found a blue metal door locked in three places. The door seemed to lead into a specially constructed space inside the bigger room. It might have been an ordinary closet if not for the metal sheeting reinforcing it and the heavily locked door. Pidge put his ear to the metal door. Inside he heard the pacing coming from within. He tried the door-knob gently but found it locked.

He took a clean index card out of his shirt pocket and wrote: *Lucy, I will try to get you out tonight. If no luck, I will be back with the police at dawn—Pidge.*

He tapped the metal door with his knuckle three times, quietly, and then waited for a response. The pacing stopped near the door. Reaching down, Pidge pushed the card partway under the door and moved it back and forth so that the person inside might hear it. But the person didn't take it. He again knocked on the door quietly. A knock came back. Pidge continued moving the card around under the door, hoping whoever was inside would take it from him.

He knocked again. This time a loud knock from inside came back, too loud considering somebody was upstairs. He froze to listen. The person inside the door knocked again.

A door on the second floor opened. Pidge bent over and quickly shoved the note back under the door and then moved toward the front door of the house. The man was rapidly coming down the stairs. Pidge burst through the front door, ran across the yard and threw himself under a fence. He ran into the woods. The lights around the house came on. The man yelled, "Who's there?"

Then somebody fired a gun repeatedly in his direction, striking branches and tree trunks around him. Pidge slipped in between two moss-covered logs and lay perfectly still. The gunfire stopped and he could hear the man running up and down at the edge of the property and then returning to his house. Dawn was starting to break, birds were singing, and white light filled the forest.

Pidge heard another car drive up to the front door. Moments later two men were talking on the lawn near where he hid. "Cops will be coming soon as that fellow gets to where he came from. You take care of the lady. The time has drawn near anyway, Johnny. At nine, you open the gates to the dam, no later than nine, you hear? Once I get up to heaven and Jesus sees what I've got for Him, He'll pave the way for you like I always promised to."

The other man murmured something. Then the first man responded.

"Don't you worry about nothing. I haven't been wrong yet, have I?"

58

Pidge heard a metal door creak open. He peeked behind him over the moss-covered logs in which he hid. Through a clearing of stumps and brush, in the green light that fell through the trees, he saw a tall man with a ponytail, Johnny Ranch, enter a large rectangular box, a meat locker. Moments later, Ranch pulled out a woman in torn rags, her hands on her head, and dragged her by the back of the collar to a tree stump where she collapsed to her knees. Pidge did not recognize her at first. She was far thinner than before. Her hair was all a mess on her head and she was barefoot. Then Pidge understood that it was Lucy and remained in disbelief. That evening he had convinced himself that she was still alive and yet to see her in the flesh seemed an almost divine revelation.

Ranch picked up his shotgun and then handed her a card from his pocket. "Who wrote this?" he yelled, pointing the gun at her as she knelt on the ground. Lucy read the note and shook her head and Pidge suddenly realized that it was the card that he had written himself that he was showing her.

Soon she was standing on her feet, and Ranch was driving her on with the barrel of his gun toward a trail on the far side of the clearing. As soon as the two figures disappeared from view, Pidge got up and began to climb among the fallen trees and thick ferns to follow them.

Before reaching the far trail, he heard a noise behind him, a girl crying. He fell flat to the ground and then raised his head. A short man with broad shoulders, a minister was lifting and shoving a young girl across the clearing toward the lake. The girl fought him, kicking and turning her head, but she was handcuffed and blind-folded. She wore just a bathing suit and the small black scales on her skin shimmered in the morning light as if she'd been coated with some kind of oil. The minister was dressed sharply in his white collar and black suit and dark shoes.

The girl screamed and called for Lucy, turning her head in the direction of the meat locker. Pidge heard Lucy scream back to her, but she had been taken in another direction and she was quite far away. Grecco shook the girl violently, pushed her to her knees and then yanked a handkerchief out of his pocket and quickly gagged her. He lifted her to her feet again and shoved her on through the clearing to another trail toward the lake and out of sight.

Pidge got to his feet and ran as fast as he could around the tree stumps and over the brush toward where Johnny Ranch had taken Lucy. The path had been recently mown and was covered with a brushy stubble as it wound through pines and hemlocks. Pidge ran recklessly down it, the feeling that it was already too late taking him over.

All at once, he stopped dead in his tracks at the edge of the woods. Below him the trail ended at a swampy pond and there Johnny Ranch stood on its weedy bank holding his shotgun to Lucy's back. She waded out into green and black water, pushing reeds aside with both hands. She was crying loudly, stuttering as she breathed in. She leaned this way and that as her feet sunk in the mud.

"That's right, that's right." Ranch was nodding his head. Lucy stopped and cried harder. "You ain't talking to her, no ma'am. You just keep going."

Pidge began walking down the hill through the grass toward Ranch, who now raised the gun to sight carefully down the barrel at the back of Lucy's head. Lucy stopped moving.

"I said keep going!"

Through her weeping, Lucy said, "Just one more time, please let me see her, please, won't you please—"

"Your girl is already on her way to heaven."

Lucy's crying grew louder to a kind of wailing that reminded Pidge of the sounds she had made when she fell down on the beach before the chimpanzee. He felt it in his knees, he felt a sorrow for her that was so wide and deep that he nearly yelled out for her at that moment.

"Quit that damn noise, you damn fool!" Ranch said. "You sound like a baby who lost her damn lollipop. You want to die with some dignity? Then quit that wailing."

Pidge slipped his hand around the dry gray surface of a rock and picked it up. He stepped through the grass, careful not to make a sound, his boots landing near dried sticks, leaves, smaller rocks.

"A few more steps. Then put your head under. I advise you to keep it there. It'll be awful ugly you bring it back up."

He moved forward, taking slow careful steps. The world seemed to change. It became bigger, far more overgrown and overly green and impossibly hazy. Waves of swamp water were bouncing the lily pads; a blue dragonfly lit by the sun buzzed by. Lucy was up to her knees, then up to her thighs in the black decaying muck of the swamp.

The sun was lighting up the frizzy brown hairs on her head as she waded up to her chest.

"Now put your head under," Ranch said.

Lucy shook her head, she had her hands to her eyes. She was crying uncontrollably.

"Did you hear what I said?"

She staggered back and forth, wailing and coughing.

"Will you swim with the critters, you ugly thing or you'll waste my damn precious gunpowder!"

Lucy only wept harder and louder, filling the little dale around the swamp with her sadness. Pidge could now see the loose threads on the back of Ranch's shirt and the coarse hair in his long knotty ponytail. He was close enough now. He cocked his hand back.

"I don't have all day, shit!" Ranch yelled. Then he swung all the way around and Pidge realized he was facing him down the barrel of the gun. Pidge flung the rock with every muscle in his body. But the shotgun went off and he felt the discharge blast deep into his chest.

59

Lucy turned around. Before her at the edge of the swamp she saw Johnny Ranch had fallen in the black water on his back, the gun next to him on top of the lily pads. She was confused, she wondered if he'd shot himself somehow. She pushed through the muck as fast as she could for Ranch's gun. Each foot oozed deep in the silt. Ranch was on his back near shore, floundering, coming up and going down, coughing, gasping for breath, disoriented, holding his forehead with one hand, grappling and finally grasping his weapon, the barrel of which was pointing down into the muck.

Lucy yanked it from his hand and Ranch fell onto his back, still holding his head wound with one hand. Then with all of her might Lucy swung the shotgun like a baseball bat across the side of his head. She connected, cracking hard into the bone and he yelled and grasped his head, then sunk deep into the weeds.

But a moment later he came up again, gasping. Lucy nearer to him, the heavy wooden handle of the gun raised directly over his head. Their eyes met as she brought it down again. It connected firmly with the crown of his head with a loud resounding crack. He sat directly down in the water and then his head slipped back, parting the lily pads, and disappearing.

Staggering out of the water, Lucy fell to her knees herself, then got back on her feet and headed toward the path where she'd heard Emma's shouts for help. She held Ranch's mud- and slime-covered shotgun in her hands. Out of the corner of her eye, she saw a work boot, a short leg, and there was Pidge's little body. He lay on his back, his open eyes glazed and still, looking up at the sky, his arm across his bloody shoulder. Blood covered his shirt. He did not blink; he merely stared up at her and she back at him. "What happened, Pidge?" she said. She knelt next to him and pressed his hand against the wound on his shirt. "I'll be back. Press your wound if you can." She got up with the shotgun in her hands.

60

As Lucy came out of the trees onto the bank of the lake, she saw them both facing away, waist deep in the clear water: Grecco in his black ministerial suit, holding Emma, half naked and gagged. It was early morning; wisps of white mist were peeling off the still water that was shimmering from the ripples around their two bodies. Grecco was behind Emma, whose scale-covered arms were fastened behind her back, a blindfold wrapped tightly around her eyes. She was gagged still. He had paused and was saying some sort of prayer. His face was upturned. Holding the shotgun out with both hands, Lucy waded out toward them as swiftly and quietly as possible, fearing that if he saw what was in her hands he would lunge with Emma into the water and vanish.

As her waves reached Grecco, he stopped and glanced at her over his shoulder.

"Let her go," Lucy said. Grecco turned back to Emma and pushed her through the water. Lucy planted herself among the slippery rocks beneath her feet.

"Did you hear me?" she called out. "I said—let her go, and I mean it!"

He ignored her and kept going. Lucy pushed farther through the water, trying to catch up.

"I'm going to shoot you if you don't stop."

But he was unaffected by her words and kept pushing Emma forward.

"I've got a gun. I've got Johnny's gun."

She stopped, found her footing again and raised the barrel of the gun toward him. The minister kept moving through the still water, grasping Emma tightly.

"All right," she said, her hand was trembling. She put her finger to the trigger and sighted at the back of his head. "All right. If you don't stop, if you don't stop this moment! Do you think I'm kidding? I'm going to shoot you!"

Still he moved forward.

"I don't want to do this. I don't want to do this!"

She aimed as carefully as she could, the gun waving back and forth.

"All right, all right, I'm going to kill you. You're not listening," she screamed.

Her finger squeezed the trigger. There was a loud click and then silence. She dropped the barrel, pulled the hammer back again with both hands and raised the gun again. She could see him moving away.

"Do you hear me? Do you want to die?"

She pulled the trigger again. Another click and silence. The gun was soaking wet.

Grecco kept going without looking back, pushing the struggling girl forward. Terrified now, Lucy dropped the gun and began to follow behind them, her bare feet pressing between slick rocks on the bottom.

"Joe," she called out. "Pastor Joe. Don't hurt that girl, please don't hurt that girl." The sound of his name seemed to stop him. "Do you know who I am? Turn around and look at me. If you really look at me, you'll see past the bruises, you'll see who you've been keeping."

Emma struggled again, tried to turn around herself, but he now held her so firmly by the back of her hair that she could not move at all.

"You'll remember me, I think you will," she said. "You befriended me when you were working out of your tent, years ago." Lucy moved toward Grecco and Emma cautiously, her eye on the backs of the two figures facing away in the glassy white water of the lake. "I'm the one, the one you asked to be your . . ." she could hardly say the word. ". . . *daughter*. You asked me to trust you . . . I started to trust you, then you took me inside your trailer." Lucy's voice became louder, it seemed that she had halted his motion, that what she was saying was getting to him. "You must not have forgiven yourself for what you did. And now you have Emma instead, even though it was me. I'm the reason you're out here. This girl has nothing to do with it; she's totally innocent."

Lucy raised her voice even higher and drew closer to him. He was listening to her. "Don't you remember that afternoon? Don't you remember Lucy Thurman? Don't you recall what you did to me when I told you I was a freak?" She was almost shouting and Emma, up to her chest in water, tried to struggle again but Grecco held her tightly. "Have you forgotten what we did together?" Lucy shouted at the top of her lungs. "I'm the one, I'm the one who gave birth to your child." He turned his head to the side. She could see his profile; he seemed frozen in place. "It was me, do you remember me? Do you?! I am the mother of your daughter, the mother of *your* daughter."

She could see sweat break out on the back of his neck. She was now within yards of him. He gripped Emma even more fiercely. "You have a daughter. A real daughter somewhere on this earth. You're a father. I know, I have proof, because I'm the mother of that child."

"You're a liar," he said.

"I'm not a liar. I gave birth to your child. I was forced to give her up."

"You're a liar, a sinful liar," he hissed.

"My mother forced me to give her up. But I had the feeling back then that you and me would meet up again. I knew it. I knew it when I escaped from your trailer, bleeding, my legs torn apart just like my life, I knew it when I hid in my room, I knew it when you lied to my mother about me, I knew it after I gave birth to my baby. I knew it when I went hitchhiking to get my daughter back and I found out she was gone, the last chair kicked out from under me. I knew there was no way to escape what you'd done to me, ever. And now I'm back. I can accept that, I can fully accept that. Here I am."

As Lucy said this, in the presence of the man who had raped her and was now trying to kill her girl, she could feel something pulse through her entire body. It was more like something was excreted, a sudden, horrific feeling that followed what she had just said, as if she didn't know the truth of her words until now. It was as if she were back in his trailer again, as if she had never left it, as if this was truly where she was destined to end up, despite her years of struggle to get away.

Grecco moved away from her. He seemed to be moving in slow motion, grasping Emma's thick hair and muscling her into deeper water, toward her death. Lucy struggled to say something to stop him but she was speechless and the distance between her and Emma seemed like an interminable dream of despair. Then suddenly something inside her took over.

"I can see what you're trying to do," she said. "You're trying to make up to God. I don't blame you. There's no worse hell than a fall from grace like that no matter how it happens."

He stopped once again. Sweat was soaking his neck; he seemed to be crying almost, trembling.

"Grace is not perfection," Lucy said. This was something that she had heard Master Howard say. Despite his misery and dastardliness, he had taught her some things. "Perfection is the invention of man. Emma's far from perfect, she's like you and me, she's a freak, too."

"Shut up!" he snapped and turned to her.

"She is."

"I don't know who you are, but get out of here, or you'll die, too."

"You know who I am."

"I said get away from here!"

"You must know who I am. I'm the girl you raped. I'm the girl that you haven't forgiven yourself for destroying. You destroyed, do you hear me? Is that not a sin? If what you did is not a sin, there is nothing in this world that is a sin. And now you're going to take my love from me."

"Get away!" he yelled, then turned as if he was going to make the final lunge with Emma. But Lucy threw herself at him, grabbed the back of his suit and yanked down with all her might, tearing his suit and then reaching for his collar and ripping that open and exposing his neck and the pinkish flaps of skin. To cover himself, Grecco threw both his hands over his neck—his gills were pulsing under his fingers.

Emma slipped away. She rushed through the water blindly, breathing heavily through her nose, coughing and choking. She seemed to instinctively know where Grecco was. He lunged at her and missed and then lunged and missed again. He tried to run through the water himself but he was fully dressed.

Lucy screamed at her. "Run away, run away, Emma as fast as you can go, please for me!"

Hiding his neck again with both his hands, Grecco turned and looked at Lucy. His gills were too large to hide with just his hands. The skin that joined his neck to his collarbone was thick and pink and alive.

He stared at her; his eyes small, milky gray. They seemed to take her in as if he were taking in not only her but everything in his life from childhood until now.

"Shame on you!" she screamed. "For what you've done to us!"

She backed up a little, facing him.

Emma must have loosened her gag. She screamed for help at the top of her lungs, piercing the still morning air as Grecco pushed through the cool water toward Lucy, a black shadow, growing taller and darker and covering the sky above her.

She saw a kind of smirk of recognition come over him. "Lucy, Lucy Thurman, I remember you," he said and nodded and closed his eyes and took a deep breath. "The Lord Jesus Christ, Our Savior, has brought you back to me. A miracle, one of the strange and beautiful and mysterious ways that Our Savior makes Himself known . . . He's brought you back to me just in time." He rolled his eyes to heaven and closed them again. "Thank you Lord, thank you for your infinite mercy."

Lucy held firmly, keeping her eyes on him. She could not turn to flee.

He threw his arms around her, grabbed her by the throat, dragged her quickly to deeper water and thrust her under, clinging to her. They slipped off an underwater ledge into deeper water and hit the stony bottom.

Grecco held fast to her neck. Lucy struggled, then suddenly realized the futility of this and stopped. She shut her eyes tightly and she could feel an almost drunken calm in her chest as if something in her couldn't fight anymore, as if something in her knew to bend into his embrace, holding onto her air and resting in this man's stronghold. She kept her eyes shut and waited patiently for the blackness to come, her breath pushing against her lungs, his fierce hands hugging her whole body.

Then she heard a burst of air rush from his lungs, then another burst and she could feel his hold on her easing. One more burst of air and she felt him gasp, convulse. Suddenly he fell back onto the rock. Opening her eyes she saw the black figure on his side, one hand holding the side of his neck where his gills were, the other grasping the yellowish stones around him. Tiny white bubbles clung to his gills.

She turned her eyes to the brightness of the water overhead. The morning sun was peering down, the ceiling of the lake seemed infinitely far away, a lifetime away, as if her swim up would be as long as the journey she had taken to get here. She pushed off and stroked upward through the bluish green water.

All of her life seemed to slip away from her as she swam, even her body, everything was left behind her. Then she was at the surface, gasping for breath, thrashing, gasping so hard that she didn't think she was going to make it. And then she was swimming, barely swimming. She could hear the screams of Emma who was standing up to her waist in the water, her hands behind her back, the gag slipped down over her chin. As Lucy's legs touched bottom, Emma broke into sobs, her eyes filled with hysterical tears.

Her eyes were locked on Lucy who staggered with the weight of the lake on her clothes and in her lungs.

Then Lucy grabbed Emma, put her arms around her, and pulled her tightly, tightly against her chest.

61

Pidge lay in the same position that Lucy left him in, shirt and pants soaked with blood, staring at the sky. After the screams there was silence and then birds began singing in the surrounding trees and frogs croaking in the swamp. And there were cricket sounds and the moist sun came out from behind the clouds. Finally, he closed his eyes. He was dying and he was sad that he had not told her what he'd meant to tell her.

As his eyes closed he saw a wide grassy plain of red grass. Far away across it he saw a circus tent, disappearing and reappearing in waves of rising heat. The plain was bigger than anything in Ohio. The clouds were low and flat and the sky seemed flat. Then he noticed that the grass was red because of his blood. He realized that if this was all his blood across this vast plain then he must be dead. The moment of death had arrived and this was what his life had amounted to—a plain of grass all muddied up with blood and nothing more.

Then he noticed an elephant with her back to him; it was Marcella, and next to her was his dog, King, looking the other way across the plain. "Hey, come here, boy," Pidge yelled. But strangely enough his shepherd did not seem to hear him. He called him again and again King merely stood next to the elephant, looking the other way. It was a strange sight, these two best of friends, something comforting about it and yet it made him feel lonelier than he'd ever felt. Then Pidge noticed a circus tent nearby and Master Howard standing at the door. "Pidge, come on, the show is about to begin, we need you in here."

"You can't mess with me anymore. I'm dead." Then as a kind of afterthought he said, "Besides, I've already told Lucy how I feel." He felt the truth of these words and it seemed a convincing argument until Master Howard asked, "How *do* you feel?"

"I feel like I—"

"You what, little man?"

"I . . ." He felt the great shame of saying this in front of Master Howard, but he went ahead and said it anyway, pushing past that thing inside of him. "I feel like I love her."

Then he turned to Master Howard and it took everything he had to raise his eyes and look at him.

But Master Howard didn't seem to notice the importance of the moment. Instead he was busy lifting the tent flap and Pidge could see blackness inside and then a white spotlight came on. Lucy was standing in the center ring in a bright white bridal gown and she was beautiful, radiantly beautiful. As she looked his way, he realized that this was his final invitation to say something to her. He started to move his lips but darkness was falling around him and he was drifting off. As he drifted off, he thought he could feel somebody holding his hand.

And it was true. Lucy was kneeling in the grass clasping his hand with both of hers. She was looking down at his face. His eyes were closed; his skin had become paler and paler so that his lips were nearly white. And under her hand she could feel the heart beating irregularly and then diminishing.

Then she reached for an index card sticking out of his pocket. She could see her name written on it.

62

It was a cold Saturday afternoon when Harold Parks crossed the parking lot and then the sidewalk to the Blue Night Mall. He pushed open the glass doors and entered the mall now as an ordinary shopper, not a security guard. The night before while on his shift he had seen through a shoe store window a pair of insulated boots on sale. He did not expect that the store would carry his large shoe size, which was often a special order item, but since it was a very cold, blustery day outside and his apartment was poorly heated he decided to take the trip anyway. Besides, he liked to see the mall filled with people after spending so much time in it while it was empty. Stamping the snow off his boots, he began to stroll across the wet floor toward the shoe store. The after-Christmas sales had drawn a heavy crowd into the mall, children were screaming and playing tag, dashing through the legs of adults, annoying the older ones who wore their caps and scarves even inside.

As Harold walked along, his hands in his pockets, he came up behind a woman and a girl who were leisurely walking just in front of him. The woman held a shopping bag and the girl had a new pair of down mittens dangling by the tag from her fingers. As they walked next to each other calmly with no particular direction in mind, something about them arrested Harold's attention. Was it the way they walked so close together that now and then they bumped into each other? The girl kept giggling at something the woman was saying and the woman laughed a little, too. Harold dropped back and followed them past the hamburger and hotdog stands, the blue jean shop, and the bookstore. Just outside of a fabric shop they stopped to confer and then the woman turned to go into the shop and the girl turned in another direction, looking behind her.

Harold turned his head quickly. He had recognized her face. It was the tattooed girl he had found near the fountain almost a year earlier. She walked right by him and turned into a used record shop and there she began browsing through the old records.

Harold stepped into the store and crossed to the opposite side of the bank of records. It was easy to observe the girl from here as she was busy lifting the covers, examining them, and then dropping them back down. He had never forgotten her face, or the mysterious feelings he had experienced that night after he had found her.

She was still beautiful, but her face had come alive. A kind of darkness remained around her eyes and cheekbones, but now the darkness had a different feeling. There were wrinkles around her eyes and lips as if she had been talking or crying or even laughing. He could see her lips move as she lifted the cards to read the covers. She did not seem interested in buying, just looking and for a long while she was very busy. Then the woman came to the door of the music shop and called for her. They left the store together and Harold followed. In the main concourse the woman stopped and shifted her shopping bags to one hand and reached out with the other to take the girl's hand. Holding hands, the two of them walked through the mall until they came to a crowd of people who had gathered around a man on a raised platform near the exit. The man was raffling off a brand new vacuum cleaner to all those who had given him their name that afternoon. The woman and girl slipped among the many people standing with their tickets in hand.

The black hair of the man on the platform was slicked back with hair gel. He wore a bright blue leisure suit. He called to the crowd through a microphone with tinny speakers. "Come on, all you folks who have taken a chance, taken a chance, round and round the cage will go and soon we'll find our lucky winner. Yes, a lucky winner for this fine machine that you see right here. Come on, all you folks, and gather around." He spun the cageful of cards and waited for it to come to a rest. Then he turned his head, reached inside to take one out and read off the winner. "Do we have a Bill Patterson in the crowd? A Bill Patterson of Morton, Ohio?" Soon an old man in the crowd held his cane up and said, "That's me. I'm Bill Patterson." The old man's face was bright with excitement. He wore loafers with thick white socks. He shuffled forward with his cane to claim his prize.

Some of the crowd applauded as they made way for him, others murmured in disappointment, then everyone began to disperse, and Harold began to look for the woman and the girl. The teenagers wandered off, and so did the families with young children. Harold's search became more urgent. Her mere presence had affected him in ways he did not know how to articulate. But he had something to tell the young girl, he was sure he had something to tell her.

Pushing past the scattering crowd, he dashed toward the glass doors. Then he was outside, and he could see the many shoppers getting in and out of their cars in the parking lot, the lake reflecting the big sky beyond.

But they were gone, the woman and the girl were no longer there.

That night after the trip to the mall, Emma had trouble falling asleep. She lay awake for a long time staring at the stars through the window. Lucy was still downstairs and she could hear the faint murmur of the television. Then the television went off and Emma could hear Lucy come up the carpeted stairs, go into the bathroom, and brush her teeth. A few moments later she came out.

"Good night, Lucy," Emma said as she passed by her door.

"You're still awake?"

Lucy came to her door, her hand on the jamb. "What is it, dear?"

"Nothing," Emma said.

"Well, you know that I'm right here. My door's open."

"Thank you, Lucy."

"Good night, darling."

Lucy went into her bedroom. A ray of yellow light from Lucy's bedside lamp fell in the hallway for a few moments, then went out.

Emma kept staring at the faint white stars, pinkish clouds drifted across the Milky Way. She was certain she would not be able to fall asleep even after Lucy's comforting words. But then her thoughts began to slip and she felt her bed moving and water come up around the sides of it, covering her arms and shoulders. Then all at once she was in a wide, blue sea of clear water, swimming swiftly like a fish. There was nobody around her to slow her down or to tell her not to do this. She was happy to be alone. She swam so hard and fast and vigorously that she vanished into the water itself.